"I won't try to sum up the plot. Some of the elements are familiar enough, but Saberhagen's writing and development of the details remove them from the obvious. And parts of the story are pure joy. There is the control of a djinn (well, call him that, though he's part Yankee mechanic and part Vulcan) who will do exactly what he's told about building aircraft for a wizard who has only a 19th-century picture of aircraft to guide him. There is a magic healing lake and the Lord Draffut, who presides over it; call him a god if you like – or try to see what Saberhagen has done with one of man's oldest servants who has evolved in mind and body. And there is throughout a marvellous analysis of the workings of magic and the true nature of demons . . .

". . . there is zest and a feel to the writing that make it irresistible to me. There are few writers who can do justice to a really rich set of characters and backgrounds, and Saberhagen has already proved he is one of the best."

Lester Del Rey

"A fine mix of fantasy and science fiction, action and speculation."

Roger Zelazny

FRED SABERHAGEN

EMPIRE OF THE EAST

Futura

An Orbit Book

Copyright © 1979 by Fred Saberhagen

First published in 1979 by Ace Books, New York

First published in Great Britain in 1984
by Futura Publications, a Division of
Macdonald & Co (Publishers) Ltd
London & Sydney

The parts of this book have been published in
substantially different form as:
The Broken Lands, copyright © 1968 by Fred Saberhagen
The Black Mountains, copyright © 1971 by Fred Saberhagen
Changeling Earth, copyright © 1973 by Fred Saberhagen

ISBN 0 7088 8101 7

Printed and bound in Great Britain by
Collins, Glasgow

Futura Publications
A Division of
Macdonald & Co (Publishers) Ltd
Greater London House
Hampstead Road
London NW1 7QX

A BPCC plc Company

Prologue

by Roger Zelazny

--- ◆ ◆ ◆ ---

Fred Saberhagen does not look like the father of the berserkers, Count Dracula's amanuensis or an authority on Inca tortures. These items do occasionally come to mind when his name is mentioned, however, because they are the sorts of things which fix themselves readily in memory. So, I wish to counter any image of a latter-day H. P. Lovecraft by remarking, for openers, that Fred is a genial, witty, well-informed individual, with a wonderful wife named Joan, who is a mathematician, and the three best-behaved children I've ever met: Jill, Eric and Tom. He likes good food and drink and conversation. His working habits seem superior to my own, and his facility with scholarly matters may even pre-date his one-time employment as a writer for *The Encyclopedia Brittanica.*

I liked Fred's writing before I ever met him, and now that we are almost neighbors, I am pleased to know him. I am just returned from a trip, and I finished reading his novel *The Mask of the Sun* on the airplane. It made me feel that he could do no wrong. It has one of the most suspenseful openings I have encountered in a long while, leading steadily and carefully into a truly exotic setting and story-situation. His management of the paradoxes it involves is an exercise in precision and symmetry. (I might as well add "colorful imagery and characterization," and for that matter "scholarship which does not impede but enhances.") And having recently read his *The Holmes-Dracula File*, I was still fresh on it for purposes of contrast and comparison. There, I was impressed by the apparent ease with which the chapters (alternately narrated by the count himself and by John Watson, M.D.) were recorded in appropriately individual styles, by the authentic feeling of his Victorian London and by the sinuosities of the plot. It was very different from *The Mask of the Sun*, but was written with equivalent skill, care and attention to detail.

All of which, upon reflection, is a way of saying that he is a versatile writer. But there is more to Fred's stuff than mere technique. Sit down and read ten pages of anything he has written, and you begin to see that he has given it a lot of thought. It hangs together. (I'm tired of the word "organic" in reference to literature. It makes me think of a book with fungus growing on it. Fred's books lack fungus but are of a whole piece — press one anywhere, and the entire story fabric responds uniformly to the tension, seamlessly — because he has passed that way many times and knows exactly why he situated every house, tree, black hole, berserker and idea just where he did.) To see, to feel, to know the world you are assembling in such a consistent and fully extended fashion has always seemed to me the mark of a superior writer. It lies beyond any surface trickery — hooks, gimmicks, stylistic pyrotechnics — and is one of the things that makes the difference between a memorable book and one that provides a few hours' entertainment and is soon forgotten.

I could simply end on that note and be telling nothing less than the truth — after announcing that here is another one, to enjoy, to remember — and then get out of your way and let you read it. But life is short, good writers are a minority group and opportunities to talk about them are few, unless you are a critic or a reviewer, neither of which hats fit me. And there is another thing about writing and Fred which seems worth saying here.

Raymond Chandler once observed that there are

plot writers, such as, say, Agatha Christie, who work everything out in advance, and then there are others, such as himself, who do not know everything that is going to occur in a story beforehand, who enjoy leaving leeway for improvisation and discovery as they go along. I've written things both ways myself, but I prefer Chandler's route because there is a certain joy in encountering the unexpected as you work. I've compared notes on this with Fred, and he is also of the Chandler school. If this tells you nothing else in terms of the psychology behind some people's creations, it at least lets you know which writers are probably having the most fun. And this is important. There are days when such a writer curses the free-form muse but the reconciliations are wonderful, and the work seldom seems a mere chore. It is good to know that beyond the place of Fred's versatility — and even beyond that special metaphysical locale where occurs the careful tightening of all story-strands into total self-consistency — there, in the secret place where he puts things together for the first time, all alone and wondering and working hard, he has this special on-the-spot joy in associating the stuff of life and ideas. For some of this, I believe, does come through to the reader in all good writing that happens in this fashion. I feel it in all of Fred's stories.

If further confirmation of the versatility of Fred Saberhagen were needed, here is EMPIRE OF THE EAST. In this unusual collaboration with his earlier self, he has produced a fine mix of fantasy and science fiction, action and speculation.

BOOK ONE

THE BROKEN LANDS

I

Hear Me, Ekuman

———◆◆———

The Satrap Ekuman's difficulties with his aged prisoner had only begun when he got the fellow down into the dungeon under the Castle and tried to begin a serious interrogation. The problem was not, as you might have thought from a first look at the old man, that the prisoner was too fragile and feeble, liable to die at the first good twinge of pain. Not at all. It was almost incredible, but actually the exact opposite was true. The old man was actually too tough, his powers still protected him. All through the long night he not only defended himself, but kept trying to hit back.

Ekuman's two wizards, Elslood and Zarf, were adepts as able as any that the Satrap had ever encountered west of the Black Mountains, far too strong for any lone prisoner to overcome, especially here on their own ground. Yet the old man fought — in pride and stubbornness, perhaps, and doubtless with the realization that his fighting could cause powers so enormous to be arrayed against him, could create a tension so great, that his inevitable collapse would bring him sudden and relatively painless death.

The intensity of the silent struggle mounted all through the darkest morning hours, when human powers are known to wane, and others may reach their peak. Ekuman and his wizards could not identify the particular forces of the West that the old man called upon, but certainly they were not trivial. Long before the end, the air within the buried dungeon seemed to Ekuman to be ringing audibly with powers, and his human eyesight misinformed him that the ancient vaults of the stone ceiling had elongated and receded into some mysterious distance. Zarf's toad-familiar, wont to jump with glee during the interrogation of stubborn prisoners, had taken refuge in a puddle of torchlight near the foot of the ascending stair, for once wanting nothing to do with the dark corners of the chamber. It crouched there solemnly, goggle eyes following its master as he moved about.

Elslood and Zarf took turns standing on the rim of the pit, three meters deep, at whose bottom the old man had been chained. They had with them talismans of their choice, and had drawn signs on floor and wall. They of course could gesture freely — though on the level of physical action the struggle was very quiet, as was to be expected when it involved wizards of this rank.

While one of Ekuman's magicians took his turn at maintaining the pressure, the other stood back before the Satrap's elevated chair, conferring with him. They were all sure that the old man was a leader, perhaps the very chief, of those who called themselves the Free Folk. These were bands of the native populace, reinforced by some stiff-necked refugees from other lands, who hid themselves in hills and coastal swamps and carried on an unremitting guerrilla warfare against Ekuman.

It was only through a stroke of fortune that a routine search operation in the swamps had netted the old man. Zarf and a troop of forty soldiers had come upon him sleeping in a hut. Ekuman was beginning to believe that if the old man had chanced to be awake, they might not have taken him at all. Even with the prisoner at his present disadvantage, Elslood and Zarf together had not even managed to learn his name.

Down in the pit the guttering torchlight flashed with unusual brightness from chains that were of no ordinary metal. Blood puddled darkly at the old man's feet, but not a drop of it was his. Lifeless before him one of Ekuman's dungeon-wardens lay. This man had approached the chained wizard incautiously, to be surprised when his own torture-knife whipped itself out of its sheath to fly up and bury its dull blade to the hilt in its owner's throat. After that, Ekuman had ordered all his human servitors save the two wizards from the chamber.

Later, when the prisoner had begun to display small but unmistakeable signs of weakening, Ekuman considered having the wardens in again, to try what little knives and flames might do. But the wizards advised against it, pleading that the best chance for a cruel prolongation of agony, for extracting useful information from the victim, lay in finishing by the powers of magic alone the process they had begun. Their pride was stung.

The Satrap thought about it, and let his wizards have their way, while he sat attentively through the long hours of the test. He had a high wall of a forehead, and a full, darkish beard. He wore a simple robe of black and bronze; his black boots shifted now and then upon the stone floor.

Only when the night outside was drawing to its end—though day and night in here were all the same—did the old man break silence at last. He spoke to Ekuman, and the words evidently formed no spell, for they came clearly enough through the guarded air above the torture-pit. When toward the end of the speech the victim's breath began to fail, Ekuman stood up from his chair and leaned forward to hear better. On the Satrap's face at that moment was a look of politeness, as of one simply showing courtesy to an elder.

"Hear me, Ekuman!"

The toad-familiar crouched lower, becoming utterly motionless, at the sound of those first words.

"Hear me, for I am Ardneh! Ardneh, who rides the Elephant, who wields the lightning, who rends fortifications as the rushing passage of time consumes cheap cloth. You slay me in this avatar, but I live on in other human beings. I am Ardneh, and in the end I will slay thee, and thou wilt not live on."

Given the circumstances, Ekuman knew no alarm at being threatened. The word "Elephant," though, caught his attention sharply. He glanced quickly at his wizards when it was uttered. Zarf's and Elslood's eyes fell before his, and he returned his full attention to the prisoner.

Pain showed now in the prisoner's face, and sounded in his voice. Defenses crumbling, powers failing, he was quickly becoming no more than an old man, no more than another victim about to die. He labored on, with croaking speech.

"Hear me, Ekuman. Neither by day nor by night will I slay thee. Neither with the blade nor with the bow. Neither with the edge of the hand . . . nor with the fist. Neither with the wet . . . nor with the dry . . ."

Ekuman strained to hear more, but the old lips had ceased to move. Now only the flicker of torch-light gave the illusion of life to the victim's face, as it did to the face of the dead torturer at his feet.

The ringing pressure of invisible forces faded quickly from the dank air. As Ekuman straightened, sighing, and turned from the pit, he could not resist a quick glance upward to make sure that the vault-ing had settled back where it belonged.

Zarf, slightly the junior of the two wizards, had gone to open a door and call the wardens in to see to the disposal of the corpses. As the magician turned back from this errand, Ekuman demanded: "You will examine the old one's body, with special care?"

"Yes, Lord." Zarf did not sound optimistic about the results to be expected from such an autopsy. His toad-familiar, however, was now grown lively again, and ready to begin the job. It burbled shrilly as it hopped into the pit and began its usual routine of pranks with the two bodies.

Ekuman stretched, wearily, and began to ascend the worn stone stair. Something had been accomplished, one of the rebel chieftains killed. But that was not enough. The information Ekuman required had not been gained.

Halfway up the first curved flight of stairs he stopped, turned back his head, and asked: "What make you of that speech the ancient blessed me with?"

Elslood, three steps behind, nodded his fine gray head, knit his well-creased brow, and pursed his dry lips thoughtfully; but at the moment Elslood could find nothing to say.

Shrugging, the Satrap went on up. It needed a hundred and more stone steps to raise him from the dungeon to gray morning air in a closed courtyard, from courtyard to keep, and from keep to the tower where his own quarters were. At several points Ekuman acknowledged, without pausing, the salutes of bronze-helmed soldiers standing guard.

Once above ground, the stairs curved through the Castle's massive, newly strengthened walls. The bulky keep was three tall stories high, and the tower rose two levels more above its roof. Most of the tower's lower level was taken up by a single large room, the Presence Chamber, wherein Ekuman generally conducted his affairs of state. At one side of this large round chamber space had been given to the wizards, covered alcoves in which they might keep their implements, benches and tables where they might do their work under their Lord's most watchful eye.

It was straight to this side of the Presence Chamber that Elslood went as soon as he and Ekuman had ascended to the tower. Around him here he had all the sorcerer's impedimenta: masks, and talismans, and charms not easily nameable, all most curiously wrought, piled on stands and tables and depending from the wall. On a stand a single thick brown candle burned, pale of flame now in the cool morning light that filtered through the high narrow windows.

Pausing first to mutter a secret precautionary word, Elslood put out a hand to set aside the arras which concealed an alcove. Within this space the Satrap allowed him to keep to himself certain private volumes and devices. The drapery pulled back revealed an enormous black guardian-spider, temporarily immobilized by the secret word, crouched on a high shelf. The tall wizard reached his long arm past the spider to withdraw a dusty volume.

When it was brought into the light Ekuman saw that it was an Old World book, of marvelous paper and binding that had already outlasted more than one generation of parchment copies. Technology, thought the Satrap, and despite himself he shivered slightly, inwardly, watching the fair white pages turned so familiarly by Elslood's searching fingers. It was not easy for one belonging to a world that thought itself sane and modern and stable to accept the reality of such things. Not even for Ekuman, who had seen and handled the evidences of technology more frequently than most. This book was not the only Old World remnant preserved within his Castle's walls.

And somewhere outside his walls, waiting to be found—the Elephant. Ekuman rubbed his palms together in impatience.

Having taken his book to the window for the light, Elslood had evidently located in it the passage he sought. He was reading silently now, nodding to himself like a man confirming an opinion.

At last he cleared his throat and spoke. "It was a quotation, Lord Ekuman, nearly word for word. From this—which is either a fable or a history of the Old World, I know not which. I will translate." Elslood put back his wizard's hood from his bush of silvery hair, cleared his throat again, and read out in a firm voice:

"Said Indra to the demon Namuci, I will slay thee

not by day or night, neither with the staff nor with the bow, neither with the palm of the hand nor with the fist, neither with the wet nor with the dry.''

"Indra?''

"One of the gods, Lord. Of lightning . . .''

"And of Elephants?'' Sarcasm bit in Ekuman's voice. Elephant was the name of some creature, real or mythical, of the Old World. Here in the Broken Lands depictions of this beast were to be seen in several places: stamped or painted on Old World metal, woven into a surviving scrap of Old World cloth that Ekuman had seen, and carved, probably at some less ancient time, upon a rock cliff in the Broken Mountains.

And now, somehow, the Elephant had come to be the symbol of those who called themselves the Free Folk. Far more important, a referent of this symbol still existed in the form of some real power, hidden somewhere in this land that refused to accept Ekuman as its conqueror—so the Satrap's wizards assured him, and so he believed. By all surface appearances the land was his, the Free Folk were only an outlaw remnant; yet all the divinings of his magicians warned him that without the Elephant under his control his rule was doomed to perish.

Still he was not really expecting the answer that Elslood gave him:

"Possibly, Lord, quite possibly. In at least one image that I have seen elsewhere, Indra is shown as mounted on what I believe to be an Elephant.''

"Then read on.''

The ominous tone was plain in Ekuman's voice; the wizard read on quickly: " 'But he killed him in the morning twilight, by sprinkling over him the foam of the sea.' The god Indra killed the demon Namuci, that is.''

"Hum.'' Ekuman had just noticed something: Indra–Ardneh. Namuci–Ekuman. Of course a power of magic could reside in words, but hardly in this simple transposition of syllables. The discovery of the

apparent verbal trickery brought him relief rather
than alarm. The old man, unable to strike back with
effect, had still managed to work some subtlety into
a dying threat. Subtlety was hardly substance, even
in magic.

Ekuman let himself smile faintly. "Fragile sort of
demon, to die of a little sea-spray," he commented.

Relieved, Elslood indulged himself in a light
laugh. He leafed through a few more pages of his
book. "As I recall the story, Lord, this demon
Namuci had kept his life, his soul, hidden in the
sea-foam. Therefore was he vulnerable to it."
Elslood shook his head. "One would have thought it
a fairly clever choice for a hiding place."

Ekuman grunted noncommittally. At the sound of
a step he turned, to see Zarf entering the Presence
Chamber. Zarf was younger and shorter than
Elslood and also resembled far less the popular
conception of a wizard. Judged by appearance, Zarf
might have been a merchant or a prosperous
farmer—save for the toad-familiar, which rode now
under a fold of cloak at his shoulder, all but invisible
save for its lidded eyes.

"You have already finished looking at the old
man's body? It told you nothing?"

"There is nothing to be learned from that, Lord."
Zarf tried to meet Ekuman's gaze boldly, then
looked away. "I can make a further examination
later—but there is nothing."

In silent but obvious dissatisfaction Ekuman regarded his two magicians, who awaited his pleasure
standing motionless but otherwise quite like children in their fear. It was a continual enjoyment to
the Satrap to have power over people as powerful as
these. Of course it was not by any innate personal
strength or skill that Ekuman could dominate
Elslood and Zarf. His command over them had been
given to him in the East, and well they knew how
effectively he might enforce it. The toad-familiar,

beneath any threat of punishment, squealed shrilly in some private mirth.

Having given the wizards time to consider the possible consequences of his wrath, Ekuman said, "Since neither of you can now tell me anything of value, you had better get to your crystals and ink-pools and see what you can learn. Or has either of you some stronger method of clairvoyance to propose?"

"No, Lord," said Elslood, humble.

"No, Lord." But then Zarf dared to attempt defense. "Since this Elephant we seek is doubtless not a living creature, but some work of . . . engineering, science . . ." The absurd words still came hard to Zarf. " . . . then to locate it, to find out anything about it more than we know already, that it exists and is important, this may be beyond the skill of any man in divination. . . ." And Zarf's voice trailed off in fear as his glance returned to Ekuman's face.

Ekuman moved wearily across the Presence Chamber, opened a door, and set foot upon the stair that led up to his private apartments. "Find me the Elephant," he ordered, simply and dangerously, ere he began to climb. As he went, his voice came drifting down to them: "Send me the Master of the Troops, and the Master of the Reptiles as well. I will have my power in this land made secure, and I will have it quickly!"

"The day of his daughter's wedding draws near," Zarf whispered, nodding solemnly. The two men looked grimly at each other. Both knew how important it was to Ekuman that his power should be, or at least appear, seamless and perfect on the day when the Lords and Ladies from other Satrapies around appeared here at the Castle for the wedding feast.

"I will go down," sighed Elslood at last, "and try if I may learn something from the old one's corpse. And I will see to it that the ones he wants are summoned. Do you stay here and endeavor again to achieve some useful vision." Zarf, nodding in agreement, was already hurrying to the alcove where he kept his own devices; he would pour a pool of ink and gaze into it.

On the first landing of the stair below the Presence Chamber Elslood drew aside to make room, and bowed low to the Princess Charmian, who was going up. Her beauty rose through the dim passage like a sun. She wore cloth of bronze and silver and black, and a scarf of red and black for her betrothed. Her serving-women, whom she chose for ugliness, came following in a nervous file.

Charmian ascended past Elslood without deigning to give him a word or glance. For his part, as always, he could not keep himself from following her with his eyes until she was out of sight.

He straightened, then, and put a hand into a secret pocket of his robe and touched the long strands of her golden hair that he kept there. Those hairs had been obtained at deadly risk, and twisted, with many a powerful incantation, into an intricate magic knot of love. And then, alas, the love-charm had proved useless to Elslood—as he had known all along, in his heart, that it would be. Any mastery of love was forbidden him, as part of the price of his great sorcerer's power.

And he thought now that the knot of Charmian's golden hair would be of doubtful benefit to any man. One as utterly evil as the Princess could hardly be moved by any charm to anything like love.

II

Rolf

When he came to the end of the furrow and swung the rude plow around and chanced to raise his eyes, Rolf beheld a sight both expected and terrible—the winged reptiles of the Castle were coming out to scour the countryside once again.

May some demon devour them, if they come near our fowl today! he thought. But he was no sorcerer to have the ordering of demons. He could do nothing but stand helplessly and watch.

At Rolf's back, the afternoon sun was some four hours above the Western Sea, the shore being several kilometers from where Rolf stood, the land between for the most part low and marshy. Looking ahead, he could see above nearby treetops part of the jagged line of the Broken Mountains, half a day's walk to the east. He could not see the Castle itself, but he knew well where it was, perched on the south side of the central pass that pierced those mountains through from east to west. The reptiles came from the Castle, and there dwelt those who had brought the reptiles to the Broken Lands—folk so evil that they seemed themselves inhuman, though they wore human form.

Spreading westward now from the direction where the Castle lay, in Rolf's eyes disfiguring all the fairness of the springtime sky, came a swarming formation of dots. Rolf had heard that the reptiles' human masters sent them out to search for something more than prey, that there was something hidden that Ekuman most desperately desired to find. Whether that was true or not, the reptiles most certainly ravaged the farmers' lands for food and sport.

Rolf's sixteen-year-old eyes were sharp enough to pick out now the movement of leathery wings. The flying creatures of the Castle swelled slowly in his vision, the thin and spreading cloud their hundreds made came hurtling toward him. He knew that their eyes were sharper even than his. Almost daily now the reptiles came, picking over the land already so much robbed and torn by the new masters from the East; a land that had now grown hungry despite its richness, with every month more farmers killed or robbed and driven from their soil. With villages turned into prison camps, or emptied out to give the Satrap Ekuman the slave labor that he must have to build his Castle stronger still. . . .

Did the foul grinning things fly ten or only five times faster than a man might run? With a big-boned hand Rolf put back a mop of his black hair, tilting back his head to watch as the vanguard of the reptiles now came nearly straight above him. A belt of rope around Rolf's lean waist held up his trousers of good homespun; his shirt of the same stuff was open in the warmth of spring and work. He was of quite ordinary height, and spare as a knotted rope. His shoulders in their bony flatness looked wider than they were. Only his wrists and callused hands and his bare feet seemed to have been made a size or so too big to fit the rest of him.

In the distance the reptiles had seemed to be flying in a compact formation. But now Rolf could see that they had been scattered widely by their differences of course and speed. Here and there a single flyer would pause, coasting in wide flat circles, to scan something on the earth below. Sometimes then the reptile would straighten out again into effortless speed of flight, having decided that whatever it had seen was not worth dropping for.

But sometimes it would dive. Stoop. Plunge wing-folded, like a falling rock—

Above Rolf's home! With a shock at his heart he saw the winged predator plummeting to strike. Before it vanished below the level of the trees Rolf was running toward it, toward his home. The clearing and the little house were invisible from here, more than a kilometer away over broken, scrub-grown country.

The reptile would be diving after the fowl in their coop, that must be it, though after the last attack Rolf's mother had tried to hide the coop under a net of strings, woven with vines and branches to make a screen. Rolf's father still lay abed with a crushed foot, mangled by a falling stone while he had been doing his stint of forced labor on the Castle. Small Lisa might be running out now as she had run out to challenge the last reptile, to strike with a broom or a hoe at a fanged intelligent killer who was nearly as big as she. . . .

Between the field where he had been working and his home, Rolf's path lay across land made unplowable by its ravines and rocks. The familiar track wound shallowly uphill and down; it leaped and bounded under him now, with the big strides of his running. Never before had he gone over this path so fast. He kept looking ahead, and his fear kept growing, because of the strange fact that the raiding reptile had not yet risen, with prey or without.

Someone might have defied the Castle's law and slain the thing—but who, and how? Rolf's father could scarcely stand up from his bed. His mother? In obedience to another Castle law, the household had already been stripped of any weapon larger than a short-bladed kitchen knife. Little Lisa—Rolf pictured her, fighting with some garden implement against those teeth and talons, and he tried to run faster yet.

So it did not seem reasonable that the reptile

should be dead. Yet neither should it be sitting at ease and unmolested, dining on some slaughtered hen. By now Rolf was close enough to his home to have heard sounds of fighting or alarm, but there was only ominous silence.

When he ran at last into the clearing and beheld the total ruin of the simple dwelling that had been his home, it seemed to Rolf that he knew already what he must find, that he had known it from his first sight of the stooping reptile.

And at the same time the truth was becoming unknowable. It was beyond anything that the mind could hold.

Smoke and flames, such as he had seen in the past devouring other houses destroyed by the invader, might have made the truth before him now more credible. But the only home Rolf could remember had been simply kicked apart, knocked to pieces like a child's play-hut, like something not worth burning. It had been a small and simple structure; no great strength had been needed to topple its thatch and poles.

Rolf was scarcely aware of crying out. Or of the reptile, flapping up in heavy alarm from where it had been crouched over a dead fowl—one of the birds set free by the collapse of the coop when the flimsy house had been knocked down. The destruction had been done before the reptile came. By some roving party of the soldiers of the Castle—who else? No one in the Broken Lands knew when the invaders might come to him, or what might be done to him when they did.

Digging wildly in the shabby wreckage of the little house, Rolf uncovered shapes that seemed misplaced as in a dream. He found trivial things. Here was a cooking pot, the worn place on its handle somehow startling in its familiarity. And here . . .

A voice that had been shouting names, Rolf's own voice, now fell silent. He stood looking down at something still and supine, a shape of flesh and hair and unfamiliar nakedness and blood. His mother had looked something like this thing of death. She had resembled this, this shape that now lay here amid all the other ruined things and shared all their stillness.

Rolf had to go on looking. Here was the body of a man, clothed, with a face very like his father's. His father's eyes, calm and unprotesting now, were opened toward the sky. No more fear and worry and held-in anger. No more answers to give a son. No more pain and sickness from a crushed foot. No more pain, though there was blood, and Rolf saw now that his father's open shirt revealed red-lipped, curious wounds. Why yes, Rolf thought to himself, nodding, those are the wounds that a sword must make. He had never seen the like before.

He shouted no longer. He looked around for the reptile but it had gone. After he had searched on through what was left of the house and the few outbuildings, he came to a halt at the edge of the clearing. He realized vaguely that he was standing in an attitude of thoughtfulness, though in fact his mind was almost entirely blank. But he had to think. Lisa was not here. If she had been hiding nearby, surely all his noise would have brought her out by now.

He was distracted by the plodding into the clearing of the workbeast he had been plowing with. The animal had developed the trick of freeing itself from the harness if he left it standing alone in the field for any reason. When it came trotting into the home clearing now it halted at once, to stand shivering and whinnying at the strangeness of what it found. Rolf without thinking spoke to the animal and walked toward it, but it turned and bolted as if thrown into panic by the very ordinariness of his behavior amid this . . . yes, it was strange that he could be so calm.

His heart gave another leap and he began again a frenzied digging through the wreckage. But no, Lisa's body was not here. He circled around the clearing, staring at everything as if to make sure of what it was. Then he began coursing in a widening circle through the surrounding woods. His mind made a motionless corpse of every fallen log. He began to call Lisa's name again, softly. Either she had run far away, or else the soldiers had . . .

It was not believable, it was not possible that the soldiers could have come here and committed all these horrors, and he, Rolf, had remained out in the fields calmly plowing. So it had not really happened at all. Because it was not possible. And all the while he knew that it was true.

. . . Or else the soldiers had taken Lisa with them. If the murders were possible, so might that be. Rolf found himself back in the clearing, averting his eyes from the nakedness of the thing that had been his mother. He did not let himself think of how her clothes had been taken from her, or why, though those also were things he knew. The men from the Castle. The soldiers. The invaders. The East.

"Lisa!" He was out in the scrub forest again, calling more loudly for his sister. The afternoon was very warm even here in the shade of the trees. Rolf raised his arm to wipe sweat from his face with his sleeve, and saw that in his hand he was carrying the little kitchen knife, which he must have picked up from amid the ruins of the house.

And then a little later, when his mind with a little inward jump moved another notch on its recovery from the craziness of shock, he found himself walking along the narrow rutted road that passed near what had been his home. The world around him looked strangely normal, as if this were nothing but another day. He was trudging in an easterly direction, taking the way that would bring him to a larger highway and ultimately to the Castle brooding on its height above the pass. Where did he think he was going? What was it he meant to do?

Again a little later, the world became thin and gray before his eyes. He felt that he was fainting, and he saw down quickly in the grass beside the road. He did not faint. He did not rest either, though the muscles of his legs were quivering with exhaustion. He saw that his clothes had recently been torn in several places. He had just been running through the woods, calling Lisa's name. But she was gone, and he was not going to be able to get her back.

Gone. All of them gone.

After a period of sitting, he became aware with a slight start that a man was standing near him in the yellow-gray dust of the road. There were sandaled feet and a pair of buskined ankles, and masculine calves with lean muscle and sparse wiry black hair. At first Rolf could think only that the man must be a soldier, and Rolf wondered if he might get out his knife and strike before the soldier killed him—he had thrust the kitchen knife awkwardly under the rope that was his belt, with his shirt closed over it for concealment.

But when Rolf raised his eyes he saw that the man was no soldier. He appeared to be unarmed, and looked not at all dangerous.

"Is there—something wrong?" The man's voice was precise, and gently accented, one of the few voices Rolf had ever heard that spoke in its tones of far places and strange peoples. The speaker's mild eyes blinked down at Rolf, from a face too woebegone in expression and too ordinary in most of its features for the hawk nose to give it pride.

The man was no peasant. Though his clothes were not the finery of an important person, they were better than Rolf's. He was dusty with long walking, and he had a pack on his back. His simple knee-length cloak was half open, and from under it one lean, dark-haired arm extended in a rotating, questioning gesture.

"There is something much wrong, hey?"

Finding an answer for that question was an insurmountable problem at the moment. Rolf soon gave up the effort. He gave up on everything.

The next thing he was clearly aware of was the mouth of a water bottle being applied to his own mouth. If his mind had forgotten thirst his body had not, and for a few moments he swallowed ravenously. Then in reaction he nearly vomited. Good clean water choked him and stung his nose, but it stayed down at last. The drink shocked him, revived him, lifted him another notch toward rational function. He found himself standing, leaning on the man. He pulled away and looked at him.

The man was a little taller than Rolf, not quite as dark. His face seemed leaner than his body, and somehow finer, as if he had trained his face to show only a part of a great and unrelenting worry— "ascetic" was not a word or concept that Rolf had at his command.

"Oh, my. Something very much wrong?" The mild eyes blinked rapidly a time or two, and the lean face essayed a tentative smile, as if hoping to be contradicted, to hear that things might prove not so terrible after all. But the smile faded quickly. The stubby-fingered hands recapped the water bottle and reslung it under the cloak, then came up to clasp themselves as if beseeching to be allowed to know the worst.

It took Rolf a little time, but he stammered out the essentials of his story. Before the telling was finished, he and the man were walking along together on the road, now going away from the highway and the Castle, heading back in the direction from which Rolf had come. Rolf noticed this distantly, without feeling that it mattered in the least which way he walked. The shadows of the trees were lengthening now, and all the winding road was cool and gray.

"Ah. Oh. Terrible, terrible!" the man kept murmuring as he listened. He had ceased to wring his hands, and walked with them clasped behind his back. Now and then he hoisted and shifted his pack, as if the weight of it was still unfamiliar after all his travels. During the pauses in Rolf's story the man asked his name, and told him that his own name was Mewick. And when Rolf ran out of speech the man Mewick kept talking to him, asking idle-sounding questions about the road and the weather, questions that kept Rolf from withdrawing again into a daze. Also Mewick related how he was walking along the coast of the great sea from north to south, offering for sale the finest collection of magical implements, amulets and charms to be found on the open market anywhere. Mewick smiled sadly as he made this claim, like a man who did not expect to be believed.

"Have you there—" Rolf's voice choked, so he was forced to start over, but then the words came out strong. "Have you there in your pack anything that can be used to track men down and kill them?"

On hearing this question the peddler only looked more gloomy than ever, and at first gave no answer. As he walked he kept turning his head to shoot glances of apparent concern at Rolf.

"Killing and more killing," the peddler said at last, shaking his head in disgust. "No, no, I carry no such things in my pack. No—but today is not your day for being lectured. No, no, how can I talk to you now?"

They came to a branch in the road, where the right-hand fork led to the clearing where Rolf's home had been. Rolf stopped suddenly. "I must go back," he said with an effort. "I must see to it that my parents are buried."

Wordlessly, Mewick went with him. Nothing had changed in the clearing except for the lengthening of the shadows. What had to be done did not take the two of them long, digging with shovel and hoe in the soft earth of what had been the garden. When the two graves had been filled and mounded over,

Rolf gestured at the pack which Mewick had laid aside, and asked, "Have you anything there that . . . ? I would put some spell of protection on the graves. I could pay you for it later. Sometime."

Frowning bitterly, Mewick shook his head. "No. No matter what I said before, I have nothing here that is worth the giving. Except some food," he added, brightening just slightly. "And that is for the living, not the dead. Could you eat now?"

Rolf could not. He looked around the clearing, for the last time, as he thought. Lisa had not answered to his renewed calling of her name.

Mewick was slowly getting into the harness of his pack again, seemingly hesitant about just what to say or do next. "Then walk with me," he offered at last. "Tonight I think I know a place to stay. Not many kilometers. A good place to rest."

The sun would soon be setting. "What place?" Rolf asked, though he did not feel any real concern for where he was going to spend the night.

Mewick stood considering the lay of the land, as if he could see for a distance through the woods. He looked to the south and asked a couple of questions about the roads that skirted the swamps in that direction. "It will be shorter, I think, if we do not go around by road," he said at last.

Rolf had no will now to debate or even to think. Mewick had helped him. Through Mewick he was maintaining some hold on life and reason, and he would go along with Mewick. Rolf said, "Yes, we can go cross-country if you like, and come out on the road near the swamp."

True to this prediction, they emerged from the scrub forest to strike the south-going coastal road, just as the sun was redly vanishing behind a low cloudbank on the sea-horizon. From the point where they struck the road it ran almost perfectly straight south for about a kilometer over the level land ahead of them, and then curved inland to the left to avoid the beginning of the swamps.

The woods having been left behind, there were open fields stretching on either side of the road, all unplowed and untended. In two places Rolf saw houses standing deserted and half-ruined in their abandoned gardens. He kept walking on beside Mewick, feeling himself beyond tiredness, feeling floating and unreal. He could generate no surprise when Mewick stopped in the road and turned to him, slipping the pack from his own back and holding it out to Rolf.

"Here, you carry for a little while, hey? Not heavy. You be an apprentice magic-salesman. Just for now, hey?"

"All right." Indifferently he took the pack and slipped it on. Geegaws and trash, his father had said, speaking of the things that the smooth-talking magic vendors peddled from farm to farm.

"What is this, hey?" Mewick asked sharply. He had spotted the outline of the handle of the little kitchen knife, made visible now by the pack straps tautening the shirt around Rolf's waist. Before Rolf could make the effort of answering, Mewick had pulled the knife out, exclaimed in disgust, and pitched it far away into the tall roadside weeds. "No good, no! Very much against the law here in the Broken Country, to carry a weapon concealed."

"The Castle law." The words came in a dead voice through a closed jaw.

"Yes. If Castle soldiers see you have a knife—ha!" Apparently anxious to defend his action in throwing away Rolf's property, Mewick seemed to be making an effort to scowl fiercely. But he was not very good at it.

Rolf stood with shoulders slumped, staring blankly ahead of him. "It doesn't matter. What could I do with a little knife? Maybe kill one. I have to find a way to kill many of them. Many."

"Killing!" Mewick made a disgusted sound. He motioned with his head and they walked on. It was the last of day, just before the beginning of dusk.

Mewick mumbled in his throat, as if rehearsing arguments. Like a man forgetful, lost in thought, he lengthened his strides until he was a couple of paces ahead of Rolf.

Rolf heard the trotting hooves at a distance on the road behind him and turned, one hand feeling at his waist for the knife that was no longer there. Three soldiers were approaching at leisurely mounted speed, short black lances pointed up at the deepening clearness of the sky. Rolf's hands moved indecisively to the pack straps; in another moment he might have shucked them from his shoulders and darted from the road in search of cover. But Mewick's hand had taken a solid grip on the back of Rolf's shirt, a grip that held until Rolf relaxed. The barren fields bordering the road here afforded next to no cover anyway, which no doubt explained why just three soldiers came trotting the road so boldly on the verge of twilight.

The troopers all wore uniforms of some black cloth and bronze helmets, and had small round shields of bronze hanging loosely on their saddles. One of them was half-armored as well, wearing greaves and a cuirass of a color that dully approximated that of his helm. He rode the largest steed and was probably, Rolf thought, a sergeant. These days the Castle-men rarely appeared on duty wearing any insignia of rank.

"Where to, peddler?" the sergeant demanded in a grating voice; he reined in his animal as he caught up with Mewick and Rolf. He was a stocky man whose movements were slow and heavy as he got down from the saddle—he seemed to be dismounting only because of a wish to rest and stretch. The two troopers with him sat their mounts one on each side of the road, looking relaxed but calmly alert, their eyes more on the tufts of tall grass around them and the marsh ahead than on the two unarmed walkers they had overtaken. Rolf understood after a moment that the soldiers must be taking him for Mewick's servant or bound boy, since he had been walking two paces behind, carrying the load, and he was poorly dressed.

But that thought and others were only on the surface of Rolf's mind, passing quickly and without reflection. All he could really think of now was that these soldiers might be the ones. These very three.

Mewick had begun to speak at once, bowing before the dismounted sergeant, explaining how he was hiking on his humble but important business through the Broken Lands from north to south, being welcomed by the valiant soldiers everywhere, because they knew he had most potent charms and amulets for sale, at prices most exceedingly reasonable, sir.

The sergeant had planted himself standing in the middle of the road, and was now rotating his head as if to ease the muscles of his neck. "Take a look in that pack," he ordered, speaking over his shoulder.

One of the troopers swung down from his saddle and approached Rolf, while the other remained mounted, continuing to scan the countryside. The two dismounted had left their lances in boots fixed to their saddles, but each wore a short sword as well.

The soldier who came to Rolf was young himself, he could have had a little sister of his own somewhere in the East. He did not see Rolf at all except as an object, a burden-carrier upon which a pack was hung. Rolf moved his shoulders to let the pack slide free and the soldier took it from him. At some time when the men of the Broken Lands still worked in the ways of peace, someone had filled and strengthened the road at this low place; under his bare feet Rolf could feel fist-sized rocks amid the sand and clay.

The sergeant was standing leaning his dull gaze on Mewick as if trying to bore through him with it; the soldier took the pack there and dumped it on the ground between then, a cascade of gimcrackery on the damp earth. There fell out rings and bracelets and necklaces, tumbling and bouncing with love-charms of anonymous plaited hair, with amulets of carven wood and bone. Most of the objects were scribbled or shallowly inscribed with unreadable markings, meaningless signs meant to impress the credulous.

The sergeant idly stirred the mess with his toe while Mewick, blinking and hand-wringing, waited silently before him.

The young soldier stuck his own foot into the scattered pile and teased out a muddied love-charm, which he then bent to pick up. With his fingers he cleaned mud from the knot of long hair, and then held it up, looking at it thoughtfully. "Why is it," he asked of no one in particular, "we never catch a young girl out here?"

At that moment the mounted man had his head turned away, looking back over his shoulder. Rolf, without an instant's foreknowledge of what he was going to do, moving in a madness that was like calm, bent down and picked from the roadbed a rock of killing size, and threw it with all his strength at the head of the young dismounted soldier.

The young man was very quick, and managed somehow to twist himself out of the way of the missile. It flashed in a grazing blur past the astonishment of his fishwide eyes and mouth. With a sensation of deep but calm regret at having missed, Rolf bent to pick up another stone. Without time for surprise, he saw from the corner of his eye that the stocky sergeant was slumping folded to the ground, and that Mewick's arm was drawn back, about to hurl a small bright thing at the man who was still mounted.

The young soldier who had dodged Rolf's first rock had drawn his short sword now, and was charging at Rolf. Rolf had another rock ready to throw, and the tactics he employed with it came from children's play-battles with clods of mud. A faked throw first, a motion of the arm to make the adversary duck and doge, then the real throw at the instant of the foe's straightening up. This way Rolf could not get full power behind it, but still the rock stopped the soldier, crunching into the lower part of his face. The soldier paused in his attack for just a moment, standing as if in thought, one hand raised toward his bloodied jaw, the other still holding out his short sword. And in that instant Mewick was on him from the side. A looping kick came in an unlikely-looking horizontal blur to smash into the soldier's unprotected groin; and as he doubled, helmet falling free, Mewick's elbow descended at close range upon his neck, with what seemed the impact of an ax.

Two riderless beasts plunged and reared in the little road, and now there were three of them as the last of the troopers finally dismounted, in a delayed slumping fall, clutching at a short knife-handle fastened redly to his throat. In another moment the three freed animals were galloping back along the road to the northeast, in the direction from which they had come.

Rolf was aware of the sudden strident calling of a reptile in alarm, high overhead. Still he could do nothing but stand watching stupidly while Mewick, his short cloak flying, hopped back and forth across the road, cutting one throat after another with the practiced careful motions of a skillful butcher. The last of the three soldiers to die was the one who had been first to fall, the stocky sergeant; he seemed to have been ripped from groin to navel in the first moment of the fight.

Rolf watched Mewick's knife make its last necessary stroke, be wiped clean on the sergeant's sleeve, and then vanish back into some concealed sheath under Mewick's cloak. His mind beginning to function again, Rolf looked about him, noted how one black lance lay useless and unblooded at the side of the road, then bent at last to pick up the young soldier's short sword.

With this weapon in his grip Rolf followed Mewick at a run, going south along the road, and then off the road on its western side, pounding across a weed-grown fallow field toward the nearest arm of swamp. Twilight was gathering, and the reptile's cries grew fainter.

Even as he and Mewick ran splashing into the first puddles of the bog, Rolf could hear distant hooves and shouts behind them.

The Castle-men made no long pursuit—not at night, not into the swamps. Still the fugitives' way had been anything but easy. Now at midnight, wading through hip-deep water, sliding and staggering amid strange phosphorescent growths, more than half asleep on his feet, ready to fall but for the support of Mewick's arm, Rolf became suddenly aware of an enormous winged shape that drifted over him as silent as a dream. It was certainly no reptile but it was far bigger than any bird that he had ever seen. He thought it questioned him with words in a soft hooting sibilance, and that Mewick whispered something in reply. A moment later as the creature flew behind and above him, Rolf could see its rounded and enormous eyes by their reflection of some sharp new little light.

Yes, on the land ahead there was a tiny tongue of fire. And now the ground rose to become solid underfoot. The winged questioner had vanished into the night, but now from near the fire there stepped forward a huge blond man, surely some warrior chieftain, to speak familiarly with Mewick, to look at Rolf and offer him a greeting.

There was a shelter here, a camp. At last Rolf was able to sit down, to let go. A woman's voice was asking him if he wanted food. . . .

III

The Free Folk

———◆◆◆———

Yes, my parents are dead and under the earth—so Rolf told himself in the instant after awakening, before he had so much as opened his eyes to see where he was lying. My mother and father are dead and gone. And my sister—if Lisa is not dead, why she may wish she were.

Having reassured himself that he was capable of coping with these thoughts, Rolf did open his eyes. He found himself looking up through the small chinks in the slant of a lean-to shelter, an arm's reach above his face. The higher side of the low shelter was braced upon some slender living tree trunks, and it seemed to have been made mainly by the weaving together of living branches with their leaves. The interstitial chinks of sky were pure with bright sunlight; the day was well advanced.

He did not remember crawling into this shelter. Maybe someone had put him to bed here, like an infant. But that did not matter. He raised himself upon one elbow, crackling the dead leaves that he had slept on. The movement awakened a dozen aches in his body. His clothing was all rips and mud. His stomach was hollow with hunger.

Lying real and solid on the leaves beside him was the short sword that he had taken yesterday from the dead soldier. He saw again in his mind's eye the thrown stone from his own hand crunching into the soldier's teeth and bringing out blood. He put out a hand and gripped the captured weapon for a moment by the hilt.

Somewhere close by, quite near outside the lean-to, a few voices were murmuring together in a steady businesslike fashion; Rolf could not quite make out the words. In another moment he got up to his hands and knees and, leaving the sword behind him, crawled out of the shelter. He emerged almost within the group of three people who sat talking around a small smokeless fire.

Mewick was one of the group, sitting cross-legged and at ease, his cloak laid aside. Also at the fire was the big blond man that Rolf remembered seeing the night before, and beside this man a woman who resembled him enough to be his sister. When Rolf appeared all three of them fell silent and turned to look at him.

Once outside the lean-to, Rolf got stiffly to his feet. He addressed his first words to Mewick: "I am sorry, for starting that fight yesterday. I could have gotten you killed."

"Yes," Mewick nodded. "So. But you had reason, if not excuse. From now on you will be sane, hey?"

"Yes, I will." Rolf drew in a deep breath. "Will you teach me to fight like you can?"

Mewick had no quick answer, and the question was allowed to drop for the time being.

The woman by the fire wore man's clothes, which was natural enough for camping in the swamp, and her long blond hair was pulled back and bound up into a tight knot.

"So, your name is Rolf," she said, hitching herself around to face him more fully. "I am Manka. My husband Loford here and I have had something of your story from Mewick."

The blond man nodded solemnly, and the woman went on: "There's a pool safe to wash in on the other side of the hummock, Rolf. Then come back and have some food, and we'll talk."

Rolf nodded and turned away, going around the lean-to and the little clump of trees which occupied the center of this island of firm ground, some fifteen or twenty paces across. On the side of the hummock away from the fire a steep short bank dropped down to water which looked deeper and clearer than that of the surrounding swamp.

Only after Rolf had washed, and dressed himself again, and climbed the bank meaning to rejoin the others, did he see a living creature perched high in the biggest of the central trees. Right against the trunk a brownish-gray mass of feathers rested, big as a small man crouching. So dully colored was this form, so motionless, so shapelessly folded upon itself, that Rolf had to look twice to be convinced that it was not a part of the tree. When he thought to look for the giant bird's feet he saw that they were three-toed, bigger than a reptile's and armed with even more formidable talons. He still could not see how, under all the feathers, the bird's head had been folded down out of sight.

He was still turning his own head to look up into the tree as he rejoined the others around the fire.

"Strijeef is our friend," Loford told Rolf, seeing where Rolf's attention was fixed. "His kind have speech and thought; they call themselves the Silent People. Like our friend Mewick here they have been driven from their own lands. Now they stand here with us, their backs like ours against the sea."

Manka had ladled stew from a cooking-pot into a gourd for Rolf. After thanking her and starting to eat, he motioned with his head toward the bird and asked, "He sleeps now?"

"His folk sleep all day," Loford said. "Or at least they hide. Full sunlight is a great strain on their eyes, so by daylight their enemies the reptiles will find and kill them when they can. By night it is the birds' turn to hunt the leatherwings."

"I'm glad to hear that someone hunts them." Rolf nodded. "I wondered why they went flapping back to the Castle every day at sunset." And then he busied himself with the plentiful good food, meanwhile listening to the others' talk.

Mewick was bringing word to the Free Folk in the swamp from other resistance bands who lived and fought along the coast to the north of the Broken Lands. That portion of the seaboard was now also occupied by men and creatures from the East, under the rule of Ekuman's peer, the Satrap Chup. This Chup was supposed to be even now on his way south, to marry Ekuman's daughter in the Castle.

And the Satraps of other neighboring lands were said to be coming here, too, for the festivities. Each of them, like Ekuman and Chup, held power in his own region, ruling with the soldiers and under the black banner of the East.

When there was a pause in the talk, Rolf asked, "I've wondered—what is the East? Or who is it? Is there some king over it all?"

"I have heard different things," said Loford slowly, "about those who are Ekuman's overlords; I know almost nothing about them. We are in an odd corner of the world here. I don't even know much about the higher powers of the West." Rolf's face must have shown a dozen more questions struggling to be formulated, for Loford smiled at him. "Yes, there is a West, too, and we are part of it, we who are willing to fight for the chance to live like men. The West has been defeated here. But it is not dead. I think Ekuman's masters will be too busy elsewhere to send any great new power to his aid—if we can find a way to bring down the power that he has already."

There was a little silence. Rolf's heart leaped up at the thought of bringing down Ekuman, but he had seen the sobering reality of the Satrap's strength—the long columns of soldiers on parade, meant to overawe, hundreds mounted and thousands more on foot; and the strengthened walls of the great Castle.

Loford, having finished some private thought of his own, resumed his speech. "If Ekuman can expect no help, neither can we. The people of the Broken Lands will have to break their own chains or continue to wear them." Shaking his great head sadly, he looked at Mewick. "I had hoped you might bring us word of some free army still in the field in the north. Some prince of the West still surviving there — or at least some government trying to be neutral. That would have been a good encouragement."

"Prince Duncan of Islandia survives," said Mewick. "But I think he has no army on the mainland now. Perhaps beyond the sea are other independent states." His mournful mouth gave a tiny twitch upward at the corners. "*I* am here to help, if that encourages anyone."

"It does indeed," Loford said. Then, with a visibly quick change of thought, he threw a narrow-eyed look at Rolf. "Tell me, lad, what do you know of the Elephant?"

Rolf was taken by surprise. "The Elephant? Why, it's some wizard's symbol. I don't know what it means. I have seen it—maybe six times in all."

"Where and when?"

Rolf thought. "Once, woven into a bit of cloth, that I saw at a magic-show in town. And there is a place up in the Broken Mountains where someone has carved it in the rock—" He went on, enumerating as best he could the times and places where he had glimpsed the strange image of the impossible beast with its prehensile nose and swordlike horns or teeth.

Loford listened with close attention. "Anything else? Any talk you might have heard, even, especially during the last few days?"

Rolf shook his head helplessly. "I spent those days plowing in the fields. Until . . . "

"Aye, of course." Loford let out a groaning sigh. "I grasp at straws. But we must try every chance to find the Elephant, before those of the Castle find it."

Rolf supposed that the big man was talking about another magically important Elephant-image. "Ask help of a wizard?" he suggested.

Loford's jaw dropped. Mewick's eyebrows went up, his face took on an odd expression, and he made odd choking gasps — it took Rolf another moment to realize that Mewick was laughing. Manka's eyes seemed to flash angrily at first, but then she too had to smile.

"Have you ever heard of the Big One, child?" she demanded of Rolf, in a voice half-irritated, half-amused.

A light dawned. Once, long ago, Rolf had been sitting in a market town on Social Night, resting from his play to listen to the talk of men. The amateur wizards of the countryside had been assembled, discussing the feats of the professionals. The Big One from south of the delta would have done such and such a thing easily, someone had said, using the name as a standard of excellence. And the men listening had nodded soberly, their farmer-beards bobbing. Yes, the Big One. The name impressed them all, and for the little boy Rolf it had for a time afterward called up a mental picture of an enormous and powerful being, nodding benignly over farm and hill and marsh.

"No, it is all right," Loford, now smiling himself, assured Rolf. "You give me good advice. I must keep in mind that I am far from being the greatest wizard in the world." His smile vanished. "I am just the best one we now have available, since the Old One was taken under the Castle to die."

Mewick said to him, "You must take over the Old One's leadership in magic. But who is going to lead in other matters, now that he is gone? I speak plainly. You are not — not too practical, always, I think."

"Yes, yes, I know that I am not." Loford sounded irritated. "Thomas, perhaps. I hope he will lead. Oh, he's brave enough, and as much set against the Castle as anyone. But to really lead, to seize responsibility, that's something else again."

The talk went on. Manka ladled out more stew for Rolf, and he went on eating and listening. Always the thoughts and plans of the others came looping back to the mysterious Elephant. Rolf came gradually to understand that they were speaking of something more than an image, that the name meant some thing or creature of the Old World still existing, here somewhere in the Broken Lands. And this creature or thing loomed in the near future with terrible importance for East and West alike. This much—but, maddeningly, no more—could Loford's powers tell him of the Elephant.

Mewick suddenly stopped talking in mid-sentence, his eyes turned skyward, one hand shot out and frozen in a gesture meant to keep the others still. But it was too late, they had been discovered from above, in spite of the trees' shelter.

Overhead there sounded a clangorous shouting of reptiles. A dozen of the flying creatures were diving to the attack, coming in at an angle under the trees, talons spread, long snouts open to bare their teeth.

Rolf dived into the shelter and jumped out again with his sword. Mewick and Manka had already caught up bows and quivers from their small pile of equipment beside the fire; in another instant one of the attackers was flopping on the ground at Rolf's feet, transfixed by an arrow.

The main target of the attack, Rolf saw, was the bird huddled in the tree. The bird roused itself as the reptiles, momentarily baffled by branches, came whirling around it; but it seemed to be blinded, rendered stupid by the light.

Before the scaly ones could work their way in among the branches, their attack was broken up. Arrow after arrow sang at them, hitting more often than not. And Rolf leaped right in among the lower branches, sword thrusting and slashing high and

wide. He could not be sure that he wounded any of
the reptiles, though he harvested leaves and twigs
in plenty. But between sword and arrows the
leatherwings were forced to retreat, whirling upward in a shrieking swarm of gray-green rage. Arrows had brought down four of them, and these Rolf
now had the satisfaction of finishing with his blade.
They screamed words at him as they died, half-
comprehensible curses and threats; still the
slaughtering meant no more to him than killing
beasts.

Having risen out of bow-shot, the surviving reptiles maintained a flying circle directly above the
hummock, cawing and screaming mightily.

"When they do that, it means there's soldiers
coming," Manka said. She had already slung her
bow on her back and was moving speedily to gather
up the rest of the camp's scanty equipment. "Quick,
young one, go and uncover the canoe."

Rolf had seen the dugout, camouflaged by
branches, floating against the bank near the pool
where he had washed. He ran now to load things
into it. Manka called to the bird. Following her voice
it descended from the tree, impressive talons groping blindly and clumsily as it walked, feeling for the
prow of the canoe. With one surprising extension of
its wings it mounted there and perched, muffling
itself in folded wings so that it resembled some
badly-stuffed figurehead.

Mewick, a bow still in his hands, was trotting
anxiously from one side of the hummock to the
other, trying to learn from which direction the soldiers were approaching. Loford, standing ankle-
deep at the water's edge beside the canoe, kept
bending and scooping up massive handfuls of
grayish swamp-bottom muck. Each time he muttered over the glob, and then let it dribble back into
the water. At last one string of droplets veered from
the vertical, went spraying out sideways as if caught
by a strong blast of wind.

Loford pointed in the same direction. "They come from that way, Mewick," he called out softly.

"Then let us go the other way, quick!" Mewick came running to the canoe.

But Loford was now muttering faster than ever, and making odd sweeping motions with his arms, like a man trying to swim backward through the air. His fingertips threw droplets of muck. He kept up this gesticulating even while Manka was guiding him to take his seat in the dugout, so that he nearly swamped it in his clumsiness, for all the others could do to maintain balance. And I thought him a warrior! said Rolf to himself with a pang, looking back impatiently from his position in the foremost seat. Then Rolf's jaw began to drop. He saw ripples growing in the swamp-water, swells that came from no wind or current. Growing in amplitude with each motion of the Big One's steadily sweeping arms, the waves followed the timing of those arms; and they did not spread like ordinary waves but instead, gathered together building higher.

Manka shoved off from shore, and then paddled from the rear seat, while the nexus of disturbed water raised by the Big One's magic followed sluggishly after the canoe. Rolf paddled in the front, his sword in the canoe bottom ready to hand. Mewick, still holding the bow with a long arrow nocked, was in the second seat, whispering Rolf directions on which way to steer among the rotting tree-stumps and the small overgrown hummocks of firm land. Rolf kept glancing back. In the third seat, Loford still labored to build his spell. He shifted his great weight awkwardly and once more nearly rolled the canoe. Rolf thought that they were going over, but a muddy projection like a sheeted hand bulged up above the surface of the water to hold, briefly but strongly, against the gunwale. Then Rolf understood that he was witnessing the raising of an elemental, and his respect for Loford jumped to a new high.

The reptiles had seen the first of the raising too, for one of them now left the circular formation that was holding over the canoe, and flew back over the big hummock the canoe had just left, crying out a warning.

But the warning might be too late to do the pursuing but still invisible soldiers any good. Urged on by the ever smaller and more precise movements of Loford's hands, the disturbance in the shallow water behind the canoe had become a slow, fantastic boil, which mounted higher and higher and now raced away, sweeping back around the big hummock, beyond which the enemy must be drawing near.

Now the water around the canoe was grown quite still again. As if by some command, Rolf and Manka had both ceased to paddle. All but the blinded bird sat looking back and waiting.

Loford's hands were still outspread. "Paddle!" he urged, in a sudden fierce whisper. For a moment Rolf was unable to obey—because he saw now, on the other side of the big hummock, and mounting almost instantly to the height of its central trees, a great upwelling structure of mud and slime and water. Shouts greeted the elemental, the startled and fearful voices of men enough to fill many canoes. Rolf could not see those men, but beyond the trees he could see the thing of mud marching among them ponderously. It was gray and black, and shiny as if with grease, and what little shape it had oozed from it as it moved.

Screams rang out that came from no reptilian throats, and then sharp splashing told of men floundering clear of overturned boats. There followed more confused yelling, and then the rhythmic work of paddles straining in retreat.

"Paddle!" Loford said. "It may turn back now after us."

Rolf paddled, at Mewick's direction steering into

a channel of sorts that ran between half-formed banks of earth.

"Paddle!" Loford urged again, though Rolf and Manka were already hard at work. Rolf's hasty glance over his shoulder showed him that the elemental, shrunken but still tall as a man, had come racing back around the hummock and was in full pursuit of its creator and the boat that bore him. The wave-shape jetted watery, unintelligible sounds in little bursts of spray; it shrank still more as it closed the distance between itself and the canoe. Loford was soothing the thing he had raised up, soothing and destroying it, his voice whispering to it once more, his hands working with firm, down-pressing gestures.

Such life as the elemental had went ebbing away from it with its volume. What finally came purling under the dug-out was no more than a sluggish wave, roiling the tiny green plants that scummed the water's surface. As it passed, lifting him, Rolf saw turning within it the thonged sandal of a Castle soldier. He watched in vain to see if any more satisfying trophy might be displayed.

Screaming in rage, but staying impotently out of bow-shot, the reptiles still followed the canoe. In a little while, trees began to close more thickly over the waterway the craft was following, and a mass of swamp-forest ahead promised almost complete shelter. Now in their frustrated fury a few of the reptiles dared to dive, screeching, at the bird which still perched motionless upon the dugout's prow.

Rolf was quick to drop the paddle and grab his sword again. With Mewick's arrows flying at them and the sword-blade singing past their heads, the leatherwings had to sheer away. They climbed again, and disappeared above what was becoming an almost solid roof of greenery.

Rolf looked gloomily at his sword, unstained in

this latest skirmish. "Mewick—teach me to use weapons?"

". . . in self-defense," Mewick muttered, sitting up. He seemed to have thrown himself into the bottom of the canoe to escape the sword's last swipe.

"Oh! I'm sorry." Rolf's ears burned. He took up his paddle and applied himself to its use, looking straight ahead.

After a while Mewick's voice behind him said, "Yes, all right, then I will teach you, when I can. Since the sword is in your hand already."

Rolf looked back. "And other kinds of fighting, too? The way you kicked that Castle-man yesterday . . ."

"Yes, yes, when there is time." Mewick's voice held no enthusiasm. "These are not things to be learned in a week or a month."

The channel they had been following divided, came together, and then branched again. Manka, now choosing their way from her position in the stern, seldom hesitated over which branch to take. Loford's magic continued to be of help; it opened walls of interlaced vines ahead of the canoe—or at least made them easier to open by hand—and then knitted them once more into a barrier after the craft had passed. Rolf paddled in the direction he was bidden, meanwhile keeping a sharp lookout ahead.

Looking ahead, Rolf was the first to see the young girl gazing down at them from a lookout's perch in a high tree; he rested his paddle and was about to speak when Manka said, "It's all right. She's a sentry of the big camp."

The brown-haired girl in the tree, dressed like Manka in male clothing, also recognized the Big One and his wife. She came sliding down from her observation post and ran along the bank to greet them. To Rolf and Mewick she was introduced as Sarah; Rolf guessed she was about fourteen years old.

And she was obviously anxious about something. "I don't suppose any of you have any word of Nils?"

she asked, looking from one person to another.

Nils was Sarah's boy friend, seemingly about Rolf's age or a little older. He had gone out on some kind of raid or scouting expedition with the other young men of the Free Folk, and they were overdue. No one in the canoe was able to give Sarah any information, but they all tried to reassure her, and she waved after them cheerfully enough when they paddled on.

Very soon after passing the sentry-post, they came to an island much larger than the one they had fled earlier in the day. A dozen canoes were already beached at a muddy landing-place, from which well-worn trails branched into the woods. Along one of these paths six or eight people came filing to greet the newcomers as they landed.

By now the afternoon was far advanced. Here in the deep shade of the island's trees the bird, Strijeef, began to come out of his lethargy. He raised his head and said a few words in his musical voice, then flew soundlessly up into a stout tree where he settled himself again. This time he did not hide his head but peered out slit-eyed from among puffed feathers. A few words of the bird's speech seemed to have been directed at Rolf, but he had been unable to understand.

"The bird bids you thanks, for fighting off reptiles," said a tall young man, taking note of Rolf's perplexity.

"He is quite welcome," said Rolf. Then in a bitter tone he added, "I had the chance to kill some of them and I failed."

The man shrugged and said something encouraging. Introducing himself as Thomas, he began to question Rolf about the events of the last two days. Thomas was perhaps ten years Rolf's senior, strongly built and serious of manner. He had greeted the other new arrivals as old friends, and had questioned them at once about the movements of the enemy.

While Rolf was giving Thomas and the others a description of his missing sister, the group walked from the landing-place to what was evidently the main camp, where a dozen large shelters had been built under concealing trees. Rolf's story was received with sympathy, but no surprise; most of his hearers could have matched it with something from their own lives. The description of Lisa would be circulated, but Thomas warned Rolf there was little reason to be hopeful.

The evening meal of the camp was just ready; there was no shortage of fish and succulent stew. A company that grew gradually to fifteen or twenty people was gathering about the cooking fire.

The food drew most of Rolf's attention, but he heard the word being passed in from a lookout that another canoe was coming. It bore only a lone messenger, who was soon being entertained at fireside. He brought some apparently routine news, and after he had spoken in conference with Loford, Thomas, and several others, another messenger was dispatched. Obviously this camp was some center of command, in contact with other groups of Free Folk. But while the message brought by the man in the canoe was being discussed, Rolf sensed something strained in the decision-making process here. Many people seemed to be taking part in it, not all of them quite willingly. They spoke with slow hesitance, each weighing his neighbors' reactions as he went on from word to word. No one seemed eager to push himself or his ideas forward.

"If only the Old One were here!" one man lamented, seemingly exasperated by the length of a debate which had sprung up, over whether or not a certain cache of weapons should be moved.

"Well, he's not," a woman answered. "And he's not coming back."

"He was Ardneh, if you ask me," said the first speaker. "And now no one is."

Rolf had not heard of Ardneh before. And so a

little later, when Loford sat down beside him to eat, he asked the wizard what the man had meant.

Loford answered casually at first. "Oh, we've come to use the name as a symbol for our cause. For our hopes of freedom. We seem to be trying to build ourselves a god."

A what? Rolf wondered silently.

Chewing slowly on a morsel of fish, Loford squinted into the firelight, which seemed now to brighten rapidly with the fading of the day. Now he spoke more intently.

"In a vision I myself have beheld Ardneh in this guise: the figure of a warrior, armed with the thunderbolt, mounted on the Elephant."

Rolf was much impressed. "But Ardneh is real, then? A living being, some kind of demon or elemental?"

The movement of Loford's massive shoulders might have meant that the question had no answer. "He was a god of the Old World, or so we think."

Curiosity left Rolf no choice but to reveal the depth of his ignorance. "What is a god?"

"Oh," said Loford, "we have no gods, these days." He interested himself more in his food.

"But were gods like demons?" Rolf asked helplessly, when it seemed that no more information was forthcoming. Once he started trying to find out about something he hated to quit.

"They were more than that; but I am only a country wizard and I know little." In the Big One's voice there sounded a momentary weight of sadness.

And then Rolf forgot about probing such deep matters, for Sarah came to join the group about the fire, having just been relieved of sentry duty. Rolf talked with her while she ate her evening meal. Her boys' clothes could not disguise the prettiness of her face nor the shapeliness of her tiny body, and he felt disinclined to seek out any other company.

She talked with him easily enough, heard his story with sympathy, listened carefully to a description of his sister—then she related almost casually how her family too had been destroyed by the men and creatures of the Castle.

Her mask of calm lifted when another messenger was reported arriving by dugout, and when this man came to the fire she listened with a bright spark of interest—which soon faded. The news had nothing to do with Nils.

The sun had now been down for some time, and Sarah grew steadily more attractive in the warm glow of firelight. But Rolf's meditations on this subject were interrupted by the arrival of yet another messenger.

This one came by air. Strijeef, who had awakened rapidly and begun to move about as the last light faded from the sky, was the first to see the approaching bird. But Strijeef had only just gotten into the air and uttered his first greeting hoot before the new arrival was down, stooping with startling speed through the leafy roof above the fires, then on the ground, shivering and gasping rapidly in what seemed near-exhaustion. People gathered around it quickly, shading its eyes from the firelight, offering it water and demanding to hear the news that inspired such effort.

The first words this bird uttered came out well mixed with gasping hoots and whistles, but they were loud and plain enough to be understood by even Rolf's unpracticed ears: "I have—found the Elephant."

The bird was a young female, whose name Rolf understood as Feathertip. Early last evening she had been prowling near the Castle. That place and its high reptile roosts were defended, by stretched cords and nets, from any bird's attack, but there was always the chance just after sunset of intercepting some reptile tardily hurrying home.

Last night there had been several stragglers, but Feathertip had been disappointed in her attempt to catch them; it had simply taken her too long to get near the Castle from her daytime hiding place in the forest. The latest of the leatherwings had got himself home safe in the darkness just ahead of her.

So it had occurred to her to try to find a place very near the Castle in which to hide during the daylight hours. With this in mind she had flown along the northern side of the pass upon whose southern edge the Castle perched. The pass interrupted the thin line of the Broken Mountains. On the northern side of the break the mountain ended in a jumble of crevices and narrow canyons which promised some concealment. In the moonlight, Feathertip flew there searching for some ledge or cranny so well hidden that the reptiles would not be likely to see it during their daylight patrols, so high and inaccessible that no patrol of soldiers would be able to get near.

The great birds' eyes were at their best by moonglow and in the tricky shadows of the night. Still Feathertip had twice passed by the opening before she paused, on her third flight through a narrow canyon, to investigate what seemed no more than a dark spot on a sheltered face of rock.

The spot turned out to be a hole, the entrance of a cave. An opening not only concealed from any but the most careful of winged searches, but so narrow that Feathertip thought that if worst came to worst, she might even be able to defend it in the light. And so she determined to stay.

Seeking out the inner recesses of the cave, to find what other entrances there might be and also to escape as far as possible the pressure of the morning sun, the bird had made her great discovery. Through a narrow descending shaft—down which one of the heavy wingless people should be able to climb if he took care—Feathertip had reached a cave as smooth as the inside of an egg, and long and wide enough to hold a house. The bird knew the sign of the Elephant, and this sign was on each flank of the enormous—creature?—thing? (Feathertip could not decide which word applied) which alone occupied the cave, and which in her opinion could hardly be anything but the Elephant itself.

Four-legged? No, it had seemed to have no legs at all. Had it a grasping nose, and teeth like swords? No—at least not quite. But never had the bird seen anything like that which waited unmoving in the buried cave.

By now Feathertip had regained her breath, and was plainly enjoying her telling of a story that made the heavy wingless people crowd around to question her so impatiently. She was established now with her back to a shaded fire, and for the most part the humans saw her as a dark soft outline, having huge eyes that now and then sparked faintly with the caught reflection of something luminescing out in the swamp.

She stuck stubbornly to her conviction that the thing in the cave could be nothing less than the Elephant itself. No, it had not moved; but it did not seem dead or ruined. On what seemed to be its head it did have several projections, all of them looking stiff as claws. No, Feathertip had not touched the Elephant. But every part of it looked very hard, like something made of metal.

Sarah was explaining to Rolf that the birds always had difficulty in describing man-made things; some of them could not distinguish between an ax and a sword. The strength of their minds just did not lie in that direction.

The questioning of the bird had begun to trail off into repetition. The air of hesitancy, of unwillingness to take up the responsibility of leadership, still seemed to dominate the group.

"Well, someone must be sent to see what this thing is," Thomas said, looking about him at the others. "One or more of us heavy wingless ones. And as soon as possible. That much is plain."

A discussion began on which of the various bands of Free Folk scattered through the countryside was closest to the cave, and which would have the easiest and safest route to get there.

Thomas cut the discussion short. "We're only about eighteen kilometers from the cave ourselves—I think it will be fastest after all if one or two of us go from here."

Loford was sitting smiling in silent approval as Thomas began to lead. Thomas turned now to the bird and said, "Feathertip—think carefully now. Is there any possible way for a human being to climb to the entrance of this cave of yours?"

"Whoo. No. Unless they made a stairway in the rock."

"How high a stairway would it have to be?"

"Eleven times as high as you." On matters of height the birds were evidently very quick and accurate.

"We are none of us mountain climbers, and we are in a hurry." Thomas began to pace nervously, then quickly stopped. "We do have ropes, of course. Is there some projection in this cave or about it, around which you could drop a loop of rope, to let us climb?"

There was no such projection inside the upper cave, Feathertip said after some thought. On the opposite side of the canyon was a pinnacle where she could hang a rope; but a human climbing there would still have to get across the canyon and in beneath an overhang.

"Could I jump this chasm? How wide is it?"

The distance of a good running broad jump, it seemed. And it would have to be accomplished from a standing start of precarious footing.

There was argument, and the rudiment of a plan emerged.

"Look, we know a bird can't lift an adult human," said Thomas. "But we've two birds here now, both big and strong of their kind."

People interrupted with objections.

"Let me finish. They can't lift a man cleanly, but

couldn't they help him jump? Swing him, delay his fall, as he jumps from atop this pinnacle of rock to get across the canyon?''

The birds both said they thought that something of the sort might just be possible. And no one was able to think of a better plan for getting a human quickly into the cave; of course the ground would have to be examined first. In any case no large party with ladders and other cumbersome equipment could be sent with any safety to work so near the Castle.

Thomas's enthusiasm was building steadily. ''It must be done somehow, and the birds' help may make it possible. We'll see what way looks best when we get there. And there's no time to waste. If I leave here within the hour, I can be hidden among the rocks on the north side of the pass before dawn. Just lie low during the daylight hours, and then tomorrow night—''

Loford asked him, ''You?''

Thomas smiled wryly. ''Well, you've been prodding me to assume some kind of leadership.''

''This is not a leader's job. It's one for a scout. Why you? You're needed here to make decisions.''

Others jumped into the argument. It was soon more or less agreed that two people ought to go, but there was no agreement on who they should be. Every man and woman who was not slow with age, or recovering from a wound, volunteered. ''Heights don't scare me at all,'' Rolf offered.

''Me neither!'' Sarah wanted to go. She claimed that she was lighter than any of the others, certainly an advantage if it came to a matter of being partially supported by birds.

''Ah!'' said Thomas to her, a spark of humor in his eye. ''But what if Nils comes back and finds that you've gone off alone with me?''

That quieted Sarah—for a while—but Thomas found the others' squabbling harder to put down. At last he had to nearly shout, "All right, all right! I know the land as well as anyone. I suppose I can decide as well as anyone what to do about the Elephant when I reach it. So I am going. Loford will be the leader here—so far as I have any authority to name one. Mewick—you must stay in the swamps for a while, to talk to others of our people as they come in, tell them about the situation in the north and elsewhere, so they'll understand we cannot expect any help . . . now, let's see. Will I be light enough to jump into this cave with a boost from two birds?"

He stretched out his arms. Strijeef and Feathertip took to the air and hovered about him, and each carefully clenched their feet around one of his wrists. Then their wings beat powerfully, the strokes becoming faintly audible, their breeze whipping up sparks and ashes from the remnants of a fire. But Thomas's feet did not leave the ground. Only when he jumped up could the two birds hold him in the air, and then only for the barest moment.

"Try it with me!" Sarah now demanded. With great exertion the birds could lift Sarah just about a meter off the ground, and hold her there for a count of three. What jumping she could manage did not help very much.

She was elated, but Thomas kept shaking his head at her. "No, no. We may have to do some fighting, or—"

"I can shoot a bow!"

He ignored her protests, and nodded toward Rolf. "Try him next, he seems about the lightest."

The birds rested briefly, then gripped the ends of a piece of rope which Rolf had found and looped around his body under his arms. "At the cave I'll need my hands free to cling and climb," he explained. Then he leaped upward with all the spring in his legs, just as the two birds lifted mightily. He rose till his feet were higher than a tall man's head, from which elevation it took him a count of five to fall to the ground against the birds' continued pull.

"Well." Thomas considered. "That would seem to be about the best that we can do."

"I'm ready to hike," Rolf told him. "I've rested most of the day. Just paddled in the dugout."

Thomas, staring at him thoughtfully, cracked a faint smile. "You call that resting, hey?" He looked across the fire at Mewick.

Mewick said, "I think the young one has got all the madness out of his system."

Thomas looked back at Rolf. "Is that true? If I take you, we may run into a fight but we're not looking for one."

"I understand that." The madness for revenge was not gone, far from it. But it had grown into something cold and patient. Calculating.

Thomas stared at Rolf a moment longer; then he smiled. "Very good. Then let's get started."

IV

The Cave

———◆———

The earliest light of dawn found Rolf and Thomas lying side by side, facing south across the pass, in the mouth of a narrow crevice between towering rocks. The pass before them was not distinguished by any name; though it was the only clean break in the Broken Mountains for many kilometers both north and south. They were both worn with swamp-paddling and cross-country hiking through the night just past—with their furtive wading crossing of the river Dolles, and their last climb, racing against the coming of dawn, to their present position.

The spot they had reached was a commanding one. By moving a meter forward, out of the mouth of the tiny canyon, they might have seen to their right the Dolles winding like a lazy snake along the foot of the mountains from north to south. Beyond the river stretched Rolf's home country of farmlands and lowlands and swamps. And in the distance, plainly visible, was the blue vagueness of the western sea.

Straight ahead of the tiny canyon's mouth, the barren land fell downward for some two hundred meters in a gradually decreasing slope to where the east-west highway threaded the bottom of the pass. And south beyond the highway the land rose again in an equivalent slope, to a foothill of the southern mountain chain; and upon that foothill stood the gray and newly strengthened walls of the Castle.

To the left of the Castle, Rolf could see part of the

desert country that rolled down from the all-but-rainless inland slopes of the Broken Mountains, and stretched on for perhaps two hundred kilometers to the high and forbidding Black Mountains. The desert looked hot already, though the sun was scarcely risen.

"The leatherwings are up betimes," said Thomas quietly, nodding straight ahead. The early sun was bright on the net-protected houses and perches clustered on the upper parts of the high Castle, showing a gray-green movement of reptile bodies under the nets. Ekuman's flag of black and bronze had evidently flown all night from a pole on the flat roof of the keep. And there were other decorations dangling high on wall and parapet; the tiny whitish stick-figures that Rolf knew had once been people, good people, who had displeased the land's new masters and had been lifted up there to be living toys and food for the leatherwings.

The only living men to be seen now on the high places were dots of black and bronze, the movements of their arms and legs barely distinguishable at this distance. They were about the morning routine of furling the protective nets from around the reptiles' roosts. Now the gray-green dots came into plainer view, swelling and contracting. The reptiles would be stretching their wings. Cawing and whining drifted faintly across the pass. In another moment the first of them were airborne, making room for more and more to appear on the perches. Soon the air above the Castle grew cloudy with their circling swarm.

"And now we had better make sure to lie low," said Thomas, casting a look around at their hiding place. To their rear, the narrow crevice in which they lay twisted back into the foot of the mountain, its sandy floor losing itself among huge tumbled boulders and splintered outcroppings of rock. A shoulder of the mountain had slumped and fallen here an age ago. Somewhere back in that jumble, this little crevice grown wider had high on one of its walls the hidden cave-entrance. Strijeef and Feathertip had taken shelter there for the day. Getting Rolf or Thomas somehow into the cave would have to wait for another night.

Directly above Thomas and Rolf, the rock-bulges of the canyon walls shut out the sky entirely. The reptile swarm centered above the Castle had now spread until its thinned edges reached this far and farther, but still there came no cawing of alarm from overhead, no gathering of faces at the Castle wall. Rolf found it moment by moment easier to believe that he and Thomas would not be seen today if they kept still.

Keeping still was not going to be hard. The folk in the swamp had given Rolf sandals, but still his feet were sore from the long, fast hike. And he was tired in every muscle.

Lying stretched out in the sand, nerves still sleeplessly taut, he let his gaze wander eastward again. In the far distance the Black Mountains looked grayly insubstantial with the morning sunlight almost at their backs. Much nearer, but still well out over the badlands, clouds were forming a high knot that promised rain. Rolf knew that under those clouds the Oasis of the Two Stones must lie, though a low elevation of the land between kept him from seeing that round fertile patch. Years ago Rolf's father had brought him here to the pass, to show him the Castle—then an innocent and wondrous ruin—and had also pointed out to him where the Oasis lay amid the desert, and had told him of the wonder of its rainfall.

Rolf suddenly realized that something strange was happening to the clouds. Instead of remaining gathered above the one always-favored spot they were moving now, coming roughly toward the pass.

This seemed to him so odd that he called it to

Thomas's attention. Thomas slid a few centimeters forward and peeked cautiously out of the canyon mouth to look for himself.

"Something must have gone awry with their magic out there," he said shortly.

"I wonder what their magic is."

Thomas shook his head. The distant knot of vapor had already darkened into a thunderstorm, and was chasing its shadow toward them across the desert, lighting itself from within by a sudden flicker of lightning.

"I suppose the invaders are holding the Oasis too," Rolf said. He thought he could hear the thunder, tiny and distant.

Thomas nodded. "Quite a strong garrison, I understand." He pulled himself back. "We'd better take turns on watch, and each get some sleep while we can."

Rolf said he could not sleep yet, so Thomas agreed to let him take the first watch. Then Thomas opened his pack and took out a marvelous thing. It was an Old World device, he explained, that was supposed to have come from beyond the western sea. It had been cherished for generations in the family of a man who now had joined a band of Free Folk.

The device consisted of a pair of metal cylinders, each about the length of a man's hand. The cylinders were clasped side by side with metal joints that fitted and worked with incredible smooth precision, as Rolf saw when Thomas let him take the device carefully into his hands. He had never before had the chance to handle anything of the Old World so freely, and he had never before seen such workmanship in metal.

Each end of each cylinder was glass, and looking through them made everything suddenly a dozen times closer. At first Rolf was less impressed by the function of the thing than by the form. But gradually Thomas made him understand that there was no magic involved here; Thomas said that Old World devices never depended upon it. Instead the illusion of closeness came somehow from what Thomas called pure technology; the thing was a tool, like a saw or a spade, but instead of working wood or soil it worked on light. It needed only whatever power eyes could give it, looking through its double tubes.

No magic needed, to move a man's point of vision out from his body and bring it back again. It was an eerie thought. Technology was a word that Rolf had heard perhaps a dozen times in his life before today, and then always in some joking context; but now the truth of what it meant began to gradually impress itself upon him.

"How do you know there's no magic in them?"

Thomas shrugged slightly. "No one can feel any. Wizards have tried."

Rolf handled the eyeglasses with an eagerly growing fascination as he drew the Castle near him and pushed it away again. He searched for the thunderstorm, but it had dissipated already. He looked at Thomas's face, a mountain-blur of nearness.

"Don't look at the sun through those, your eyes will burn out."

"I won't." Rolf already felt an affinity for technology deeper than any he had ever felt for the things of magic; he had known enough not to look at a sun made a dozen times more dazzling.

Something in the satisfaction of the glasses eased the tension that had so far kept him from feeling sleepy; he yawned and felt his eyelids drooping. Thomas announced that he himself had better take the first watch after all.

Rolf rolled against the rock wall of the canyon, put down his head and at once dropped off to sleep, to awaken with a violent start when his arm was touched. He had little sense of time having passed, but he did feel rested, and the sun was near the zenith.

Having the Old World glasses to use, Rolf found the time of the afternoon watch passing quickly. At the main gate of the Castle, there was a more or less continual coming and going, of both soldiers and civilians. A few wagonloads of provisions came jolting over the bridge that spanned the Dolles in the midst of what was now a half-deserted village at the foot of the Castle's hill. Barrels and bales and sacks were carried up on slave-back to the Castle from the barges moored at the village landing-place. Only slaves labored now in what Rolf remembered as a free and thriving town. Dots of bronze and black stood guard with whips that became visible only through the glasses.

Rolf did not watch that for long. Each time a party of soldiers came down from the Castle, or passed below him in either direction through the pass, he watched them tensely, ready to rouse Thomas in an instant should any turn upslope toward these rocks.

Thomas had rolled under a bulge of rock as far as a man could get, and there he slept. Now and then he would utter a faint groan and make abortive motions with his powerful arms. Somehow it seemed wrong and discouraging to Rolf that a man healthy and strong, a successful leader, should have to put up with bad dreams.

Rolf swept the landscape once more with his glasses. Here was something new, coming toward the Castle from the southwest, the general direction of the swamps. In a little while Rolf made out that it was a group of slaves or prisoners being marched along a road. First he had seen only the dust raised by their slow progress; now through the glasses he could see that they were men and women both, chained or roped together, perhaps fifteen of them. Now he could see the arm of a bronze-helmed guard rise and snap and fall back again. A long time later the faint pop of the whip came drifting across the intervening valley of the pass.

He did not want to watch this and yet could not keep from watching. The prisoners' faces became visible. More bewildered conscripts for the endless building . . .

Rolf nearly dropped the glasses. He raised them again quickly, and with shaking fingers turned the knurled knob that Thomas had taught him to use for greatest clarity. Still the image wavered before him, until he remembered to rest his elbows once more in the sand.

A little behind the other prisoners, and bound more lightly if at all, was a young girl who looked like Sarah. She was riding, mounted on a huge beast behind a soldier. She looked like Sarah all the more as they came slowly closer. If it was not some terrible trick of these demon-begotten glasses . . . Rolf kept trying to tell himself that it was only that.

At last he woke Thomas. Thomas was instantly alert, but still just too late to see the girl as the Castle's maw swallowed the last of the prisoners and their guard. The teeth of its portcullis snapped shut behind them.

Thomas put down the glasses he had just raised. "Are you sure it was Sarah?"

"Yes." Rolf stared at a double handful of sand and pebbles, into which he was digging his fingers until they hurt.

"Well." It seemed to Rolf that Thomas was taking the news with unnatural calm. "Did you recognize anyone else?"

"No. I don't think any were people from our camp."

"So. There might have been some word about Nils come into the swamp, and Sarah went out to try to make sure of it—whatever it was. And she just got picked up. Those things happen. Anyway, there's nothing we can do about it, except to go on with what we're doing now." When Rolf nodded, he put a hand on Rolf's shoulder for a moment, then turned away again against the rock. "I should sleep a little longer. Be sure and rouse me before the sun goes down."

But Thomas could scarcely have fallen asleep before Rolf was shaking him again. More people were approaching the Castle, and had popped suddenly into Rolf's view, their earlier progress having been hidden from him by the rock he sheltered against. Not in chains did these folk come, but in great splendor, on a gaily-painted river barge descending the Dolles, escorted on each shore by a hundred mounted men.

This time Thomas looked long before handing the glasses back to Rolf. "It's the Satrap Chup, coming down from his own robber's roost in the north. Ekuman's son-in-law to be."

The barge tied up at the central landing-place. In the center of those who disembarked was a powerful-looking man in black trousers and cuirass trimmed with red, mounted on a magnificent riding-beast. And beside him on a white animal came riding a young girl with blonde hair of marvelous length; so fair was her skin, so beautiful her face, that Rolf wondered again, aloud, if the glasses might not add a shading of magic to the things they showed.

"No, no," Thomas reassured him, dryly. "You'll not have seen her before, because her habit is to stay in the Castle or very near it. But that's Charmian, Ekuman's daughter. She evidently went halfway to meet her bridegroom, and now comes finishing his journey with him. It might be an interesting wedding; I've heard there's another in the Castle who dotes on her."

"How could you hear that?"

"The Castle servants are human if the masters are not. They're too frightened to talk much, but sometimes a single word can travel marvelously."

Rolf had heard of Charmian's existence, but had not really thought about her until now. "I thought that Ekuman had no wife."

"He had once, or perhaps she was only a favored

concubine. Then he went East, to perfect himself in
. . . the ways that he has chosen."

Rolf did not understand. "He went East?"

"From where he came to begin with I do not know,
but he has been to the Black Mountains, to pledge
himself to Som the Dead."

That name was new to Rolf. Later he would seek to
learn more, but now he took a turn at thoughtful
silence. It was beyond his understanding that a
fiend like Ekuman should have a lovely daughter, to
be given away like some kindly farmer's, with a feast.

Thomas's thoughts were evidently running along
the same lines. "I wonder sometimes why such as
these bother to marry. Hardly to pledge their love. I
think not even to pledge each other any kind of
honest help in life."

"Why, then?" Rolf wanted to think of anything but
what might be happening to Sarah.

Thomas shrugged. "It's hard to remember sometimes that Ekuman and those about him are still
human, that the crimes they commit are human
crimes. I've heard Loford say that if the Satraps live
for many years, growing stronger in their evil, it
sometimes happens that they are summoned East
at last, to stay."

"Why?"

"To become something more or less than human,
I think that was the way Loford put it." Thomas
yawned. "Loford wasn't sure, and I'm talking in
total ignorance. You want another nap?"

"No. I don't feel tired."

So Thomas did sleep again, but he roused himself
well before sunset, and then Rolf was willing
enough to take another nap himself. He only dozed,
and got up without being wakened as the shadows
began to deepen.

Like the humans of the Castle, the reptiles had
been coming and going in small numbers all
through the day, but now they came from all direc-

tions, in haste to reach their roosts before night. Now was the time when Feathertip, if she had been following her original plan, would have come soaring forth. Tonight she could have caught more than one straggler made careless by the Castle's nearness. But with a far greater enterprise hanging in the balance, the birds would not hunt reptiles tonight. The leatherwings came home unmolested, to slowly blacken the rooftops of the Castle with their clusters.

And in the earliest of the true night the two birds came silently down the canyon, following the dim twisting channel of it with scarcely a wing-movement. Their huge shapes were over Rolf before he had more than imagined that he saw them.

Rolf and Thomas were each carrying ropes, long and strong but thin, wound about them under their shirts. Thomas unwound a long rope now from his ribs, and tied one end of it into a loop, of a size Feathertip directed.

The two birds then flew back up the canyon. Behind them a trailing end of rope tickled over the sand and over shadowed, broken rocks where human feet must move with caution.

Rolf and Thomas followed. The looped rope had already been hung for climbing when they caught up with the birds, who sat waiting on the canyon floor.

"Well," said Thomas. He set down his pack, then tugged hard on the rope, to make sure that the loop was holding solidly on the invisible peak, about eleven times his height. Then he hesitated. At last he said, "If I'm killed or left unconscious beyond rousing—I've seen men that way after a fall— then you must just go on as best you can."

"I know."

After that Thomas delayed no more but climbed, swiftly and surely; Rolf envied the strength of arm that could swing a big man up like that. For a few moments Thomas's climbing figure was outlined vaguely against the stars. Then he passed out of sight above a convexity of rock. Soon after that, the hanging rope's gyrations ceased.

From where he stood Rolf could see only that loose descending rope, and nothing of what was going on above. He could see where Thomas would come down, if he fell. At that place a hard flat surface would have been bad enough, but the actuality was worse, a jumble of sharp upjutting stony corners.

The rope hung still, and held time with it. Then the long line started swaying again. Rolf let out his breath in a huge silent puff. The birds were first to settle to the ground, and then the man, who slid the last distance with his sandaled feet clamping the rope.

Having got down, Thomas leaned as if for needed support against the face of the rock he had just quitted. Then he wiped at his face with his sleeve and said, "I didn't try it. The only way is with the birds."

Strijeef hooted, "Tooo heavy." Feathertip made a nodding motion that she must have adopted from humans.

"Then I'll go." Rolf looked at the birds, telling himself how strong they were, especially now when they had just had a good day's rest. But he could not keep his eye from moving beyond them to mark how the sharp rocks stood in the bottom of the crevice. "That's what I came along for."

"Yes." Thomas now sounded stubbornly angry. Rolf found himself half-wishing that the man might change his mind and, after all, attempt the leap himself—and make it, of course. But Thomas did not change his mind.

Rolf divested himself of his pack, and his extra ropes. Such things could be lifted easily to him later, if he—after he had reached the cave. He kept the short length of rope for the birds to grip and swing him by.

"Good luck," said Thomas.

Rolf nodded. And then he was climbing the long rope, hauling with his hands and walking with his feet against the rock. He remembered you were not supposed to look down from a high place, so he did not.

And then before he had any time to think about what came next, he had reached the pinnacle. There was just room for him to crouch on the peak of the tall rock. The world looked unreal from here—the stars above, the sparks of torches on the distant Castle. The moon, huge and nearly full, was just starting up across the desert.

The birds were hovering at Rolf's sides. He handed each of them an end of the short rope looped under his arms. His eyes were searching downward among the deceptive shadows on the cliff-face opposite. "I don't see the cave. Where is it?"

"Hoo. Stand up."

He stood, holding out his arms for balance. With gentle pulls at the rope the birds turned him, facing him in the right direction. They had wound the rope-ends tight in all their talons.

"I still don't see it."

"We will bring you to it. Jump high, jump far, and then grab rock when you can."

He remembered when he was a child, jumping on a dare from a tree tall enough to offer a frightening drop. Take no time to think, and jump straight out, then you could do it . . . delay, and you might never go . . . and after the bold jump had come the hard triumphant landing . . . don't look down.

"This way?"

"This way." Their wingtips multiplied soft blessings near his head. "Now bend and jump!"

Giving himself to the birds, he leaped, fear adding spring to his legs. The lifting power that he could feel on the ropes was heartening—for a moment. Then he was falling. It was not the sheer empty dropping from the tree, but neither was it flying, or being held. Rolf's arms turned panicky and thrashed ahead of him for something to grip. Impossible for human eyes to judge a distance here at night. The enormous wings worked on above him; their wind and that of his falling whirled against his face, while the horizontal momentum of his leap still carried him toward the wall of stone where the cave must be. That wall was moving upward frighteningly as his fingers scraped it. It bulged toward him, and his fingers were free in the air of a sudden aperture—and then Rolf jolted to a halt, arms thrusting into the cave over its lip which struck him in the chest. His knees banged painfully into the wall below. He clung there seemingly without a grip, held by his extended arms' friction on smooth rock. The supporting pull on the ropes ceased while the birds walked over him and into the cave. Then they pulled again, from in front. With beak and talon they helped him drag his heaviness up and into the safe hole.

Once he had solidity under him he sat without moving, trying to get his hands to loosen their compulsive gripping of whatever came in reach. To the panting, quivering birds he said, "Tell—tell Thomas I made it."

"He has seen youuu did not fall. Hoo. He knows you made it." But after only a moment's rest the birds took to the air and left him. They would be back very soon with his tools and supplies. Rolf swore that by then he would be able to let go the rock and do something useful.

It was a mighty good thing that Thomas had had the guts not to attempt the jump. His weighty muscles and his big bones would have pulled him down for sure, down to be broken on the rocks . . . but there was no point in such thoughts now. Rolf forced himself to relax.

Strijeef was back even before Rolf had expected him, dropping a rope-tied pack hastily at Rolf's feet.

"Rooolf, big patrol from the Castle is coming on the ground. Thomas will run away, so if he is caught it will not be here. We Silent People must help him, we will come back when we can. Soldiers cannot climb here. Thomas says find out what you can."

"Yes," Rolf stammered after a moment. "All right. Tell him don't worry. I'll find out." There seemed to be nothing more that needed saying.

The bird waited just a moment longer, gazing at Rolf with its wide wise-seeming eyes, swollen drops of ghostly light here in the dim cave. "Good luck," it said, and brushed him with a wingtip.

"You too."

When Strijeef had vanished, Rolf sat in silence, listening. After what seemed a long time he heard hooves passing somewhere below, making muffled sounds in sand and scraping very faintly over rock. For a while the movements seemed to slow down, to pause; then they proceeded at a faster rate that soon took them altogether out of earshot.

Straining to hear more, he told himself that Thomas certainly could not have been taken without a struggle and outcry. The birds would be eyes for Thomas. He must certainly have got away.

Time passed, bringing no further sounds. Rolf undid the rope from around the pack, and found food and water, more rope, flint and steel, small waxy torches, and a small chisel wrapped against clinking. With this last tool he was to carve in the rock some sort of notch in which a climbing rope could be anchored. The madness of birds and jumping would not have to be repeated.

He thought it over. The soldiers who had passed below were evidently gone now, either back to the Castle or in pursuit of Thomas, or simply continuing their patrol. They would not have left only one or two men here, not at night, and if they had left more than that he should be able to hear something from them. But they might well send men here in the morning. And in the morning the reptiles would be out. All in all, it seemed that now was the best time for stonecutting.

To muffle the sounds he emptied the pack and set the chisel under it. Then he chose a rock for his mallet and got to work, pausing after every tap to listen. The rope he meant to anchor here was already fastened to the middle of a short stout stick, and he needed only to reshape a wrinkle in the floor a bit to have a place where this anchor could be solidly fixed.

So his noisemaking was soon over. He repacked his gear and sat listening for another while. Once he thought the wind brought him some distant cry, whether animal or human he could not say. He shivered slightly. He felt wide awake. Should he start now on his exploration of the inner cave?

He could make a tentative beginning anyway. He crawled away from the cave mouth, going into utter darkness, groping before him with his hands. He had gone only a few meters when his foremost hand came down on nothingness. He stretched himself out on the brink of a vertical shaft and reached forward as well as he could, but could not touch the other side.

He went back to his pack and got out one of his torches. These were stiff-stemmed wax-rushes from the swamp, dried and dipped in animal fat, then cast by Loford under some kind of fire-spell that was meant to make them burn smokelessly and bright. But at last Rolf decided not to light the torch, to put off further exploration until morning. Daylight would doubtless filter even into the lower cave, so he might climb down without having to hold a torch. And besides, he kept expecting one of the birds to come back at any moment, bringing him word of what had happened to Thomas. And besides that—he was reluctant to go down to face the Elephant alone at midnight.

He sat down near the cave mouth and, despite his situation, easily fell asleep. Twice he awakened with a start from dreams of falling, to find himself clutching at the rock. And each time he woke he worried a little more because the birds had not yet come back. Surely Thomas must have got away by now, or been caught? And had the birds been shot down too, by luck and by torchlight?

Rolf passed the time dozing and waking, until a more violent start after a period of deeper sleep roused him to the awareness that daylight was at hand. At least now he could feel certain that the birds would not come, not until another evening had arrived.

He had cut his socket into the rock so that it would hold the anchor stick firmly against a pull from either direction. He set the stick in place now, and from it hung his longest rope into the inner shaft. With full daylight he started the descent, pack strapped firmly on his back.

The chimney at its top was perhaps three meters wide; it narrowed irregularly as he went lower. It had the look of a natural fault, some splitting of the hill that perhaps had happened at the same time as the dumping and scattering of the rock-jumble outside.

As Rolf moved further down the daylight lessened, but still for the first twenty meters he did not need a torch. Then, at what he thought was approximately the level of the ground outside, the chimney ended in a hole, through which the rope went vanishing into blackness. Supporting himself on feet braced on opposite sides of the diminished shaft, Rolf freed his hands and struck fire to a rushlight. It burned cleanly. He thought the flame and trace of smoke showed a gentle upward movement of the air around him.

Rolf followed his rope, gripping it between his sandaled feet, keeping one hand free to hold the torch. He was in a huge wide hollow place. After descending only a few meters more, he could set his feet on a floor of smooth and level stone.

The rays of his rushlight fell across the cave, upon a closed pair of enormous doors. Before him stood a motionless rounded shape, twice taller than a man and perhaps a thousand times as bulky.

Rolf knew that he had found the Elephant.

V

Desert Storm

———————◆◆◆———————

Thomas could see nothing of Rolf's bird-supported leap across the chasm, and could hear only the faint scrambling noise of his arrival at the cave. But that, at the moment, was quite enough. Thomas allowed himself a single sigh of relief.

It took the birds only a few more moments to put an end to his relief, by descending with the news that a mounted patrol was moving in his direction from the Castle, was in fact already crossing the highway at the bottom of the pass.

That meant they were not much over two hundred meters away, and Thomas got moving even before he spoke. "If they catch me here they'll keep poking around in these rocks. I'll head for the western slope. Tell Rolf to find out what he can in the cave. And make sure no ropes are hanging out in sight."

He was just working his way out of the rocks on the western side, thinking to get back to the swamps if he could, and communicate with Rolf for a day or two by bird, when Strijeef came spinning above him again, with word that more men were approaching from the west, coming uphill from the riverbank. "You must go east, Thomas. We will help."

He hated to leave Rolf, but the youngster in the cave would just have to depend on his own brains and nerve. Thomas got out of the rocks at last on the eastern side, and started moving furtively down the first open slope of the vast desert. He had a water bottle with him, and could lie low in the wasteland for a day. When night fell again he could work north and get back across the mountains somewhere; the Broken Mountains were nowhere high or wide enough to keep an agile man on foot from finding his way through.

He cursed the brightness of the moon as he angled down the long open slope, heading away from pass and Castle. After going something over a hundred meters he paused and listened. He thought he could hear the muffled sounds of soldiers in considerable numbers moving in the area he had just left. He would have given much to know whether it was just a routine patrol, or whether they had seen or suspected something. Sarah was in the Castle. If the enemy had the least reason to connect her with the Free Folk, she might easily have been forced by now to tell everything she knew. It was Thomas's own fault, doubtless, that she knew so much. He supposed that he and the other leaders would have to be more secretive in their planning, hide themselves from their own people half the time, keep the rank and file from knowing anything beyond what they were absolutely required to know. There had to be ways to organize a rebellion properly. To install a rigid command structure and iron discipline. Such things were probably vital and would have to be used—if Ekuman let the Free Folk survive long enough to learn them.

If he meant to survive he had better get on with his retreat. He had gone only a little way further when, looking back, he saw the enemy begin to come out of the rocks, tall wraith-like shapes on riding-beasts emerging in the moonlight. Thomas crouched down again and kept on moving slowly away. The enemy troop fanned out as they left the rocks, riding slowly in his general direction. Obviously they hadn't seen him yet, but neither were they ready to go home for the night.

Their apparently random choice of a direction to search further was uncomfortably accurate. With an underhand fling Thomas pitched a pebble way out to the southeast, at right angles to the line of his retreat. They heard it, all right; he saw some of them stop at the sound. They would think it was probably an animal, but would be suspicious. Now their whole rank of twenty men or thereabouts came to a halt. Thomas continued to pace softly and steadily away from them. When they got underway again they were headed more to the east.

He might have lain still now and let them pass him at a little distance, but there was always the chance that they might turn again, and he didn't want them pinning him against the mountain. So he kept on retreating along his original line, getting a little farther out into the desert and breathing a little easier. He was just congratulating himself that the pebble-tossing had been exactly the right move, when one of the birds came drifting swiftly over his head, hooting to him in the lowest of warning notes. Thomas turned, and what he saw in the moonlight froze him in midstride. He felt himself suddenly huge and nakedly exposed. The long open slope that a moment before had been so free and sheltering in its distance was now a barren trap.

A vast fan-formation of a hundred riders or more was coming down on him from the north. Their line extended from the side of the mountain, sheer and unclimbable just here, out into the desert farther than a man could see at night from where Thomas stood. It was now all too plain to him that the smaller force which had chased him out of the rocks was intended only to drive the game into the net. They might be only engaged in training exercises, but the trap was very real.

He was one man, and unmounted; they could scarcely have seen him yet. Both birds came over Thomas's head for a moment, but they only turned together there in silence and rose again. There was nothing that needed to be said; they would do what they could, he knew, to help him get away.

The trap looked very tight. He had stopped moving now because there was no place to go. If he was taken alive . . . he knew too much to risk that. He drew a long knife, his only weapon, from his belt. It would be utterly foolish to try to dash through the enemy line. As the noose drew tighter he huddled down, making himself as small as possible, in the moon-shadow of a tiny bush. With one hand he scraped up sand, trying to cover his legs sticking out of the shadow. It was not going to be enough, and yet there was nothing better he could do. Unless the birds could create some distraction.

The ghostly-looking line of troopers came on at a walk that looked unhurried but still covered ground. At the point of their line nearest Thomas, they were so close together that a bush-bounder could not have crept unseen between them. The cursed moon seemed growing brighter by the moment. Surely they must all see him now, they were only playing with him. With only a knife he might not even be able to kill one of them. He ceased trying to cover his legs, and held his breath and waited. The line was almost upon him.

Suddenly the rider nearest Thomas stood up straight in his stirrups. He had grown a monstrous winged helmet, a blot of darkness that dragged and lifted at him, tearing from him a terrible cry of pain and fear. His riding-beast panicked and bucked, and those next in line on either side reared up, their masters struggling to control them. "Birds!" The word was passed in low voices, quickly, to the right and left.

The first man who had been struck drove off his attacker somehow. The line continued to move forward. There was another flurry of movement a little distance off, and then another. Both birds were now attacking, making it seem that there were more than two of them. Ranging up and down the line from the spot where the first man had been struck, Strijeef and Feathertip spread pain and confusion, dragged one man from his saddle, got home on others with beak or talon, veered off from the attack if they found a man ready to meet them with sword or short lance.

There was no telling how long the birds could keep it up. Thomas forced himself to move toward the enemy, out of the shadow of the bush, flat on his belly. It seemed unbelievable that they did not see him. But the riders were looking up into the starry air, guarding themselves. Their beasts were all prancing now, uncertainly if not in downright panic.

On his belly Thomas slid forward one meter after another, keeping his face turned down and hidden. A riding-beast snorted almost over his head, and hooves trampled past, almost hitting him. If the beast saw him, the rider did not.

He heard a grunt of triumph from one of the men in the line that had now drawn past him, and simultaneously a scream whose like he had never heard before from the throat of man or beast. A little scuffle ended in a fluttering sound that he had never before heard made by the wings of the Silent People. And then very quickly the desert was once more almost silent.

Thomas now lay on his face without moving, without trying to look around. The knife-handle in his hand was slippery with sweat. He breathed the dust of the desert floor. His ears told him that the line of troopers was moving on still, going away from him.

When the sounds were far away he rose cautiously to knees and elbows, and turned his head. The mounted men were many meters distant now and still receding; he could not see that any of them carried a feathered trophy. He crawled, circling as widely as he dared over the area where the birds had fought the men. But he could find no trace, not even a feather.

The birds had saved him, whether they had died

for him or not. Dead or wounded, they were gone. Thomas crawled out into the desert until he had put sufficient distance between himself and the enemy to feel safe in standing up. Looking back, he saw that the noose had tightened all the way. The enemy force, once gathered, seemed to be breaking up into smaller bands. There was no telling how they might move next to scour the plain. The only course for Thomas was to keep moving away from them, farther and farther out into the desert. Well, so be it, then. He would turn back westward when he could. Maybe it would have to be tomorrow night. He had his water bottle.

At dawn he was still walking; by now the Castle and the pass were many kilometers behind him. The Black Mountains ahead were not perceptibly closer. Nearly barren, the land around him undulated to the horizon in all directions, without a sign of men or man-made things.

Daylight was liable to bring reptiles. The notch of the pass behind him was too distant for him to see the leatherwings rising above the Castle, but he knew they would be there. He would soon have to hole up for the day.

The scanty vegetation here offered no really promising place to hide. He would go on a little, looking for a bigger bush. Now in the growing light he began to notice an odd thing. The sand in places had a crusty, pocked, granular look, as if it had recently been rained on. Yes, just a day ago he and Rolf had seen the improbable rainstorm moving over this part of the desert. The Oasis of the Two Stones was in this general area, though Thomas could not see it for the rolling of the land between.

He went on, still searching for a good hiding place, and casting frequent anxious glances up at the brightening sky.

Then he saw a reptile, but it was on the ground, and dead—and, like the rain-stippled sand around it, something of a marvel. He stepped over a low dune to find the reptile's body there in the hollow before him. It lay sprawled and twisted, gray-green no longer but swollen and black.

The death was not the marvel—reptiles had their diseases and misfortunes, and certainly their enemies—but rather the manner of the death. The body was swelled enough to split the scaly skin, but not with decay, rather as if the creature had been roasted alive. Yet the sand around showed no signs of fire or great heat, only the faint marks of yesterday's rain.

Around the swollen body stretched a strap that held a pouch—the reptile had been one of Ekuman's couriers. Thomas turned the child-sized body over with his foot. The pouch itself was burned black and torn; the charred fabric crumbled further at his touch. There was no heat left in it now. Inside, his gingerly probing found what had doubtless been a written message, but the paper dissolved into ash-powder at a breath.

There was something in the pouch, however, that did not dissolve. A closed case of some heavy metal. It was of a shape that might contain some precious jewel, but the size of Thomas's two fists. He turned it over carefully in his hands. It was not an Old World thing, he decided, for its shape and joining lacked the incredible precision that distinguished the metalworking of the ancients. It was blackened and battered. Thomas could not read the signs that were graven on it, but as he weighed it in his hands he felt certain that he held some powerful magic. The enemy would hardly freight his couriers with mere gimcracks.

So the thing must be taken to Loford. Thomas buried the reptile and its emptied pouch with hasty scrapings of sand, to keep the others of its kind from finding it.

Walking on, he shook the strange case in his hands and could feel a shifting weight inside. He turned it over and over, and felt the natural temptation to open it. But caution prevailed over curiosity, and he thrust it unopened into his pack.

Looking up again for reptiles, Thomas was pleased to see that the sky was clouding over. If there was to be a peculiar rainy season this year in the desert, well, he would take advantage of it; clouds would hide him from the reptiles better than any of these scanty bushes could.

As the sun came up a rim of clear sky brightened all around the horizon; but directly overhead a solid low overcast a couple of kilometers in diameter developed. The grayness of it thickened and darkened in swirls and ominous gatherings of vapor, while Thomas mentally cheered it on. A good rain would not only protect him from aerial observation, but could eliminate any chance of his running out of water.

Thomas sat down for a rest. The clouds showed no inclination to blow in any direction today, the air seemed windless. The first grumble of thunder sounded overhead; the first big drops came pelting down. He put out his tongue to taste them.

There was a flare and flicker above, then thunder once again. Sullenness growing in the atmosphere, and an electric pause. And then a high-pitched scream, that brought Thomas leaping to his feet and spinning around. From the same direction that he had come, a young woman was now running toward him, some fifty meters away. She wore a simple farm-girl's dress, and a wide hat such as the folk of the Oasis wore when working their unshaded fields. As she ran toward Thomas she was crying out, "Oh, throw it! Throw it away from you!"

Some buried part of his mind must have been aware already of the danger, for now he did not hesitate an instant. He scooped the blackened thing of power out of his pack and in the same motion of his arm lobbed the weight of it away from him, putting all his strength into the effort. And then the air seared white around him, and a shock great beyond hearing seemed to tear apart the world.

VI

Technology

With slow steps Rolf walked twice around the Elephant, keeping a cautious distance from it, holding his torch high.

Except for the impression that it gave of enormous and mysterious power, this before him did not much resemble the creature depicted in the symbols. This was a flattened metal lozenge of smooth regular curves, built low to the ground for something of its massive size. Here could be seen no fantastically flexible snout, no jutting teeth. There was no real face at all, only some thin hollowed metal shafts projecting all in one direction from the topmost hump. Looking closely Rolf could see that around that hump, or head, were set some tiny glassy-looking things, like the false eyes of some monstrous statue.

Elephant was legless, which only made it all the more impressive by raising the question of how its obvious power was to be unfolded and applied. Neither were there any proper wheels, such as a cart or wagon had. Instead Elephant rested on two endless belts of heavy, studded metal plates, whose shielded upper course ran higher than Rolf's head.

On the dull metal of each flank, painted small in size but with Old World precision, was the familiar sign—the animal shape, gray and powerful, some trick of the painter's art telling the viewer that what it represented was gigantic. In its monstrous gripping nose the creature in the painting brandished a

sharp-pointed spear, jagged all along its length.
Under its feet it trod the symbols:

426th ARMORED DIVISION

—whose meaning, and even language, were strange
to Rolf. Now, holding his breath, he ventured to put
out a hand and touch a part of one of the endless
belts, a plate of armor too heavy for a man to carry or
for a riding-beast to wear into a fight. Nothing
seemed to happen from the touch. Rolf dared to lay
his hand flat on the featureless surface of the
Elephant's metal flank.

Then he stepped back and looked around the rest
of the cave. There was not much to see. A few openings in the curving walls, holes too small for men to
enter. Maybe they were chimneys of a sort; the air in
the cave was good. And there were the huge doors
set in the wall just ahead of Elephant—if "ahead"
was the direction in which the projections on the
topmost hump were pointing.

These doors were flat expanses of metal, seemingly covering an opening of just the right size to
permit Elephant's passage. The vertical cracks of
imperfect closure at the doors' edges were noticeably wider at the bottom than at the top, as if the
great panels had been slightly warped. Through
each widened crack a small heap of pebbly dirt had
sometime trickled to the floor below.

Rolf knelt thoughtfully to finger some of this debris. As nearly as he could calculate, the floor here
was at approximately the same vertical level as that
of the canyon outside. The same landslide that had
made the rock-jumble out there might easily have
buried these doors.

He closed his eyes for a moment to better vis-
ualize the various distances and directions of his
movements in coming into the cave. Yes, it seemed
so. Let these doors be opened, and some of the
house-sized rocks outside them cleared away, and
Elephant would be free.

His rush-light had burned down to a finger-searing shortness and he lighted another from it. The air in the cave seemed as fresh as ever, and what little smoke his torch gave off was rising steadily. It would be far too much dispersed and faint for anyone to notice at the outer entrance of the cave.

Rolf walked again around Elephant, running his hand along its surface. On this circuit he paid much closer attention to details. This was like handling Thomas's eyeglasses; there was no feeling of magic here, but a sense of other powers that somehow seemed to suit Rolf better than wizardry.

High on one vast armored flank, just above the covered upper level of the endless tread, was a barely perceptible circular line, like the crack of a very close-fitting door. Recessed in the surface of this circle was a handle that might tug it open, if it was indeed a door. And now Rolf saw there were four small steps, set into the solid metal, ascending from floor level to the circle.

He took a deep breath, gripped his torch precariously between his teeth, and climbed. The handgrip on the door accepted his fingers easily. Deep in his throat he muttered a protective spell, half-forgotten since his childhood—and then he pulled. His first tug was resisted, and his second. Then, when he dared lean all his weight outward from the handle, ancient stiffness yielded with a sudden crack of sound. The door, incredibly thick, swung open on a hinge. In that moment a sharp, straining click sounded somewhere in Elephant's inside, and there was light, striking out of the door like the golden beams of the sun.

Already off balance, Rolf half-leaped, half-fell from Elephant's side, his torch landing on the stone floor beside him. He did not need the torch, with the flood of true illumination washing out of Elephant's opened side. That golden glow was not as bright as sunlight, he saw now, but it was as steady as the sun, without smoke or flames or flickering

Now Ardneh will appear, Rolf thought, and made

himself stand up. He had some idea, or thought he
did, of how a demon should look, but no ideas at all
about a god. He waited, but no creature of any sort
appeared. Elephant was as immobile as ever.

He chose to take the light as a favorable sign, and
once more climbed the steps, pausing to marvel at
the balance of the heavy door that he had opened.
He paused again with his eyes just above the lower
rim of the doorway, for the shapes inside were of a
bewildering variety and all at first seemed utterly
strange. Printed or graven symbols, not one of
which Rolf could read, were sprinkled thickly
everywhere. Nothing moved; nothing was clearly
menacing. The light as steady as the sun came from
little panels that glowed like white-hot iron but yet
seemed to radiate no warmth.

Pulling himself up gradually until he was halfway
into the doorway, Rolf listened. From somewhere
deeper inside Elephant came very faint murmuring,
a little like running water, a little like soft wind.
Wind it was, perhaps, for air was moving faintly out
of the doorway, past Rolf's face.

He sat in the doorway a little longer, probing the
strangeness before him with busy eyes. Actually the
open space inside Elephant was not very big. Three
or four men would pretty well fill it, and be crowded
among all the strange objects that were already
there. But now Rolf could see certain indications
that humans were meant to enter. The door itself
had an immensely strong but simple latch that
could be worked only from inside. And the narrow
clear paths of the metal floor had been roughly surfaced, as if to provide good traction for human feet.
And from the fixed furniture of peculiar objects
there extended several projections that looked like
tool-handles, made to fit the grip of human fingers.

Soon Rolf was crouching entirely inside the
doorway, bathing in the heatless light, continuing
to marvel. From here he could see more. Three ob-

jects that had puzzled him at first he suddenly understood to be chairs. They were low and stoutly
made, faced not toward one another but side by
side, turned in what seemed to be the direction
Elephant was facing, toward the huge flat doors.

With gradually increasing boldness, Rolf carefully
stood upright—though he was not tall, he had little
head-room—and made his way step by step, touching things with deliberate caution, to the central
chair. This chair was thickly surfaced with stuff that
might once have been good padding but was now
hard and brittle. It cracked at his touch and sent up
a cloud of dust when he at last dared to sit on it. The
dust made him sneeze, but soon it was borne away
by the mysterious whispering circulation of the air.

Around the three seats and in front of them were
ranged many incomprehensible objects, made of
metal and glass and substances more difficult to
name. Here were several of the handles that might
have been those of tools or weapons; experiments
first cautious and then more energetic convinced
Rolf that none of these handles were intended to be
pulled free to reveal simple tools of some sort on
their working ends.

Elephant seemed to be accepting Rolf as some
huge placid work-beast might tolerate a baby's
prodding; when this comparison occurred to Rolf he
smiled. A feeling of possessive power was growing
in him. All these wonders were becoming his—
already they belonged more to him than to any
other living man. Suppose Thomas were here now,
or Loford. Suppose one of the clever and mighty
wizards of the Castle. Would any of them dare do
this? And Rolf raised a hand, and touched casually
one of the light-panels, which gave off only the faintest warmth.

Sitting in the middle chair, he noticed that above
each seat there hung a mask. Each mask had a strap,
as if to hold it on a human head, and two glass

rounds for eyes. From each mask's nose there curled away a snout of more than Elephantine length, to fit into a socket in the wall. Rolf's first touch made the face of the mask that rested above his chair crack dryly, and broke the long snout into a shower of dust and brittle fragments.

Blinking his eyes and brushing powder out of his hair, he looked around him apprehensively. But still nothing happened. Even the murmuring whispering seemed to be smoothing itself down nearer silence.

Rolf sighed out a long shuddering breath and was aware that, for the moment at least, the last of his fear had left him. His being here was all right, all right with whatever powers were in charge. He waited. The quiet air seemed pregnant with importance. The movement of the air carried the fresh dust away. A broken mask perhaps did not matter to Ardneh, for Ardneh was not a demon. He was — something more than that. If he was anything at all.

On a sudden impulse Rolf spoke soft words aloud. "Ardneh? You were a god in the Old World, where this Elephant was made. I know that much. I don't know any spells to call you up. Since you're not a demon maybe spells aren't needed — I don't know."

He paused. Encouragement seemed to wrap him, through the softly moving air.

"Loford says that you have come to stand for freedom, and so I . . . I wish that you would work through me. Someone said that the Old One was Ardneh, in a way, and in the same way I want to be Ardneh too." For a moment Rolf in his imagination saw himself as the warrior of Loford's vision, mounted on Elephant, armed with the thunderbolt in his hands. And for a moment the dream did not seem ridiculous.

Still no voice but the steady fading murmuring answered him. Rolf twisted in his seat, suddenly feeling like a fool kid playing, talking to himself. He sneezed again in the fresh dust raised by his movement. So much for that. It would be nice to have a sorcerer's power, but there was no point in playing at it like a child. He had no real control of demons, nor of gods either, whatever they might be.

He decided to get on with the job. Again he began to test the objects before him and around him with his hands, pulling and prodding and twisting carefully. If there was a magical aspect to Elephant, he was incapable of dealing with it. He would just have to approach it like a farmer confronted with some strange and enormous tool, trying the handles that should make it work—

Rolf grunted in surprise, and snatched his hands away from the table-like thing before him. Within a glassy panel on that table a series of dots of light had suddenly appeared, all regular in form and spacing though no two alike in color. Above and around the dots and also limned in pure light were sets of characters, in a language unreadable to Rolf. The largest said: CHECKLIST.

After contemplating this for a little time, and reassuring himself that nothing more serious had happened, Rolf was emboldened to put his hand back on the control he had last touched, and push where he had just pulled. The lights in the panel before him obediently died away. He turned them on and off and on again, savoring new power.

The upper most dot on the panel was bright orange. A small knobbed lever at the side of the panel, near Rolf's right hand, had also acquired a marking of orange light. He pushed it, and it moved with a click.

NUCLEAR POWER IGNITION sprang out in orange characters beneath CHECKLIST on the panel. And at the same moment Elephant grunted.

The grunt came from deep in Elephant's guts. It repeated itself, and turned into a groan, like the agony of some deep bellyache. Rolf, stricken suddenly by all old fears redoubled, grabbed at the little lever to reverse what he had done. His shaking fingers missed, as the whole bulk of Elephant lurched beneath him. The groaning divided itself into divers voices, like those of a cage full of demons all in torment and wrestling one against another. Rolf sat paralyzed, afraid to try to stop them now, afraid to let them go. The voices slowly managed harmony in their wrath, their shouting racing faster, blurring into a single shuddering roar.

NUCLEAR POWER ON

Rolf might have leaped up and fled, but for the thought that he could never get out of the cave before Ardneh struck him down. He clutched his dust-exhaling chair and waited.

Nothing struck him. Instead, Elephant's shaking gradually diminished. The roaring deepened, becoming smoother and more certain. An exhilarating sense of enormous power being delivered into his hands blended with Rolf's returning confidence, making it stronger than ever.

The orange dot was gone now from beside the NUCLEAR POWER ON legend inside the glass panel, and the markings of orange light were gone from the little lever. The next highest dot in the panel was purple, and now purple markings glowed on another small handle, this one at Rolf's left.

This time he closed his eyes in wincing anticipation as the control clicked under his fingers. When he opened them again he knew another brief spasm of fear. A ring like a giant's collar, nearly a meter in diameter, was descending from above his chair to encircle his head.

The ring came to a halt, not touching him, at the level of his eyes. The inner surface of it was flat and bright, shot with moving patterns of light, the way he supposed a wizard's crystal might look if the visions were uncertain. But soon this confusion cleared away, and Rolf found that by some power he was looking through the surface of the wide ring as if it was a window. This was something more impressive than Thomas's far-seeing glasses. He could see the cave around him, the big flat doors ahead, with perfect ease, as if the solid mass of Elephant had become transparent as water.

Purple was gone. Now there was a red dot on the panel, and a red-lit control to handle.

ARMAMENT INOPERATIVE

A pair of thin red lines, crossing each other at right angles, had appeared on his vision-ring. Rolf pressed at the red control again, and a spurt of what looked like liquid fire came lashing feebly from one of the projections on Elephant's snout. It was as if Elephant had retched up a mouthful of pure flame, and fouled its own forequarters with its spitting. Only one drop of the flame shot as far as the doors ahead, where it hung heavily, oozing lower like a fire-tear, leaving a blackened trace above it.

Now Rolf sat still for some time, watching the spattering of fire cool and blacken on the door and on Elephant's impervious metal hide. At last he tried again the control that had brought the fire, but this time nothing came. The red dot, unlike the previous ones, stayed on the panel, along with ARMAMENT INOPERATIVE, though he could make the thin red cross-lines on his vision-ring come and go.

He decided that he would go on anyway to the next color, which was a spring-sky blue. He got the blue dot to go out, and went on, testing control after control. There were others that stayed lighted, turning red. Some caused strange rumblings or cracklings around him. Some controls produced no effect that he could see, except for changing the lights on the panel.

When finally the lowest dot in the sequence winked away, the CHECKLIST legend vanished with it. And now for the first time light appeared on the two most prominent handgrips within his reach, outlin-

ing them in bright green. These two handles, sturdy
enough to have fit a plow, stood one on each side of
his chair. He had tried moving them before, without
result. Now he tried again.

At his first gentle pressure on the levers, the roaring beneath him, which had gradually been smoothing itself down to a lower level of noise, came swelling up. Rolf hesitated, waited, and then stiffened his
arms, pushing the two levers forward. Groaning
anew, Elephant gave a lurching start and moved.
Suddenly the doors were very close ahead. Startled,
Rolf yanked both levers back. His great mount
bucked, with a sound of studded metal plates laboring like monstrous claws on the stone floor, and
then lurched into reverse. It gathered speed. Now
the rear wall of the cave was very close behind.
Again Rolf over-reacted, pushing the levers forward
hard. In his haste he moved them unevenly this
time, the right farther than the left. Elephant
skewed toward his left as he advanced again. His
right shoulder touched a door just as Rolf, fighting
against panic, once more reversed his two hand
controls. Any child could use a pair of reins. You
had to let the creature you were driving know that
you were boss. The homely thought-pattern helped
him get himself under control, and when he had
done that he found that the control of Elephant was
easy.

Carefully, with the beginning of skill, he eased his
great mount forward and backward. There did not
seem to be room for a full turn, but he started a turn
to the left and stopped and came back and began
one to the right. At last he brought Elephant back to
somewhere near his original position, standing still
and quietly vibrating.

He dared then to let go of the controls, to wipe
sweat from his face. He nodded to himself—quite
enough for one day, yes. He had probably pushed
his luck too far already. He had to find out now if he
could put Elephant back to sleep.

Following what seemed to him the commonsense way to accomplish this, Rolf began to return the controls he had moved to their original positions, in the reverse order from that which he had used to wake the Elephant up. The system worked. The colored dots began reappearing on the panel, bottom to top. Soon the vision-ring dimmed, became opaque, rose up away from his head. And soon after that the roar of power mumbled down into silence, and all the characters and dots of CHECKLIST vanished behind dark glass once more.

Slowly, trembling with a tension he had not fully realized till now, Rolf climbed out of the hole in Elephant's side. At first he left the door open, the light pouring out, while he stood on the stone floor marveling. Yes, it had all really happened. There was a fresh gouge-scar where Elephant's shoulder had touched the surface of the enormous door; there were blackened spots on the door and on Elephant's own surface, where the spattering of fire had fallen—maybe Elephant's thunderbolts had grown feeble with the passing of the years. If so, it hardly seemed to matter. The size and power and metallic invulnerability of the Elephant seemed weapons great enough for any battle.

In a moment of imagination he saw himself battering down the Castle walls, rescuing Sarah. But he must rest, to be ready for the night, when surely birds would come, and possible human help as well.

He lighted a rush, then climbed the Elephant's flank again to push shut the massive door, the door's last closure shutting off the light inside. Going up the rope with the torch between his teeth, he could envision Loford and Thomas and the others refusing to believe all he had to tell.

The upper cave was bright with midday. He took off his pack, and ate and drank a little. There was only a mouthful of water remaining in the bottle. Probably the birds would bring him more, as soon as darkness fell. Yes, they would certainly be back to-night.

Excited as he was, Rolf soon fell asleep sitting on hard rock in the high cave, and awoke only as the first darkness was welling up outside. He shook the water in his bottle, and then drank down the last of it, for now the birds would surely be here soon.

Full night came, and he looked for them with every passing moment, and yet they did not come.

Sitting now in the cave's very mouth, he could see some of the sky, and mark the stars. Let that bright blue one, he thought, pass from sight behind the pinnacle opposite, and time enough will have passed. I can be sure then that there's something wrong. But they must be here before the heavens have turned the star that far. Surely any moment now . . .

The blue star rode its measured course and vanished. Half-relieved at being forced to action, Rolf stood up, biting his lip. All right, then. Something was very wrong. He was going to have to leave the cave and try to get back to the swamp and find his friends. Not only was he out of water, but the information he had gained was too important to be delayed.

Still nothing but the night-wind seemed to be stirring in the dark outside the cave. He anchored his climbing rope again, put on his pack, and then began to lower himself outside. He kept the free length of the rope coiled up, paying it out only as he went down. Looking down now at what the moon-light showed him of the rocks below, he thought he must have been a half-wit or a great hero, to have made that jump that got him into the cave.

His feet touched down at last. Now was the time for the enemy, who had been waiting patiently, to rush out . . . but no rush came. They had never known that he was here.

After several tries he managed to whip his rope

free of its anchorage above; he reached as best he could, balanced on the tumbled stones, to catch the anchor-stick as it came falling. But he failed to catch it, so it made a soft clatter when it hit. But no one came, only the night breeze still whispering softly along the canyon.

He made a quick job of coiling the long rope into his pack. And then he set off for the swamps, working his way cautiously out of the canyon and the rocks to emerge on the western slope of the mountain's foot with the river below him. He angled northward down this slope, heading away from pass and Castle. He had gone only about a hundred meters when the feel of sandy soil under his feet suggested that it might be a good idea for him to bury his pack with all its equipment. He could hardly keep quiet about where he had been if they caught him with all of that, and he would travel lighter and faster without it.

When he had covered up the pack he went on, getting down toward the east bank of the Dolles, still half-expecting to be greeted at any moment by the hooting of a bird.

He avoided the places where he and Thomas, on their way up to the pass, had seen soldiers. After a couple of kilometers he got down to the water's edge. Here he knew the river was shallow clear across; he waded in, clothes and all.

He had hardly climbed out on the eastern bank before the Castle soldiers sprang out of hiding to seize him. He turned at once to flee, but something that felt incredibly hard and heavy struck him on the side of the head.

He was face down in the riverside mud. As if through a muffling fog he could hear the voices over him.

"That settled 'im down good." A brief laugh.

"Did this one get t' the barges? See if he's got any loot on 'im."

Hands turned and shook and prodded him. "Naw, nothin'."

"What'll we do, hang 'im in a tree? We haven't hung a thief on this side of the river yet."

"Um. No, they need workers, up at the Castle. This 'un looks healthy enough to be some use. If you didn't scramble his brains."

VII

The Two Stones

Thomas, still dazzled by a dance of luminous afterimages before his eyes, his ears ringing, raised his head and began to try to regather his wits. He was lying on the desert, where a moment ago he had fallen or had been flung. It was raining hard. He wiped a hand across his eyes, trying to see more clearly. A little distance away the farm-girl in the wide hat knelt, looking at him.

"You are not dead," she was saying. "Oh, I'm glad. You're not one of them, are you? Oh no, of course you're not. I'm sorry."

"Of course I'm not." Let the young woman be dried out a little, he thought, and she would be quite good looking. He noticed that there was no wedding ring on her finger. "Why did you yell a warning? How did you know what was going to happen?"

The girl had turned away from him, and was looking around her now, as if for some lost object. "Since I did save your life, will you help me now, please? I've got to find it."

"The thing that was in that case, hey?"

"Yes, where did it go?"

"If it was mine I'm not sure I'd ever want to see it again."

"Oh, but I—must." She stood up, peering this way and that.

"My name is Thomas."

"Oh—I am Olanthe."

"Of the Oasis? I see you wear one of their hats."

"I . . . yes. Now will you help me find the Stone?"

She seemed to realize too late that the last word had let slip another bit of information.

"The Stone, hey?" An idea struck him. "The Oasis of the Two Stones; I suppose the name means something. Would this Stone you're looking for be one of those? I'd just like to know what it was that nearly killed me."

The rain was slowing down. Olanthe turned away from him, searching, walking a widening spiral over the sand.

"Olanthe? I have good reason to be curious, don't you think? I wish you no harm out in your Oasis. I was a farmer once myself. Say, how did you get out past the guards?"

"You were a farmer? What are you now?"

"Now I fight."

She gave him an appraising glance. "I hear the real fighters are in the swamps."

"And I do want to thank you for shouting a warning. You could have done it sooner, though, hey?"

Her eyes turned away, roving distractedly over the nearby dunes and bushes. "I . . . did see you, bending over the dead reptile. At first I thought you might be only a bandit."

"This Stone of yours draws lightning somehow, and it killed the reptile. You followed me, waiting for the lightning to come again, so you could pick up the Stone from my burned body. And then you couldn't do it."

"I didn't know you, I was afraid," she said in a small voice. "Help me find it, please, it's very important."

"I can understand that. Look, you don't have to be frightened of me, farm-girl, if what you say is true. Keep your Stone. We in the swamps don't need its rain." The rain had all but stopped; Thomas looked up at the sky, where rents and gaps of blue were showing through the cloudy mass. "Since you seem to be no better friend than I am of the reptiles, you'd better take shelter under one of these bushes, as I intend to do."

"First I must find the Stone! It can't be far."

"All right, I give up. If they see you running around here they'll find me too. Does the thunderbolt actually hit the Stone? At least you can tell me something about it while we search."

They were both casting over the mounded desert now, eyes on the ground, walking in loops and circles that moved them apart and brought them together again. Olanthe spoke rapidly. "The bolt always hits the Stone directly, yes, and sometimes throws it for many meters. After that the storm can end." She added what was probably a warning: "You see, whoever formed the Stone meant to make it proof against any one creature's greed. Only when possession of it passes from one to another does its virtue take effect, and summon up a thunderstorm."

Thomas had just seen something, twenty meters away. It was the Stone in its case, if he was not mistaken, but picking it up was not going to be easy.

In a moment Olanthe had noticed his fixed attention and was walking at his side. "Oh!" she said, seeing what he saw. The blackened metal case was half-submerged under what appeared to be the flat shimmering surface of a pool of water some eight meters across, filling a small hollow between dunes. "Mirage-plant!"

Thomas nodded. "And about the biggest one I've seen." There was no doubt about what the thing was; reason told that any such flourishing pond of real water here was totally improbable.

In itself, the illusion was flawless. Sunlight sparkled off the seeming surface of the pond (though the rain, which had now stopped, would have fallen through without splashing and shown the pond not to hold water.) Small green plants, genuine enough, living on moisture doled out by the quasi-intelligent masterplant below, rimmed around the illusive pool. This camouflage gave an appearance of coolness to the surface of the pond, which was in fact only a plane maintained between layers of air of different temperatures. This surface rippled faintly, like real water, with the wind. Thomas knew that if one bent to drink and brought his eyes within a meter of the surface, the illusion failed. Man or animal would jump back, once that point was reached; but if they were that close, none lived who could jump fast enough.

Thomas frowned at the sky, where the clouds were still dispersing, not gathering anew. "Did you not tell me that a new storm was summoned up every time the Stone changed hands, and that a bolt must come to strike the Stone itself? If so, we need only wait, and our little pond here will be safely boiled."

They had stopped about ten meters from the mirage. Olanthe shook her head. "A storm comes only when the Stone is taken up by human hands, or by a creature like the reptile that is capable of speech."

The Stone rested in a shallow part of the seeming pool, under the surface. It would seem to be very easy simply to step forward and pick it up.

Thomas got some rope out of his pack and made a lasso, with which he had a try at casting around the case. The loop sank silently through the surface of the "water," and then at once snapped taut. Thomas dug his heels into the sand; Olanthe came to lend her slender strength to his aid, but shortly it was either let go or be dragged in. From just outside the zone of real danger, the two of them watched with fascination while the rope's tail whipped out of sight like that of a plunging snake. But there was evidently little to the mirage-plant's liking in the rope—a few moments later it was spat out, wound into a knotty ball and looking otherwise the worse for wear, spat or tossed through the air to land a dozen meters away.

At Olanthe's suggestion they next had a try at filling in or smothering the mirage-plant with sand. But the sand was flung back at them faster than they, keeping at a safe distance, could scoop it into the depression. And there were no rocks available to throw.

"If only it would spit out your Stone, as it does sand and rope," Thomas griped. "But no, it must have a taste for magic."

Now that she knew where the Stone was, Olanthe did not seem much worried about retrieving it. She said, "Well, then, one of us must just try to distract the creature, while the other rushes up and grabs the Stone."

"Oh, just like that? Your life is not overly important to you?"

"The Stone is life, to the people at the Oasis." She looked at him haughtily. "Oh, I will be the one to expose myself to danger and create a distraction. It is my property that we are trying to save. And your plan of lassoing it did not work out very well."

The last accusation was undeniable, but he still had not connected it logically to the new plan when he found himself volunteering insistently to create the distraction himself—though if he gave himself time to think about it, he was not at all sure which of the two roles was the more dangerous. The girl couldn't have maneuvered him into taking the part she wanted him to have, could she? Just that quickly and easily?

Having rehearsed their plan briefly, Thomas and Olanthe separated, then approached the innocent-looking pool from opposite sides. After an exchange of nods, Thomas rushed forward shouting. In one hand he was carrying his knife, in the other the chewed-up rope, which he had partially untangled. He braked to a halt at the last instant, going down on all fours in the sand. He reached forward and lashed with the rope at the surface of the mirage. It seemed that the trick might work, for the creature beneath began grabbing again at the once-rejected fibers.

Olanthe was very quick, and her timing perfect. Unfortunately however she fumbled the Stone in the instant of picking it up, and was forced to reach for it again. Looking across from the other side of the pool, Thomas for the first time saw the deadly tendrils of the mirage-plant as they shot above the surface of the illusion, looping and snapping about the girl's body with marvelous speed. He shouted. He hurled himself around the edge of the pool and plunged into the struggle, slashing with his knife.

Only when he was enmeshed himself did he realize that, incredibly, the deadly network had not been able to hold the girl, that she was backing away quite free. He had no time to wonder about her luck, for his own was not so good. He was gripped around the waist and head. His blade severed one of the tough, elastic tendrils, but two more snapped around him, their suckers thirsting for his blood. One curled around his right arm, in which he held his knife. His left hand was already caught behind his back. He was sprawled on the sand, only his feet, dug in desperately, keeping him from being dragged to his death. The apparent water-surface had entirely vanished now, as the carnivorous plant devoted its full energy to hauling in this stubborn prey. When the pull of it dragged Thomas half upright again he could see down into the hollow, see the nest of writhing mouths and the white animal-bones between them, where the illusion had shown nothing but a sandy bottom.

Thomas cried out something. He saw the girl, a look of anguish on her face, reaching into her small pack. Her hand emerged holding a grayish, egg-shaped object which she thrust out toward him. "Here!"

He had to drop his useless knife to take the thing she pressed into his clutching fingers. It was hard and heavy in his grasp. Before he could wonder what he was supposed to do with it, he felt the mirage-plant's grip loosening. It was as if his skin and clothing had suddenly developed surfaces of oil and melting ice. In a moment he had pulled free and was several meters away. He lay gasping on the sand while he watched the frustrated tendrils wave about disconsolately and then withdraw.

Olanthe, the Thunderstone in its battered case still under her arm, came to kneel beside him; she reached out a tentative hand to take back the small gray Stone that Thomas still held; but instead he shot out his own hand and took her by the wrist.

"One moment, my girl. Bring out yet another Stone and destroy me with it, if you will, but first I will have some explanations."

Still, when she made no answer but only struggled silently to pull away from him, he let her go. When he had done this, she was willing to sit on the sand nearby, looking apologetic. "I—I have no more Stones. There are no more."

"Aha. That's something. Yes, that's good. If it were the Oasis of the Dozen Stones, I don't know what—" He broke off suddenly and looked up. "The sun is being hidden once again. I take it we may soon expect another thunderbolt?"

She waved a slender hand impatiently. "Oh yes, of course, since the Thunderstone has changed hands again in coming back to me. But that's all right. I'll leave it here on the sand, and we'll just go a little distance off and wait. Then after it's been hit I'll be able to carry it safely."

"May I suggest that you leave it at a safe distance from the mirage-plant? So that we won't have to . . . hey? And while we sit through another rainfall, you might explain to me the virtues of this other Stone."

The clouds were swiftly thickening once more. Thomas and Olanthe, their clothing not yet dried from the previous storm, left the Thunderstone in a gentle hollow between dunes and went a few score paces distant to sit together under the useless shelter of a desert bush.

She blurted out, "I didn't want you to know about the Stone of Freedom too. Otherwise I could have simply walked up to the mirage-plant and taken my property back."

"Yes, I see that, now."

"I'm sorry. Those suckers didn't draw any blood, did they? Good. Well, now you know our secrets, and I must trust you. We need help at the Oasis. The invaders are—we can't endure them."

"Who can? We may be able to help each other." The new rain began to fall. Thomas was thoughtful. "Tell me more about these Stones."

The origin of the two Stones, Olanthe said, was lost in the past. Since the beginnings of the history of the Oasis the farmers there had possessed them both. The folk of the Oasis for the most part lived in harmony with one another, content to stay half-isolated from the rest of the world, though they had been friendly and hospitable to visitors and exhausted travelers who strayed in from the desert. The secrets of the two Stones had been kept within their settlement.

The desert soil was rich, lacking only water. And whenever the fields of the Oasis needed rain, he who held the Stone of Thunder at the time would present it to his neighbor; so water came just to suit the farmers' wishes, and drought and flood were alike unknown. The other talisman, called the Stone of Freedom or the Prisoner's Stone, was kept hidden, and only the elders of the Oasis knew of its existence. It was of little use to honest men as long as freedom ruled the land.

Then the foul invaders from the East had come, in force too strong to be resisted. The elders had somehow managed to preserve the secrets of both Stones.

"Alas, it was my own father who broke the pact of secrecy. Oh, he acted not through any wish to help the invaders, no, the very opposite." After saying that Olanthe fell silent for a moment, her eyes downcast, rain dripping from the brim of her wide fieldworker's hat.

"How, then?" Thomas wiped rain from his own eyes. This was becoming a soggy desert indeed. He felt vaguely cheered by the reflection that a certain mirage-plant might be the first of its species ever to drown.

Olanthe was looking down at her hands folded in her lap. "The commander of the invaders' garrison . . . that is . . . he wanted . . ."

"Something to do with you?"

"Yes . . . me." She nodded, and looked up. "When I was unwilling, they made threats . . ." She fell silent, until Thomas reached out and took her hand.

"Afterward—" She had to clear her throat and start over. "Afterward, my father was—he happened to have the Thunderstone in his fields at the time. He unearthed it from its hiding place—"

The latest bolt came smashing down at the Stone forty or fifty meters away, making Thomas jump for all that he had been expecting it, jarring his teeth and bones anew.

"—and, pretending to curry favor, he gave it to the garrison commander. My father acted as if he was pleased that the pig had taken a fancy to me. My father told him that the Stone had something to do with the Oasis' rain, but of course he never mentioned lightning.

"They—they stood talking inside the invaders' compound, there, in what used to be a park. My father said later that he could hear the thunder starting overhead while they stood there, and he smiled at his enemy, the man who had . . . and then the commander turned away, with the Thunderstone under his arm, to walk across the parade-ground to his quarters. He never finished his walk."

Thomas nodded. He squeezed Olanthe's hand slightly. She went on: "Next day a soldier picked the Stone up and brought it right to the one who had been second in command, and was now in charge. They knew it was something of magical importance, but they guessed no more than that. Before another storm could break over their heads they had put the Thunderstone into the pouch of a courier reptile and dispatched it to the wizards at the Castle. We knew this because we could see the growing storm follow the reptile out over the desert. We knew the storm must catch up before the leatherwing reached the Castle. It was necessary for someone to go out and recover the Stone, before it fell again into the hands of enemies or strangers. Without it, the Oasis would die for lack of water."

"How were you chosen?"

"A girl can search as well as a man. And others of the enemy would be — would be after me, now that the old commander is dead. And my father would do something else — and perhaps bring destruction on us all.

"So the elders were willing enough that I should leave, and they gave me the Stone of Freedom, which for its bearer sets fences and guards and all confinements at naught. Now I must return the Thunderstone to the Oasis somehow, and then — I don't know what I'll do."

"I see." Thomas shifted in his drenched clothes. The rain was thinning again. The Thunderstone had not been moved far by the latest bolt — he could see it, a small dark lump on the sand.

He stretched out his hand with the Stone of Freedom in it to Olanthe. "The Stones are yours. But tell me, what use are they, what use is life itself, to your people, as long as the invaders are there?"

She accepted the Stone. "What can we do? What are you getting at? I must take back the Thunderstone or all will perish."

"The Oasis can live for a few more days at least without it. And remember this: while it's there, the enemy may find it, realize what it is, and perfect his power over you."

She asked again, pleading now, "What can we do?"

Thomas smiled. He stood up, just as the sun broke out once more. "I can think of several things. And I know those who will be able to think of more. Come with me to the swamps!"

VIII

Chup

——◆◆——

Dazed as he was by the blow on the head, Rolf still had wit enough left to realize that the soldiers thought him nothing more than a thief, who had been trying to get aboard one of the barges in the river. They asked him no questions, and he said nothing at all.

Feet hobbled and hands bound painfully behind him, he was taken to a command post concealed in trees right by the riverbank. His head throbbing, he sat on the ground and tried to think of nothing. There were too many soldiers for him to have a hope of getting loose, and they seemed discouragingly capable as they went about their routines of duty.

At earliest daylight the watch was changed. The soldiers who had caught Rolf now tied a leading cord around his neck, freed his legs, and took him up the road to the Castle, tethered behind a riding-beast like some small animal being led to slaughter.

The journey was not long. The road followed the west bank of the Dolles for a couple of kilometers, joining on the way with other roads that converged toward the pass. Shortly the pass came in sight, with the village and its bridge in the foreground, and the Castle brooding above.

Crossing the bridge, Rolf raised his eyes to the northeast, looking at the high, distant rocks that only a day ago had hidden him in safety. Now he saw that which deepened his despair—reptiles were on those rocks, and in the air above them, thick as flies on dead meat. And, marching up that slope, like bronze-black ants, a company of soldiers.

The enemy had found the cave, then. That must be it. Rolf brought his eyes back to the bridge under his feet, hardly aware any longer of his surroundings. He was lost, and all else too.

Once over the bridge, the soldiers began to relax their vigilance. In the nearly deserted village square they halted, straightening their uniforms, evidently getting in proper shape for appearance in the Castle.

Rolf stood staring dully at the rump of the riding-beast that he was tethered to, until a movement at the corner of his eye caused him to turn his aching head. The village inn, a two-story timber structure, was evidently still in business, for two men were standing on its porch.

His heart leaped when he recognized Mewick. There could be no mistake, the lean figure was the same, though liberal streaks of gray in the dark hair had added twenty years of age—added them credibly, when seen above the lined gravity of Mewick's face. The short cloak and the magic peddler's pack were gone. Mewick was wearing moderately rich clothing now, putting Rolf in mind of merchants he had seen now and then, who were said to be from far islands in the sea.

Rolf looked away, holding his face blank. Let him make one blunder now, and Mewick could be dragged away beside him, both to meet some grimmer fate than that of a mere thief. Desperately, Rolf tried to think of some way of passing on to Mewick his new knowledge of the Elephant.

The porch of the inn was not ten meters distant. He could hear Mewick talking with a rotund man, perhaps the innkeeper, about problems of trade and shipping, the prevalence of bandits. Mewick sounded gloomy as ever. Let him ask something about the soldiers swarming on yonder hill—let

him ask *something* that I can answer yes or no,
thought Rolf, and I will nod my head or shake it,
enough for him to see.

But Mewick asked no such thing—dared not, or
could not think of a useful question that could be
made to sound innocent. Rolf could not either. Tonight when he was in the dungeon they would both
think of ten questions Mewick might have asked. Or
of some other way of passing information. But at
least Rolf knew that Mewick must have seen him—
that was something, that his fate was not entirely
unknown to his friends. Staring straight ahead, Rolf
made one nodding motion of his head.

The soldiers were ready now, and dragged him on
again. Once out of the little village, the road ascended, worn deep here by the daily passage of an
army. The walls and towers of the Castle swelled
with nearness now. The main gate stood open, the
portcullis looking more than ever like the teeth in
some vast jaw.

In an inner courtyard, where the stables were,
Rolf's bonds were taken off, and he was given to
guards who wore no bronze helmets and carried no
swords, but had only keys and cudgels at their belts.
These pushed him into a doorway at the base of the
keep, and from thence led him downward over
worn, damp stairs. Just underground, the passage
became level, dark and narrow. It was lined with
cells, separated by heavy grilles of iron. Some of
these were crowded with wretched figures while
others waited empty, doubtless for the return of
slaves who labored somewhere up above. The smell
was worse than that of any animal pen that Rolf had
ever visited. Rolf was sent with an impersonal kick
to join the apathetic bodies in one cell, and the door
was made fast behind him.

The morning light that entered so poorly into
those upper dungeons had little better success in
penetrating the richly curtained windows of the

upper tower. It was not the sun that awoke the
Satrap Ekuman today, but voices, quietly excited,
just outside his chamber door.

Blinking, he roused himself in his vast bed. When
his concubine of the night, who was curled sleeping
like some soft beast at her master's feet, made a
movement that impeded his stretching, he kicked at
her irritably. Once on his feet, he wrapped his body
in a fur gown, then spent a moment in setting aside
the magical defense that guarded the door of his
bedchamber from within, before he called out to
know whose business brought them to him at this
hour.

It was the Master of the Reptiles who was passed
in by the guards. This Master was a small man, usually phlegmatic in his manner. But his face was now
aglow with triumph, so that the sight of him made
Ekuman's hopes blaze up before the man had spoken.

"Sire, we have found the Elephant for you!" That
said, the Master rushed quickly on with explanations, as Ekuman's expression bade him do—how
he had zealously investigated yesterday's report of
a strange rumbling noise, heard by reptiles, coming
from under the ground on the north side of the pass.
And then birds had attacked troopers, during last
night's maneuvers in that area—

"The Elephant, the Elephant! Have you news of it
or not?"

"Yes, Lord!"

At break of dawn the Master had sent hordes of
reptiles to those rocks, under orders to cover them
centimeter by centimeter, crawling if need be, to
find the cause of the strange noise. They had found,
first, the entrance to a cave, holding signs that at
least one human had recently been there, and birds
as well—

Observing the countenance of his Lord, the Master of the Reptiles swallowed some words, hastily
condensing his story further. One reptile at least

had seen the Elephant in that cave—a thing of metal, huge as a house, with the familiar symbol painted on its flanks.

"Very good. You will be well rewarded, if all this proves to be the truth." Ekuman tossed the man a jeweled ring, in token of more to come. Then the Satrap, half-dressed as he was, descended to the lower level of the tower. Here a doorway brought him out onto the flat roof of the keep, from whence a good view could be had of the country across the pass.

The Master of Reptiles, basking in his favor, hurried just behind. His other chief subordinates, he knew, would be gathering round him momentarily, as soon as they heard the tidings of the great discovery. And in fact Ekuman had no more than rested his hands on the northern battlement, when there came the sound of many climbing feet upon a nearby stair. Turning, he saw the Master of the Troops coming up, with his officers and aides behind him.

Frowning at the Master of the Troops, a tough graying soldier named Garl, Ekuman demanded, "Just what are all those men doing over there?"

Garl's face, which had been set to join in his Lord's triumph, quickly sobered. "Lord, we are . . . consolidating the position against possible enemy action. And I am waiting only for your word to send men into the cave itself."

Ekuman nodded. "You do well to await my word before taking such a step."

Zarf had come up just in time to hear the last exchange of speech. "Lord," he volunteered, "it will be best if I am first into this cave." Then he bowed slightly as the older wizard came puffing unimpressively up the stairs. "Or Master Elslood, of course. If he is not required to be busy elsewhere."

Ekuman turned away from his wizards. Elslood and Zarf were well and firmly under his thumb, and through them, all the others here. Yet he had heard of other Satraps who doubtless had been as firmly seated and still had been overthrown by intrigues in their own households—Som the Dead never seemed to care, if the usurpers served him with equal or greater dedication.

So Ekuman did not mean to trust a power as great as the Elephant's under the personal control of anyone except himself. At least, he meant to reserve that option until he had learned much more about the Elephant than his wizards had yet been able to tell him.

Ekuman said to Garl, "Signal at once to those across the pass. No human is to enter that cave until I personally have given permission."

This signaling was promptly attended to. Then noticing the Master of the Harem hovering in the background, Ekuman was reminded of another matter to be taken care of. He beckoned to the eunuch and said, "That girl I had last night acted like one half-sick. Dispose of her."

"At once, Lord." Then the eunuch reached behind him and with a conjurer's motion pulled forward a short slender figure, garbed in a harem gown—until now the girl had been hidden behind his bulk. "This girl I think will be very lively, Lord. She was brought in two days ago, and at my direction has been examined carefully and reserved for you."

"Hm." Engrossed as he was with other matters, Ekuman took time to look at this girl. Dark-haired and very young and certainly attractive. Her face colored when the eunuch opened her gown. Silent, yet brave enough to scowl openly at him in hate—yes, she was interesting. "Very well. But now is not the time for harem matters." He dismissed the eunuch with a wave.

The Master of the Reptiles stood now at Ekuman's side, and put what seemed to be a new sense of his own importance into a tiny sound of throat-clearing. "Lord? Is it your wish that I should make ready a courier to send East? With word of our discovery?''

The man was already grown presumptuous. But Ekuman would let him puff a little yet, that correction when it came might be the more precise and salutary. "No, I will send no word of this discovery yet. Not until I am more certain of just what has been discovered yonder.'' If Elephant's power was all that had been hinted, it was just possible that with it under his control he might even be able to face east one day without cringing in utter subservience—but no, he would not let even his inner thoughts follow that line. Not yet.

From the direction of the ascending stair, a loud masculine voice said, "Well! The prettiest little piece I've seen in about a month!"

Ekuman turned once again, to greet his neighbor and son-in-law to be. The Satrap Chup was just mounting to the roof-terrace, golden Charmian on his arm. Ekuman knew quite well the signals of his daughter's face; and glancing at her now he felt immediately certain that Chup's thoughtless exclamation of praise for the new young dark-haired slave would cost Chup some future moment's peace if nothing more.

Ekuman's chief sensation as he thought about his daughter's impending marriage was one of relief; her dedication to petty malice was so strong that he felt sure her departure would rid his household of a whole vortex of minor intrigues. In fact he thought with some approval that Charmian's presence might ultimately weaken Chup, and that would bode well for Ekuman's own ambition. There were recurring whispers on the wind saying that some one of the coastal Satraps might soon be promoted to a position of suzerainty over all the others. These were whispers only, perhaps meant merely to keep them all vying with one another to serve the East, but still . . .

Chup came pacing to Ekuman's side. He leaned his tall warrior's frame, dressed in rich cloth of red and black, upon the parapet, and looked out at the activity of men and reptiles on the north side of the pass.

Ekuman said conversationally, "I thought, brother, that I might ride forth this afternoon, to oversee this treasure-hunt my men are on. No doubt you've heard the tales? If you would care to ride with me, of course, you will be welcome."

Ekuman had phrased the invitation in a style that left it quite open to acceptance or polite refusal, and Chup elected to return the latter. "Naturally, elder brother, your company is always a delight. And riding, even to poke around among some rocks, would be a form of exercise. But—well, unless you—"

Ekuman let himself suddenly remember something. "In truth it was a rather poor suggestion for amusement. I have another, much more suited to a true warrior's taste. You might divert yourself and at the same time render me a true service in preparing for the wedding celebration. As you know, I plan some gladiatorial entertainment on that day—nothing professional, just some of these sturdy farm lads—"

"I like to watch amateurs go at it, if they've any spirit."

"Just so, Brother Chup. Would you deign to visit the dungeons with my Master of the Games? I'm sure no one in my employ could pick out fighting men as well as you can. You may even find one or two with real training—if not, I know you'll spot the raw ability . . ."

Chup was nodding agreement, though with little enthusiasm, as Ekuman maneuvered him away toward the stair. The Master of the Harem trailed in the rear, the arm of the dark-haired slave-girl firmly in his massive grip. Charmian, her ethereal face disfigured by one of her petty rages, was staring after them. The princess was now alone upon the roof-terrace, except for her personal maid—and one other.

Elslood the wizard stood before Charmian and bowed his massive gray head slightly. He was marking the hatred with which her eyes followed the lovely slave-girl. "My Princess?"

Her eyes turned on him, losing their look of hate but remaining as hopelessly distant as ever. "Well?" she demanded. Soon she would be gone, and he unable to follow. While she was yet here, he would take great risks, hoping nothing more than to please her. Such was his doom, and he could do nothing about it but try to conceal it from others; he could not even do that, he knew with a sinking feeling, the very maidservant was now smiling at him openly.

Elslood said, "That new harem-slave, my Princess; there is a circumstance I now of, that I might be able to turn to your amusement—"

Listening, Charmian began to smile.

Following the jovial Master of the Games and the sallow chief warden through the low-roofed dungeons, Chup wrinkled his nose and tried to hold his breath against the stench. So far he had had nothing to say about the prospective gladiators but a few terse expressions of scorn. Sturdy farm lads they might once have been, but now they had rotted in their cages overlong. He suspected that all the hale ones were up above, unloading barges or building walls. Faugh! What did it serve, to pen men up like this? It served no aim that Chup could see, but only created a foulness. If the men were objectionable and useless, let them be killed. If good work was to be gotten from them, then at least house them in fresh air and feed them, like draft animals of some value.

Chup had as yet made no pilgrimage to the East, had pledged no allegiance to Som or the other mysterious lords. He supposed he would go, some day soon. All men must serve some master, or so the way

of the world seemed to be. Charmian was already
egging him on, to get his wizards to arrange the
matter. Charmian . . . *why* did he want to marry her?
He had women enough—ah, but none so fair. And
the greatest warrior must have the fairest princess,
that was one of the things a man fought for. So, once
again, was the way of the world.

The warden stopped before yet another dim and
noisome cage, and delicately reminded Chup of the
fact that no gladiators had as yet been chosen:
"We'd best pick out today whatever your Lordship
decides should be reserved for the games. I think
the foremen of the work-gangs will be down here
soon enough, taking all the bodies that can be made
to lift and haul." And then the warden fell abruptly
silent, having just got a dirty look from the Master of
the Games. Probably new work-gangs were going to
be sent across the pass to dig, and that business was
not something to be discussed before a visitor.

Chup had a fairly good idea of what the Ele-
phant-search was all about, and of course he was
keen on learning more. He knew that if he had ridden out with Ekuman, he would not have been taken
where there was anything worth the seeing. But he
meant to learn in good time about whatever they
found. Charmian, who would certainly have her
uses, wanted very much to be the queen of an over-
lord. Chup's wizards had heard hints that one of the
Satraps here along the coast might soon be raised to
such an eminence. . . .

"This lot here is a bit fresher than the last," said
the warden hopefully, looking into the cell.

Chup sniffed. "If no sweeter." The cell was pretty
well filled up with ten or a dozen men who at first
glance looked like nothing much; but with only a
quick look you could never be sure. Chup was ines-
capably interested in fighting and in fighters, even
only in potential. The Master of the Games began to
harangue this lot of wretches: brave lads raise your
hands, who will step out and have a chance for

glory, and so forth. If Chup had been in a cell he would not have believed a word of it for a moment. Neither did those who were in fact inside; though it stood to reason that any who were real men in there would seize even the faintest chance to take revenge for their evil fate.

On impulse, Chup took charge. "Open the door," he ordered. He got a startled glance from the warden, whose speech he interrupted, but such was the Satrap's voice and bearing that he did not have to repeat himself.

As the warden was swinging a segment of the grillwork back, Chup drew out his sword and set it on the dirty floor. This was not his prized battle-winning weapon, of course, he would not treat that in such a style. This was a fancier-looking blade that he wore on dress-up days like this — it was service-able enough, of course.

All were gaping at him. "Now let me borrow this," he said. And he took the cudgel from the startled warden's belt, tried the grip of it in his hand, whipped it once or twice through the air. Then he held it down at his side.

He addressed the sullen, unbelieving faces inside the cell. "You men in there! Or whatever you are. If there be a man among you, let him come out and take this up." He shoved with his elegant toe at the bare sword, moving it a hand's breadth nearer them. "We're at the end of a passage here, and you can set your back against a wall and hack away at me — these two with me will give us room, I doubt not. Well?"

No answer.

"Come, come, you fear to soil my fine garments? Let me tell you, I raped a dozen of your sisters this morning, ere I had my breakfast. Look, the sword is real. D'you think I'd stoop to playing pranks on such as you — well, here's a bantam with some life in him, if we can't get a man full grown."

Putting one foot slowly in front of the other, Rolf

was coming out of the cell. As soon as he was out, the warden sprang forward and clanged shut the door.

Whether it was the power of Ardneh that possessed Rolf now, or only the power of hate, it left no room in him for fear. Without taking his eyes from Chup's, he squatted and rose up again, the sword's hilt now gripped tight in his right hand. The weapon felt wonderfully deadly, longer and heavier than the only other sword that he had ever held.

The warden and the Master of the Games retreated; with cautious outrage they peered around the Satrap at this strange creature, an armed prisoner. At another time Rolf might have laughed at their expressions. The Master of the Games had one hand half-raised, almost but not quite daring to pluck at the Lord Chup's sleeve; and the warden kept muttering, something about calling for a couple of men with pikes.

Chup's eyes were locked with Rolf's, a resonance between them. In the tall Satrap's face there was a life that had not been there before. Without looking around he answered the blithering behind him: "Oh, go away if you like, and stand behind your pikemen. Only let me have a few moments' life at least out of this deadly boring day."

And Chup was thinking: *Mountains of the East! Look how ready this one is to carve me! See in his face how little he values his own skin at this moment. If he but knew how to hold that sword, I'd be looking for pikemen myself. Ah, to lead into battle an army of men who all had something like this one's will to fight!*

The youth was coming forward now, moving slowly at first, convincing himself that there was no hidden trap laid for him here. In a moment he would lunge, or hack. Chup waited, poised, holding the cudgel loosely, waist-high, pointing it horizontally like a dagger. He had grown happy, moved into the true intense life of physical danger, so much more real than any other part of life. He was going to have to exert all his powers, to win with the short stick of wood against the long keen blade and the earnest clumsy hate behind it.

Rolf's intent to attack showed itself in his face an instant before he lunged, and Chup was very glad to have the warning; he knew the young could move very fast, and utter ignorance could wield a sword with deadly unorthodoxy. Dodging back, Chup made the awkward downcurve of the blade's path miss him by something less than he in his bravest moments would have planned. Chup counter-attacked, stepping in with his best speed, whacking down with the cudgel against the blade to keep a backstroke from coming up into his legs or groin, then dagger-thrusting with the blunt club. He aimed just below the youth's breastbone; he did not want to do this brave one any permanent damage.

Rolf never saw the counterthrust coming. He only felt the murderous impact of it, paralyzing him, knocking out his wind. His hand let go the sword. His knees betrayed him also, so that he fell slumping down onto the dirty stones, seeing through a reddish haze, fighting now for nothing greater than to draw a breath.

The warden and the Master of the Games, in voices loud with relief, clamored their praise for his Lordship's bravery and skill. His Lordship spat. His toe prodded Rolf, gently. "You there—you'll have another chance in a few days to draw some blood." He handed the cudgel back to the warden, and accepted the sword the man had picked up for him.

"Feed and exercise him," Chup ordered, nodding at Rolf. Then he surveyed for the last time the other prisoners, who were now moving restlessly inside their fetid cage, awake now when it was too late and the door was once more shut upon them. So Chup had expected, knowing men. "Faugh! Pick out what other ones you will!" He stalked away.

Rolf was not put back into the cell, but instead, when he could walk, led to a stair and so up into full daylight. Then through one small courtyard after another, amid a warren of walls and sheds and gates. By turning his head to look up at the keep and its tower, he tried to get his bearings; he was now on the eastern side of the keep, still of course within the mighty outer walls. And just as his breath was coming back strong enough to let him walk easily, Rolf saw that which made him feel that Chup's club had struck again—a small face, framed in dark hair, in a narrow window high up in the keep.

He tried to delay to look a moment longer, but the guards dragged him on. Still out-of-doors, they brought him at last to a cell that stood alone against the wall of a shed, a stone-walled cell just about big enough for a man to stand up in and long enough for him to lie down. It was quite windowless, but the door was an open grillwork of hardwood and iron bars.

Small as this cell was, it gave him more room than had the crowded one below. And this one was free of filth, and open to the air. Looking out through the grillwork of the door into the sunlight, Rolf could not see much more than the wall and corner of the adjacent shed, and more blank walls a few meters distant. The keep and its windows were not within his range of vision.

He had not been sitting long on the straw-littered floor when a warden came, bringing him a jug of water, and a plate of food surprisingly substantial and clean. Rolf drank and ate, and tried to keep himself from thinking of anything beyond the moment's satisfaction.

He was startled awake from a nervous, twitching doze by the grating of the cell's lock. One man stood at the opened door, a tough-looking soldier with a tanned, lined face, not one of the dungeon wardens. This man wore the bronze helmet of the troops, and under his arm he carried a pair of mock swords, having true handles but blunt wooden shafts instead of blades.

"All right, kid, fall out."

Saying nothing, Rolf got up and went with him. The man led him around a corner into a small closed yard. Along one wall stout butts of timber had been set firmly in the ground; they were much hacked and splintered.

The man held out one of the practice swords to Rolf, hilt first. "Take this and come at me. Let's see what you can do." When Rolf did not instantly obey him his voice shifted effortlessly into a heavy, threatening tone. "Come on! Or maybe you'd rather go up on the roof instead, and fight the leather-wings? Up there you won't get no sword to use — you'll be strung up by your fingers."

Slowly Rolf took the proffered weapon. Evidently seeing by Rolf's manner that he was genuinely ignorant and puzzled, the soldier ceased threatening him and explained: "Kid, you're lucky. You're gonna be put into the arena to fight. Do a good job and you'll see no more dungeons. How'd you like a chance to join the army? Have a real man's life?"

"If I get into the arena with Chup," said Rolf, his voice low, "I'll carve his guts out if I can. He'll have to kill me. So either way I won't be in your army after that."

The soldier rubbed his jaw. "The Lord Chup," he said.

"He picked me out. He said I'd have another chance at him, in a few days."

"Yeah. Yeah, well, he's like that. A real man, a real fighter, admires anybody who'll put up a scrap."

As much as he hated the invaders, Rolf had to believe in the honesty of the man who had just beaten him, wooden stick against sword. He had been granted clean air and water and good food, and now, it seemed, one to teach him swording. He was being given a real chance, if a small one, to strike back before he was destroyed.

"All right, kid, make up your mind."

Rolf smiled, looking down at the wooden sword in his hand. Maybe he could strike back more than once. He lunged forward suddenly and struck, aiming with his best intent to hit the other's face.

The old soldier's weapon slid easily up into place to block the blow. He returned Rolf's bitter smile. "That's it, hit first and hit hard when you can. Now let me show you how to hold a sword."

IX

Messages

———◆—◆—◆———

"We must strike first, and strike hard." Thomas spoke in a low, heavy voice, knowing their truth and at the same time knowing the grim risks that they implied.

Around him in the huge lean-to were assembled such leaders of the Free Folk as had been able to respond in time to his summons to a council. Olanthe sat at his left hand, and Loford at his right. The bird Strijeef had a place in the circle, sitting sideways and with his unwounded wing raised to shield his eyes from the firelight.

Around the island the night noises of the swamp rose and fell. Thomas went on: "When Ekuman has the Elephant, and has made himself its master—then it will be too late for us to attack or defend, even if we could raise ten thousand men. Is this not true?"

Loford nodded his great head at once. Others in the circle added their agreement. None could deny what had been said.

Thomas went on: "If we are daring enough, we may let Ekuman dig away the mountain first, then strike to take the treasure from him. But even that moment lies only a few days in the future."

"The very day of the wedding," said someone.

"Very likely," Thomas agreed.

Another man, the leader of a band from the delta region, shook his head. "You want to attack him on his very doorstep. How many men can we raise in a few days, and march there with any secrecy? Hardly more than two hundred, I think!"

There was some discussion. No one could really dispute that the figure of two hundred must be approximately correct.

"Ekuman will have the Elephant-diggings guarded heavily," the man from the delta predicted. "He must have a thousand men available, in and around the Castle."

"Still, do you see any alternative to attacking?" Thomas asked him. Then Thomas looked around the fire-lit circle, questioning each person with his eyes. None had anything to suggest. Loford's visions, and those of the Old One before him, had convinced them all that the Elephant was the key on which the future rested.

"Then, since we *must* attack, it only remains to determine how. Don't forget that we now have new powers of magic on our side. The Thunderstone — we've already discussed some plans for that. And we'll find a way to put the Stone of Freedom to work, too. There are plenty of prisoners needing to be freed. One of them, especially, would be important to us now."

"The boy who was in the cave," said Olanthe.

Thomas nodded.

Mewick spoke up; with the gray still painted in his hair he looked like some grave tribal elder. "I think the soldiers who had him knew nothing of his importance, of where he had been. On his clothes was much mud, so likely they took him at the riverbank. And they had tied him most casually behind a beast, and they were in no hurry. Also Rolf was smart, he looked at me but once. If he stays smart I think they will just be using him as an ordinary slave."

Thomas added: "The birds are watching for Rolf in the work parties that go out of the Castle at night. There are some now." He hesitated. "Of course we can't be sure he really learned anything about the Elephant."

"He nodded to me," said Mewick sadly. "How could he talk? What other signal could he give? So I think that the nod means something."

Olanthe said: "It might have meant only that he saw you."

"Maybe."

"Well." With a gesture Thomas put the problem of Rolf aside. "With more knowledge of the Elephant or without it, we still must get the thing out of Ekuman's hands, or else overthrow him before he can put it to use. Now consider that our friend Ekuman is not stupid, nor are his chief officers. They know that we must act."

"All the more hopeless then," said the pessimistic delta-man.

"Not at all," returned Thomas firmly. He looked round the circle and saw faces steady in their support. "For one thing, we'll arrange diversions. Draw troops from the Castle if we can, at least keep any more from being sent there. For another, we'll come at Ekuman in a way he doesn't expect."

Bending, he scratched on the bare earth beside the fire a rough map of the Broken Lands. "Here, and here, are the likely places for us to cross the river, to get near the Castle for an attack. Ekuman will be strengthening the night patrol in those places. But we'll avoid them."

"How?"

"It'll mean a long hike, but we can do it. Go farther south, cross the Dolles in your country, the delta. Move in small groups, mostly at night of course. Get across the mountains there in the south. Reassemble, somewhere on the desert . . ." Thomas's voice slowed. He felt a new idea taking shape.

Olanthe seemed to be reading his thoughts. "That's not far from the Oasis."

Thomas faced her. "Olanthe, how many of the Oasis farmers would be willing to join us, against the odds that we'll be facing?"

"How many? Every one of them!" Her face had

lighted. "Two hundred and a few more, men and boys. And some of the women will come too. If you once get the invaders off my people's necks, they'll go to the Castle and fight, they'll follow you to the Black Mountains if you like. They'll fight with their pitchforks and reaping-hooks!"

"They'll have swords and shields and arrows for the picking-up, if we can hit the Oasis garrison the way they should be hit!" It was a heady thing for Thomas to see, the hope coming into the faces of these strong people who now depended so much on his words.

The objector from the delta was ready and willing to act as an anchor on Thomas's soaring dreams. "Aye, suppose we do attack the Oasis at night! Suppose we win! Then, what, next day, when the leatherwings come out from the Castle and see what's happened? We're out there, in the midst of the desert; we'll not get back to the swamp or the mountains before Ekuman's cavalry has gobbled us up." His voice became sarcastic. "Or maybe you think we can raid the Oasis and wipe out the garrison, and march away from it again, all in one night?" The man snorted his scorn. "It would've been done already if it was so simple."

"We've got new powers now, remember?" Thomas pointed again to the Thunderstone, in a new pouch at Olanthe's side. "It will bring not only lightning, but sheltering clouds and rain as well. And I mean for us to use every power that it has!"

On his first night within the Castle walls Rolf in his great exhaustion could do nothing but sleep. In the morning he was well fed, and again at noon. And in both morning and afternoon the old soldier came to take him to the practice yard, where they spent an hour or two each time. In the afternoon they practiced with real shields as well as the mock-swords, and Rolf was given a gladiator's barbut-helm to accustom himself to wearing.

His hands were callused by farm work, and he had thought his arms well toughened too. But this new unfamiliar weight of weaponry seemed to discover new muscles and set them aching. His tutor drilled him mainly in endless repetitions of simple lunge and parry, retreat and counterstroke. It was work that soon grew dull; and for all Rolf's sullen urge to hurt his enemies, he could not manage to hit this man while the old soldier corrected Rolf's technique by jabbing and thwacking him in the ribs, seemingly at will.

As if Rolf's lessons were something semi-secret, the practice sessions were ended whenever other soldiers came to the yard to carve at the timber butts, or spar against one another. Rolf felt some curiosity at this, but there were more demanding burdens on his mind. Escape was much in his thoughts, now that he was nourished and had rested. But the high walls were all around, and only his thoughts could leap them.

Looking up from the practice-yard from time to time during the day, Rolf marked the growing preparations for the approaching wedding. Flowers and gay banners were being brought by the wagonload into the Castle, where they were at once made grotesque by their surroundings. At the direction of the Master of the Games, these were displayed on walls and parapets and railings. Rolf wondered if the bleaching human bones hanging beside the high reptile-roosts would be bedecked with flowers as well.

And somewhere not far from his cell, lively music was being rehearsed throughout the day. The Castle was preparing to work at being joyful, but Rolf could see no joy in any face, as he had seen during the preparation of farmers' weddings. Here even the Master of the Games had a prisoner's countenance.

On his second night in his privileged cell, Rolf saw the labor-gangs returning just after sunset from their work, being driven stumbling and staggering back to the dungeons from which they had been routed in the early morning. There was rockdust and sand on them tonight, not river-mud—he knew by this that most of them had been working on the north side of the pass, lifting off the mountain from Elephant's resting place.

Leaning against the cell wall beside his door, Rolf listened as two of the overseers trudged past wearily. One said that today the digging had uncovered the corner of a door, but there was days' work yet remaining. Aye, said the other. Not until after the wedding would they be done.

The voices faded. Rolf threw himself down on his bed of straw. The mount of Ardneh was almost freed—the Elephant, that belonged more to Rolf than to any other. Even his coming duel with Chup faded to secondary importance in his thoughts.

During this night a second shift of slaves went out from the dungeons to labor, a column of soldiers at their side, marching as sullenly as they. The courtyards were ablaze with torches through most of the night. Workers and messengers kept coming and going, and even the singing practice went on, so the business of the digging seemed all mixed with that of the wedding. Rolf could sleep but little with the noise and the light. And he was worried again, for his life no longer seemed valueless. He must not die, just for a chance of scratching Chup—not when the Free Folk might be facing slaughter for want of knowledge of the Elephant, knowledge that Rolf alone could give them.

When morning came and he was taken as usual from his cell to go to the barracks latrine, Rolf noticed more than one tiny burnt-out stub of torch amid the night's casual litter on the paving stones. The guard who was escorting him today had taken on either too much work or too much wine, or both, last night, so that his eyes were closed as much as they were open. Coming back, Rolf contrived to stoop and fiddle with his sandal-straps. When the door of his cell swung shut on him again, he had a little charcoal-stick closed safe within his sweating hand.

Again he was given water and good food. And again, the old soldier came to take him to practice. Rolf had contrived to hide his piece of charcoal inside a seam of his shirt. And the impulse that had prompted him to pick it up had begun to grow in his mind into something of a scheme.

Today his tutor brought swords, though dull of edge and blunt of point. During the practice Rolf's mind was kept too busy to elaborate on schemes. He was beginning to appreciate the truth of Mewick's warning—that the martial arts were not to be learned in a week. Just as he thought his sword arm had finally developed some cunning, his teacher's weapon would thump against his ribs once more.

But during the break at noon, and when he was locked once more into his cell at nightfall, he was free to think. The idea had already occurred to him that the birds must certainly come reconnoitering at night, probably every night, above the Castle. He saw that the defensive cords and nets were always carefully spread on the high places after the reptiles had come thronging back at sunset. But there was nothing to stop the birds from passing over, higher still. There would always be some scrap of information that they might gain, using their sharp eyes and their wits. Now, if he could only display some sort of message for them to read. . . .

That night within the Castle walls was quieter than the last; it seemed that the attempt to work a double shift in clearing Elephant's hiding place had been abandoned. Maybe there were not enough slaves still driveable. Tonight there was no prodigality of torches in the courtyards, and Rolf's cell was unobserved, save by the sentry who passed by a few meters away, at reasonably predictable intervals. Rolf had realized that no one could see the roof of his cell. The adjacent shed kept it from being seen from the height of the keep.

Turning his comparatively new shirt inside out gave him a nearly white surface for a slate. After pondering for a while on how to get the most information into the fewest words possible, he set down:

I RODE ELE. IN CAVE

And then he was stuck for a way to convey what should be said of the power that he had seen and sensed. Finally all he could add was:

SAVE IT FROM EKUMAN
ROLF

He thickened and darkened the letters with double strokes of his writing-stick, and worked them into the fabric with fingers and spit. He rolled up the garment and unrolled it again; his message seemed to have a fair degree of permanence.

Now he had only to display it on his cell's flat roof, spread out straight and unwrinkled enough for a bird to read. After a little thought he reached out through the bars at the bottom of his door and gathered in some traces of the recent construction that lay there, small stones and little chunks of dried mortar. Choosing from these several that seemed of proper size, he made shift to attach them as weights to the lower edge of the shirt, loosening threads from the garment to tie them on. It took some time to make them all secure, but of hours he had plenty.

He rolled up the shirt then like a scroll, and made several practice openings of it, snapping it out to unroll quickly on the floor. One of the weights came loose and had to be retied, but he saw no reason why the scheme should not be successful.

Meanwhile he had been counting silently, roughly timing the passages of the sentry. Now Rolf waited until the man had passed once more, then went to the door. He thrust his rolled-up shirt out through the high bars, then held it by the shoulders and unrolled it with a backward snap. He heard the little stones strike with tiny clacks on the flat roof above his head.

Leaving the shirt spread out—as he hoped—upon the roof, he went to huddle in the cell's darkest corner. So grimly was he forbidding himself to indulge in any hope that when there came another tiny clack on the roof he jumped to his feet, convinced that the sound must somehow mean that his signal had been discovered by the enemy. But no outcry followed. There came no rush of raging men with torches.

He realized gradually that the tap on the roof had been like the sound of a tiny pebble, dropped from a great height.

The sentry was nearly due again. Rolf made himself lie quiet on the straw until the man had shuffled past. And no sooner had the guard vanished than another pebble came, this one bouncing on the pavement before his cell, rising to ping faintly from a bar of the grillwork; Rolf could not see it but there was no doubt at all about the sound. He jumped to the door, reached out and up to grab his shirt and sweep it from side to side, waving it across the roof. Then he pulled the garment quickly into the cell, tore off the stones and threw them away. He rubbed and crumpled his message into an unreadable smudge and put the shirt on again.

He had living and watchful friends. He was not forgotten, not entirely alone. He pulled the shirt around him tightly. Only then did he realize that his sudden shivering was not due to cold or fear, but to a triumph that must be kept in silence.

On the next day Rolf practiced his swording with a will, winning some mild praise from his tutor. On the following night Rolf made no attempt to signal again—it was very dangerous, and he had nothing new to say—but he lay wide awake, listening, until the hour when the exchange of signals had taken place on the previous night.

Click. Click. Click. Evenly matched and spaced, three tiny impacts on his roof. He sat upright with a jerk, then waited, propped on one elbow in the straw. Did the bird expect him to reply? He went to the door and put his arm out and waved it slowly back and forth, once, twice, thrice. Then he lay awake listening and wondering for a long time, but no further signal came from above.

X

Fight For The Oasis

———◆—◆◆—◆———

Lying sprawled near the top of the gentle dune, peering over its crest, Thomas could see the dark island-like mass of the Oasis of the Two Stones spread before him in the moonlight, its nearest boundary less than a hundred meters away. The night made the outlines of the great circle of fertile land uncertain, and gave it a half-magical look. Still, since Olanthe had schooled him in the matter, he could pick out where the different areas of the settlement were.

Most of the Oasis' area was in the wide outer ring of cultivated fields. The invaders, Olanthe said, had at first wanted to fence in the whole fertile circle, but fence-building materials were hard to come by here in the desert, and they had concentrated on finishing their inner works.

On one side of the central area of the Oasis all the farmers' dwellings, semi-permanent structures of wooden frames and stretched hides, had been moved together, crowded close to one another, and a strong fence built around them. In this compound the people of the Oasis could be confined every night at sunset. And by night as well as by day strong mounted and foot patrols of Castle-soldiers roamed the fields and paths around the perimeter of the watered land.

Stretched out on the dune with Thomas, and on the dunes immediately to east and west, were the two hundred men and women of his attacking force, resting now in silence from the hard march that had brought them out here from the mountains. Olanthe lay at his left side, and on his right was Mewick, face darkened with earth for the night attack until it looked like the visage of some carven demon of melancholy.

Beyond Mewick, Loford lay, the faint wheeze of his breathing carrying in the stillness to Thomas's ears. Olanthe's hair blew in the night breeze, touching Thomas on the cheek. She was leaning toward him to whisper, and stretching out an arm to point. There, she was showing him, in the Oasis' central area, lay the defensive compound of the enemy. That was where the bulk of them must be taken by surprise tonight and slaughtered. Two corners of its high palisade were marked now by the distant sparks of torches. Olanthe had explained earlier that the gate of it usually stood open, though of course there would be a guard.

Thomas knew there were a score of birds over the Oasis now, invisible to human or reptilian eyes. They were marking for him the positions of the enemy patrols, and once the attack began it would be the birds' job to prevent the escape of a single foe, on wing or foot. For the Castle to learn of this attack tonight, or even tomorrow, would probably mean disaster; the Free Folk meant to rest in the Oasis for a day and a night before beginning the march that would take them straight into the decisive battle for the Elephant. Tonight's fight could be decisive only if the Free Folk lost.

"Pass the word again," Thomas whispered now, repeating the message both to left and right. "No burning." Any great fire would surely be seen by the watch on the battlements of the distant Castle; then morning would surely bring reptiles, to investigate; and after reptiles would come the cavalry in force. Ekuman would need no Elephant to win a battle fought by day and in the open.

Loford was crawling toward Thomas now. A few moments ago the Big One had gone back down the dune, and now was coming up again, between Thomas and Mewick. The wizard moved, Thomas thought, with all the stealth of a foundered plowbeast; but even he could not make a great deal of noise in soft sand, so this time it did not matter.

"I have been trying this and that," Loford rumbled softly, collapsing with a grunt to lie beside him at full length. "But things are just not favorable for magic. Too many swords are out, I suppose."

"Not even an elemental?" Thomas wanted all the help that he could get, and he knew that Loford had a knack for elementals.

Loford shook his head. "I might draw up a good one from the desert. But not at night. The desert is day. Sun, and heat, and a withering wind throwing a blast of sand—aye, I might fetch up something to please you! But not at night." The wizard sounded guilty and defensive.

Thomas hit his shoulder gently. "I wasn't really counting on your powers tonight. We made need that sand-elemental more, to screen us when we're crossing the desert toward the Castle day after tomorrow. In case the Thunderstone doesn't draw enough rain for us to hide in."

"I am thinking about that march; tossing the Stone ahead of us to keep drawing rain, and dodging thunderbolts. It should be as adventurous as some battles. And you want an elemental to keep us company too. Ho!"

"Sh!" hissed Mewick.

In a very low whisper Thomas added: "And I am thinking that we will fight no more swamp-battles. One way or the other."

The shadow of a bird came drifting down in ghostly silence to stand just below Thomas on the dune. Wings proudly spread, it reported on just how many enemy patrols were out, and where. Thomas hurriedly made decisions, and passed orders to his squad leaders down the line. One squad he detailed to positions along the western rim of the

Oasis, to be ready to intercept any of the enemy who might try to flee toward the Castle.

"And we are ready in the air, Thomas," the bird assured him. "If the reptiles dare to arise, not one of them will escape."

Orders acknowledged, the long rank of human figures began to break up, drifting away in silent clusters, half-visible under the Moon. "Go now," said Thomas to the bird, "and bring me word as soon as our squads are in position of the far side of the Oasis." The separate attacks on enemy patrols must be made as nearly simultaneous as possible, and at the same time the entrance to the inner compound should be seized.

With a sweep of wings the courier drifted up and away. Now, if anything had been forgotten, it was too late to mend. Thomas thought to himself that being a leader gave one advantage anyway: there was no time for a man to worry much about his own skin.

His eyes met Olanthe's in the moonlight, and they looked at each other for a time. Neither felt need to speak.

The bird was back before he had really started to expect it. "They are ready on the far side, Thomas. And along the western edge."

"So. Then we are ready too." He drew a deep breath and looked at the remnant of his force that was still near enough for him to see. "And we attack."

With a wave of his arm he motioned forward the dozen who were to accompany him closely into the fight, to try to seize the inner compound's gate. Another squad of the same size, led by Mewick, would be following closely, hoping to be able to rush through the gate and kill sleeping invaders in their barracks.

The outer boundary of the Oasis was marked by a ditch that, according to Olanthe, served to keep the desert from drifting in. Crossing it now, she whispered to Thomas: "Nearly dry. We must use the Stone for rain while we are here."

Once past this outer ditch, Thomas led his squad between rows of knee-high plants toward the Oasis' center. He motioned his people to spread out, and at first set the pace across the level ground at a crouching run. When they had covered a few hundred meters he slowed to a walk, and a little while later dropped down to crawl between the rows of plants. There would be a patrol of eight foot-soldiers not far ahead. Thomas's and Mewick's squads were supposed to sneak past this patrol, leaving it to be ambushed by other Free Folk a little farther on.

Thomas saw the patrol, walking in slow single file on a course at right angles to his own. The moon turned the bronze helms into ghosts' heads. He stopped crawling, and around him his squad melted into the soil and the night.

The enemy passed. Then their leader took an unexpected turn. Raising his head a few centimeters, Thomas saw them now heading straight for where Mewick's squad had gone to earth. Only let it be silent, Thomas thought, when an encounter appeared inevitable.

The soldiers' leader stopped, making a startled, turning movement. Around him and his men, Mewick's people rose up like dark and silent demons. They had the advantages of numbers, twelve to eight, and of surprise, and it was no wonder that they cut down the Castle-men without loss to themselves. Still, silence had been too much to expect, and a pair of screams went drifting in the night.

Thomas stood up tensely, looking toward the center of the Oasis, now less than half a kilometer distant. Olanthe's hand was on his arm. "That may not alarm the central compound," she said softly. "They may think only that some fugitives are being chased through the fields, or that birds are harassing a patrol. That sometimes happens."

"There may be noise from the other patrols at any moment. We'd better hurry." Thomas waved his own squad forward. He motioned Mewick to follow closely, and got an acknowledging wave.

Thomas's short-sword rode in a scabbard strapped against his leg. He saw Olanthe loosening a long knife in its sheath at her hip as they walked.

Now the Oasis' central area grew close enough for details to be visible. There was the barrier of sharpened stakes, forming a prison compound where the Oasis-folk were penned at night. Thomas could see clay silos, barns, and storage bins. And, straight ahead, the invaders' defensive palisade, wherein the torches still burned. The gate was open. No trees were to be seen; Olanthe had said they had all gone to make the stockade. No humans or reptiles were in sight.

"Let the two of us go first," Thomas whispered when his squad had gathered round him. Then he took Olanthe by the hand and walked with her along the dark path that led almost straight from where they were to the open gate of the palisade. Now he could see the arm and part of the uniform of a soldier who seemed to be lounging just inside the gate. The hope was that the first few soldiers who saw Thomas and Olanthe would take them for nothing more dangerous than a young couple trying to sneak in after curfew.

On the right side of the path ran the barricade enclosing the houses of the farm folk, and on the left side were tall storage bins. From behind one of these a soldier stepped out suddenly to bar their way.

He showed a pleased grin at their starts of surprise. "Looking for a hole under the fence somewhere? I hope your frolicking half the night was worth it, because—" He peered more closely at Olanthe's hand. "What've you got there?"

From somewhere out in the fields came a yell of fear, agony weakened and purified by distance. The soldier saw Olanthe's long knife, and his mouth was forming for an echoing yell as he started to draw his sword; he meant to step back, but Thomas's blade was already between his ribs.

Thomas heard two dozen feet come shuffle-pounding speedily on the path behind him as he sprinted for the palisade gate. A pair of sentries came into view, alarmed—too late. They had time to yell, but no time more.

The gate taken, Thomas cast one look backward. Mewick's squad was coming on the run, only a few meters down the path. Then he put Olanthe aside with one arm and turned and ran on into the compound, sprinting for the open doorway of the nearest barracks. On the right as he faced inward from the gate he saw stables along the palisade, and then the barracks, a long low timber building big enough for nearly a hundred men. On the left side of the compound were similar stables and barracks, and on the side opposite the gate another long low building that Thomas knew housed the officers and served as headquarters. All the center of the compound was bare sandy earth, pounded flat by marching feet. Before the headquarters building a flagpole held a limp banner of Ekuman's black and bronze. And in the very center of the parade-ground, upon a sort of cruciform gibbet, there was a man bound living—a naked man with the wounds of whipping striped across his body, who raised his gray head now to stare at Thomas. Thomas had no time now for a close look at the victim; his running strides were carrying him on toward the barracks' open door.

A man came stepping out of this doorway, half-naked and half-awake, buckling on a sword. He stumbled to a halt, eyes and mouth widening at the sight of Thomas, charging, huge, black all over for the night attack.

Thomas aimed for the middle of the body, drove his short sword in nearly to the hilt, shoved the dead man back into the barracks and went in after him. Right at his back his raiders poured after him through the narrow door, all bellowing now to raise up terror and panic. Before him, only a few of the enemy as yet had weapons in their hands. Thomas was no master swordsman, and he knew it. So he used the advantages he did have, his strength and size, for all that they were worth. With two hammering strokes he beat down his next opponent's guard, and with the next stroke cut his arm off near the elbow.

In a moment the raiders controlled the door, and the weapon-rack that stood beside it, from which Thomas grabbed himself a shield; in a few moments more what was going on could no longer be called a fight. Castle-men were killed in their hammocks, stabbed crawling in corners, died while playing dead, were slaughtered like scrambling, squealing meat-beasts in a pen.

The killing was still unfinished when Thomas scrambled over the slippery floor back to the door again. By now more than a score of Free Folk were inside the compound, and in front of the other barracks a fierce fight raged. Mewick was there, thrusting with a long dagger, swinging a war-hatchet that looked like some peasants' tool save for its swordlike basket-hilt.

Even with one barracks cleaned out, the Free Folk inside the stockade were still outnumbered. Yelling, Thomas led his own squad charging to Mewick's aid.

The men in the second barracks had been given just a few more moments to rouse themselves than the men in the first barracks had enjoyed, and that made a great difference. These men were just starting to pour out and fight, but when Thomas charged they began retreating into the barracks again, probably not realizing in the confusion that the advantage of numbers was still theirs. Arrows began to come singing out of the slits in the barracks' timber wall. The barracks was a solid structure, built right against the strong high palisade.

"Remember, no burning!" Thomas shouted. He could see two of his men down already with arrows in them. But welcome reinforcements were now charging in at the palisade's gate, Free Folk who had evidently finished their ambush of one of the outer patrols.

Olanthe popped up from somewhere to stand at Thomas's side. "Keep down!" he barked, gripping her protectively. He reached into her pack and took out the Thunderstone, and rolled it toward the barracks. The battered metal case bounced to a stop just at a corner of the low building.

It would take some little time for the storm to develop. Meanwhile, Thomas disposed some men to discourage those inside the barracks from sallying; that done, he turned the greater part of his attention to the headquarters building. He saw that Mewick had already led men onto the roof of it, where they were fighting with some bronze-helmets who had climbed up from inside. Others were trading spearthrusts and missiles at the doors and windows.

Yet another squad of Free Folk came pouring into the compound now, and with them the first of the farmers to rise in arms—pitchforks and reaping-hooks, as predicted, and a raging joyous fury. Thomas ran to meet these, and led them to the headquarters building.

On the headquarters roof, guards and officers and orderlies in bronze helmets were holding off the Free Folk with pike and sword and mace, protecting one corner of the palisade. There one of their number was waving torches to drive off birds, while another tried to pull the protective net away from a reptile-roost; they meant to get a courier away to Ekuman.

The soldier waving torches went down, struck by a pitchfork hurled up from the ground. Thomas

skipped quickly over the shingles to kick the flaming
brands off the roof before they could set fire to it.
The man struggling with the net at last succeeded in
getting it out of the reptiles' way—but not one of
them ventured out of the doorway of the roost. The
night belonged to the birds, and well the reptiles
knew it.

Thunder grumbled overhead. Suddenly there was
no one but Free Folk left standing on the roof,
though others were still lying there. Blood slicked
the shingles underfoot and trickled in the rain-
gutters. Someone had taken up a captured pike and
was starting to try to prod the reptiles out of their
little house. Birds were landing at the doorway,
their soft voices vibrant, urging those within who
had eaten birds' eggs not to be shy now, but come
out and welcome their guests come to return the
call.

Men down on the ground at the entrance to the
headquarters building were calling for Thomas. He
swung over the edge of the roof and dropped down
to discover that some of Mewick's squad thought
they had nabbed the garrison commander. They
shoved forward a gray-haired fellow with a thin
ropy neck. They had caught him in a store-room,
putting on a private soldier's uniform.

Rain pattered down, then drummed. Lightning
was marching closer. In one sudden white opening
of the sky, Thomas looked up and saw Strijeef, old
wound still bandaged on one wing, eyes mad and
glaring, emerging from a reptile-roost. Leathery
eggshell clung to the talons of his upraised foot. His
beak and his feathers were stained with purplish
blood.

"See to the other roost!" Thomas shouted up.
Then he dragged the gray-haired prisoner to
Olanthe, and some of the other Oasis-folk, to make
absolutely sure of who he was. Olanthe was out in
the center of the parade-ground, in range of arrows
from the still-resisting barracks. A couple of farmers

were standing by with captured shields, ready to deflect any shafts that came at those working to take the old man down from his scaffold. Olanthe was weeping, oblivious of arrows; Thomas realized that the man on the cross must be her father.

The victim was just being lowered when the Thunderstone got the lightning it was calling for. The bolt followed the corner of the barracks from eaves to ground, opening the structure like a great egg carefully topped at table. The rain, pouring now, prevented any fire from catching. Thomas ran to join his men entering the breach, but his leadership was not needed. His force swept in through the riven wall and completed the night's work without further loss to themselves.

And so ended the battle for the Oasis. Olanthe's father and the other wounded freedom fighters were carried out of the invaders' compound to be cared for in the farmers' homes. From the farmers' compound, a prison no longer, voices began to rise, men and women and children singing in the gladness of their deliverance.

At a touch on his shoulder Thomas turned, to see Loford standing there, grinning hugely; on the upper part of the wizard's big right arm a small wound was bleeding.

"How was the fighting?" Thomas asked.

"Oh, very good! Oh, excellent! I tell you I was once facing two of them—but I am come to remind you, this time the Thunderstone is yours to pick up."

"That's right." Thomas, grinning, thinking how he would torment Loford by never asking him how he had got his glorious wound, trotted over to the shattered barracks and picked up the graven case from a puddle.

While he was there a bird came down to him, bringing the good report that not a single enemy had escaped the slaughter. Several members of the patrols ambushed in the fields had tried to get away, to reach the Castle, when they saw that the whole Oasis was under attack. All but one of these had been cut down by Thomas's men left along the Oasis' western boundary for the purpose. The one man who had got past them, mounted, had been dragged bloodily from his saddle while at full gallop, by three of the Silent People who had overtaken and fastened on him from above. And now even the terrified beast he had been riding was caught and being brought back to the stables.

Though the fighting was over, no one who was not wounded could be allowed to rest. There was too much to be done before dawn. The wounded must be moved out of sight and cared for, the dead must be buried and then all traces of their graves effaced. Any couriers from the Castle must not be allowed to suspect what had happened—not until they had landed, or at least descended within certain arrow-range.

The wall of the riven barracks was hastily propped up in place, and the gaps mended as well as possible. At dawn the farmers would go to their fields in the usual numbers to do their ordinary tasks. Men of the Free Folk would put on uniforms of bronze and black for incoming reptiles to see, and would march or ride or stand on watch. The mess of shattered eggs and purplish reptile blood was scraped and scrubbed from the outer porches of the roosts.

"One thing more," said Olanthe. And she nodded at the empty gibbet in the center of the parade-ground, from which her father had been taken almost too late to save his life. In her voice was a hardness that Thomas had not heard there before.

"A dead man will do," Thomas said. "A gray-haired one." He tried to remember some corpse among those now being buried that would be a fair match for Olanthe's father; it was a hopeless effort. He turned to look over the handful of prisoners who were still alive, awaiting some questioning; there hung the long disheveled locks of the garrison commander.

Thomas nodded at him, and the men who had the prisoners in charge immediately caught his meaning. Grinning, they pulled the waxen-faced officer forward. "We'll mount him for you, Chief! And we'll see to it that his hide's decorated properly first!"

That was exactly right. That was the best thing to do. But Thomas turned away. He saw Mewick, sad-faced as ever, turning also. But Mewick was not the one who bore responsibility. Thomas made himself turn back and watch, and listen to the whipping. He was surprised at the effort it took him—as if he had never seen blood before. Olanthe was watching, with a look of remote satisfaction. But Thomas was afraid. He feared the urgings and the delights of power, that he could feel stirring within himself like the pangs of some glamorous sickness.

The whipping of the garrison commander was useless. All through the next day, while he hung dead on the cross, no couriers from the Castle came. The Free Folk, and the Oasis farmers who were going to march with them, half-rested through the day, and then relaxed more completely on the following night.

On that night the birds brought word that they had learned Rolf's whereabouts in the Castle, and repeated his message to Thomas. They had tried to alert him that the attack was coming in three nights. If Rolf was ever taken out of doors after dark they would try to put the Prisoner's Stone into his hands.

XI

I Am Ardneh

———————◆▶◀◆———————

Three pebbles on Rolf's cell roof one night, and at the same hour on the next night, two. He waved back twice.

On the morning after that, Rolf for the first time was given a genuine keen-edged sword and, with this weapon he spent the morning lunging and hacking at the timber butts. His tutor stood by criticizing, flanked by a pair of pikemen who held their long weapons at the ready all the time that Rolf was truly armed.

In the afternoon Rolf and his tutor were alone again, once more dueling with the dulled and blunt-tipped blades. And during this session the tutor's parries were in several instances too low, and Rolf managed to poke him in the belly or hack him bloodlessly on the arm. Rolf drew small satisfaction from this, being thoroughly suspicious that the soldier was letting him win to build his confidence. If the tutor had but known it, the two pikemen in the morning had gone a long way to accomplish that.

That night there came the signal of a single pebble, which Rolf answered with one wave. Three, two, one, the count had gone, from night to night.

On the morning of the following day, Rolf knew, the wedding would take place. In the afternoon he would face Chup in the arena. Certainly it was neither of these things that the Free Folk were signaling to tell him—therefore something else of great importance was coming, tomorrow or tomorrow night.

He meant to be alive to see it.

He was awakened early on the wedding-day by loud shouts, and by music that sounded like the accompaniment of some bawdy dance. He thought again that today's festivities could not be much like those of the simple pledge-weddings he had seen and attended. On those occasions the company maintained at least an effort at solemnity until the middle of the day, until vows had been exchanged and perhaps some amateur wizard of the countryside had tried to put a spell of happiness upon the rings. After that the dancing and the drinking started, and the games, and whatever feasting the people could afford. . . .

The day wore on. Rolf was given a fresh surcoat of cheap black cloth to put on over his own clothes. There was no sword practice, no sight of his instructor. He was fed as usual and escorted to the privy. About the courtyards there were men in liveries that Rolf had not seen before—in each the color black was matched with one other, red or green or white or gray. It was true, then, that wedding guests were here from all the Satrapies nearby.

In the later afternoon the Master of the Games came with two wardens to Rolf's cell, and he was hurried out of it. First to the privy once more—he supposed so their Lordships should not be disgusted if fear overcame him utterly in the arena. And then he was led under the keep, to a small windowless chamber with an overhead of oddly slanting timbers. Through the cracks in this ceiling, and around a closed door opposite the one they entered by, sunlight filtered in. Feet tramped overhead, the sound of laughter came from very near above, and Rolf realized that he was already under the seats ringing the arena. His soldier-tutor had given him some description of the place.

A bronze helm and a shield and sword were waiting for him. While the Master of the Games hurried off on some other errand, Rolf's guards handed him the first of two of these items at once. They eyed him critically while he took the shield on his arm and set the barbut on his head; he supposed they wanted to see whether he was likely to collapse with fear.

From against the wall they swung out a cunning sort of cagework, meant to hold him against the door leading to the arena. Only after he was thus restrained did they put the naked sword into his hand. Some signal came to them almost at once when that was done, and one man hauled on a chain to make the door in front of Rolf fly open, while the other took up a spear to urge him, if need be, out onto the sand.

The spear was not needed. Rolf's legs carried him out into the glare of the low sun. Through the T of his helmet's opening he had a glimpse of a ring of faces above him, gay colors, movement; he was greeted with a burst of brutal noise. He stood at one end of a sandy oval, some twenty meters long and proportionately wide, surrounded by a high smooth unscalable wall.

There came another roar of applause, and Rolf saw the tall, black-clad figure of his opponent stalking toward him, coming from the opposite end of the flat little world in which the two of them were now alone. A red mask painted on the front of a black barbut-helm concealed Chup's face. Holding sword and shield ready, he came straight forward; in his gait there was a swaying movement that Rolf could interpret only as some intended mockery.

Rolf put out of his mind everything but: *strike first, and strike hard.* His knees that had been quivering now bore him forward steadily.

His enemy was taller, and longer of reach, and so had the privilege of striking first; an option he chose to exercise. The straight overhand cut seemed a mockery also, for it was slower than some that Rolf had parried from his tutor's blade. Rolf caught the downstroke on his shield, and perhaps he shouted—he had thought earlier that when this moment came he should shout something, so the evil ones who watched would know that he was dying for the cause of freedom.

Later, he did not know whether he had cried out anything at all at this moment. He knew only that he deflected the clumsy downstroke with his shield, as he had been taught to do, and thrust straight in to kill.

His point slid so easily through the black cloth and between his opponent's ribs that for a moment Rolf did not believe in his success. He retreated a step, thinking only: *What trick is this?*

But the man in black was not shamming. A spurting stain of red spread down his front. His arms sagged with his weapons in them, and with what seemed infinite weariness he went down upon his knees. Then, turning sideways, he toppled out full length upon the sand.

Victory still seemed unreal to Rolf. The gay throng encircling him above the wall were cheering, a sound was made even more incredible by the groans that mingled with it—not laments of rage or shock, but whines of mere disappointment, the sounds of watchers cheated by the sudden ending of a show.

Taking off his helmet, Rolf looked up. Chup sat there, in the first bank of seats, looking down at Rolf, smiling lightly and applauding. Beside Chup was his golden bride; even now Rolf noticed that Charmian was looking across the arena and up, with expectancy in her face.

Rolf turned and looked down again at the figure on the sand. He scarcely noticed when soldiers came to take his weapon away; he was watching two dungeon-wardens approach the fallen man. One of them cautiously kicked away the dropped sword while the other turned the body on its back and pulled off the demon-painted barbut. The face revealed was young, and quite unknown to Rolf.

One of the wardens had begun to raise a heavy maul, to give the quietus. His motion was stopped on the backstroke by a scream—a woman's shriek so sudden and so terrible that it sent reptiles cawing up in startlement from their high perches on the overlooking keep.

And Rolf knew whom he had stabbed; he knew when he looked up and saw that the screaming girl was Sarah.

The Satrap Ekuman, twisting around in his cushioned seat of honor under a bronze-black awning was looking at Sarah also. Plainly the girl was screeching the name of the man who had just fallen in the oddly unequal bout. Something more than a coincidence, thought Ekuman. With a look he ordered the Master of the Harem to be quick about quieting the girl, getting the nuisance of her shrieks and her contorted face out of the presence of the guests. And then he faced forward again, looking across the arena to where his daughter sat beside her bridegroom. It had become almost a reflex for Ekuman to suspect his daughter, whenever some nasty internal intrigue threatened the peace if not the very security of his household. And the expression she was wearing now, a look of slight aristocratic puzzlement at the disturbance, was quite too good for him to believe in it for a moment.

So.

The Satrap was not, of course, concerned about the bereavement of a harem slave. Nor, really, about the fixing of a gladiatorial contest, though that was an annoyance. What bit him was the discovery that an intrigue of any kind could be accomplished, in his own Castle and without his knowledge, by one who was departing, who tomorrow would presumably have no power here at all. It meant that there were people in his establishment, in positions of responsibility, whose first loyalty was to his daughter today and would be so tomorrow, when she would be Lady in a rival house, when there would be things of infinitely greater moment at stake.

He would impress his guests. He would find out, today, who those folk were, and today he would be rid of them.

Already he was leaning forward, with an outstretched hand staying the wardens in the arena from disposing of the fallen man, who might be saved for questioning. Garl, Master of the Troops, having seen from his Lord's expression that something was amiss, was already at his side. Ekuman issued quick orders that both gladiators, and those who had had them in charge, should be brought before him at once. "In my Presence Chamber."

Turning his head, Ekuman said to the Master of the Games, "See that some other entertainment is set before my guests, and then do you attend me also." He shot his glance across the arena, and raised his voice from its confidential level: "My dear daughter and my son, please come with me."

But as Ekuman arose he had to delay, for now the Master of the Reptiles was pressing toward him along the aisle before the lowest tier of seats, creating a fresh wave of puzzled comment among the guests. The Reptile Master's face showed clearly that he thought his errand urgent. In his hands he held a reptile courier's pouch, that had some bulky weight inside.

"Bring it along," Ekuman told him, and strode along the passage that opened for him between courtiers, heading for the keep. He noticed clouds coming with portentous suddenness over the lowering sun, and behind him he heard the Master of the Games call out, "Lords and ladies, I pray you come inside! The weather conspires with other disturbances against our celebration here. My Lord Ekuman bids you make merry in his hall, where he will join you when he can!"

Once inside the keep, Ekuman drew the Master of the Reptiles aside.

The Master of the Reptiles whispered, "My Lord, this pouch was most likely sent toward us from the Oasis, for it was found in the desert. It was sent some days ago, for the fallen courier's body was decayed when one of my scouts discovered it during this last hour. The courier may well have fallen in one of those untimely rainstorms that have raged over the desert for the past few days."

"What's in it?"

"There must have been a message, Lord, but — see? — the pouch's lock is broken, from storm or fall, and the desert wind has left no paper. Only this." The Reptile Master let the torn pouch fall away; his hands remained holding up a weighty case of metal, the size of two clenched fists. It looked as if it had come through fire and battle both.

Ekuman took the thing. The graven markings tickled his stroking thumbs with power; he knew strong magic when he felt it in his hands. "You did well to bring this straight to me."

Problems were encircling him like armed men, attacking all at once. He would just have to fight them all off as best he could, dealing a stroke here and another there, till he could pin one down and settle it; it was a common predicament for a ruler.

"Summon Elslood to the Presence Chamber too," Ekuman ordered a soldier who was standing by. The man saluted and ran off. Ekuman let two more soldiers pass him, bearing between them the fallen gladiator on a litter. Then he walked himself in the same direction. Passing a narrow window, he marked how sudden a gloom had fallen outside. The Master of the Games had been right to summon the guests into the hall.

Rolf had been willing enough to be disarmed; at the moment he wanted never to touch a sword again. He stood there in the arena, not knowing whether he wished to live or die. Only once since Nils had fallen had Sarah looked in Rolf's direction, and that look had stabbed him like a blade.

At least Nils still lived—whatever his life might be worth. A pair of robed men came to minister to Nils and supervise his being carried off. Rolf was soon prodded on to follow. Under a suddenly threatening sky, all the gaily appareled spectators were also starting to file into the keep.

Rolf was marched indoors and upstairs. Gradually he began to understand that something about his fight with Nils was perturbing the great folk of the Castle; the faces of his guards were concerned about something more important than avoiding a rainstorm.

An officer came to search Rolf, then preceded him and his escort through a large and richly furnished hall, filling up now with the spectators from the arena. They stared at Rolf as he passed and whispered curiously, while the Master of the Games called to them, trying to rouse interest in his jugglers. Servants were putting torches in wall sconces, against the sudden onslaught of the night.

One more flight of steps, then a wait in a rich antechamber. Then Rolf was brought into a large circular room, the lower level of the squat tower that crowned the keep. Against one wall was Ekuman, enthroned on a great chair. In flanking chairs sat Chup, and golden Charmian, haughty as a statue. At Ekuman's back the curving wall was hung with many trophies, of war and of the chase, and among these were some Old World things—Rolf thought he could recognize them as such, seeing their precise smooth workmanship, like that of the far-seeing glasses and the Elephant.

Nervous attendants milled about. On the floor of inlaid wood before Ekuman was set the stretcher with Nils on it, the robed men bending over him to stanch the flow of blood. And standing before Ekuman was the soldier who had taught Rolf his swordplay, at attention now, quivering with a rigidity of discipline. And there was Sarah, between two soldiers who gripped her arms to keep her from collapsing or going to her lover on his pallet.

Rolf had only a moment to look at these others, as he was hurried forward to be confronted by the Satrap himself. Ekuman's baleful eye swung round on him, and the two men who held Rolf's arms forced him to kneel.

The Satrap's voice struck him all the more impressively for seeming mild. "You fought well today, sirrah. What would you have by way of reward?"

"I would have—only what I thought I had. The chance to fight against the one I thought was wearing that devil-painted helmet!" Rolf did not look at Sarah, but he could hope that she had heard him.

"And whom did you think you were fighting?" Ekuman asked him calmly.

Rolf turned his head to look at Chup.

It was a moment before the warrior-lord understood just what the prisoner meant. Then Chup sat up straight in his chair. "Me? You clod of dung! You thought that *I* had arrayed myself in helm and shield to descend and fight a formal duel with *you*?"

Thinking back, Rolf realized that it had been only his own foolish assumption, that Chup would fight him. Others had used his foolishness to lead him on, to make him murder Nils to give them sport.

"Clod of dung?" mused Ekuman. "Yes, a peasant, by all signs—but that stroke was well put that felled the other. Young master, where were you taught to use a sword?"

Intrigue was foreign to Rolf's experience, but he could feel very plainly the mutual distrust and malice of all the evil folk around him. He could sense divisions arraying each of them against the others. If he had known what lie would be most like to set them on to mutual destruction, he would have tried to tell it. As matters stood, he instinctively chose the truth as his weapon.

"All that I know of swordplay," he said clearly, "I was taught here in the Castle." And he realized the truth had scored, somehow; if Charmian's eyes could kill he would have died in that moment.

"Taught by whom?" asked Ekuman reasonably.

"By this one." Rolf leveled a pointing arm at the old soldier. The man did not look at Rolf. Behind his stoic front he seemed to quiver neither more nor less than before.

Lightning came, not far away. An easy ripping crackle at the start, and then a giant tore the sky in two from top to bottom, letting through a momentary blaze that seemed to come from some furnace-glare beyond. The light was strong on Charmian's face, as she raised her eyes with an expression of relief. She was looking over Rolf's shoulder. Rolf turned his own head for a moment; a tall gray figure, wizard if there ever was one, was standing now within the door.

"Face the Satrap!" A guard's fist struck Rolf's face; Rolf turned back. Somehow an afterimage of the gray wizard's hollow eyes came with him, superimposing itself on Ekuman's face.

"And you were well fed?" Ekuman asked, as if all that moved him was some mild concern for Rolf's welfare.

"I was."

One of the robed men by the stretcher turned up his face, and Rolf saw with fascinated horror that a creature that was a toad and something more than a toad crouched half-hidden on the wizard's shoulder, under his cloak. "Lord, I am sure now, this man who lost was starved and weakened. Deprived of rest. The signs are very plain."

After that Rolf could hear nothing more for a few moments. In the very abyss of his fear and hate he came near feeling pity for people grown so pettily malignant, to play such games with helpless slaves. But he had believed them—that he would have a chance at Chup—he had wanted to believe. He felt himself swaying on his knees. Just now he could not have turned to face Sarah to save his life—his life?

No, that was not worth turning his head to save. If only Nils had killed him, instead!

When he could think again, when his self-disgust was turning wholly outward against those who had so tricked and used him, he saw that his tutor was being made now to kneel at Rolf's side. The man spoke at last, in a muttering voice. "Mercy, Lord." But he did not raise his eyes to look at Ekuman.

"Tell me, my loyal sergeant—who gave the orders for this method of training the two gladiators?"

In answer the old soldier gasped. His head twisted around, eyes staring, as if he wanted to see something invisible that had fastened on him from behind. In the next moment he was toppling forward from his knees, much as Nils had done in the arena. But this man was smitten by no blade, only stiffening and straining in some sort of fit, gone foaming and speechless.

Ekuman was on his feet, barking angry orders. The man with the toad-creature watched the fit, then raised his head frowning as he who had been in the rear of the chamber came forward at a majestic pace, tall and gray.

Ekuman held out to this one a blackened case of metal, and said, "Elslood. Tell me quickly what you can make of this."

Frowning, the wizard Elslood took the thing, weighed it in his hand, muttered over it for a moment, then raised the curved lid, while some around shrank back. He stared at the lump of blackened stone that lay inside. "I can tell you nothing quickly, Lord, save that there is some real power here."

"That much I knew. Put the thing in some safe place, then, and attend me here. I mean to get to the bottom of this game that was played in the arena today."

Elslood shut the case with a snap. He looked down once—as if indifferently—at the fallen soldier, who was still writhing feebly on the floor while others tried to minister to him. Elslood looked at

Rolf, and again, stronger than before, the image of his eyes burned brilliant and gigantic in Rolf's mind. Then he handed the case to the man with the toad, at the same time indicating the far side of the chamber with a motion of his head. The man with the toad-creature accepted the case and started across the chamber with it. On the far side was an arras which might hide a closet or a separate apartment.

Through the window nearest him, Rolf heard rain roar suddenly upon the flat roof-terrace just outside. Servants had just finished lighting torches, and the flames smoked fitfully. Rolf had the sensation that the sky, like some great flat coffin-lid, was pressing down upon the tower.

"Now, sirrah!" Ekuman was speaking to him again. But this time the Satrap's voice seemed to be coming and going, issuing from behind a barrier and then emerging once more, echoing through an immense distance. Rolf did not seem to be able to answer. The image of Elslood's eyes, growing and swelling, remained like some malignant growth within his head, clouding thought and vision alike. The tall gray wizard was standing nearby, but Rolf dared not look up at him again.

"Answer me, sirrah!" Ekuman was almost shouting. "Good answers now will save some pains when you are taken down below!"

Whether it was the boldness of utter despair that now settled on Rolf or whether some outside power came to his aid and he managed to put away both the terror that Ekuman wanted to fasten on him and the imposed vision of the wizard's eyes that would compel him to be silent. The Satrap's face grew clear before Rolf and he stood up from his knees.

Ekuman's voice was clear and ordinary once more, coming with the drumming of the rain through a heavy silence. "Tell me, master swordsman, whose agent are you?"

Beyond all fear now, Rolf smiled. "I? I am Ardneh—"

The night pressing on the Castle was destroyed. The light that rent it was as sudden as that which had blazed out of Elephant's side, and a thousand times, a million times, as bright. The concussion that came with it was beyond all sound.

Rolf was aware only that something had hit him with force enough to knock him down, nay, turn him inside out as well. Other people had been hit also, for a voice was screaming, over and over. No, it was more than one voice. Some of the women's voices had turned guttural, and there were masculine ones gone high and childish.

By some means that Rolf did not understand at first, the window nearest him had just been widened, so that rain drove in on him where he lay on the floor amid loose stones and broken wood. The noises of human agony went on. Could that be Sarah screaming, Chup stabbing her with his punishing cudgel?

When Rolf raised his head a ball of lightning was still adrift in the middle of the room. He watched it dancing about there, lightly and hesitantly, as if it looked to see whether any chance for destruction had been missed, before it skipped to the wall and vanished up a chimney.

A path of ruin had been plowed straight across the center of the room. From the blasted window nearest Rolf to the flaming arras of the distant alcove, human bodies and furniture had been treated like the nestings of mice turned up by a furrowing plow. The wooden floor was marked with a blackened path, smoking and smoldering. The incoming rain hissed on this scar where it was near Rolf's head, but could not reach it elsewhere.

The smoke oozing up from the floor was forming a thick cloud in the higher air, so Rolf did not at once attempt to stand. Crawling would serve, for the moment. Where was Sarah? She was gone, like his sister and his parents. On hands and knees he moved dazedly over wreckage, seeing without emotion the twitching dead and the struggling injured, hearing the lip-licking crackle of the hungry bright young flames.

Not finding Sarah, he went on dazedly following the black burning furrow of the lightning-plow. At the end of the path he came to Zarf's roasted body; Zarf smelled of cooked meat now. In death his face no longer ordinary, and the dead thing at his shoulder was no longer a toad, but an odd terrible little creature like a bearded human baby. And here was a monstrous spider, sizzled crisp; and none of these were stranger than other things that were strewn across the floor, amid tumbled shelves and fallen, burning draperies.

Not having found Sarah, Rolf turned back again. He saw now that there were new people in the room, moving capably about, and he got himself to his feet. More he could not do. Now soldiers and servants were pouring into the chamber, from the stair and from the roof-terrace.

And Ekuman himself was on his feet. His rich garments were torn, his face begrimed, but the vigor of his movements showed that he had taken no serious hurt. In his hands he now held one of the Old World things that Rolf had earlier noticed on the wall behind the throne—one of a pair of red cylinders, whose mate still hung there on a strap. At one end of the cylinder was a black nozzle which Ekuman aimed at the burning floor. With his other hand he gripped a trigger that reminded Rolf of some of the controls inside the Elephant.

From the black nozzle there shot out a white rope that looked hardly more substantial than smoke, but remained coherent and opaque and was heavy enough to sink to the floor. There it expanded. Like some magic pudding the whiteness spread itself across the burning floor, flame and smoking wood vanishing beneath it. The wounded lying on the floor brought their heads above the white blanket to gasp for air—but they need struggle and cry no longer for fear of being burned. The fire was quickly being put out.

There was Sarah, beside Nils' stretcher, holding up his head above the whiteness. The sight of her alive was joy to Rolf, even though a soldier had her in charge, and even though two more of them seized him as he took his first step toward her.

Ekuman worked on, a diligent laborer. From the seemingly inexhaustible device he held there spread out a white carpet to cover all the fire. His soldiers and his servants took heart from the sight of their Lord standing calmly unharmed in the midst of it. Soon, at his orders, the wounded were being lifted up, the damage assessed, order reestablished.

Only one voice went keening on in mindless fear, the voice of one who had not been hurt. Rolf saw Chup draw back his hand and coldly slap his smudge-faced wife. The one blow brought her to a silence of astonishment, utter and open-mouthed.

Now there were only the purposeful noises of workers in the chamber. The fire was dead; Ekuman shut off his foam-thrower and set it down. Nils was still alive, and the tall wizard Elslood seemed unhurt.

Out on the terrace the rain was trailing off to nothing, but daylight was not returned. The sun, Rolf thought, must be already down.

It was not light that burst in next at the exploded window. It was a patch of darkness, darkness not black, but gray-green scale. The reptile flapped to a halt in the midst of the white floor, cawing out to Ekuman:

"My Lawrd! M'Lawwrd! The enemy attacks, acraaws the pass!"

XII

To Ride The Elephant

———— ◆◆◆ ————

Rolf lunged and twisted in the soldiers' grip, trying to see outside. Peering through a narrow north window into the deep dusk, he managed to see only a few distant sparks, fires or torches, before he was wrenched away.

"Take this one back to his cell," an officer was ordering. "Keep him alone until the Lord Ekuman has time to question him again."

Rolf's guards hustled him downstairs. Several times they paused, making way for messengers dashing up or down. Rolf could see nothing but elation among the soldiers at the news that the Free Folk were attacking in force. The Castle-men had no doubt that they could win a battle in the open, even at night.

Each time he passed a window Rolf tried futilely to get a look at what was going on outside. Three, two, one—so the count had gone, aiming at tonight. The signals must have been meant to tell him of something that involved him more directly than the attack across the pass. Something would be expected of him. And now he was going back to his cell, where his friends would expect him to be.

Extra torches had been lighted in the courtyards, which were filled with a confusion of hurrying people and animals. Three, two, one, the time had come, and he was still alive to see it. Rolf was at a peak of alertness, and his ears at once caught the high clear hooting that drifted down to him from above. He did not look up, for on the instant a small object struck the paving near his feet and bounced up right before him. Tied to the missile was a note, a paper—at least a white tail of some kind.

Rolf caught the stone on its first bounce, thinking meanwhile that the bird was mad to drop a message to him in this way. His guards' hands grabbed at him, then unaccountably slipped away as the stone came firmly into his grasp. He twisted free, hoping to gain a moment to discover what words were worth getting him killed in order that he might read them.

"Put that down!" a guard bawled, and followed this urging with a string of demons' names, directed at his mate who for some reason had come blundering awkwardly into him. Rolf skipped away farther, and got the paper open, but before he could try to read it the two men were coming at him, hands outstretched. Rolf raised the rock, on the point of trying to brain one of them with it, but in that instant a door opened in the wall just at his back. The door was left ajar by the soldier who came running through it on some urgent errand; as if he did not see them, he ran right in the way of the two coming after Rolf.

Seizing the opportunity, Rolf dodged through the door. It slammed shut of itself behind him, then creaked with the weight of his shouting pursuers. He was in another courtyard, this one nearly filled with soldiers just forming up for roll call. There were no more open doors in sight. Rolf darted past a gaping officer and then, since there was nowhere else to run, went dodging through the ranks, looking frantically for some way out. Men stared at him, some cursed, some laughed.

"Seize that man!"

"He's greased!"

"Ensorceled!"

"What's up here? *Seize* that man!"

"It's some slave, kill him and have done."

"No, that's one of those the Satrap wants to question! Take him alive!"

Holding up his arms to shield his face, smarting from the slapping hands that could not hold him, Rolf emerged from the gauntlet—on the wrong side, he saw now. In his confusion he had turned back toward the keep. Aware now that some magic was protecting him from capture, he turned again.

The company of soldiers had turned into a mob, shouting, roaring, floundering into one another's way. Rolf slipped past and through them. Their fingers lashed him like so many branches, powerless to grab. The disgusted officer, even as he bellowed to his men to form a ring, stepped aside himself, as if absentmindedly letting Rolf run by.

A low wall loomed ahead, the side of a one-story shed. Rolf sprang atop a barrel sitting near the wall, and from there leaped again without pausing. The springy wood of the barrelhead seemed to add unnaturally to his momentum. Scarcely did his hands need to touch the eaves before his feet were on the gentle slope of the roof; he bounded on across it, not slowing for an instant. The Stone was tingling in his fingers. A present from Loford; he should have understood that at once.

Between him and the Castle's mighty outer wall was one last courtyard, and at this courtyard's farther end the postern gate—a narrow door, now closed, barred heavily, and guarded on the inside by a pair of sentries. These looked up in astonishment as Rolf came leaping lightly from the low roof, bounced to his feet and raced toward them. He was trusting utterly in the power of the magic that had been given him. As he ran he heard voices raised behind him crying, "Ho, guards! Stop that fugitive! Kill him if you must but stop him!"

One of the sentries began to draw his sword. Rolf came running on, holding the Stone before him in two hands, as if he charged the gate behind a battering-ram. Indeed, the effect seemed much the same. When Rolf was still five running strides inside the gate, the giant bar that held it shut went flying, spinning high into the air. In the same instant, with a booming sound, the door itself flung wide. The sentries cringed away and it took them an instant to recover. As Rolf's strides carried him through the gate the corner of his eye showed him a sword-stroke coming; he felt only the merest touch, below one shoulder blade, and then he was free, flying safe into the enveloping dark.

The descending slope outside the Castle walls soon gentled beneath Rolf's feet. The stars were coming out now, and he very quickly had his bearings. He was on the east side of the Castle. He would have to circle to his left, giving the walls a wide berth, to come to the north side of the pass and the Elephant-cave. Looking that way now, he saw fewer torches than he had seen earlier from the Castle window. Shouting, terrible and vague, drifted to him from that direction. Rolf began to trot, listening each moment for another sound—but the voice of Elephant had not been reawakened yet, for all that he could hear.

Almost at once he was forced to slow down again to a cautious walk. Guarded human voices were audible, not far ahead. As Rolf's eyes adjusted to the night, and the starry sky grew brighter with the clouds' dispersal, he could see human figures, vague and distant shadows, moving in the same general direction as he. He could not see whether they were friends or enemies. Probably the whole valley of the pass was crawling with moving troops belonging to both sides.

"Roolf!" This time the hooting cry was soft, quivering as if with delight, and very near, just above his head. "Well done, well flown, oh heavy egg!"

He looked up at the dark hovering shape.

"Strijeef?"

"Yes, yes, it is me. Hurry on, hurry! More to your right. Is Ekuman dead?"

"Not when I saw him last. The lightning missed him, though it did his friends no good. Where's Thomas? Strijeef, you must guide me to the Elephant."

"I have come to guide you there. Run, the way ahead is clear just now! Thomas is busy fighting. He asks if you can wake the Elephant and ride him into battle."

"Tell him yes, yes, yes, if I can get into the cave. And get the Elephant out. Is anyone in there now? Is there fighting?"

"Nooo. The fighting has been in front of the big doors; they are still closed. The Stone you carry will help you thrust them open from the inside. Ekuman would trust none of his people to enter the cave without him; so I have been able to fix a rope in the place you carved to hold one. When we get there I will let it down for you to climb."

Several times Strijeef had him detour around enemy troops, or wait for them to pass. In the intervals when it was safe to talk Rolf could move swiftly, while Strijeef told him much of what had happened; how Feathertip had been killed and himself wounded, helping Thomas, and Rolf therefore left to himself in the cave. How the Thunderstone had been found, and used to cover the Free Folk's passage across the desert today; and when they were hidden at the side of a mountain, how it had been returned, in a captured pouch, to the body of the reptile that had fallen with it, and that body uncovered again for Ekuman's scouts to find.

"And this Stone you dropped to me, Bird. What's this note tied to it? Do you know I was nearly killed trying to get it open to read it?"

"Whoo!" Strijeef thought that was funny. "The note just tells you what the Stone is; you found that out for yourself. Hoo! it was fun to watch the way you flew, over a roof and through a wall!"

By this time Rolf had crossed the road at the bottom of the pass, and now the northern slope was steepening under his feet. He passed a nearly-burned-out signal torch, still casting brightness on the sand in a little circle which included the dead hand of the soldier who had held it. Rolf would have stopped to grope around the dead man for weapons, but Strijeef chided him to hurry. "The enemy is still holding in front of the big doors. The fighting there has stopped right now and our men have pulled back a little. I'll guide you around them all."

They went on up the northern slope. Once more Rolf had to stop and wait, crouching in silence, listening to a file of the enemy go past him, moving west to east across the slope. When the last sound of them had died away, the hovering bird plucked at Rolf's shirt with a silent claw, and he arose and followed Strijeef on up the hill. Now he recognized the silhouette of the familiar towers of rock against the sky. Now around him in the darkness there rose the pitiful loud moaning of the wounded.

"How has the fighting gone?" Rolf dared to whisper, once when the bird's wing came near enough to brush his face.

"Not too bad, not too good. The Castle-men have no eyes to see for them in the dark, but still they have the greater numbers. Quiet, now."

Strijeef led Rolf by one of the eastern crevices into the complex of tumbled rocks. Rolf groped his way, climbing over boulders and squeezing between them. At last he felt the canyon's familiar sandy floor beneath his feet, and then the jagged rocks that he knew were right below the mouth of the high cave. Strijeef went rising silently ahead of him, and a moment later the climbing rope came hissing and uncoiling down the cliff to touch Rolf's face.

He gave the rope a hard precautionary tug, then went up swiftly. From the wound on his back there was a light tugging pain, too small to be worrisome. Once having gained the high cave—with Strijeef fluttering nervously just outside, still urging him on—he quickly pulled up the rope. Leaving the anchor-stick in the notch, he crawled through the blackness to the chimney and let the rope down again. On the descent into the lower cave there was no room for the bird to guide him, but he could easily feel his way. Soon he could lay first his hand and then his forehead against the cool solidity of Elephant's flank.

At that moment all exhaustion seemed to drop away; and only as his weariness left him did he realize how great it had become. Now it seemed that some of Elephant's age-old power came flowing into him, the strength of some fantastic metal army descending to his muscles and his hands. His hands, moving caressingly rather than groping over Elephant's cool side, quickly found the recessed steps and grips. Before he tugged open the circular door, he remembered to close his dark-adjusted eyes, and to warn Strijeef to do the same.

The expected shock of light from within came redly through his eyelids. He climbed inside and tugged the door tightly shut behind him, squinting to make sure the massive latch was caught. With an odd feeling of homecoming he made his way to the seat that he had occupied before, meanwhile gradually getting his eyes opened. The familiar whisper of air was moving around him. His hands at once began their half-remembered task of goading Elephant up out of his slumber.

Blinking sleepy panel-lights at Rolf, Elephant uttered his first groan. This wakening was not so shuddering and agonized as his last had been—Rolf supposed Elephant had not had time to sink age-deep in sleep again. The CHECKLIST symbols lighted reassuringly, and once more Rolf began the ritual of wiping out the colored dots. The vision-ring descended as before to make a circle around his head. Through it the cave grew visible around him, and Strijeef flying in the cave in anxious circles. The bird's eyes were open wide, black fathomless pupils dilated as Rolf had never before been able to see them; every feather of the bird's spread wings, and the bandage on one wing, were plain. Elephant's night-seeing was evidently as good as any bird's; if Rolf could once burst from the cave, he would need no guidance to find the enemy.

Dot by dot CHECKLIST vanished. This time the process went much faster than before. Elephant's unbreathing voice roared strong and sure. Strijeef said the sound of that voice had led the enemy to the cave. Well, let them hear it now. Let it shake the ground beneath their feet, all across the valley. Let it vibrate in the dungeons of the Castle, and quiver in the bones of those who stood commanding in the proud tower above!

Suddenly the green tracery of light showed on the two big levers, standing one on each side of Rolf's chair. He reached inside his shirt, to touch again the Stone of Freedom where he had it tucked away. And then he gripped the levers and gently pulled.

Elephant backed up, grumbling, turning at Rolf's direction to aim head-on at the doors that must be opened. Strijeef's flying circle in the air blurred with the speed of his excitement. Rolf shoved both levers hard forward.

His huge mount shouted out, as if in rage and charged like a raging beast. Rolf seemed to feel the Stone he carried twitch inside his shirt. Before Elephant had touched the big doors they were opening, jerking sideways like cloth curtains before the invisible influence of the Stone. Elephant's impatient shoulders caught them even as they parted, and Rolf heard the metal barrier give way, like paper tearing noisily.

The boulders that Ekuman's slaves had not yet

been able to remove slowed Elephant as he went
tilting out upon the open slope. But they could not
stop him; they slid or rolled or bounded, making
way.

Startlingly plain, the Castle was suddenly in front
of Rolf. And visible were both armies in the field,
spread across the valley of the pass in groping files
and squads and ambushes. All of them were still
now, waiting for the outcome of this moment, hearing the mighty unseen crashing and bursting out of
Elephant, knowing what it was but not what it might
mean. Elephant's buried voice had warned them all
a little distance from the doors, but still some, both
friend and foe, were near enough for Rolf to see their
wonderment and fear. All their faces, blind with
darkness, were turned straining toward him.

Rolf kept his two drive levers pushed well forward. Bellowing out his rage across the valley,
Elephant charged down the slope, rapidly picking
up speed. Rolf had selected his first target—a company of enemy cavalry. They were just starting to
walk their mounts upslope from the bottom of the
pass, coming too late to reinforce their mates in the
fighting near the cave.

Rolf steered to hit their file head-on. He jounced
and bounced with his mount's increasing speed but
kept his seat. Hearing Elephant's approach if still
unable to see it, the company mounted. But in
another moment their animals were uncontrollable, they panicked and fled before the earthshaker
hurtling at them through the night.

Those who galloped to one side or the other escaped Elephant, but those who fled straight back
could not run fast enough. Beasts and riders alike
went down under the wide, swift-racing treads. Rolf
looked back, but only once.

The cavalry company scattered or destroyed, Rolf
crossed the highway. Seeing no more enemies before him, he pulled back on his left-hand lever, guiding Elephant through a thundering, jolting turn that

brought him back onto the road. He followed the road westward, passing below the Castle. Now the enemy in the field seemed no more than scattered ants. As targets they were unworthy of his wrath, as long as the anthill itself was still standing, arrogant as ever.

He thought of turning Elephant straight uphill, charging at the Castle wall by the shortest route. But despite himself he was dissuaded by remembering the awesome thickness of those high, gray walls, the hugeness of the slabs of stone that formed their base. In his concentration of fury and joy, he scarcely noticed excited birds come sailing round him and depart again. No, he would take the Castle at its weakest point. He would ride the highway into the village, and turn onto the road that led up to the gate through which he had once been dragged behind an animal.

Let the teeth of that portcullis bite down upon him now!

Thomas stood halfway down the northern slope of the pass, straining his eyes to see through the night, and heard the mighty voice and tread of Elephant go past.

"Where's he going now?" Thomas demanded of a bird who hovered near. "Tell him to wait, till I can talk with him!" Tonight, naturally, the Silent People were Thomas's eyes and communications system. Thanks to them, he held in his mind a picture of the battlefield very nearly as complete as Rolf's view through the vision-ring. To Thomas, accustomed to thinking in tactical terms, it was obvious that Elephant's first charge had outflanked the enemy in the field, cutting them off from the Castle and completing their demoralization, begun by the night itself. The Elephant with its demonstrated night-vision, speed, and invulnerable strength, seemed quite capable of mopping up the enemy, completing their scattering, sending the survivors fleeing in exhaustion and panic into the river or the desert to be hunted down later by Thomas's own rested men. . . .

But Rolf was simply driving along the road.

Strijeef came dropping out of the sky, crying, "We cannot speak to him! Elephant seems to have no ears, though its eyes must be as good as mine!"

Thomas demanded, "Where's he going? It sounds like he's in the village now."

"He is." Strijeef rose higher, looked again, cried out, "He turns with the road! He's going up toward the Castle!"

After thinking for a moment, Thomas ordered, "Then you and the other birds gather all our people to me, here, as nearly as you can. If Rolf can't hear us—well, he who can't take orders must be the leader, if he fights."

Rolf was not yet expert at guiding Elephant through sharp turns; though he passed through the village at a moderate speed, a brush of Elephant's flank still tumbled one deserted-looking house. He saw no people tumbling with the house; the village seemed already depopulated. He was soon out of it, on the road that climbed upward to the Castle. The great gate at the road's end was open, a company of fleeing foot soldiers pouring into it; the last man was barely in before it was pushed shut. Now the bars as thick as tree trunks would be dropping into place to hold it fast. Let them work at making their defenses all secure. Yes, let them think that they were safe.

With the drive levers only half-forward, Elephant came up the ascending road at the pace of a trotting man. The Castle walls grew. Even now, Rolf felt a shadow of his old awe at their size. Now the defensive towers that flanked the great gate seemed to be leaning almost over his head, their height reaching the blind spot that the vision-ring left directly above.

Still, as he halted a little distance from the gate, he could see that there were men atop the towers. Arrows and slung rocks began to spray down over him. Elephant did not notice such things; Rolf could scarcely hear them. He urged Elephant forward, thinking to request admittance, and the men above began to pour some sort of liquid fire; Elephant minded it no more than rain.

There was no room on the small level space before the Castle to build up headlong speed. Still, at Elephant's first knocking, the iron teeth of the portcullis bent in like so many straws, and the great gate itself sagged in with timbers cracked and splintered. Elephant was stopped from pushing through not by the gate's strength but only by its narrowness; the broad bulk of Rolf's mount was caught and held by the towers on either side.

The burning liquid from above came pouring in an orange glow across Elephant's eyes, then dribbled harmlessly away, leaving Rolf's view as good as ever. Rolf pulled his levers back, backing Elephant up. He wondered briefly that the gate should be able to resist him, with the Prisoner's Stone still in his pocket. But it occurred to him that he was a prisoner no longer; he was trying to break in, not out. Delicately he worked his levers, turning Elephant slightly to the right, aiming him head-on at the tower on that side. He charged again.

The massive tower stopped Elephant, and sent Rolf sliding unsuspecting forward in his seat. His forehead struck against the inner surface of the vision-ring. He was half-stunned for a moment, then roused to a fury of frustrated anger. Growling and muttering, he hauled back the levers. Elephant, quite unhurt, responded; when they had backed up Rolf saw with satisfaction that several of the great stones in the tower's base had been shifted and loosened. The battered gate was now leaning more crookedly than before, and its timbers were beginning to burn from spatterings of liquid fire.

Again Rolf charged, hurling Elephant's brute power against the strength of the gigantic masonry.

This time he braced his legs as strongly as he could against the lower part of the panel before him, setting himself to meet the impact. More stones caved in, like teeth before a club. Working in a cold rage, Rolf again and again drew Elephant back, and again and again rammed him forward. Elephant did not tire or weaken. Parapet-stones began to tumble, from atop the shaken tower, and now fell jumbled with contorted men and bundles of unshot arrows and a spilling cauldron of the liquid fire. *Ekuman, where are you? Hide in a bigger tower than this, or burrow into your deepest dungeon, if you will. Ardneh has come to find you out!*

The impact of the next charge burst in the gate completely, sending burning timbers bounding and spinning with seeming slowness across the deserted yard. But still the towers stood, narrowing the gap enough to keep Elephant from passing through.

Elephant's last charge at the damaged tower did not come to a sudden stop. Instead it lurched on through a long satisfying yielding grinding thunder of collapse. Elephant's eyes were covered for a time—first by rebounding blocks of stone, and after that by a fog of dust so thick that no bird or machine might see through it. Covering his ears with hands and arms, Rolf bent over in his seat, hearing the tower come falling on his head.

His progress having ground at last to a halt, Elephant stood tilted somewhat on one side, his belly-voice droning on imperturbably. Rolf had just regained a firm seat in his chair, and was reaching for the drive levers, when he was surprised to feel a new current of air come swirling around him. The draft brought with it outside noises and the smell of rock-dust. He turned to look back at the door and saw with utter astonishment that it was open. A warrior stood there. His garments and his helm and shield were black and red; he held his sword out in a half-extended arm, so that the point was scarce a meter from Rolf's heart. The warrior's face was hidden in a barbut helm, black with a demon-mask outlined on it in red; Rolf had not a moment's doubt that this was Chup.

Even Chup, entering the Elephant for the first time, must pause for an instant in sheer awe and bewilderment. And in that instant Rolf slid from his chair on the side away from the sword.

The sword came flicking quickly after him. But the Stone of Freedom was still inside Rolf's pocket, and even now it opened a way out for him. A panel whose existence he had never guessed swung open in the floor beside him. A head-first dive into the dark space thus revealed took him into a cramped place surrounded by strange heavy machinery. Even as the panel closed itself over his head, the surface on which he was crouching parted, made way for him to exit. He wiggled out, straight through a solid slab of armor thicker than a man; the metal sealed itself perfectly again behind him.

He was sprawled on one of the stones of the fallen tower, lying half under Elephant's tilted body. Dust still hung thick and choking in the air. There was some light to see by, from wood amid the ruins caught ablaze by the spilled fire.

Here, Elephant's voice was deafeningly loud; but as Rolf slid out from under the tilted bulk he could hear shouts in the middle distance. He rose to a crouch, looking this way and that for some kind of weapon; Chup would be on him at any moment. At least there were no other soldiers in sight; Chup's degree of courage seemed unique among the defenders of the Castle.

No, here was one Castle-man who had stuck bravely to his post—or else had simply been too slow in taking flight. He was under some rocks, now. His protruding hand still clutched a sword; Rolf bent to take it and found that he must pry the spasmed fingers loose.

He had just got the weapon for himself when

Chup came into sight around Elephant's forequarters, stepping over wreckage. The warrior chief had evidently given up trying to follow Rolf's magical exit and had backed out of Elephant through the ordinary door. Rolf had no time now to puzzle over how Chup had opened that door in the first place.

"There you are, young one!" Chup's voice sounded almost jovial, but he moved carefully as he came toward Rolf. Even Chup was wary of one who had mastered the Elephant's power. "My infant gladiator—a precocious wizard also, it seems. Come now, you have fought well, you have fought like a giant, but you have lost. Give me the spell, the rein, the whip, whatever it is you use to bridle this monster to your will."

Rolf wasted no breath on words, only bent and picked up a rock with his left hand, meanwhile holding his borrowed sword ready in his right. Now some of the shouting voices were coming very close, sounding from just outside the ruined gap where the gate had been, the gap now half-blocked by the tilted Elephant.

Chup was staying between Elephant and Rolf. Rolf retreated a little deeper into the courtyard, to get his feet on flat ground rather than the rubble of the tower.

Chup was going to tolerate no stalling; he came at Rolf steadily and quickly. There would be no getting away; the light wound on Rolf's back reminded him that the Prisoner's Stone gave no protection against a blade. Rolf threw his rock as best he could left-handed, and lunged straight in behind it with his point. He saw the rock bounce from Chup's raised shield, and then Rolf's sword was knocked from his grip by a short parry of such violence that it numbed his hand. Chup came charging like a human Elephant, and down Rolf went. He knew his life was spared only because his secret must be learned; Chup's demon-masked figure towered over him, Chup's swordpoint rested at Rolf's beltline.

"Now give the secret of this Elephant to me! Or I will slowly—"

The screech of a battle-cry warned Chup, sent him spinning around only just in time as Mewick came leaping at him. Mewick was carrying no shield but matched the short sword in his right hand with a basket-hilted hatchet in his left.

Rolf managed to roll away. He saw Chup somehow weathering the first assault, giving a little ground, then standing and fighting back. Sword and shield, sword and hatchet, rang together in a blur of speed, separated briefly, clashed again on a higher level of violence.

Now there were more of the Free Folk coming in around Elephant's bulk, through the gap that had been the gateway. And bronze-helmeted soldiers from within the Castle were rallying to meet them. Amid the confusion Rolf crawled over the littered earth, trying to get back to Elephant, whose belly-voice droned on beneath the growing clamor of the fight. But he found bronze helmets always in his way. He couldn't fight his way through to Elephant without a weapon. Where was the sword Chup had knocked from his hand? It seemed that he could never manage to keep a sword.

Dodging and jumping to keep himself alive, Rolf worked his way around the fringe of the melee to a point from which he could see that Elephant's door still hung invitingly open. He tried to shout to some of the Free Folk to enter it, but the din of battle drowned his voice. And none of them had ever even seen Elephant before—small wonder if they did not rush to climb into the noisy cave of its inside.

Rolf at last managed to grab another weapon from another fallen soldier's hand. But then, as for fighting his way through, he had all that he could do to defend himself against the nearest of the soldier's mates. This opponent had nothing like Chup's power and skill, but he was still less of a novice with the sword than Rolf. Rolf found himself being forced farther from the breached wall and the Elephant.

His duel reached no clean conclusion; he and his opponent were swept apart by the confused, headlong retreat of the soldiers to an inner courtyard. Knocked to the ground again, Rolf played dead while the throng stampeded over him. He had a moment in which to wonder if all battles were as mad and stupidly desperate as this one. When the rush had stopped and he raised his head he found that his friends were in possession of the field around him.

All was not well, though. The last of the Free Folk to come pelting through the ruined gateway were not charging forward, but rather in retreat. Right on their heels there sounded trumpet calls, and a thunder of arriving hooves—cavalry, and in substantial force.

The first few of the riders entered the courtyard, but their mounts stumbled in the ruins of the tower, and shied from the Elephant and from the burning timbers that lay about. Thomas rallied his men to hold back the cavalry at the gate. The enemy dismounted, and with leveled lances held the breach from their side—held the Elephant too, though none of them would touch it. The hundred fighters who had rushed in with Thomas were now effectively trapped inside the Castle. Cheers echoed back and forth, between Ekuman's men at the gate and their mates atop the keep.

The thicket of lances defending Elephant looked impenetrable. "Toward the keep, then!" Thomas shouted, making a quick decision. Before Rolf could reach his side to argue, the Free Folk were charging deeper into the Castle, and Rolf could do nothing but join them. His sword remained unblooded, for the charge met little resistance until it had swept the warren of walls and sheds up to the forbidding mass of the keep itself. At that point the Free Folk met doors as strong as the outer gate had been, closed and barred against them. And missiles began to drop on them from above.

This courtyard held many carts and other objects under which men might shelter. Rolf had just scrambled under a cart, panting, when a big man with a sword in hand came crashing down beside him. Turning, Rolf recognized Thomas.

Laboring for breath like Rolf, Thomas demanded, "The Elephant's wrecked? Crippled?"

"No . . ."

"*No?* Then what demon possessed you that you left it?"

"The demon Chup. He got the door open—I don't know how—"

Thomas groaned. "Never mind how. But the enemy can use the Elephant, then? It'll obey them if they dare to try?"

"It might." Rolf started trying to explain the controls.

"All right, all right. Then we must just get you back into it. Take good care of your life until we do. What's that? The birds! There's a distraction for us, if we can use it!"

A mighty polyphonic shrieking had burst up from the high places of the Castle. The defensive system of nets and cords, probably weakened by the fall of the tower beside the gate, was now under heavy assault by birds, who seemed to be carrying some edged weapons for the work. Sections of severed net came sagging and dangling into the courtyards, brushing Thomas's men as he led them out in another charge against the outer gate.

There was too much fire there for the birds to be of help. And in the light of burning timbers the backs of the Free Folk were exposed to the missiles that now hailed more thickly from the roof of the keep. And the dismounted lancers' long weapons, pointed as thick as hedgethorns into the yard, still formed a wall proof against sword and mace and farmer's pitchfork. "Back! Back inside!" Thomas bawled out.

Once more they scrambled panting into the relative shelter of the inner court. Now Thomas cried out, "Find a timber! We must break in the door of the keep!" And at last the desperation was plain in his voice. This door would sturdily resist the biggest ram that men might lift; and the missiles would keep coming down from above; and, given time, Ekuman could summon more reinforcements.

Rolf felt the weight of the Prisoner's Stone, still inside his shirt. It was no help in breaking *in* a door . . .

There came a sudden flash of understanding. Rolf seized Thomas by the sleeve, at the same time holding up the Stone of Freedom. "It was this that opened the door for Chup, when I was in the Elephant! No doors will hold, that guard whoever holds this Stone!"

Thomas stared at him blankly for just a moment, then understood. He raised his arm and signaled urgently, calling down a bird.

XIII

The Morning Twilight

Scowling, intent on his labors, Elslood stood at a table flanked by torches, at the side of the lightning-blasted Presence Chamber opposite the empty throne. The floor around him was still strewn with stones from the riven window, with clots and patches of the durable fire-extinguishing foam, and other debris of the afternoon's disaster, a corpse or two included. But the bodies of Zarf and Zarf's familiar had been removed; a wizard's corpse was still a thing of power, liable to disrupt another man's magic.

Here in his own place, where his closet had once been covered by rich hangings and protected by a spider, Elslood had set up his worktable and reestablished a measure of order. Gesturing and reciting now over the diagrams and objects he had disposed upon the tabletop, Elslood foresaw that his labor was likely to be futile. The subtler arts were hard to use against an enemy in the field, when swords were out and blood a-spilling. Elementals were sometimes employable in such situations, of course — his industrious opponent Loford had quite a knack for raising them, though he was hardly Elslood's match in other ways. But no one could raise an elemental from the worked stones of the Castle, nor from the man-trampled patch of earth the Castle stood on.

On the table was a flat-sided crystal, which had been darkening steadily as Elslood worked. He could not bring the darkness to fruition, could not summon out of it the dread power that he wanted—but the crystal in its present state did act prosaically as a mirror. The mirror distracted Elslood with its reflection of a tableau set on the far side of the chamber, not far from Ekuman's empty throne. Soldiers were constantly coming and going through the room on various errands, but always one of them stood guard there, over the litter holding the prisoner who today had fallen in the arena. And always the dark-haired girl was there, keeping her gentler watch.

Elslood knew that even battle and invasion had not made Ekuman forget the warning of the day's intrigue. Ekuman never forgot. And when Ekuman had won the night's battle, as it seemed now that he would, he would take up the investigation as before.

Elslood had effectively silenced the sergeant by inflicting fits of madness. And the mysterious youth who had called himself Ardneh had escaped. The one on the litter, though, might still give testimony that would ultimately involve Elslood. Certainly the one on the litter should be silenced. But there was the soldier on guard, and the dark-haired harem-girl presenting a greater if unconscious obstacle. Her devotion radiated like a torch to keep the dark arts of madness at a distance. Still it should be possible to do *something*, to finish off one who was so gravely hurt. . . .

So it happened that Elslood, distracted from his duty to his Lord, was looking behind him through the crystal's mirror, and in one flat surface of it saw a winged shape enter at the blasted window. At first he thought it was a reptile; then he heard the sharp, loud hoot. He spun around, in time to see the great bird's taloned foot fling into the room an object that looked insanely like an egg. The thing skittered and bounded a short distance over the burned floor, straight to the girl beside the litter. She leaned across the litter and caught it; more, it seemed to keep it from hitting her beloved, than for any other reason.

The bird was already gone from the window. The girl, standing up like a frightened awkward doe, took a step backward with the unknown object clutched against her breast. She did not want the thing. Elslood saw in her face that she wanted only to get rid of it, to hide it, to get back again unnoticed to her job of nursing.

The soldier standing guard had yelled at the bird, which was gone again before he could do more. Now he grabbed at the girl. Though she made no attempt to flee, his hands only slid from her arms and clothing as he grabbed again and again, so he seemed to be attempting some sort of frantic caress. Frightened at running into magic, the soldier jumped back just as Elslood came stalking up.

He did not try to restrain the girl. She did not want to flee, not without her man. The birds had blundered, this time, trying to rescue the wrong prisoner. Towering over the terrified girl, Elslood did nothing but extend his open hand, palm up.

She gave the Stone to him. At that moment a great crash and a burst of wild yelling mounted up from somewhere at the base of the keep. The shock, first of suspicion and then of understanding, hit Elslood's mind, as the girl dropped back on her knees beside the litter. Elslood's skilled fingers swept hastily over the blurred and ancient carvings on the thing that she had given him: ". . . *neither by spell nor by chain, neither by moat nor by cliff, can the holder of this Stone be confined. Not lock nor key nor bar can bind him in. Now powerless be all doors and sentries, all watchers and all walls, that are set to guard him round about . . . .*"

Elslood stood for a moment staring blankly at nothing, then on his face there grew a twisted smile: *So, Loford. I was too contemptuous of you, and you have won after all.*

Out on the roof terrace Ekuman was bellowing in bewildered rage, and on the stairs below the clamor of a panicked retreat already mounted closer. There were not enough soldiers left in the keep to hold it, with the great doors they had relied upon suddenly burst open.

The thought of Charmian brought all of Elslood's energy back. Ignoring Ekuman's shouts, ignoring everything else, the tall gray wizard ran from the Presence Chamber to the stair. On legs as springy as a youth's he bounded down one flight, passing visiting Satraps who were reeling upward in retreat, grim-faced and bloody in their battle-harness.

Elslood left the stair on the level of the keep just below the roof-terrace. He raced down a corridor that was thick with the smell of dying flowers, and burst without ceremony into Charmian's exquisitely decorated rooms. From the corridor he had heard women already screaming within.

The uproar ceased abruptly on his entrance. The enemy was not here yet; it was only some hair-pulling fight. During the fighting all the Ladies of the visiting Satraps had been gathered here for safety, here amid the mocking gaiety of massed flowers, in the rooms that were to have been tonight a bridal suite. And some of the Ladies and Charmian had fought. She raised her head now in the midst of an ugly wrestling group of them, her own face as near to ugliness as ever it had been in Elslood's eyes. Her long hair had just been pulled into a painful disarray, her face was swollen with her tears and rage—none of these things did Elslood wholly see. For he saw that his Princess was, for whatever reason, overjoyed to see him.

"Change them!" she shrieked at him. "Blast these bitches with your spells, wither them into hags and crones—"

Elslood had no time to be subservient or soothing. He raised his voice, overriding hers even as his hands held out the Stone of Freedom to her.

"My Lady, take this! The ruler's doom, but the blessing of the fugitive. As you pass from power to wretchedness, its constant effect will change from harm to help. It is all that I can give you now."

Her face softened with fright at his tone. She took the Stone obediently. " 'Wretchedness'? Then we have lost?"

He had heard her voice sound just like that when she was ten years old. While the other women cowered away from him in terror, he took Charmian by the wrist and led her out of the suite. He knew where Ekuman's secret passage of escape began, and how that passage ran, dark and windowless beneath the other stair all through the Castle's wall, to emerge from under ground only when it was kilometers out in the eastern desert. And he knew of the secret cache at the tunnel's end, the water and food and weapons laid by for just such a time as this.

Ekuman was waiting for them on the first curve of the stair above the Presence Chamber, near the entrance to the secret way.

"So," the Satrap said, and not another word, at first. But the golden child-woman and the towering gray man both stood mute and quivering before him.

Charmian broke the silence. "Father?" she pleaded in her frightened child's voice. And when Ekuman, who was staring at Elslood, did not move his eyes or speak, she pulled her hand free of Elslood's grasp and darted forward, past her father, on up the stair and around its curve and out of sight.

"I thought it was you who had betrayed me," said Ekuman. His eyes locked Elslood's. His face was granite. "When the soldier fell in his strangling fit, I thought so. Yet I delayed, wanting to make sure." The Satrap shook his head in wonderment. "You may have destroyed me — for nothing. For an infatuation."

Elslood had long schooled himself, not to bear fear, but to avoid it. So it struck him now as a sudden overburdening weight would hit the muscles of a man grown slack and soft with long neglect of exercise. Looking now at Ekuman, he could see his own certain fate, and he felt the great fear rushing up like vomit from his middle to his head. It could not be that this thing was really going to be done to him, no, not now; there was always one more cranny of escape. . . .

In a defensive reflex Elslood began the casting of a spell of his own, but he could not finish it. Great as his powers were, they were helpless against those that Ekuman had been given, for this one purpose, by Som the Dead in the Black Mountains. Still Elslood could not comprehend that this was really happening. Unbelievingly he watched as the Satrap's hand made the gesture of power, he listened as Ekuman's voice uttered the one necessary word.

The Elslood's vision left him — for a while. He still remained conscious. It seemed to him that he could feel the water gushing from every pore of his body, the bulk that made him tall and strong rushing away in liquid and in steam to leave him infant-sized. His brain knew that it shrank, keeping in close proportion with his every other organ. More horrible yet, he knew even as it happened that his mind was shrinking with his brain. The intellect was aware, step by step, of its own maiming.

His senses were disorganized then, but they came quickly back to him, to his new-shaped body muffled under the heap of human clothes collapsed upon the floor. The thing that regained sense had forgotten what magic was, and even speech. But its memory still held, and knew that it would always hold, the knowledge that once it had been man.

Ekuman kicked at the creature and it flopped away from him in terror, struggling to master its new webbed feet. It croaked and bounded and hopped away, as if it would flee its very self. The Satrap wasted no more thought on it, for the sounds of violence on the stair below were drawing nearer.

He spun around and followed the way his daughter had taken, into the secret passage. He took care that the door was tight shut behind him. Charmian's footsteps had already gone ahead out of hearing in the darkness. Ekuman followed, needing no light. But he was scarcely thinking of Charmian. He was not heading for the desert, no, not yet. There was a chance yet of his saving all.

His mind was still fixed on the Elephant. He had been watching from atop the keep when the fearless Chup entered the Elephant and drove out the youth. Then he had watched it standing open, riderless, watched balanced between rage and satisfaction when he realized that none of his men who could reach it dared to enter.

Ekuman would dare anything now. His secret passage had another door, hard by the ruined gate where Elephant sat.

When someone's hands inside the keep took up the Prisoner's Stone, and its power burst in the great door of the keep, Rolf was one of the first of the Free Folk to enter. In the lower halls of the keep he used his sword—as inconclusively as before. But there were stronger fighters at Rolf's sides. The enemy was rapidly pushed back, cut down, being taken by surprise, being outnumbered now in the stronghold where they had thought themselves finally secure.

Rolf joined others then in pressing up the stairway, fighting now against the last desperate defense of the visiting Satraps and their bodyguards. Chup was not among them. Rolf had not seen Chup, nor Mewick either, since the two of them had begun their duel in the outer court.

When resistance had failed completely, Rolf, who knew the lay of the land better than anyone else, led the advance into the upper level of the keep. Sword in hand, he was the first of the Free Folk to enter the Presence Chamber, the room from which he had been taken under guard only a few hours earlier. His

knees quivered with his relief when he saw that
Sarah was alive and unhurt. She was still where
Rolf had seen her last, kneeling beside Nils's
stretcher—as if all the time between had found her
immune to danger and had flowed around her.

She raised her eyes joyfully at the entrance of the
Free Folk—but when she recognized Rolf under the
blood and grime that masked his face, her eyes
turned cold. Nils still breathed; he turned drained
but living eyes to his rescuers as they entered.

Thomas swept his glance around the chamber,
then faced Sarah. "Did you see which way our gracious Lord Ekuman retired?"

She could only shake her head, no. The Free Folk
spread out, searching. Some went out onto the
roof-terrace. Others poked among the hangings on
the wall and tested corpses with their blades.

Rolf chose to follow the stairs that went up to the
top-most level of the tower. Only a few steps up, a
bundle of clothing lay. He lifted the upper garment
with his sword. It was a long gray robe. It caught at
his memory, but for the moment he could not remember who. . . .

A small circlet woven of the sun fell from the robe
and dropped upon the stair just at his feet. It
flashed across his mind how cold and deadly
Sarah's eyes had been just now, looking at him. Her
hair was dark, not at all like this. It was Sarah that he
loved, so why should he bend swiftly and pick up
this yellow charm?

The circlet was soft and flawless and intricately
knotted, and he thought he could feel power in it.
But why should he quickly put it into the inner
pocket of his shirt?

Thomas came up beside him then, and together
they went on up the stair. When they saw the richness of the furnishings in the apartment at the top
they felt certain, it was Ekuman's. But the Satrap
was not there. In a small anteroom two harem girls

were cowering; they screamed in terror when Rolf
and Thomas came bursting in on them.

"Where is he?" Thomas demanded, but the girls
could only shake their heads in fear. Rolf noticed
that one of them had red hair, the other brown. It
seemed there had been only one girl in the Castle,
perhaps in all the land, with hair of the particular
golden—

Outside there burst up a roaring cheer, drawing
Rolf and Thomas to a window. On the roof-terrace
there were torches enough to show them how Ekuman's banner of black and bronze was being hauled
down, torn to ribbons, spat and stamped upon.

The sight was witnessed by others, the last of
Ekuman's troops to hold a portion of the field.
These were the lancers, still huddled together
around the Elephant. The fall of the tower, attested
by the tearing down of the flag, was enough for
them. They abandoned their wounded, and some of
them their weapons, and they turned and fled.

Here high in the tower the windows were broader
and shallower than those in the lower walls. Here
Thomas could lean out and strike his fist upon the
sill. "Fewer of 'em than we thought! We might have
got to the Elephant with one more push. Well, it's
ours now—"

The fire that had started with the breaching of the
gate was still spreading slowly among the sheds just
inside the outer Castle wall; so there was firelight
enough in the courtyard to let Rolf and Thomas see
the sudden lifting of a paving stone from below. A
man's head and shoulders rose out of the ground,
followed by the rest of a tall spare body. The man
turned his head this way and that, then sprinted for
the Elephant.

"It's Ekuman!" Even at this distance, Rolf knew he
could not be mistaken.

Thomas was shouting something incoherent.
Ekuman's figure seemed to grow tiny as it raced

beside the Elephant's bulk. The Satrap found the hand-grips, climbed, scrambled through the light-circle of the open doorway, reached back to pull the door's round slab closed behind him. He was only just in time — a farmer broke his pitchfork hurling it at the door, and another came running up quickly to beat on the door uselessly with an axe. But Ekuman was now established where no man might pluck him out; and Rolf knew how ready were the reins for the Satrap's hands, or anyone's, to take them up.

Rolf was running down the stair already, Thomas at his side demanding, "Will the Elephant obey him?"

"*I* learned very quickly how to give Elephant orders. And now it is already awake."

On impulse Rolf turned aside from the stair at the level of the Presence Chamber. He came to a halt in the middle of the huge, once-splendid room. Across the floor the path of the thunderbolt, was etched black, zig-zagging slightly through patches of persistent foam. . . .

With a bound Rolf was standing on the throne, reaching to take down from the wall the twin of the red cylinder that Ekuman had used in putting out the fire. It was not heavy.

Thomas was still right at his side. "Will that thing stop the Elephant? I doubt if the Thunderstone itself could do so."

"Nothing that I know can stop the Elephant." Rolf spoke with conviction. "It can batter down this keep, I think, if the driver's arms don't get too tired to work the levers back and forth. But I may be able to blind the Elephant for a little while. Maybe long enough for our people to get to some high mountain, or else back to the swamps."

Rolf had thrown down his sword. As he started down the stairs he was already slinging the red cylinder across his back by the leather strap that had been made to hold it on the wall.

Once sealed inside the Elephant, Ekuman could slow down, think, and be cautious. There must be dismay and uproar among the rebels outside who had seen him enter, but here there was no sound but the grumbling drone of the mysterious power under his feet, and his own heavy breathing. With steady hands he approached and then touched the strange lights around him, so bright and yet so cool. His nerves felt very good, now that there was nothing left for him to lose.

He soon noticed that someone had recently been sitting in the central chair, cracking and flattening the ancient cushions. He knew who had occupied this seat more powerful than a throne — he had been watching from the roof-terrace when Chup forced Rolf out of the Elephant. He had recognized the same youth, outwardly no more than a peasant, who had been involved in Charmian's petty intrigue — and who, during questioning, had suddenly risen from his knees and looked Ekuman fearlessly in the eye. "I am Ardneh," the boy had said, and then it was as if he had thrown the thunderbolt with his right hand.

But the Satrap Ekuman had survived the bolt, as he had so far survived all of Ardneh's blows. And now the throne of Elephant's power was Ekuman's. Whether Ardneh was only a symbol or something more, Ekuman meant to crush him yet.

He let his weight down, gingerly, into the chair where Rolf had sat. Nothing happened but the rising of a small cloud of dust, prosaic and somehow reassuring. Now he could perceive the vision-ring, and marveled at it.

And now, cautiously but steadily, he reached to touch the drive levers. They were the obvious places for a man sitting here to put his hands.

Rolf ran out through the open doorway of the deep, jumping over bodies and debris. He was just in time to see Elephant make its first slow tentative movements under the control of its new master. He dodged through the ravaged courtyard, trying to keep the red cylinder as much as possible behind him, so that Ekuman might not see it and know what Rolf intended. Whether Ekuman saw Rolf coming or not, Elephant gave a sudden grinding lurch and freed itself of the ruins of the tower, then with a mumbling roar went backing out of the breach it had created in the wall.

Elephant vanished from Rolf's sight, but the noise of Elephant receded only a little way; and when he had run up to the debris of the fallen tower he saw the huge vague armored shape standing motionless a little way ahead, as if waiting for him, on the road that curved down toward the village.

Rolf knew that the new driver could not yet have much sureness of control. He ran straight toward the Elephant, and Ekuman made it roar and lurch toward him. He waited until the mighty circling treads were almost upon him, until they were shaking the ground violently under his feet; then he sprang out of the way and turned and ran in at Elephant's flank.

Before the metal beast could pass him, Rolf's hands and feet had found the tiny inset steps and he was climbing toward its head. Ekuman made a sudden turn off the road and onto the rougher slope. The move came very near throwing Rolf off, but he clung on grimly, the red cylinder dragging on his back. He leaned his weight outward on the door handle when he reached it, but of course Ekuman had latched the door inside—and Ekuman had no Prisoner's Stone with him to betray him now.

When Ekuman reversed his turn, Rolf was able to shift his grip, and with a desperate upward lunge to seize one of the rods projecting from the front of Elephant's head. In another moment he was able to pull himself up onto that head. Sitting on the topmost hump, he contrived to grip the projecting rods with his legs, so that his arms were free to bring around the red cylinder from his back. He gripped the black snout of it and aimed it as he had seen the Satrap do, and the fingers of his right hand found the trigger. He played the jet from the nozzle over the tiny insect-eyes that were spaced around Elephant's head. The foam as it went splattering away was the color of nothingness in the dead light of pre-dawn morning.

The stuff would not cling to Elephant's eyes as Rolf had hoped it would. The metal and unbreakable glass were very smooth, and with Elephant's jouncing motion and the wind of his rush the foam fell quickly away. Still, Elephant's eyes were covered as long as Rolf kept playing the jet on them. Ekuman would not be able to see where he was going, let alone hunt down running targets; Rolf remembered, from his own time in the saddle, how dust, and falling stones, and liquid fire, had each momentarily blinded Elephant.

Ekuman, who could do nothing else till he had thrown Rolf off, kept Elephant stopping, starting, turning, going down the long slope toward the bottom of the pass. The red cylinder kept on spewing foam at a tremendous rate. Rolf swept the nozzle in a circle, trying to keep foam covering the eyes in the back of Elephant's head as well as those in the front. When he took a moment to lift his own eyes, he could see numbers of Free Folk scattering and streaming away from the Castle. He was giving them a chance to fight again someday—to fight against a Satrap who rode the Elephant, and the forces that such a man could rally to him.

But Rolf had no time now to lament the bitter future. Elephant's turning, twisting run down into the pass continued, with maneuvers that grew more violent as Ekuman gained a better feel of the controls. Several times Rolf was nearly thrown off, had to drop the nozzle of his foam-thrower and use both hands to save himself. But each time he recovered in a moment, and once more covered Ekuman's eyes.

Ekuman suddenly abandoned his weaving tactics, and turned for a straight run west. He must have had a few moments of clear vision, enough to give him some idea of directions, but still he chose a course that would soon bring him through the outskirts of the village and ultimately to the river. Was the Satrap grown so desperate to rid himself of Rolf that he would risk the miring of his heavy mount in mud and water? Why?

The red cylinder gushed on as if it could never empty itself. Now in the first forelightening of dawn the foam covering the great hump of Elephant's head was white, a white hood spreading and streaming continuously down to hide the eyes. And now Rolf noticed a curious thing; at one small spot, right at the back of Elephant's head, the foam instead of being blown away was rushing inward—as if Elephant's nose was there, and he continually inhaled. And Rolf then remembered the circulation of fresh air inside with the door shut tight.

He twisted around as well as he could on his difficult, bouncing perch, aiming his jet of foam to keep that gasping nostril covered, even if he must let the eyes in front begin to see again.

Rushing at full speed now down the western slope, Elephant raised its bellowing voice to its loudest roar. Though its eyes were now uncovered it still weaved like a blinded beast. Rolf was bounced back and forward and up and down, bruising his lean bones. He clung on, somehow, and kept his foam-nozzle aimed at the little orifice that sucked so greedily for air. When he looked back he saw that Elephant, like some sickened animal, was now leaving a continuous trail of dropping. A line of foam was dribbling like dung from somewhere under its belly.

The riverside village was just ahead. Trees rushed by. Rolf bent, clinging desperately to the rods on Elephant's head, as great branches whipped past just above him. Other trunks were flattened like grass before Elephant's charge. A low retaining wall was trampled under the treads.

The scrape of Elephant's rushing flanks dragged down the walls of houses. There seemed now to be no hand at all upon the reins.

Rolf saw then that the last steep plunge into the river was unavoidable, and that it was certain to throw him off. Just as Elephant tilted down the bank, he leaped clear. He jumped forward and to one side, as high and wide as he could, hoping for deep water where he came down. The red cylinder was still with him, held by its strap going around his body. His feet were just touching down on the calm surface of the Dolles as the great sheet of Elephant's oceanic splash began to rise behind him.

The sound of Elephant's plunge roared at him while he was underwater. The cylinder was now light enough to float and his treading water brought him easily to the surface. It seemed that the whole riverbed was still rocking, sloshing water like a hand-held basin, with the force of Elephant's dive.

Elephant, half submerged, had come to a struggling, straining halt. Its forequarters were evidently forced against some underwater rock, some firm fixed bone of earth. The endless driving treads still spun, like tail-swallowing snakes, flinging up gobs of mud and hurling ribbons of water, digging Elephant deeper into the bottom of the river.

Exhausted, Rolf struggled back toward the shore. In thigh-deep water he took a stand, and set to work again with his red cylinder. Until the cylinder at last ran empty, he kept the narrow gasping throat of Elephant filled with foam.

Not that breathing foam seemed to do metallic Elephant any harm. His voice was still as loud, its treads still spun as rapidly as ever. Rolf, though, was thinking of the inside of the cabin. In there, now, all the cool lights would be glowing still, glowing faintly through the solid insubstantial whiteness that was filling all the space there was, filling eye and ear and nose and lung. . . .

When the cylinder was emptied Rolf dropped it from his deadened arms and let it drift away. He had only just strength enough left to get himself ashore. Once ashore he lay in the mud, hardly able to lift his head at the sound of running feet. He knew his friends as they came in sight. Down the long trail of foam and through the shattered village they had followed him, though Elephant's mad descent had left them far behind. They were gathering around Rolf now in the morning twilight, lifting him up and crying out the triumph that he was too weak to shout.

It was about noon on that day when Elephant suddenly died — or once more fell asleep. At any rate the droning voice coughed once or twice and ceased, and with it ceased the endless mindless working of the treads. Instantly the gentle river healed over its torn surface, leaving only one ripple-scar bent around the motionless metal hulk. Those who were standing guard first backed away, then crept closer. But still the round door that they were watching never opened.

When Rolf woke up, near sunset, they told him about Elephant. Rolf was up in the Castle when he awoke. He vaguely remembered being helped back up the hill by men only just less weary than he was; he did not even remember lying down to sleep.

There was other news. The troops who had been coming to Ekuman's reinforcement from outposts scattered throughout the Broken Lands had turned and fled when they saw the Castle lost, and heard from their scouts that the Satrap himself was dead. All of Ekuman's high commanders were fled or fallen. More important, not one of the visiting Satraps had escaped; so with today's one blow, all the powers of the East here along the seaboard had been shaken. And here in the Broken Lands, farmers and villagers had seen victory in a sky that was for the first time in years empty of reptiles; and the people were hunting the remnants of Ekuman's army or driving them on into the eastern desert.

After enjoying a meal from what had been meant as Ekuman's festive table, Rolf mounted to the Castle's battlements to take a turn as lookout. The high roofs and walls had been cleaned of the last reptile's corpse, and the last bleaching bones of the reptiles' victims had been removed for burial. Now on all the roosts were birds, beginning to stir with the sunset; Rolf could pick out Strijeef, stretching his bandaged wing.

Rolf turned in all directions, looking out over the battlements. It seemed to him odd that the new air of freedom should be invisible over distant swamps and farms, villages and roads, the pass, the desert, the Oasis of the Two Stones.

The Thunderstone was safe, though the Prisoner's Stone had not yet been found. Nor had Charmian.

Looking from the roof-terrace into what had been the Presence Chamber, Rolf could see that Sarah was still there. There were many wounded now for her and the other women to tend; but still she spent as much time as she could beside one pallet. Nils still lived. And Mewick still lived, and even walked a bit, though he bore five or six wounds and had been drenched in his own blood.

And Chup survived—or half of him, at least. He lay on one of the pallets that had been set in rows in the Presence Chamber. Most of the time he kept his arms raised to cover his face. His legs and all below his waist were dead, unmovable, since Mewick's hatchet had at last come looping around his guard and bitten at his spine.

Sarah's eyes would not meet Rolf's. He turned away and looked down into the courtyards. Thomas, his broad shouldered figure tirelessly erect, was down there directing the building of a temporary barrier across the breach that Elephant had made in the outer Castle wall. If some surviving band of the enemy should think to take surprise revenge, they would not take the leader of the Free Folk unaware.

Though Thomas was ceaselessly giving orders, still he did not hesitate to stoop and lift a timber himself. A girl Rolf did not know, wearing a wide Oasis farmer's hat, was staying close to Thomas's side. And there was yellow-haired Manka, stewing food in a huge caldron—and there stood Loford, displaying a bright bandage around the upper girth of his right arm.

Rolf had a bandage too, over the wound on his back. A dozen smaller hurts all throbbed and nagged. But these discomforts were no burden now; other things, more lasting, had happened to him.

He still had no clue to what had happened to his sister Lisa; he no longer had a real hope that he would ever learn her fate.

His fingers kept straying to the inner pocket of his shirt, to touch the knot of golden hair concealed there. He would speak of the charm to Loford—yes, when he had a chance.

Alone on the battlements Rolf stood the day's last lookout, gazing levelly across the desert. The mountains of the East were black even now, with the rays of the setting sun thrown full upon them.

BOOK TWO

THE BLACK MOUNTAINS

I

Tall Broken Man

The great demon came to Chup in the middle of an autumn night of howling wind. It came in the midst of a torrent of air, whose vortices rose seemingly within a single gasp or howl of attaining life; it came with a blast that shook Chup's hovel of a shelter, pitched against the inside of the Castle wall. Lying sleepless with the nagging of his ever-painful wound, for many nights, Chup had heard time and again the screaming passage of things that from their sound were on the verge of becoming elementals of the air. So it was that he paid little heed to the demon's first shaking of his lean-to.

But soon the shaking grew more violent. A prolonged pounding against one end of his little shelter bounced its crooked boards against the wall of enormous stones. Raising his upper body on his elbows, Chup looked down the length of his paralyzed legs in the direction of the sound. And he saw, like smoke flowing through the crevices of his patchwork dwelling, the demon coming in.

Involuntarily he stiffened. The thing from the East would have been his ally, in his days of power; what business it might have with him now he did not know. And even a strong man, thinking demons were his allies—even such a man, when a demon came to him at midnight, and at hardly more than arm's length distance, might know himself strong indeed if he resisted the urge to run, or to cover his eyes and flatten himself on the ground.

As for being able to run, Mewick's battle-hatchet

had seen to that. And as for covering his eyes —well, he was still Chup. Raised on his elbows, he kept his gaze fixed steadily upon the smoky image coalescing in the close space before him. Outside the wind moaned softly, relieved of bearing that which had come in to Chup. Rain began to spatter on the lean-to.

Inside the hovel, space changed and distance grew as the face of the demon began to take its shape. Chup could scarcely make out on it anything like a human feature, and yet he knew it was a face. As it became a little more distinct there grew in Chup the fear that he might understand what he was looking at, that at last he might perceive the features rightly and that when he did they would be too horrible to see.

Nothing but demons could shake him like this. Now his eyes demanded, if not closing, at least to be allowed to slide out of focus. With a sigh he at last let them do so.

Only then, as if it had waited for that token yielding, did the demon speak. Its voice was a skeletal hand, searching furtively through dead leaves: "Lord Chup."

The power tapped by this pronouncing of his name made its image plainer in his sight. With a shudder he gave up trying to face down the thing, and let himself sprawl back on his rude bed, a forearm flung over his eyes. "I am Chup. But Lord no longer."

"But Lord again, mayhap." The dry leaves rustled, stirred by finger-bones. "Your unclaimed bride, the Lady Charmian, does send you greeting now through me."

"A greeting —from where?"

"From her place of power and safety in the Black Mountains."

Of course, the demon could be lying. It could have come merely to torment a cripple, like some nasty child on a romp; sometimes no meanness was too small for them to bother with. But no, on second thought. It would not have come so lightly to this castle now, filled as the place was with an army of wizards and warriors of the West; even demons had to heed some dangers. It was here, then, on important business.

Without lifting his arm from his eyes, Chup asked: "What does my Lady want of me now?"

The image of the demon's face began to form inexorably inside Chup's eyelids, under his forearm that could not keep it out. Moving what did not seem to be a mouth, it said: "She wishes to share with you, as with one worthy of her, her present power and glory and delight."

Now whether he opened his eyes or shut them, the demon's face, like some hideous afterimage, remained the same. "Power?" Suddenly shaking-angry, Chup raised his head and glared. "Power is mine, you say?" His enemies had not heard a groan or a complaint from him in half a year, but now the fullness of his bitterness burst out. "Then show me that I have just the power to move my legs — can you do that?"

Below the monstrous face the darkness worked. There appeared a pair of hands, roughly manlike but deformed and huge. They were visible in the light that sprang out when a cover was removed from an object held in one of them. It was a large, thick goblet or bowl, dark itself but holding a bursting warmth of multicolored light. That glow ate away the darkness, and seemed to half-obliterate the demon's image, and yet it did not dazzle when Chup looked directly at it.

The demon's free hand reached for Chup. He uttered an involuntary grunt, but did not feel the repulsive contact he expected. There was only an impersonal force that spun his body halfway round. Now he lay face down, with his dead feet still pointed at the demon. On his back, right in the old unhealthy wound where Mewick's hatchet had bitten at his spine, Chup now felt a cold touch as of icy water. A moment later there followed something, some kind of shock, that might have been pain of terrible intensity but was ended so quickly that even the timidest man could scarcely have cried out.

When that clean shock had passed, Chup realized that it had burned away the nagging gnawing that had lived in the wound almost since it was made. Before he could think beyond that point, the next change came, a dazzling tingling down the great nerves of both thighs. Automatically he tried to move his legs. Still they would not stir; it was long months since those wasted, shrunken muscles had contracted, save for painful and uncontrollable twitchings. But even now he felt those muscles try.

With his arms he turned himself again upon his back. The demon, withdrawn slightly, was recapping the vessel from which it seemed to have poured his healing. Warmth and light vanished. Chup again faced only a distorted presence, dim in darkness. The only sounds in the hovel were those of rain and autumn wind, and Chup's lonely, ragged breathing that now gradually grew steadier.

"Is this a true healing?" he asked at length. And then: "Why have you done it?"

"A true healing, sent to you by your bride, that you may come to her."

"Oh? Why, then, she is very gracious." Chup could feel the coursing life down to his toes; he tried them, but they were still too stiff to move. He did not dare accept this miracle as true; not yet. "She is full of unexpected kindness. Come, messenger, I am no child. This is some prank. Or—what does she need me for?"

With the speed of a blow, the demon-face came looming over him. He was Chup—but he was no more than human. He could not, with all his will, keep from turning his head away and lifting up an arm as if to ward a blow. His stomach, that had never troubled him before a fight, now knotted in spasm.

His eyes clenched uselessly upon the demon-image looking through their lids.

Unhurriedly, the voice of dry leaves scraped at him. "I am not to be mocked, lord though you were, and lord you are to be. Not to be called 'messenger' in insolence. Much less shall you scorn those who sent me here."

Those? Of course, Charmian herself was no magician, to have the ordering of demons. She would again have charmed a wizard or two into helping her, with whatever scheme she played at . . . The demon would not let him think. He was to be punished for his disrespect. He had the sensation that the demon was starting to peel away the outer layers of his mind, with no more effort or concern than a man toying with an insect. They could change men. If it kept on it would turn him into something far less than a cripple. Unless they really needed him—he cried out. He could not think. He was Chup, but he could not stand against an avalanche.

"You are not to be mocked," he whispered, through clenched teeth. "Nor are your masters to be scorned."

The effortless onslaught faded. When he was master of his eyes again, there was nothing to be seen but the bearable dim face.

The demon then began impersonally to tell him why he was needed. "Among the forces of the West now gathering in this castle, there is a peasant youth named Rolf, born here in the Broken Lands."

There could have been more than one fitting that description, but Chup had no doubt who was meant. "I know him. Short and dark. Tough and wiry."

"That is his appearance. With him he now carries, always and everywhere, a thing that must be taken from him. It must be brought to the Lady Charmian—and to no one else—in the Black Mountains, and soon. When the youth goes into battle, what we seek may be destroyed or lost. Here the power of the West is too strong for me or any other to take the thing by force; stealth must be used."

"What is it?"

"A small thing in size. A knot woven from a woman's yellow hair. A charm of the kind that men and women use when they seek from one another what some of them call love."

Yellow hair. Charmian's own? He waited for the demon to go on.

It rasped: "Tomorrow your legs will bear your weight, and soon they will be strong enough for battle. You are required to get this charm before the Western army marches—"

"They may move any day!"

"—and bring it to your Lady. Men in her service will be patrolling in the desert, a few kilometers to the east, watching for you. Beyond that you must expect no further help." The hugeness of the demon's face was growing less; Chup saw how far the space beneath his slanting roof had stretched, now it was coming back.

The dry voice too was fading. "I will not come to you here again. Except to punish you for failure." And then the face and voice were gone, the hovel it had occupied was ordinary. The wind outside went howling loud again. Chup lay without moving until it had become an ordinary sound, burdened with no more than the rain.

The rain and clouds delayed first entry of the morning's light into the long and crowded barrack-room. When Rolf woke all was still in darkness, round him the familiar jumble of packs, equipment, weapons, and bunks and hammocks with their load of snoring bodies.

He who had roused him, without touch or word, stood at the foot of Rolf's bunk, a tall and bulky figure in the gloom.

"Loford? What—" And then Rolf guessed what

had brought the wizard to him. "My sister? Is there something?"

"There may be. Come." Loford turned away. Rolf was into his clothes and had caught him up before Loford reached the door.

The wizard turned to a stair, and as they climbed the rising turns of stone toward the Castle roof, he explained in a low voice: "My brother has arrived. He is speaking much of technology and how we may be able to use it. Of course I mentioned your experience, and your handiness along that line, and he was interested. I told him also how I have tried with my poor spells to learn what happened to your sister. Beside my brother I am a backwoods dabbler. Certain powers that I never could have commanded, he has called up and set to work. Understand, the answer we get may be incomplete, or . . ."

"Or may not be one I want to hear." They were starting up the last steep stair, leading to the battlemented roof of what had been Ekuman's private tower. "Still I thank you. It will not be your fault if the news is bad."

Emerging on the roof, Rolf pulled his jacket tighter against the dying drift of rain, and through habit, without thinking, made sure that something in an inner pocket was safe. Mist hung like wet garments round the tower, and no sentry had been posted here in this hour before the dawn. Near one battlement a tripod supported a brazier in which glowed a green, unearthly-looking fire. Besides the fire a motionless figure in wizard's robes stood looking out away from the Castle, into the rainy night.

Loford raised one finger to his lips, gave Rolf a warning glance, then led him forward. The green fire flared up once, the waiting figure turned, tall and spare. Hood and shadow concealed the face of Loford's brother. His fingers moved as if he tested some invisible quality of the air. Arrayed on the paved roof around him, Rolf now saw, were some of

the things that good magicians used: the fruits and
flowers of autumn, what looked like water and milk
in little jars, small heaps of earth and sand, plain
wooden twigs, some bent, some straight. The green
unsteady light had changed them all, but they
looked innocent and simple still.

The hooded figure beckoned, with a turning of its
head, and Rolf went to stand beside it, still keeping
silence as he had been signed to do. Now, looking
out across the battlement into the east wind and its
drifting rain, he saw the clouds and tendrils of
lethargic mist speed faster past him. In a moment it
seemed to Rolf that he stood on the prow of a racing
ship of stone, driving into a gale. A vase holding
flowers was blown in from the parapet, to land at
Rolf's feet with a tiny smash.

Rolf put out his hands to grip the stone before
him. The man beside him raised a long arm, pointing nearly dead ahead. Just at that point the driving
mist flew faster still, became a gray smooth blur that
was not mist, and then tore soundlessly from top to
bottom. Rolf peered into the opening, leaned into it,
and then for him the wind and rain were gone. A
vision engulfed him while it seemed that he hung
bodiless in space.

A forest clearing, that he had never thought to see
again. A house of thatch and poles, simple and
small, the garden, the familiar path, fowl in a pen
beside the house. The vision was utterly silent, but
it held life and movement, sun and shadow shifting
with a breeze. Then in the shaded doorway a dim
figure moved, one hand with a gesture that Rolf had
seen ten thousand times wiping itself on his
mother's familiar ragged apron.

Rolf cried out then, as in a nightmare, knowing
and enduring the worst before it happened. And
someone, disembodied too or at least invisible, was
gripping his arms, speaking with Loford's kind
whisper in his ear: "It is all written! All unchange-

able! They cannot see or hear you. You can only watch, and learn.''

His mother had shaded her eyes, looking out; then she stiffened with alarm, hurried inside, and shut the useless door. Rolf did not know how he could keep watching. But he had no choice. He must learn Lisa's fate. And he must learn who *they* were, the ones who came. Soldiers of the East, of course. But Rolf wanted their faces and their names.

In the foreground of the vision now the first of them appeared, a mounted trooper wearing black and bronze, his back to Rolf. Behind him came another and another, the beginning of a line. There were six of them in all. Their mouths were wide, with soundless shouts or laughter, their weapons were held ready. And now the door was opening, Rolf's mother standing there again.

A time came presently when Rolf could no longer look. He shut his eyes and floated in a void, but could not flee the thought of what was happening. At length there came what must be Loford's hand, large and unseen, to clamp his chin and shake his head gently, trying to force him now to see.

The hut had already been contemptuously kicked to bits. The bodies of his mother and father were hidden in its small ruin, for the son to find when he came running home. Here was Lisa, twelve years old, long hair still neatly bound up in peasant style but her garments torn and smeared, her face as pale and blank as death, hoisted awkwardly up before a soldier's saddle. Wiping blades and straightening clothing, the marauders were almost ready to leave. He who carried Lisa must be their officer, for he alone wore half-armor, and he rode the tallest steed. Now as he turned his mount out of the yard toward the road, he showed Rolf his youthful, unlined, and harmless-looking face. There was a soft, proud, almost pouting look about the mouth.

If she were seriously injured, dying, they would

not have bothered carrying her off. " . . . alive?" So choked was his throat, Rolf had to try twice before he could speak intelligibly. "Is she alive now? Will I find her?"

Loford, at a little distance, murmured something, and Rolf understood that his question was being passed on. Then Loford brought back an answer, which he whispered to Rolf slowly, like one who did not understand the message he conveyed: "She lives. You must get help from the tall broken man."

"What? Who?" This time there was no reply. Rolf drifted, bodiless and alone. "Then what of those who took her?" he demanded. "There were six. How many of them still breathe?"

The vision changed. Rolf now beheld a portion of a simple, unpaved road, running through green, wooded land. Rolf recognized the spot as one near where his home had been.

A trooper in black and bronze came riding into Rolf's field of view. Gone were his cheeks and eyes and nose, and his jaws of weathered bone gaped wide, showing missing teeth. What might have been dried leather clung in fragments to his skull and to his skeleton's hands. Rolf understood that he was answered regarding this man's fate.

The second mounted trooper hove into view. He grinned, for he too was a skeleton, although it seemed he had good grounds for peevishness. Straight before him there extended the long handle of a farmer's pitchfork, long tines vanishing in his tunic's front, and coming out his back as fine, sharp points. Rolf had one third his answer now.

The third wore flesh upon his bones, and breathed, but only in a vision could anyone so wasted sit on a beast and ride. His scalp was marked by an old wound, his eyes rolled vacantly. The fourth man came, a handless skeleton: had he survived his maiming, and fled with other of Ekuman's people to the East, there to discover no one could be bothered feeding him? The fifth man rode past jauntily, a hatchet buried in his fleshless skull. The overthrow of Eastern power in the Broken Lands had taken heavy toll.

The tallest beast came last, with Lisa still carried unconscious before the saddle. She lived—but Rolf saw with a shock that she was changed. Her body looked the same, and her ragged garments and her dark-brown, bound up hair. But her face had been transformed, from its familiar homeliness to beauty that awoke an echo from Rolf's dreams and made him catch his breath. This was the girl whom he had called his sister, yet it was not. He called her name out, once, and then fell silent, marveling.

Her captor, too, was live and whole. His full-fleshed image with its proud, bored face watched indifferently the ghastly capering before him of his slaughtered men.

"Does he live, then?" Rolf demanded of the air.

He will be slain and he will live, he thought the answer came.

"Loford?" The vision was suddenly spinning before Rolf like a reflection in a whirlpool. He staggered, drew in a deep breath, and found himself firmly in his own body once more, standing on the solid Castle stone. Loford and Loford's brother were close beside him, and the light of day had come, to make the green fire ghostly dim. The last torn ribbons of the fog were swirling far above them now, borne by what seemed no more than a natural wind.

A wizard's or a statue's face, that of Loford's brother, lined but somehow ageless, loomed over Rolf. "Call me Gray," the statue said. "You will understand I cannot casually use my real name. How is it with you?"

"With me? How would it be? Did you not see?" Then Rolf felt Loford's grip upon his arm, and fought to calm himself. "I am sorry. I give you thanks, and ask your pardon, Gray."

"I grant it," Gray said solemnly.

Rolf turned from one of the wizards to the other.

"She lives, then. But where? Tell me, could he still have her with him? The one who took her?"

"I do not know," said Gray. "You heard the only guide that we were given to further information: 'get help from the tall broken man.' I expect that will prove decipherable to you. I am not sure what powers we reached today, but at least they were not definitely evil, and I would tend to trust them. Though they were strange . . . it seemed to me I spoke with one who held the lightning in his hands . . ."

A little later, Rolf stood on the tower alone save for the sentry who had come with day to scan the desert. While he was deep in thought, gazing out over the complex crowded courtyards of the castle, Rolf saw a familiar figure by the newly rebuilt main gate in the outer wall, dragging crippled legs out of a beggar's lean-to.

A broken man, who once was tall.

When it had become apparent that Chup was not going to die, he had been placed under close guard by the new masters of the land. Thomas and other leaders of the West had come many times to question him. Chup had told them nothing. They had not tried to force answers from him; new to revolution and to power, they probably were not sure what questions needed answers, nor what information Chup was likely to possess. Probably he could not have told them much of any use. He knew little of Som the Dead, of Zapranoth the Demon-Lord, and of the Beast-Lord Draffut, the powers of the Black Mountains, two hundred kilometers distant across the desert. They were the powers that the folk of the Broken Lands and the other newly freed satrapies must fear, and must eventually defeat if they were to retain their freedom. Unlike most others of his rank in the Eastern hierarchy, Chup had never formally pledged himself to the East, never passed through the dark and little-known ordeals and ceremonies. He had never visited the Black Mountains.

A few of the Free Folk, as the successful Western rebels in the Broken Lands did sometimes call themselves, had perhaps been willing to show some mercy to a fallen enemy, at least to one who had never been known to dabble in pointless cruelty himself. Perhaps for that reason Chup's life had been spared. Chup himself thought it more likely that after the physicians and the wizards had looked many times at the ill-healing wound on his back, had jabbed pins and burning sticks at his useless unfeeling withering legs, and had decided that no herb nor surgeon's knife nor wizard's spell could ever mend what Mewick's flashing hatchet-blade had severed, then the Free Folk of the West were quite content for him to live. Existence as a cripple among enemies might well be thought a punishment worse than death.

So they let him go, or rather one day they dragged him out of the cell in which he had been guarded. Explaining nothing to him, they simply dragged him out and walked away. When he was left alone, he used his hands to drag himself on. When he got as far as the great new gate where the road came in through the massive outer wall, he could see the empty distances the road ran to, and found no point in trying to crawl on.

When Chup had been sitting for half a day beside the gate, preparing himself to starve, there came one he had never seen before, an old man, to leave beside him a chipped cup with some water in it. Having set this down as if he were doing something shameful, and hardly looking at Chup, the old man walked quickly on.

Thinking it highly unlikely that anyone would trouble to poison him in his present state, Chup drank. Somewhat later, a passing wagoneer, perhaps a stranger, looked down from his high seat, perhaps saw only a beggar instead of a fallen enemy, and tossed Chup a half-gnawed bone.

Chup propped his torso erect against the castle wall and chewed. He had never been too finicky about his food when in the field. Turning his head to the right, he could squint across two hundred kilometers of desert to a horizon darkened by the Black Mountains. Even if he could somehow get there, the East that he had served had little use for the crippled and the failed. That was of course quite right and realistic, fitting with the way the world was made. Where else? A few kilometers to the west was the sea, to north and south, as here, his former enemies were in power.

The village just below the Castle was in ruins from the fighting, but people were already moving back and rebuilding. The road here promised to be a busy one. It seemed that if he must try to live on handouts he was not too likely to reach a better place than this.

By the night of that first day he had gathered scraps of wood and had begun to build his lean-to near the gate.

On the morning after the demon's visit, Chup had life back in his legs. Before emerging from his shelter he had tested them, gritting his teeth and laughing with the glorious pain of freely coursing blood and thawing muscles. Whatever the source of the healing magic, it was extremely powerful. He could bend each knee slightly, and move all his toes. His fingers told him that the wound upon his back had shriveled to a scar, as smoothly healed as any of his other battlemarks.

Now he must earn what the East had given him. He knew them too well to think for a moment that the demon's parting threat of punishment for failure had been an idle one.

Emerging at the usual hour from his shelter, he took care to give no slightest sign that anything of moment had occurred during the night. The light drizzle was fading as he dragged himself to his usual station at one side of the great gate, which had just been opened for the morning. As usual, he held in his lap his beggar's bowl, chipped pottery salvaged from a dump. His pride was too great to be destroyed by taking alms; it had been easier because he had never been forced to really beg. The weather had been good, and food plentiful throughout the summer. People came to look at him, a lord humbled, a villain punished, a terrible fighter beaten. People whom he never asked or thanked put in his bowl small coins or bits of food. There were no other beggars at the gate, and not many in the land. Western soldiers maimed in the fighting were still being cared for as heroes, and the others of the East, of less importance than Chup, had evidently been slain to the last man.

Sometimes people came to gloat, silently or loudly, at his downfall. He did not look at them or listen. They were no great bother. The world was like that. But he was not going to give them the satisfaction of dying, starving, or even showing discomfort, if he could help it.

Often it was the soldiers, even those who had fought against him, who gave him food and drink. When they spoke to him civilly he answered them in the same way. Daily he dragged himself to get water at their barracks well.

This morning, Chup had hardly taken his place beside the gate, when he saw the youth Rolf pacing across the outer courtyard toward him. Rolf stepped quickly but deliberately, frowning at the puddles, evidently on serious business. Yes, he was coming straight toward Chup. The two of them had not spoken since Chup was a Lord and the other a weaponless rebel. This visit today could not be coincidence; the demon must have somehow arranged it. Chup's chance was coming sooner than he had dared to hope.

Rolf wasted no time in preliminaries. "It may be you can tell me something that I want to know," he began. "About a matter that is not likely to mean anything to you, one way or the other. Of course I'll be willing to give you something, within reason, in return for information."

Not for the first time, Chup found himself somewhat taken with this youth, who came neither bullying the cripple nor trying to be sly. "My wants these days are few. I have food, and little need of anything else. What could you give me?"

"I expect you'll be able to think of something."

Chup almost smiled. "Suppose I did. What must I tell you in return?"

"I want to find my sister." Speaking rapidly, saying nothing of his sources of information, Rolf described briefly the time and circumstances of Lisa's vanishing, her appearance, and that of the proud-faced officer.

Chup scowled. The tale awoke real memories, a little hazy though they were. Better and better, he would not have to invent. "What makes you think that I can tell you anything?"

"I have good reason."

Grunting in a way that might mean anything or nothing, Chup stared past Rolf again as if he had forgotten him. He must not seem eager to do business.

The silence stretched until Rolf broke it impatiently. "Why should you not help me? I think you no longer have any great love for anyone in the East—" He broke off suddenly, like one aware of blundering. Then went on, in a slower voice. "Your bride is there, I know. I didn't—I didn't mean to say anything about her."

Here was a peculiar near-apology. Chup looked up. Rolf had lost the aspect of a determined, bitter man. He had become an awkward boy, speaking of a lady in the manner of one who cherished secret thoughts of her.

Rolf stumbled on. "I mean, she—the Lady Charmian—couldn't be harmed in any way by what you tell me of my sister or her kidnapper." One of Rolf's big hands rose, perhaps unconsciously, to touch his jacket, as if for reassurance that something carried in an inner pocket was safe. "I know you were her husband," he blurted awkwardly, and then ran out of words. He stared at Chup with what seemed a mixture of anxiety, hatred, and despair.

"I *am* her husband," Chup corrected drily.

Rolf came near blushing, or did blush; it was hard to tell, with his dark skin. "You are. Of course."

Though Chup preferred the sword, he could use cleverness. "I am so in name only, of course. You came breaking in the Castle gates before Charmian and I could do more than drink from the same winecup."

Rolf looked somewhat relieved, and utterly distracted now, despite himself, from whatever his original business with Chup had been. He sat down facing Chup. He wanted, needed, to ask Chup something more, but it took much hesitation before he could get it out.

"Was she really . . . I mean, there have always been bad things said about the Lady Charmian, things I can't believe . . ."

Chup had to conceal amusement, a problem he had not faced in quite a while. He managed, though. "You mean, was she as evil as they say?" Chup looked very sober. "You can't believe all that you hear, young one. Things were very dangerous for her in the Castle." Though not as dangerous as they were for others, living with her. "She had to pretend to be something different than what she truly was; and she learned to dissemble very well." Rolf was nodding, and seemed relieved; it amused Chup to have answered him with perfect truth.

"So I have thought," said Rolf. "She seemed so . . ."

"Beautiful."

"Yes. So she could not have been like her father and the others."

Of course, Chup thought, suddenly understanding the boy's monumentally innocent stupidity about the Lady Charmian. He was befuddled by the love-charm that he carried; the same that Chup would have to carry, later. However, time enough then to cross that bridge . . .

Rolf was saying, more calmly: "Nor were you, I think, as bad as Ekuman and the others. I know you were a satrap of the East, oppressing people. But you were not as vile as most of them."

"The most gracious compliment I have enjoyed in some time." Chup rubbed a flea-bitten shoulder against the cool, damp stone of the sunless wall. The moment seemed favorable for getting down to business. "So, you would like me to tell you where your sister may be found. I can't."

Much of Rolf's original businesslike manner returned. "But you know something?"

"Something that you'll want to hear."

"Which is?"

"And, since you are in earnest, I will tell you what I want in return."

"All right, let's hear that first."

Chup let his voice fall into a grim monotone. "If I can help it, I do not want to die like this, rotting by centimeters. Give me a rusty knifeblade, so I can at least feel like an armed man, and take me out into the desert and leave me there. The great birds are gone south on their migration, but some other creature will find me and oblige me with a finish fight. Or let thirst kill me, or a mirage-plant. But I am loath to beg myself to death before my enemies." It came out quite convincingly, he thought. Yesterday, there would have been more truth in it than fiction.

Rolf frowned. "Why must it be the desert, if you can't bear to live? Why not here?"

"No. Dying here would be a giving in, to you

who've made a beggar of me. Out there I'll have gotten away from you."

So long did Rolf sit silent, pondering, that Chup felt sure the bait was taken. However, the fish was not yet caught. Chup volunteered: "If you want to make sure of my finish, bring along a pair of swords. I think the chances would now be somewhat in your favor. I'll tell you what I can about your sister before we fight."

If Rolf was outraged by this challenge from a cripple, he did not show it. Once away from the subject of Charmian, he was adult again. Again he was silent for a time, watching Chup closely. Then he said: "I'll take you to the desert. If you lie to me about my sister, or try any other sort of foolishness, I won't leave you in the desert, dead or living. Instead I'll drag you back here, dead or living, to be displayed beside this gate."

Chup, keeping his face impassive, shifted his gaze into the distance. In a moment Rolf grunted, got to his feet, and strode away.

II

Duel

———◆———

In midafternoon Rolf came back, leading a load-beast. The look of the animal suggested it might be a reject from the Castle stable that could not be expected to give useful service in the coming campaign. Slung on it were several containers that might hold food and water. Rolf had also armed himself, but not with two swords. A serviceable sword and a long, keen knife hung from separate belts cinched round his waist.

The time since morning had tested Chup's patience to the limit. First, of course, because he was not sure his fish was wholly caught. Secondly, the urge to move his legs had become almost overwhelming. Under his ragged trousers their muscles were far looser, and even seemed thicker, than they had been yesterday. The ache and tingle of returning life had turned into an itch for movement.

Rolf said nothing but halted his feeble-looking animal just beside Chup. Then he came to catch Chup under the armpits, and with wiry strength heave his half-wasted frame erect. The gate sentries turned their heads to watch, as did some passersby. But no one seemed to care if Chup departed. He was a prisoner no more, only a beggar.

Once standing, Chup gripped the saddle with his strong hands and raised himself, while Rolf guided his dangling legs into the stirrups. Rolf asked: "Are you going to be able to hang on, there? I wouldn't want you to fall and split your head. Not just yet."

"I can manage." Chup had forgotten how high

riding raised a man. Rolf took the loadbeast by the bridle, and they were off, down the sloping switch-back road that led first to the village and then the world.

Rolf walked with long strides beside the load-beast's head: a position that let him keep the corner of one eye on Chup. Chup, for his part, breathed deeply with the joy of seeing the Castle gradually recede behind him, and the greater joy of surreptitiously testing his legs in the stirrups and feeling them respond.

Before they reached the village, Rolf turned off the road. He led the animal down a slope of wasteland to the beginning of the desert. The autumn day had cleared, and had grown almost hot. Ahead of them, gently rolling flatness shimmered with mirage. Sparsely marked with vegetation, it stretched on to the horizon, where towered the Black Mountains, jagged and enigmatic. Rolf had chosen the only di-rection which led quickly to solitude, and was head-ing straight east from the Castle.

Men in the service of the Lady Charmian were to be patrolling in the desert. That might or might not mean some help for Chup. He could not count on any.

Neither Chup nor Rolf spoke again until the Cas-tle had fallen nine or ten kilometers behind them. At this distance it plainly overlooked them still, from its perch on the low flank of a mountain pass. But the eastward of this point where they now were, the lay of the land was such that a man going east could take advantage of declivities and brush, and perhaps never see the Castle or be seen from it again.

Here Rolf stopped the beast, and, still warily hold-ing its bridle, turned to Chup. "Tell me what you know."

"And after that?"

Touching a water bag slung on the animal, Rolf said: "This I'll leave with you, and the knife. The beast goes back with me, of course. You won't be able to get anywhere, or to stay alive out here for very long, but that's what you asked for."

Chup was curious. "How do you plan to judge whether or not what I tell you is the truth?"

"You have no cause to seek revenge on me in particular." Rolf paused. "And I don't think you lie just for the sake of lying; do harm just for the sake of doing it. Also, I already know, on good authority, a few things more than what I've told you about what happened to my sister. Whatever you tell me should match with that."

Chup nodded several times. He had intended anyway to tell Rolf the truth; he could almost regret that Rolf would not live long enough to benefit.

"The name of the man you want is Tarlenot," Chup said. "He served as an escort commander and a courier between the Black Mountains and outlying satrapies. He may still; whether he still is alive I have no idea."

"What did he look like?"

"His face, as you described it. I've heard that women found him handsome, and I think he shared their view. He was young, strong, of middling height. An uncommonly good fighter, so I've heard."

"And when did you see him last?" Rolf might have had his questions on a written list.

"I can tell you that exactly enough." Chup turned his face to the north, remembering. "It was on the last night of my journey southward from my own satrapy, coming here to the Broken Lands to take my charming bride.

"I came on river barge down the Dolles, escorted by two hundred armed men. Tarlenot, with five or six, going northward, met us on the last day before we reached the Castle. He and his troop, being so few in unfriendly country, were glad to spend the night in our encampment."

"Who or what was he escorting then?" Rolf, listening eagerly, leaned forward. But he was not near enough, as yet, for Chup to lunge at him.

"He was escorting no one. Perhaps he carried messages. Anyway, he had with him one captive girl who might have been your sister. As nearly as I can recall, she must have been about twelve years old. Dark-haired, I think. Ugly. Whether she had any closer resemblance to yourself I can't remember."

"True, she was not pretty," Rolf said eagerly. He shook his head. "Nor was she my blood relative. What happened then?"

"I had other things to think about. I remember Tarlenot, if I am not mistaken, saying something about selling her, in the north. There was a tavernkeeper up there at a caravanserai—" Chup stopped, caught by a sudden thought. "Why, it comes back, now. On that night I dreamt, and it was most odd. I thought I wakened, while all the men in the encampment, even the sentries, lay sleeping all around me. Tarlenot rose up from his blankets, but I could see his eyes were closed and he was still asleep."

"What happened then?" Rolf was utterly intent, but none the less alert. And still no closer.

Chup thought he might better have kept quiet about the dream. It must sound like some devious lie or stalling tactic. But now he had begun it.

"I dreamt there came one from outside the firelight, taller than a man and dressed in full dark armor that hid his face and all his body. A great Lord, certainly, but whether of East or West I could not say. The earth seemed to sink down beneath his feet, as stretched cloth would yield to the weight of a walking man. He stood before the sleeping, standing Tarlenot, and stretched out his hand toward— yes, toward where the girl must have been lying.

"And the dark Lord said: 'What you have there is mine, and you will dispose of it as I wish.' Those were his words, or very like them. And Tarlenot bowed, like one accepting orders, though his eyes remained closed in sleep.

"Then all became confused, as in dreams it often does, you know? When I awoke it was morning. The sentries were alert, as they must have been all through the night. The girl was still asleep, and smiling. That recalled to me my dream, but then I forgot it again in the press of the day's business." The dream had been very vivid, and the way he had forgotten and then remembered it was odd. Quite likely it had some magical importance. But what?

Chup asked: "The girl was not blood relative, you say? Who was she?"

"I call her my sister; I thought of her that way." Seeing how intently Chup leaned forward, gripping the saddle, Rolf went on. "She was about six years old when she came to us, the year I was eleven. The armies of the East had not yet reached here, but they were in the country to the south, and people fleeing north sometimes passed along our road. We thought Lisa must have come from some such group passing through. My parents and I woke up one spring morning to find her standing naked in our farmyard, crying. She could remember nothing, not her name or how she'd got there. She could hardly talk. But she had been well fed and cared for up till then; my mother marveled that she had not a bruise or scratch."

"You took her in?" Chup would find out all he could from the young fool. Before he should come close enough . . .

"Of course. I told you, that was before the East had come upon us; we had food in plenty. We named her Lisa, for my true sister, that had died as a baby." Rolf scowled, running thin on patience. "Why are *you* questioning *me*? Tell me what happened to her."

Chup shook his head. "I told you, what happened to her finally I do not know. Except for this: when we

separated in the morning, Tarlenot spoke no more
of going north and selling his captive, but of going
east to the Black Mountains." Weary of talking,
Chup reached for the waterbag and got a drink.

After probing Chup with his gaze for a time, Rolf
nodded, "I think, if you were making up a lie, you
would make one that was more satisfying and believable." And yet Rolf hesitated. "Come, if this tale
just now was a lie, tell me. The water and the knife
will still be yours. And freedom, whatever it may be
worth to you out here."

"No lie. I've done my part of the bargain, told you
all I know." Chup gripped his left leg with his hands
and pulled it free of the stirrup, and then the right.
He made them dangle lifelessly. "Come, get me
down. Another moment or two, and this animal will
fall beneath my weight."

"Swing yourself off with your arms," said Rolf.
"I'll hold its head."

Chup, had he been honestly trying, might not
have been able to manage getting off without using
his legs. Whichever side he lurched toward, one of
his limp legs hooked over the saddle, while the
other dangled awkwardly in such a position that it
was likely to be broken under him if he just let go
and fell. Even a man seeking to be left alone in the
desert to die would not like to start his ordeal with a
broken ankle. The beast grew restive, while Rolf held
its head.

At last Rolf muttered impatiently: "I'll lift you
down." Still holding the bridle with one hand, he
stepped to the side of the animal opposite from
where Chup was clinging at the moment. He freed
Chup's leg so it would slide easily over the animal's
back. Then, bridle still in hand, he moved back
around the loadbeast's head.

He found Chup standing free.

Rolf's moment of surprise was time enough for
Chup to half-lunge, half-fall, upon his victim. Chup

learned in that first moment that his legs were still far from their full strength. They could do little more than hold him up.

But they had served him well enough for a moment, and that moment was enough. Rolf's hand had moved quickly, but still he had hesitated fractionally between drawing sword and dagger, and by the time his choice had settled on the shorter blade it was too late. Chup's hand was there to grip Rolf's wrist and argue for the weapon. Grappling as he fell, Chup dragged the other down upon the sand.

The youth had wiry strength, and two good legs. He writhed and kicked and struggled. But already Lord Chup had the grip he wanted, on Rolf's dagger arm. Rolf's tough arm muscles strained and quivered, fighting for his life; the Lord Chup's brutal power, methodical and patient, wore them down.

The captured arm began to bend. It was near the breaking point before its hand would open and give the dagger up. Chup caught the weapon up, reversed; he did not want to kill Rolf until he had made absolutely sure the charm was still with him. If it was not, Rolf would have to tell him where it was. He clubbed Rolf along the skull with the butt of the knife, and Rolf went limp.

Inside Rolf's jacket, in an inner pocket buttoned shut and holding nothing else, Chup found the charm. No sooner had his fingers touched it than he snatched them back. When he took it, would it work on him as it seemed to have on this young clod? Turn him misty-eyed and doting over the treacherous woman whom he had wed for nothing but political reasons?

Only briefly did he hesitate. If he would be a Lord once more, he had no choice but to take the charm into his possession and carry it to the East.

The loadbeast, decrepit and lethargic as it was, had run off a few strides and was still stirring restlessly. Chup called to it in a soothing voice. Then he muttered the three brief defensive spells that sometimes seemed to work for him—he was a poor magician—and drew the coil of hair out of Rolf's pocket.

It was an intricately woven circlet of startling gold, large enough to fit around a man's wrist. Chup had no immediate feeling of power in it, but obviously it was no mere trinket; it was not dull or crumpled, though an oaf had kept it in his pocket perhaps for half a year, and had probably given it much secret fondling.

Chup did not doubt for a moment that it was Charmian's hair. It brought her beauty sharply to his mind, and he stood up, swaying on his reborn legs, gazing at the charm. Aye, his unclaimed bride was beautiful. Whatever else was said of her, no one argued that. Charmian's was the beauty, made real, that lonely men imagined in their daydreams. He recalled now the ceremonies of their wedding. There had followed half a year of death, for him. But now he was a man again . . .

Eventually he took note of Rolf's stirrings at his feet, and tucked the charm into a pocket in his own rags, and bent to put an end to his victim. On Chup's still-unsteady legs it was a slow bending. Before he could complete it, one of his victim's feet was hooked behind his right ankle, and the other came pushing neatly at the front of Chup's right knee. The warrior-lord had no more chance of remaining upright than a chopped-through tree.

When he landed on his back he lay still briefly, raging at his own foolishness while he pretended to be stunned. Pretending did no good, for the peasant was not fool enough to jump on him. Instead, Rolf was crawling and scrambling away, dazed-looking, but also plainly full of life. Chup struggled erect, and tried to hurry in pursuit. But instead of lunging and pouncing he could only stumble on his traitorous legs and fall again.

Quickly he was up once more, holding his captured dagger. But Rolf too was now on his feet, sword drawn and pointed more or less steadily at Chup's midsection.

Something he had almost forgotten began to grow in Chup: his old happiness of combat. "At least," he observed, "you have learned how to hold a blade since last we fought."

Rolf was not minded to talk or even listen. His face showed how he, too, raged at himself for carelessness. He lunged forward, thrusting. To Chup, his own response seemed horribly slow and rusty; but still his hand had not forgotten what to do. It came up of itself, bringing the knife in an economical curve to meet the sword. The long steel sang, shooting two centimeters wide of Chup's ribs. Then quickly the sword slid back, to make a looping swing and cut. Chup saw it was coming downward toward his legs. They had no nimbleness to save themselves. He let himself drop forward, reaching down with his short blade to parry the stroke as best he could. He caught the sword blade in the angle between hilt and blade of his dagger, caught it and tried to pin it to the ground. But Rolf wrenched the sword away again. Rolf feinted twice before he struck again, but there was not much skill in his pretense, so Chup had time to get back on his feet, parrying the real cut even as he rose.

Chup saw as they circled that the loadbeast was moving steadily away. No help for that. His eyes were locked on Rolf's, and both of them were breathing harshly. So it went on for a little time, with nothing said. Rolf would advance and strike, or sometimes only feint. Chup parried, and faked attacking in his turn. With his short blade he could not very well attack a sword, held by a determined foe. If Chup had had his strong legs he could have tried and might have won—skipping back when the sword cut at him, driving forward then at the precisely proper instant for striking. Without perfectly dependable legs it would be suicide.

A first-rate swordsman in Rolf's place would have driven in on Chup, trying to stay just at the distance where the sword could strike but the dagger could not, pounding one stroke upon another until at last the shorter blade must miss a parry. Though Rolf was dangerous with a sword, he was far from masterly. Chup watched and judged him critically. Rolf was evidently determined he was not going to be tricked again into rushing to too close quarters with the Lord Chup. So he stood just a fraction of a meter too far away before he struck; and he failed to press his attacks. Against his efforts the knife in Chup's hand could, with a minimum of luck, stand like a wall of armor.

At last Rolf drew back a further step, and dropped his sword point slightly. Perhaps he hoped to provoke Chup into something rash.

But Chup only dropped his own arms to his sides and stood there resting, panting honestly. His legs were stronger than when the fight had started, as if exercise were an aid to the demon's magic. But in the joy of fighting, with health and strength and freedom come again, he had no great wish to kill.

He said: "Youngster, come with me to the East. Follow and serve me, and I will make you a warrior. Yes, and a leader of warriors. You may never be a great one with the sword, but you have the guts, and if you live long enough you may absorb a little knowledge."

The murderous determination frozen in the young face did not thaw for an instant. Instead, Rolf closed again, and struck, once, twice, three times, with greater violence than usual. The blades rang, rang, rang. Ah, Chup thought, it was too bad, a good man wasted as an enemy. Chup would have to kill him.

If he could. The desert this near the castle must be patrolled. Should a squad of Western cavalry appear, that would be all for the Lord Chup and his

ambition and his golden bride. And, too, the sun
was lowering. Suppose they kept on duelling here
until nightfall? To fight with blades in darkness was
more like rolling dice than matching skills.

Rolf circled round him now, struck less frequently, and appeared to be thinking more. It
seemed that he was searching for the proper way,
trying strategies in his mind. He might hit on the
right one. He would have the guts to try it if he
decided it was best. Chup therefore had better get
the initiative, and soon. How? He would dare Rolf,
anger him, play on young impatience.

"Come here to me, child, and I will impart a little
knowledge. Just a little spanking is all that I intend.
Come, no reason for you to be so much afraid."

Rolf was not even listening. He was looking eastward now, past Chup's shoulder, and there was a
change toward desperation in Rolf's face.

Chup carefully backed up a step, to insure against
surprise, and took a quick glance behind him. A thin
cloud of dust rose from the desert, a kilometer or
more away. Beneath the dust he glimpsed movement as of riders; and he thought that the riders
were garbed in black.

Rolf, too, thought that he saw black uniforms, and
plainly they were coming from the east.

Chup had lowered his blade again, at the same
time stretching himself up to his full height. His
beggar's rags were suddenly completely incongru-
ous. In a lofty and distant tone, he said: "Burrow
into the sand, young one."

Rolf's thought, like a cornered animal, jumped
wildly this way and that. It would be hopeless, in
this barren country, to try to run from mounted
men. The approaching riders now seemed to be
coming straight on, as if they had already spotted
Chup, at least. He stood quite tall and willing to be
seen.

"Don't be an idiot. Hide, I say."

Bending low, Rolf scrambled around the nearest

hummock, threw himself down there, and dug himself as rapidly and thoroughly as possible into the sand between two straggly bushes. Not much more than his head, emerging amid roots and wiry stems, was left unburied when he ceased his work and froze, hearing hoofbeats nearby.

Looking out over the top of the hummock, he could see the head and shoulders of Chup, who stood facing away from Rolf with chin held high. And in that moment Rolf felt a chill brush over him, a shadow unseen by eyes yet deeper far than any simple lack of light. Something enormous and invisible brushed by him, something that he thought was searching for him. It missed him, and was gone.

The many hoofbeats, their makers still unseen by Rolf, had halted. Dust came drifting above Chup. Now an unknown, deep, and weary voice called out: "And are you Chup? The former satrap?"

"I am the Lord Chup, man."

"Where is it? Were you able to—?"

Chup in his best commanding voice broke in: "And your name, officer?"

For a moment the only sound was the shifting of hooves. Then the deep tired voice said: "Captain Jarmer, if it makes any difference to you. Now quickly, tell me whether you—"

"Jarmer, you will provide me with a mount. That beast you see wandering away there will not support me longer."

Some of the mounts shifted their positions, and now Rolf could see the one he took to be the captain, scowling down at Chup. Mounted beside the captain was one in wizard's robes of iridescent black, with the hump of some small beast-familiar showing under the loose robes at the shoulder. The wizard juggled something like a crystal in his cupped hands. A facet of it winked at Rolf, with a sharp spear of the lowering sun; again he felt the sense of something searching passing by.

Chup in the meantime was continuing his debate

with Jarmer: "Yes, I have it, and it is not your job to ask for proofs of anything, but to escort me. Now the sooner you provide me with a mount, the sooner we will be where all of us want to go."

There was a murmuring of voices. Chup vanished from Rolf's view, to reappear a moment later, mounted. "Well, captain, are there any more problems I must solve before we can be off? A Western army lies within that fortress, and if they've eyes they've seen your dust by now."

But still the captain tarried, exchanging glances with his wizard. Then he spoke to Chup once more, in the tones of one who knew not whether to be angry or obsequious. "Had you no companion on your way out here from that castle? My wise man here says his crystal indicates —"

"No companion that I mean to tarry for. That ancient loadbeast, mirages, and a skulking predator or two." Unhurriedly, but ending all delay, Chup turned his new mount to the east and dug his heels in.

The captain shrugged, then motioned with his arm. The wizard put away his jiggling piece of light. The sound of hooves rose loudly for a moment, then rapidly declined, with the settling of the light dust they had raised.

Almost unbelieving, Rolf watched and listened to them go. When the last sound had faded he pulled himself out of the sand and looked. The riders' plume of dust was already distant in the east from which the night was soon to come. Turning back to face the castle, he saw that some sentinel had—too late—given the alarm. A heavy stream of beasts and men, a mounted reconnaissance-in-force, flowed from the main gate toward the desert.

Rolf stood there numbly waiting for them. He had been given back hope for his sister's life, but robbed of something whose importance he had not understood until it was taken from him . . . though in truth his feelings were more relief than loss, as if an aching tooth had been pulled. His hand returned again and again to the empty pocket. His head ached from the robber's blow.

Ask help of the tall broken man. Why had Gray's powers told him that?

III

Valkyrie

On the first night of the long flight into the east there had been only brief pauses to rest. During the following day their toiling across the enormous waste of land seemed to bring the Black Mountains no closer. Jarmer during daylight slowed down the pace somewhat, pausing for long rests with posted sentinels. Chup at each stop slept deeply, lying with his golden treasure beneath his body, where none could reach it without waking him. When he awoke he ate and drank voraciously, till those of the black-clad soldiers who had been ordered to share provisions with him grumbled—not too loudly. His legs grew stronger steadily. They were not yet what legs should be, to serve the Lord Chup properly, but he could stand and move on them without expecting to fall down.

The second morning of the journey, the sun was very high before it came in sight; the Black Mountains of the East were tall before them now, casting their mighty shadows many kilometers out upon the desert. Clouds draped their distant summits. Seen from this near, they were no longer black, nor particularly forbidding. What had given them the hue of midnight from a distance, Chup saw now to be the myriad evergreen trees that clothed the middle slopes like blue-green twisted moss.

The troop now traveled upon a long, slow rise of land by which the desert approached the cliffs. The chain of peaks ran far on either flank to north and south, and curved ambiguously from sight in both

directions, so Chup was hard put to guess how far
the range might stretch.

Straight ahead was one of the higher-looking
peaks, sheer cliffs rising to its waist. Now from
somewhere on the tableland above the cliffs it dis-
gorged a dozen or so flying reptiles. Down to inspect
the mounted troop they flew, on laboring slow
wings; the air here must be high and thin for them,
and the season of their hibernation was approaching.

Looking more closely at the cliffs as he rode
ahead, Chup saw that they were not after all a perfect barrier. To them and into them a road went
climbing, switchback after switchback. Toward that
road and half-hidden pass Jarmer was leading his
men. And indeed the frayed-out start—or ending—of that climbing road seemed to be appearing
now, beneath the riding-beasts' hurrying hooves.

Chup was observing all these matters with alert
eyes and mind, but with only half his thought. A
good part of his attention was focused inward, upon
a vision that had grown in his mind's eye through
the two long nights and single day upon the desert.

Charmian. The weight of the knot of his wife's
hair, swinging in his pocket as the wind and motion
of the ride swung his light and ragged garments,
seemed to strike like molten gold against his ribs. He
remembered everything about her, and there was
not a thing that made her less desirable. He was the
Lord Chup again, and she was his.

The gradually steepening slope slowed down the
tired riding-beasts. The road they traveled, empty of
all other traffic, veered abruptly away from the cliffs,
then toward them again, on the first winding of the
steep part of its ascent. The cliff tops must be a
kilometer above their heads.

Chup drank again from the borrowed waterskin
he had slung before his saddle. His thirst was marvelous; the water must be going, he thought, to fill
out his recovering legs. Their muscles still seemed

to be thickening by the hour, though the speed of recovery was not what it had been at first. He stood up in his stirrups now, and squeezed the barrel of the beast beneath him with his knees. The skin on his legs ached and itched, stretching to hold the new live flesh.

On the next switchback the road climbed past a slender, ancient watchtower, unmanned on this road where scouting reptiles perched and the defenders above held such advantage of position. In Chup's mind the slender tower was an evoking symbol of the slenderness of his bride. Again, with another turning of the road, the riders passed shabby, dull-eyed serfs at labor in a terraced hillside field. Among them were a few girls and women young enough to look young though they labored for the East; but Chup's eyes passed quickly over them, only searching for one who was not there, who could not be.

Oh, he knew what she was like. He remembered everything, not just the incredible beauty. But what she was like no longer seemed to matter.

It was a long and arduous climb, up through the narrow pass. As soon as they had reached the top, men dismounted wearily, and animals slumped to their knees to rest. They faced a nearly horizontal tableland, rugged and cracked by many crevices. Across this wound the road they had been following, and at its other side, two or three hundred meters distant, sprawled the low-walled citadel of Som the Dead. Several gates stood open in the outer rampart of gray stone. It did not look particularly formidable as a defense. There was no need for it to be; a few earthworks, now unmanned, stood right at the head of the pass where Chup and his escort had stopped. It needed no shrewd military eye, looking back and down from here, to see that a few men here could stop an army.

Beyond the citadel, the mountain went on up, to lose its head at last within a clinging scarf of cloud.

This mountain, unlike most of those surrounding, was but little forested. Above the citadel, the rock itself grew black. The more Chup looked up at that slope, the better he perceived how odd it was. On that dark, dead surface—was it perhaps metal, instead of rock?—there were a few tiny, even blacker spots, that might be windows or the entrances of caves. No paths or steps led to them. They might be reptile nests, but why so high above the citadel, already at an altitude where the leatherwings had hard work to fly?

Jarmer was standing beside him now, looking forward as if half-expecting some signal from the citadel. Chup turned to him and asked: "I suppose that Som the Dead dwells there above the fort, where all the signs of life are gone?"

Jarmer looked at him oddly for a moment, then laughed. "By the demons! No. Not Som, nor demons either. Quite the opposite. That's where the Beast-Lord Draffut dwells—you may meet him one day, if you're lucky." Then worry replaced amusement. "I hope you're what you claim to be, and what you bring is genuine. You seem quite ignorant . . ."

"Just bring me to my lady. Where is she?"

Shortly they were mounting up again. Jarmer turned away from the largest gate, and chose a path that followed close beneath the wall, round to the south flank of the citadel. There a small gate was open, just wide enough for the troop to enter in a single, weary file. They dismounted in a stableyard, giving their animals into the care of quick-moving, dull-eyed serfs.

Scarcely had Chup got his feet upon the ground when there came hurrying to him a man with the indefinable air of the wizard about him. He gave this impression more powerfully by far than the one who had accompanied the patrol, though the newcomer had no iridescent robes and no familiar on his shoulder. He was slight of build, with a totally bald head that kept tilting from side to side on his lean, corded neck, as if he wished to view from two angles everything he saw.

This man caught Chup's ragged sleeve, and in a rapid low voice demanded: "You have it with you?"

"That depends on what you mean. Where is the Lady Charmian?"

The man did something like a dance step in his impatience. "The charm, the charm!" he urged, with voice held low. "It's safe to speak. Trust me! I am working for her."

"Then you can take me to her. Lead on."

The man seemed torn between his annoyance and satisfaction at Chup's caution. "Follow me," he said at last, and turned and led the way.

A series of gates were opened for them, first by black-garbed soldiers, then by serfs. With each barrier they passed, the aspect of their surroundings grew milder. Now Chup followed the wizard along pleasant paths of flagstones and of gravel, across terraces and gardens bright with autumn flowers and fragrant with their scent. They passed a gardener, a bent-leg cripple with a face like death, pulling himself along the path upon a little cart, his implements before him.

The last barrier they came to was a tall thorny hedge. Chup followed the bald wizard through a gateless opening. They came upon a garden patio, built out from a low stone building, or from one wing of it; Chup could not see how far the house extended. Here was the grass thicker and better cared for than before, and the flowers, between a pair of elegant marble fountains, brighter and more numerous.

By now the sun come round the mountain's bulk. It made a flare of gold of Charmian's hair, as she rose from a divan to greet her husband. Her gown was gold, with small fine trimmings of dead black. Her grace of movement was in itself enough for him to know her by.

Her beauty filled his eyes and nearly blinded him. "My lady!" His voice was hoarse and dry. Then he remembered, and regretted, that he stood before her in the rags and filth of half a year of beggary.

"My husband!" she called out, in tones an echo of his own. Mingled with the tinkling of the fountains, it was her voice as he had dreamed of it, through all the lonely nights . . . but no, he had not dreamed of her. Why not? He frowned.

"My husband. Chup." The very sunlight was not brighter nor more joyful than her voice, and in her eyes he read what all men want to see. Her arms reached out, ignoring all his filth.

He had taken three steps toward her when his feet were pulled out from under him and a rough gravel path came up to strike him in the face. He heard a shriek of laughter and from the corner of his eye saw a dwarfish figure spring up and flee away from a concealing bush beside the path, trailing howls of glee.

The unthinking speed in his arms had slapped out his hands in time to break his fall and save his chin and nose. Gaping up now at his bride he saw her beauty gone—not taken away, or faded, but shattered in her face like some smashed image in a mirror. It was, as usual, rage that contorted her face so. How well he knew that look. And how could he have forgotten it?

She glared at him as he regained his feet. She screamed out her shrewish filth and hate—how often he had heard it, in the brief days he had known her before their marriage ceremony. He had not been the target, then, of course; she would not then have dared.

Now why was she screaming all this abuse at him? It neither hurt nor angered him. He had no intention of striking her or shouting back. She was his bride, infinitely beautiful and desirable, and he would have her and she must not be hurt. Yes, yes, all that was settled. It was simply that this side of her character was annoying.

She was screeching at him. "—Filth! Carrion! Did you ever doubt I would repay you triply for it?"

"For what?" he asked deliberately.

A vein of anger stood out in her lineless forehead. For a moment she could not speak. Then, in a choking voice, not unlike a reptile's caw: "*For striking me!*" A tiny drop of spittle came far enough to strike his cheek, the touch of it a warm and lovely blessing.

"I struck you?" Why, that was mad, ridiculous. How could she think—but wait. Wait. Ah, yes. He remembered.

He nodded. "You were hysterical when I did that," he said, absently trying to brush the dust from his rags. "I did it for your good, actually. I only slapped you with my open hand, not very hard. You were hysterical, much as you are now."

At that she cried out with new volume and alarm. She backed away toward a doorway that led into the building. From a gap between hedges there came running three men in servants' drab clothes. One of them was quite large. Together they ran to make a wide barrier between him and his lady.

"Take him away," she ordered the servants in a soft and venomous voice, regaining most of her composure. "We will amuse ourselves with him—later." She turned quickly to the bald wizard, who was still hovering near. "Hann. You have made sure he has it with him, have you not?"

Hann tilted his head. "I have not yet had that opportunity, my lady."

"I have it," Chup interrupted them. "*Your* lady, wizard? No, she's mine, and I have come to claim her." He stepped forward, and saw with some surprise that the three fools in his way stood fast. They saw only his dirt and rags, and perhaps they had seen him fall when he was tripped.

He scorned to draw his knife for such as these. He

heeled an ugly nose up with his left hand, and swung his fist into the stretched-up throat; one man down. He grabbed a reaching hand by its extended thumb, and broke bone with one wrenching snap. He had only one opponent left. This third and largest fellow had got behind Chup in the meantime, and got him in a clumsy grip. But now, with his fellows yelping and thrashing about in helplessness, the lout realized he was alone, and froze.

"I am the Lord Chup, knave; let go." He said it quietly, standing still, and he had the feeling that the man would have done so if he had not feared Charmian more than Chup. Instead the big slave cried out hoarsely, and tried to lift Chup and throw him. They swayed and staggered together for a moment before Chup could shift his hips aside and snap a fist behind him, low enough for best effect.

Now he was free to turn once more to claim his lady. She once more howled for help. The wizard Hann hauled out a short sword from under his cloak—evidently feeling his magic had turned unreliable with the onset of violence—and threw himself between Chup and his bride. But Hann was not the equal of the last swordsman Chup had faced, and Chup was stronger now than then. Hann dropped his good long blade and fell down screaming, when he felt the knife caress his arm.

This time, however, Charmian did not resume her noise-making, nor did she try to flee. Instead she stood with bright eyes smiling past Chup's shoulder. He heard a foot crunch gravel behind him on the path.

It was Tarlenot who stood there. He had already drawn his sword, at sight of the lawn littered with writhing, groaning men. His eyes lighted unpleasantly in recognition as Chup turned round to face him. Tarlenot was not a tall man, but powerful and long of arm. His short pink tunic showed bare legs as muscular as Chup's had been in his days of full strength. Around his thick neck was clasped a thin collar of some dark, plain metal, a strangely poor-looking thing for one to wear who was otherwise garbed luxuriously. Tarlenot's face was haughty now, more so than Chup remembered; the countenance of a pouty child grown big and muscular; his fair hair fell with a slight curl round his ears. He nodded his head lightly in recognition to Chup, and gave him a little smile. But he made no move to sheathe his sword.

"Tarlenot," said Charmian's ethereal and tender whisper. "Make this one a gardener for us."

Chup bent and picked up the sword dropped by the wizard Hann, who still sat moaning, bleeding lightly, on the flagstones. The sword seemed stout enough, though its twisted fancy hilt was not much to Chup's liking. It did feel better than it looked.

"That is no gardener's tool," Tarlenot observed. "And here we do not need another lord."

Charmian giggled quietly. "Tarlenot, his legs have grown too straight. Bend his knees for him. We will get him a little cart, and he will tend our flowers."

Chup sighed faintly and moved a step farther from his lady. It was hard, when the woman you were devoted to might stick a knife between your ribs. She was his bride, and the only woman he wanted, but there would be no trusting her.

"Tarlenot," he called, waiting while the other made up his mind. "One questioned me about you. Only a few days ago."

"Oh? In what connection?" The mind had been made up. "First, though, would you rather I only cut your tendons, or took your legs clean off? They say that useless limbs are worse than none at all. You should know, is it so?"

"He was one who meant to do things to you that you would not like." Chup stepped slowly and easily forward. "Now he will never have his chance." His legs were working very well, but he could have wished to give them their first real test in practice. He raised his blade as he advanced, and Tarlenot's

sword came up in a motion quite gentle and controlled, and with a careful metal touch the duel was
joined.

With the first preliminary touches and feints
Chup knew that he had met a formidable enemy,
and one cautious enough not to be deceived by
Chup's scarecrow appearance into taking the
scarecrow lightly. And when Chup had to make a
really quick hard parry for the first time, he realized
there was no great endurance left in his own body,
long underfed, but newly healed, and just finished
with a long ride.

Tarlenot was fresh and vigorous. Had it not been
for the residual effect of the healing elixir—fading
now, though the good work it had done remained—Chup might have been quickly beaten.
His muscles were left aching and quivering by two
or three exchanges at full power and speed.

They circled slowly on the gravel path and
flagstones, and felt for cautious footing amid the
flowers between the tinkling fountains. Chup as he
turned saw Charmian pass within his range of vision; he saw her with a gesture stay her other attendants, now running up, from any interference. He
saw how bright her eyes were, and the expectant
parting of her perfect lips. She would take the win-
ner, but only to use him and discard him when it
was to her advantage or merely suited her whim.
Chup knew that, if Tarlenot perhaps did not. But
she was Chup's . . .

And then in front of her face came Tarlenot's. "Let
me see," said Tarlenot, "if I can hit the old wound on
your spine, within a finger's breadth. How was it
done? Like this?" And he attacked.

Chup parried desperately, and riposted; his
weary arm thrust wide. "Not like that, no," he said.
"But with some skill." Demons and blood, but he
was tired.

And Tarlenot knew it. He was now carefully making sure that Chup's tremulous near-exhaustion

was no sham. Now that Tarlenot had measured Chup's reach and something of his style, he began to push the fight harder. Harder, till he himself began to puff.

Now Chup gave ground steadily as they circled. Sheer desperation kept him going, now. He might back into a corner . . . he saw before him the gardener on his cart, with lifeless eyes . . .

No, he was the Lord Chup, and he would win or die. And just then Tarlenot's sword came flicking in a little faster than before. Chup saw the danger but his weary, tardy arm could not make the parry quite in time, and he felt the hot bite of the wound along his side.

With that hurt there came before Chup all the blackness of the past half year, all of it seemingly alive before him in the person of his foe. The hurt was rage, the rage was fuel, the only hope and power he had left. He let his fury drive him forward, striking fast and hard, stroke after stroke—and then he staggered, halting. He feigned a final exhaustion before his ultimate reserve of energy was quite gone. Tarlenot, with triumph too early on his face, came thrusting in as Chup had thought he would. Chup parried that thrust and spent his final strength in one last blow, straight overhand, cleaving downward at the angle of his enemy's shoulder and neck.

The sword touched glancingly the blackish metal collar, and then bit down through garments, flesh, and bone. He saw Tarlenot's eyes bulge out, and the red fountain leaping from the wound. Clear down to the breastbone Chup's sword smote, and Tarlenot was driven to his knees, and then fell backward dead, his arms flung wide.

Chup found the strength to set his foot upon the ruined tunic that had once been silken pink, and wrench to get his swordblade free. He staggered back, then and got his back against a wall. He leaned there choking while the world grew gray and dim before him with the throbbing of his heart, as if it were his own blood puddling up the walk.

But he was not bleeding much. His searching fingers told him that the cut along his side had parted little more than skin.

Charmian . . . but she was gone. That was all right. Let her play any game she wanted, but he was going to have her now. As soon as he had rested for a bit. A sound made him turn. A small mob of lackeys were goggling timidly at him from a distance. The odd sound did not emanate from them. From where, then?

Straight up. A flying reptile had emerged from one of the windowlike openings that marked the mountain's dead black upper slope. It was winging down toward where Chup stood—but not on reptile's wings, he realized. Its rounded, headless body, dead and rigid, considerably bulkier than a man, hung beneath a speed-blur such as the wings of hummingbirds drew in the air. But this blur was a thin, horizontal disc, a spinning, not a vibration up and down. The noise it made, growing now into a whining roar, was like no sound of life that Chup had ever heard. The thing came rushing, almost falling, down toward the garden.

Chup pushed himself away from the wall. He had seen something of the magic that the Old World had called technology (though never a machine that flew), and knew the hopelessness of fighting with a sword against machines. He moved toward the doorway beside Charmian's empty divan; the flying thing looked too big to get in there. But before Chup reached the door, the wizard Hann was coming out to meet him, not as a foe but welcoming, with a flushed maidservant skipping beside him awkwardly, trying to finish tying a bandage on Hann's arm.

"The Lady Charmian sends you greetings . . ." Then Hann noticed the flying machine's approach, and Chup's attention to it. "No, no, Lord Chup, do not concern yourself; it is not a fighting device. Put up your sword. Come in! The Lady Charmian greets you, as I said, and expresses her apologies for all of this unfortunate . . . she will soon receive you. You have the golden charm with you, I trust? She begs you, let her maidens tend you now. When you are rested and refreshed . . ."

Chup was not really listening as he went on with Hann inside the door. Anyway the machine was not coming to Chup. Instead it descended close beside the corpse of Tarlenot. Just above the ground, the flyer hovered, while the shining whirl of speed on top roared down a blast of air that pressed down bushes, kicked up dust, and rippled grass. Along the headless metal body there stood symbols, meaningless to Chup:

VALKYRIE MARK V
718TH FIELD HOSPITAL BATTALION

In another moment the rounded metal body opened six secret holes, three on a side, and from them came extending hidden legs, sliding jointed things like insects' feelers grown monstrously large. These reached for Tarlenot and probed him, one delicate leg-tip clinging to the dull metal collar beside the great leaking leer of his wound. Then suddenly and effortlessly the flying thing gathered up Tarlenot's dead weight with its slender legs, drew it up and swallowed it into a coffin-sized cavity that gaped suddenly in the metal belly and as suddenly closed again. The six legs retracted and the Old World thing shot upward once again, roaring a louder noise and blasting the garden with a greater rush of air. It raced up toward the place whence it had come. Turned insect-sized again, it vanished into one of the windows where, according to Jarmer, the Beast-Lord Draffut dwelt.

Chup had stepped outside again, and remained

gaping upward until prompted by Hann's diploma-
tic voice. "When you have rested and refreshed
yourself, Lord Chup, and dressed in finer garments,
your lady waits to see you."

Lowering his eyes, Chup saw six serving girls approaching. All were young but ugly; his lady preferred her servants so, he knew, to heighten by contrast her own beauty. Carrying towels and garments
and what might be jars of ointment, the girls advanced very slowly, looking almost too frightened to
put one foot before another. Chup nodded. He
would have to relax his guard sometime. "I would
put down this sword that I have won, but I seem to
have no scabbard."

Hann hastened to amend this lack, unburdening
his own waist, wincing when he moved his
wounded arm. "Here, take all. Indeed I think I am
well rid of it. Let the shoemaker stick to his last."

When he had wiped and sheathed his sword,
Chup let the servants of Charmian lead him along a
short path into another garden, and from that into
another wing of the same low, sprawling building
that Charmian had entered. He could not yet see its
full extent; perhaps all of Som's court lived in its
separate apartments. In a luxurious room the servants stripped away Chup's filthy rags, and tended
the light cut along his side with what seemed ordinary ointments, not the demon's cure. The girls'
fear of him abated rapidly, and by the time they had
immersed him in hot water in a sunken marble tub,
they were talking almost freely back and forth
among themselves. After serving Charmian, he
thought, any other master must be a relaxation and
a pleasure.

He hung the love-charm of springy golden hair
upon the twisty hilt of his captured sword, and set
both close beside him as he soaked and washed and
soaked again. He was too weary to give the least
thought to his attendants as females. Amid their
nervous chatter, though, he caught their names:

Portia, with the blackest skin and hair that he had ever seen, and a bad scar on her face; Kath, blond and buxom, with eyes that looked in different ways; Lisa, shortest and youngest, nothing quite right about her looks; Lucia, shaped well enough except for her huge mouth and teeth; Samantha and Karen, looking like sisters or even twins, with sallow skins, pimples, and stringy hair bound up in the same peasant style as that of the other girls.

When Portia and Kath had finished scrubbing his back, Lisa and Lucia poured on rinse water, and Samantha and Karen held a towel.

When he had been clothed in rich garments, Karen and Lucia fed him soup and meat and wine. Between mouthfuls he touched the golden charm, safe now in an inner pocket of his tunic of soft black. He only tasted the wine, for already sleep hung like weighty armor on his eyelids. "Where is my Lady?" he demanded. "Is she coming here, or must I go to her?"

There was a moment's hesitation before Kath, with noticeable reluctance, answered: "If my Lord permits, I will go and see if she is ready to receive you." At this the other girls relaxed perceptibly.

His weariness was great, and he reclined on a soft couch. Though he had much to think about, his eyes kept closing of themselves. "Keep talking," he ordered the five girls. "You there, do you sing?" And Lisa sang, and Karen fetched out an instrument with strings. The music that they made was soft.

"You sing quite well and easily," Chup said, "for one who serves the Lady Charmian. How long have you been her servant?"

The girl paused in her song. "For half a year, my Lord, since I was brought to the Black Mountains."

"And what were you before?"

She hesitated. "I do not know. Forgive me, Lord, my head was hurt, my memory is gone."

"Sing on."

And then he was waking, with a start, the golden

harm clenched in his hand inside his pocket. It seemed that no long time had passed, for the sun still shone outside, and the young girls still made their soft music.

His tiredness was like the hands of enemies gripping all his limbs, but he could not rest until he had made sure of her, at the very least seen her once again. He arose and walked out of the building, into the garden under the upper mountain's looming bulk. On legs that pained but could not rest, he paced the paths and lawns, emptied now of men and cleaned of signs of violence. He entered the building where she had gone in. In a narrow passage he caught a whiff of perfume that woke old memories clamoring, and at a little distance heard Charmian's well-remembered laugh. He put aside a drapery.

Some distance inside a vast and elegantly female room, Charmian sat on an elaborate couch. She was facing Chup expectantly, though his coming had been soundless. The man who sat there with her, facing her, had fair hair that fell with a slight curl around his ears. His long, strong arms emerged from the short sleeves of a lounging suit of black and pink. As this man arose, turning toward Chup the wary, pouting eyes of Tarlenot, Chup could do nothing but stand frozen in the doorway, marking well the scar, wide and long but neatly healed, that ran down from the joining of neck and shoulder to vanish on the hairy chest—ran down from just below the metal collar that bore a little shiny spot left by a sword.

IV

Djinn of Technology

———————◆━◆◆━◆———————

The army of the West lay camped for the night, a day's march to the northeast of the Castle. Around them the plain was no longer a true desert, but a gentle sea of sparse grass, now drying and dying before the approaching winter. Once long ago the flocks of peacetime had grazed here.

Thomas now had with him more than four thousand soldiers, all holding in common a hard hatred of the East. The ranks of his own fighters of the Broken Lands had been greatly swollen by volunteers from Mewick's country and others in the south, from the offshore islands, and from the north, whence came warriors who wrapped themselves in unknown furs and made strange music from the horns of unknown beasts.

In the early evening the camp murmured with the feeding of the army and the digging of temporary defenses for the night, with the hundred matters of organization and repair that must be tended to before the second day's march. Inside Thomas's big tent were crowded the score of leaders he had called into a meeting.

The first matter that Thomas raised with them was the golden charm, and its sudden departure to the East. That the charm was magic of great power was obvious to all, and none blamed Rolf for having fallen so deeply under its influence that he had not spoken of it during the long months since he had found it, while it forced him to cherish secret thoughts of a woman he would otherwise have hated. Still he was downcast and somewhat ashamed as he sat at one side of the circle in the tent. Thomas, Gray, and a few others were at one end of the long test, their chairs around three sides of a plain table, the fourth side being open to the wide circle of onlookers who made themselves comfortable upon the matting of the floor. Thomas sat at the center of the table looking up at Gray who was on his feet and holding forth.

"Some of you know, but some do not," Gray was saying, "that I and other wizards of the West have for some years spent most of our time in a desperate search for the life of Zapranoth, the Demon-Lord in the Black Mountains."

There was a faint murmur round the tent. Rolf felt a little better, seeing how many of the others' faces mirrored his own ignorance of what the higher wizards did.

"It now seems possible," continued Gray, "that I stood next to the life of Zapranoth where I had scarcely thought to look for it: inside the walls of that strong Castle we left yesterday. It is possible—I think not likely—that the Demon-Lord's life was hidden in that twist of hair."

Eyes turned to Rolf, enough of them so that he felt he had to speak. "I had no thought or feeling of any demon near me, before or after the charm was taken from me."

Gray had paused to survey his audience. Now he said: "A number of you are still looking at me blankly, or frowning suspiciously at that young man. I am convinced that a short lecture on the ways of demons is in order." Having received a nod of agreement from Thomas, he went on. "The ordinary layman, soldier or not, has little hard knowledge of magic, though it almost daily influences his life. And to him the ways of demons are as unaccountable as those of earthquakes.

"I must make sure you understand me when I speak of our search for the life of Zapranoth. Now that we are on the march and can hope that spies have been left behind us, I can speak somewhat more freely. If you understand it may be that you can help, and if you help we may still succeed, and if we succeed in slaying the Demon-Lord of the Black Mountains it will count for more than would grinding the walls of Som's citadel to powder. Depend on that.

"Now. When I speak of finding a demon's life, I do not mean his active presence but his essence, secret and vulnerable—what the Old World seems to have called the soul. A demon's soul is separable in space from his personality. It is invisible, impalpable, and of vital importance, for only through it can he be destroyed. To keep his soul safe, he may hide it in any innocent thing: a flower, a tree, a human's hair, a rock, the foam of the sea, a spiderweb. He may keep it far away from him, where his enemies will not think to look for it, or near at hand where he will more easily know when it is threatened, and take steps in its defense. What is it?"

One of the fur-garbed Northmen got to his feet. "Is not Som the Dead the viceroy of the East, in the Black Mountains? And the Demon-Lord only his subordinate? Well, then. It would seem to me Zapranoth's life must be in Som's control."

Gray shook his head. "We think not. Those who rule the Empire of the East would not care to give any underling as much power as Som would have if Zapranoth were absolutely at his mercy. Therefore they have given Som only a lesser power of punishment over the Demon-Lord; so the two of them are constrained to eye each other jealously. It is a common pattern in the organization of the East."

Thomas and other senior leaders nodded. The man from the north sat down, and one from the south, from Mewick's country, asked: "If you wizards are baffled, trying to get at Zapranoth, how are we supposed to help?"

"How? First, understand the great importance of

our search. Then, if our campaigning takes you among strangers, friendly or neutral-seeming, say nothing of this matter, but listen carefully for any hint that there is information to be had. We will pay for it. We make no broadcast offers of reward, or half the fools and swindlers in the world would come to clog our path and waste our time, with spies and agents of the East among them. The chance that you will hear any clue is doubtless very small; but we must take every chance that we can get. Our search is desperate."

Gray took his seat, and Thomas rose. "Any more questions on our magic? Then let's go on to something else." He looked round as if gauging the temper of his hearers before continuing. "Though we are a real army now, it will be plain to all of you that our numbers are insufficient to storm any citadel as strong as Som's. You must know also that I have sent far afield, to every source of Western strength we are aware of, looking for help. You have been asking yourselves, and me, who may be sending troops to help us and where we are to meet them. The answer is: no troops are coming, or very few. We go on this campaign with no more men than we have now. Yet we are attacking the Black Mountains."

Thomas paused there, with every eye fixed on him intently. There was no murmur in the tent, but rather a deep hush; somewhere in the camp outside a blacksmith was shouting coarse imprecations at an animal.

He went on. "After, we make a feint to the north and perhaps a few skirmishes there with Som's outlying garrisons. In the Black Mountains is his power rooted, and only there can it be destroyed."

Someone urged: "Wait for the spring, then, for the birds' help! We cannot scale Som's cliffs against him. The birds could lift rope ladders for us, scout, bear messages, drop rocks upon the enemy, and use their talons, too!"

Thomas shook his head inflexibly and the murmur of approval that had started up died down. "We thought once that the Silent People might have stayed; we would have tried to warm them through the winter; but it is written in their bone-marrow, it seems, that they must fly south each autumn. There was nothing we or they could do about it. However, if the birds of the West will be absent from this campaign, at least the reptiles of the East will be sluggish and thick-blooded. And it is all very well to say, wait for spring, for the Silent People to fly north again. But so might Som be stronger then. And what of this human army we have gathered here and now? Shall we sit on our tails for another half year, hoping for improvement in our luck?"

That got something of the response Thomas must have hoped for. Folding his arms before him once again, he went on in a milder voice. "As for getting at Som in his citadel, we think that we have found a way. Gray?"

Once more the wizard arose, and spoke. As the plan he was proposing became clear, they cast looks at one another across the circle, with slowly lengthening faces. When the wizard paused, there were no questions. Probably, Rolf thought, because the only ones that came to mind were bluntly insulting about Gray's sincerity or sanity.

"As I said before, we are now on the march, away from prying eyes. Now the time has come to test what I propose, and if the test succeeds, to practice it. It will not be a usable technique till it is given considerable practice."

The stunned silence continued. Thomas dismissed the meeting, and while the others were filing out, called Rolf to one side where he stood with Gray. "Rolf. You have more experience with technology than anyone else we know of in our army. Gray will need an assistant in the project he just spoke of. I think you could do a good job of helping him."

Rolf grunted. "I don't know much, really."

"You have a knack." Thomas clapped both their shoulders, and said to Gray: "Take him, if you will, as your helper for the first experiment." Then Thomas turned quickly away, answering voices that were already calling him to see about some other business.

Gray and Rolf were left confronting each other in what was apparently a mutual lack of confidence. "Tell me, young one," the tall wizard said at last. "what do you know about the djinn?"

"Much like demons, are they not?"

Gray's gaze grew harder. "May you never be called upon to suffer in proportion to your ignorance of the world! Djinn are no more like demons than men are like the talking reptiles."

Continuing to talk Gray led Rolf from the tent. "Demons are, without exception, of the East. But the djinn are rather like elementals, neither good nor evil in themselves, and a human may call on them without being corrupted or consumed thereby."

"I see." Rolf nodded, not seeing much. "But what has this to do with technology, and the scheme you were proposing?" They were walking now through the uneven rows of tents, Gray heading for the outskirts of the camp.

"Just this. The djinn I plan to call upon for help is unique, so far as I know, among his kind. He is a technologist, a builder and designer, I think superior in those fields to any human who has lived since the Old World. Now help me with some preparations, if you will."

It seemed to Rolf that he had little choice. Besides, the djinn as Gray described him was certainly intriguing.

They had got past the tents now, to a place near the camp's edge, not far from the latrines. It was a clear, open area perhaps fifty meters across, badly illuminated by a couple of torches on poles stuck in the ground. Rolf had earlier heard casual speculation that the place was being kept reserved for some magical purpose. Near its center was tethered a sullen-looking loadbeast wearing panniers that were bulky but did not seem heavy. From these Rolf and the wizard gathered bags and parcels which Gray opened on the sand. From them in turn he took small objects which, Rolf again helping as directed, he set out on the ground in a regular and careful pattern. The things looked to Rolf for the most part like toys for some carpenter's child: there were miniature hammers, wooden wheels, a tiny saw, small brace and bit, and other little tools.

"Rolf, once you rode upon an Old World vehicle that moved across the land without a beast to pull it; you learned its secrets of control, and rode it into battle."

"That is so." Rolf had finished laying out his portion of the pattern.

"Had you ever any indication that it might fly?"

"No, Gray." His answer was emphatic. "It was of metal, and heavier than a big house, and it had no sign of wings."

Gray shrugged. "Well, certainly they had many machines that did not fly; but they had some that did. And some of them still do, I think, though that does not concern us at this moment. What I proposed in meeting just now was not as mad as some thought. Machines can fly, and I intend that we shall use them to assault the cliffs of the Black Mountains." Squinting at the arrangement of toy tools on the ground, Gray grunted with satisfaction, and began to draw with his staff (it occurred to Rolf that he had not noticed any staff in Gray's hands until just now) a diagram of straight lines surrounding the symbolic tools. "The djinn that I will summon up will build for us a vehicle which we will then operate ourselves. I think its pilotage will not be too difficult, for intelligent men who have a little nerve and imagination."

Gray stood his staff beside him on the ground;

there it remained, as if it had taken root. He rummaged in the beast's panniers again, and produced a paper that he unrolled and showed to Rolf.

"I have made this sketch from drawings left by the ancients of some of their simpler flying machines. Other types they made as well, that were heavier than air, and winged like birds, but the technology of those remains somewhat beyond my grasp; and what I cannot understand, I cannot order the djinn to build. However, the type that I have shown here should suit us well."

Rolf studied the sketch. It showed, apparently in midair, a rimmed platform or shallow basket, supported at each of its four corners by a cluster of lines, the lines in turn reaching tautly upward to four great globes above. A mast rose from the center of the platform; small sails bellied, and pennants fluttered, showing the direction of the breeze. Inside the basket, four men rode.

"These globes from which the flying craft depended were made of some elastic fabric" Gray explained. "Sometimes filling them with hot air was enough to make them rise."

Rolf considered silently. *Was* Gray mad? But wait—hot air did rush up the chimney.

"But with the djinn to labor for us, we shall do far better. Our globes will be made of thin metal, much stronger and safer, and in them there will be nothing."

"Nothing?" Rolf tried to make the question sound intelligent.

Gray studied him, and sighed. Perhaps he wondered if he should request a more intelligent aide. "Consider: Why does a ship, or any chunk of wood, float on the water?"

"Because—because it is lighter than water. Too light to sink."

"Ah. Very true." Gray smiled, and tapped the paper with his finger. "Now, when all the air has been exhausted from these metal spheres—experiments have already shown me that air indeed has weight—when the weight of this whole apparatus is thus made less than the weight of an equal volume of air, what will this flying craft do?"

"It will weigh less than air?" Yes, it all sounded mad; but Rolf despite himself felt some enthusiasm growing for this mad scheme. Wild as Gray's ideas were, they somehow began to feel right in Rolf's mind.

Gray spoke more rapidly, pleased that someone could halfway understand him. "Air is very light, true. But nothingness is lighter still. I tell you, the ancients made the idea work. Are you ready to try it with me, young technologist? I will need quick hands to help me and a quick mind, too, perhaps; Thomas tells me you have both, and I believe him. Of course you will help, you are ordered to. But are you really *with* me in this enterprise?"

Rolf took the time to give the question honest thought. "I am."

Gray nodded. With a flourish, then, he beckoned to his balancing staff—that sprang lightly through the air into his hand. "Be silent for a moment now, while I evoke the djinn. He is an odd creature, even of his kind, irascible and not well-meaning. But he must labor for us, though he cares nothing for East or West, or for any man or demon."

The calling-up was accomplished with quick confidence. After making a few controlled gestures over the array of toy tools and drawn lines, Gray uttered in a low rapid voice words that Rolf could not quite hear. Fire appeared in the air before the wizard, with a belching of soot and acrid smoke, and accompanied by a sound of rapid pounding, as by unseen, crude and heavy implements. The voice of the djinn rolled forth, sounding one moment like splintering wood, the next like clashing metal. "I come as bidden, master. What is your command?"

Gray unrolled his sketch and held it forth toward the flaming image of the djinn, meanwhile intoning:

"I first let be created four such great hollow spheres such as you see represented here—"

The djinn's voice hammered, interrupting. "You *let* be? That means you do not hinder?"

Asperity was in Gray's voice. "It means that I command! I order you to do it, and be quick! The specifications for the globes are as follows . . ."

The djinn did not dispute him further, but maintained its sooty glow in silence, evidently listening. A moment after Gray had finished detailing his order, there appeared from nowhere four crude blocks of metal, each half as big as a man. In another moment the blocks were glowing hot. At once there arose a mighty screeching, and a banging as of invisible hammers.

The few soldiers who had been standing in the middle distance, watching, were being joined momentarily by ever-growing numbers of their fellows, drawn by the prospect of seeing something spectacularly unusual in the way of magic. The camp had doubtless heard by now several versions of what had happened at the meeting in Thomas's tent. Rolf, for his part, backed up a few paces, and considered putting his fingers in his ears to dull the noise. The blocks of metal glowed incandescent and expanded under the powerful working of the djinn. They stretched out and up into enormous sheets of fiery metal, which then began to curve themselves, perfectly and surely, into spheres.

When the spheres, each the size of a small house, were almost completely closed, the djinn left them to cool on the sand. Meanwhile he received from Gray the specifications for the platform of the flying device, and for the ropes and sails and their attachments.

"So I let it be done!" Gray concluded.

The djinn began to work again, extruding from its smoke long coils of twine. And as it worked, it grumbled. "Just so you understand that it is I am gathering all the stuffs and doing all the work that you are letting. It does not come from nothingness, you know.''

''Nothingness,'' said Gray sharply, ''is what I want inside the spheres—when the craft is finished, we are aboard, and all's in readiness for flight. Then will I give you the order to empty them and seal them.''

The djinn emitted a burst of noise somewhat like the working of a broken sawmill. It took Rolf a little time to understand that this was laughter. ''Nothingness! You do not know what you are ordering—beg pardon, what you are letting, master.''

''Contrary dolt!'' A vein now stood upon Gray's forehead. Rolf made a prudent mental note that the wizard was not notably long on patience. Gray went on: ''By nothingness I mean a lack of air, a vacuum, nullity; such as you yourself will soon become if you irritate me too sorely!''

The djinn evidently did not regard the threat as idle, for the work did pick up speed, and for the time being at least there were no further grumblings. What seemed to be a multitude of invisible hands spun twine into stout ropes, and fastened ropes to the basket as it was fabricated. It was of a size to hold three or four people without crowding, with a waist-high rim all round, woven of tough, flexible withes, and seemingly very light. Each corner of the square basket was secured with several ropes to one of the great metal spheres. Their overshadowing bulks creaked as they cooled, and all but hid the basket from observation. At Gray's direction, a central mast was now stepped in, and sails and pennants made and stowed folded in the bottom of the basket. Water and provisions, from more commonplace sources, went in also.

Full night had come when Gray was satisfied that all was in readiness for flight. He himself was the first to step into the basket, with a somewhat cautious scissoring of his long legs. ''Now master Rolf, if you will.'' And Rolf, feeling almost evenly balanced between eagerness and reluctance, hopped nimbly aboard.

Thomas and several others had drawn near, to wish the voyagers well and to observe at close range whatever might happen next. When the last word of encouragement had been called in between the surrounding metal globes, Gray gestured for silence. Facing the smoky glow of the djinn's image, he swept his pointing hand to one after another of the four spheres as he cried out: "Now, let there be exhausted from them all the air and other vapors, and let them then be sealed shut!"

A quartet of hissing noises suddenly surrounded the basket, issuing from the four orifices left in the spheres. Rolf felt his hair stirred by one of the jets of air. Tensely he gripped the basket's railing, waiting for the first surge of flight.

And almost at once the four enormous globes did stir themselves. But not to rise. Instead, as their hissings began to be drowned out by ringings and portentous metal groans, they rolled from side to side on the sand, they lurched and crumpled and deformed themselves. The sphere in front of Rolf seemed to be struck by some giant and invisible mace; it sounded a deafening clang as it drew into itself a vast dent that bent its surface to its center. Then all four spheres, in a great blacksmith's uproar of tortured metal, were shrivelling and flattening like so many fruit-husks thrown into a fire. As their obscuring bulks shrank down, Rolf saw Thomas and others tumbling away with as little thought of dignity or face as they would have shown before an enemy ambush that caught them unarmed. Rolf had one leg over the basket rim again, and would have fled himself, but one direction looked as perilous as another. Meanwhile the basket stayed firmly seated on the sand, only swaying with Gray's vociferous anger. The wizard spouted words at a tremendous rate, while Rolf dodged this way and that to avoid his gesturing arms.

Silence returned as suddenly as it had fled. The metal spheres, now reduced to shrunken, twisted wads of scrap, were still. Gray's speech faltered and ran down, and for the moment silence was complete. There quickly ensued a murmur of laughter from part of the watching army, a murmur that dissolved before it could grow too large, when Gray swept his glare around him like a weapon. The dim masses of people beyond the torchlight began to scatter and drift off; a number of them, once they had got some distance away, seemed compelled to utter muted whooping noises.

Thomas and others, drawing near once more, spitting dust and brushing it from their clothes, did not seem much amused. But none of them dared yet say anything to Gray.

Gray drew in a big breath, and shouted one more outburst at the djinn. Its flaming, fuming scroll flared on apparently unperturbed.

"Oh great master," it answered in its clattering voice, "such a curse as you have just delivered would pain me like the grip of Zapranoth—if I were in fact such a disobedient traitor as you say I am. But, as things are, I feel no ill effects. I have followed your instructions to the letter."

"Ahhg! Technology!" Gray flung down his arms. He climbed out of the basket, in his excitement of disgust catching his foot on the rim and nearly falling. Lowering his voice, he said to those nearby: "It speaks the truth. Technology! How can any man who means to keep his sanity go far in such an art?"

Rolf, having got out of the basket too, was thinking. Hesitantly he asked: "Can I put questions to this djinn?"

"Why not?" Gray snapped, as if answering only with the easiest thing to say.

Rolf turned to address the fiery image. "You, there. What made the balls crumple up like that?"

There was a brief silence, as if the djinn were

assessing its new questioner. Then with a clatter the answer came: "Little master, they crumpled because the air was taken out of them."

"Why?"

"Why not? The outside air pushed in with all its weight, and there was only thin metal to resist it."

Gray had spoken of his experiments, showing that air had weight. The wizard looked uncomfortable, but with a sharp motion of his head he signed Rolf to go on with his questioning.

Rolf considered. It seemed to him that Gray's theory was basically correct: a machine made lighter than air should rise in air, as wood rose in water; and air most certainly had weight. But obviously there were traps and dangers awaiting the technologist.

Rolf asked Gray: "Must it speak the truth to us?"

"Yes." Gray sighed. "But not the whole truth; that's the catch. Go on, go on, ask it more. Perhaps you have a better head for this than I."

Rolf took thought, tried to put from his mind the fact that everyone present was watching and listening to him, and faced the djinn again. "Suppose you make the walls of the globes thicker and stronger. That should keep them from being crushed when you take out the air."

"You are right," said the djinn immediately. "Shall I rebuild them so?"

"And would they still be light enough, when emptied, to lift us and the basket with them?"

There was a short delay. "No." This time Rolf thought he detected disappointment.

He folded his arms, and took a few short paces to and fro. "Tell me, djinn, what did the folk of the Old World do when they wished to fly?"

"They made a flying machine, and rode in it. I myself was born with the New World, of course, and never saw them. But so I have been told, and so I truly believe."

"How did they make these flying machines?"

"Describe a way, and I will tell you if it is right or wrong."

Rolf looked at Gray, who shook his head and told him: "I cannot compel it to greater helpfulness. The djinn must give us what it knows of the truth, in answer to our questions, but if it wishes to be grudging it can yield only a small fragment at a time."

Rolf nodded, accepting the rules of the game, which he found more and more fascinating. "Djinn. Were these flying devices lighter than the air?"

"Some of them."

"Had they lifting spheres, as big as these were?"

"Sometimes."

"Yet their spheres were not crushed."

"That is true."

The audience was silent. The time of half a dozen breaths had passed before Rolf chose his next question. "Were their lifting spheres empty?"

"No." The monosyllable had a forced, reluctant sound.

"They were filled, then, with something lighter than the air?"

"They were."

It was midnight before Rolf had extracted from the djinn what seemed to be the last necessary bit of information, and Gray could issue new orders: " — that the new spheres be made of fabric such as you have described, airtight and capable of stretching; and that they be filled, by this lighter-than-air gas that will not burn, to the point where they will lift the basket with us in it."

Shortly before dawn, having managed a few hours' sleep in the meantime, Gray and Rolf were once more in the basket, attended by an audience much smaller and less hopeful-looking than that of the previous evening. Once more Gray gave orders to the djinn. The new balloons, that had replaced the crumpled metal spheres, rose from the sands as they inflated, then tugged boldly at their strong tethers, pulling them taut. The basket creaked and moved, and Rolf beheld the desert floor go dropping silently from beneath his feet.

The few who watched the launching cheered and waved. The camp was already astir with preparations for the day's march, and now a wider cheer went up to greet the swift-ascending flyer. Looking down upon an earth much darker than the lightening sky, Rolf saw his comrades' breakfast fires shrink steadily. The airborne flying machine was drifting slowly but steadily to the north. Gray was issuing sharp orders, planned beforehand, to the djinn, whose smoky image drifted without weight or apparent effort beside the basket. There came a hiss as flying gas was vented from the bags. Their giant shapes were spheres no longer but pressed together above the mast by their own bulging.

The hissing continued, as Gray had ordered, until their ascent had been stopped, or so the djinn informed them. Rolf could not say from one moment to the next that they were really on the same level, and he would have been hard put to judge exactly how high they were. The fires of the camp were now a scattering of sparks at some distance to the south, and the last people Rolf had seen there had been shrunken to the stature of small insects. Not that he was worried about their height. The tight grip he had taken on the rim of the basket when it lifted, was now loosening. Enjoyment was winning out steadily over fright.

Gray, too, seemed pleased. After exchanging with Rolf opinions that all was going well, he resumed giving orders to the djinn, for the attachment of rigging to the mast, and the readying of sails.

The wizard called out jovially: "Rolf, have you ever steered a sailing ship?"

"No. Though I have lived my whole life near enough to the sea."

"It matters not, I have experience. Once we get up a sail, I'll show you how to tack against the wind.

We'd best not fly by daylight, there may be reptiles scouting."

Things did not immediately go right with the rigging. Rolf was called upon to hold lines, tie knots, and pull. A sail soon rose upon the mast, but then hung in utter limpness. Gray, scowling again, hauled this way and that on lines and cloth, but the sail would not so much as flutter. He hoisted a pennant, but it too drooped like chain mail. Clenching his fists, Gray muttered: "Is this some countering magic? I sense none. Yet there was a breeze before we lifted from the ground."

"There is one yet," said Rolf, nodding to the ever-shrinking pattern of the camp's cookfires, dimming now with the approach of dawn. "Or what is carrying us northward?" But he could not feel a breath of moving air upon his face.

Gray took one look back at the camp, and called the djinn to question. "Why does the wind not belly out my sail?"

"Name a reason, and I will say if it be true." The clatter of the djinn's voice became something like a cackle.

Gray sputtered.

Rolf asked: "Djinn. Are we becalmed because our whole craft is already moving with the wind, like part of it? Instead of the wind pushing past us?"

"It is so."

Angrily Gray flared up. "There were sails drawn in the Old World pictures—" Then a thought struck him silent; after a moment he grumbled: "Of course, those drawings may have been sheer fancy; they did that sometimes. But they *did* have real airships. How then did they steer them? Rolf, question it some more. And I will think, meanwhile."

Rolf tried not to think of how fast they might be drifting, and how high. "Djinn, tell me. Did the ancients ever use sails?"

Clatter, cackle. "Not to fly."

"Did they use paddles to propel their airships?"

"Never."

"Rudders to steer them?"

There was a reluctant-seeming pause. "Yes."

"Yes?" Rolf pounced without a second thought. "Then fetch us such a rudder, here, at once!"

The air around them seemed to sigh, as with a giant's effort, or perhaps the satisfaction of a djinn. Then arrived the rudder, here and at once indeed; it was a wall of metal, curving, monstrous, overgrown, wedged between balloon and basket so that it bent the mast and stretched the ropes and all but crushed the occupants. Shaped roughly like a door for some great archway, the rudder was a good twelve meters long. Its longest, straightest edge, turned downward now, was nearly a meter thick; coming out of the flatness of this edge were festoons of cabling and the ends of metal pipes.

The balloon sank horrendously under the huge load. Gray, bent double under the slab whose main weight was fortunately carried by the basket's rim, cried out an order. In an instant the great mass was gone. The airship leaped up again, Gray stood, and Rolf recovered himself from the position into which he had been forced, almost entirely out of the basket.

There was silence for a little while, except for gasps and wheezings. When Gray spoke at last, his voice was icily detached. "In magic, hasty words are ill-advised. So I learned long ago."

"I will not utter any more of them. Believe me."

"Well. I have blundered too, this night. Let us learn from our mistakes and then forget them, if we can."

"Gray, may I ask the djinn a cautious question?"

"Ask him what you will. Our troubles seem to stem from giving him orders."

Turning to the unperturbed scroll of smoke, Rolf asked: "Did the Old Worlders ever use such a rudder as you brought to us to steer a flying craft like this one, lighter than the air and with no means of making headway through the air?'' He was imagining himself in a boat, drifting with a current; and he saw clearly in his mind that the rudder in the boat was useless, for there was no streaming of water around it.

''No.'' The monosyllabic answer seemed all innocence.

Gray asked: ''Did they ever steer craft like this at all?''

''No.''

The two humans exchanged a weary look. Gray said: ''I had better give orders for the gradual deflation of the bags, so that we drift no farther. It will take our men a while to reach us as it is.''

''I see no danger in that order,'' Rolf approved cautiously. As gas began to hiss from the bags again, he turned to the east, where now the sun lanced at him from above the distant range of black. There was one peak that seemed to tower above the rest, its head lost in a wreath of cloud that looked much higher still than the balloon.

Gray seemed to know where he was looking. ''There lies the citadel of Som the Dead. On those cliffs—can you see them?—that rise up halfway on the highest mount. There's where we must somehow land part of our army.''

And somewhere there, thought Rolf, my sister may be still alive. ''We will find a way,'' he said. With his hand he struck the basket rim. ''We will make this work.''

''Here comes the ground,'' said Gray.

The landing was a tumble, but it broke no bones.

V

Som's Hoard

———◆———

Chup stood frozen in the doorway, watching as the man whom he had killed stood up, fresh and healthy as when their duel had started. Tarlenot, starlted by Chup's entrance, turned and got up quickly. But when he saw Chup's paralysis of astonishment, he relaxed enough to offer him a slight bow and a mocking smile.

Charmian, who had looked up as if expecting Chup, said calmly: "Leave us now, good Tarlenot."

Tarlenot, with the air of one who had completed his visit anyway, bowed once more, this time to her. "I shall. As you know, I must soon give up this happy collar for a while, and take to the road again. Of course I mean to see you again before I set out —"

She waved him off. "If not, you shall when you return. Go now."

He frowned briefly at her, decided not to argue, and gave Chup one more look of amusement. Then Tarlenot withdrew, going out through a doorway at the long chamber's other end.

Charmian now turned herself completely toward Chup, and at the sight of him began to giggle. In a moment she was rolling over on her couch, quite gracefully, in her mirth. And she laughed with a loud clear peal, like some innocent teasing girl.

Chup moved unsteadily toward her. Still looking after Tarlenot, he said: "My blade went this far down in him. This far. I saw him die."

She still laughed merrily. "My hero, Chup! But

you are so astonished. It is worth all the vexation, just to see you so.''

For his part, Chup was very far from laughter. ''What powers of sorcery do you have here? What do battles mean, and warriors' lives, when dead men jump up grinning?''

Her mirth quieted. She began to eye Chup as if with sympathy. ''It was not sorcery, dear Chup, but his Guardsman's collar that saved him.''

''No collar stopped my blade, I cut down to his heart. I know death when I see it.''

''Dear fool! I did not mean that at all. Of course you cut him down. He died. You beat and killed him, as I knew you would. But then he was restored by the Lord Draffut.''

''There is no way of restoring . . . '' Chup's voice trailed off.

She nodded, following his thought. ''Yes my Lord. As it was done for you, by the fluid of the Lake of Life. Since you do not wear the collar of Som's Guard, I had to risk the Beast-Lord's great displeasure by having the fluid stolen for you—by one of the demons he so hates. But I would face greater risks than that, to have you with me.'' Her face and voice were innocent and proud. ''Come, sit beside me here. Have you the little trinket with you, that was woven of my hair?''

He walked to the soft couch, and sat down beside his unclaimed bride. From his pocket he brought out the golden charm, clenched in his hand.

''No, keep it for me, my good Lord, until I tell you how it must be used. Keep it and guard it well. With no one else will it be so safe.'' Charmian took his hand, but only to press his fingers tighter around the knot of yellow hair.

He put the thing back in his pocket. Still foremost in his thought was the resurrection he had witnessed. ''So, Tarlenot will be magically healed, whenever and however he is slain?''

''If he falls here, in sight of Som's citadel and with

his collar on. Did you not hear him say just now that
he will leave his Guardsman's collar here when he
goes out as a courier again? The valkyries will not fly
more than a kilometer or two from the citadel.''

"The what?"

"The valkyries, the flying machines of the Old
World, that take the fallen Guardsmen up to Draffut
to be healed. They get but little practice now."

"What is this Guard of Som's?"

"An elite corps of men he thinks reliable." She had
released his hand and was talking in a businesslike
way. "They number about five hundred; there are no
more collars than that."

He observed: "You have not yet managed to get
one of these protective collars for yourself."

"I will depend upon my strong Lord Chup for
protection; we will see that you have a collar, of
course, as soon as possible."

"You have been depending on the strong Lord
Tarlenot till now, I gather. Well, I will wait and catch
him with his collar off."

Charmian laughed again, this time even more de-
lightedly, and curled up amid her silks. "That messenger? Why, you are joking, lord. You must know I
am only using him, and to make him really useful I
must lead him on. My only true thoughts are for
you."

Grimly and thoughtfully, he said: "I remember
that you do not have true thoughts."

Now she was hurt. Her eyes looked this way and
that, then sought him piteously and fluttered. One
who did not know her as he did might easily have
been convinced. He knew her, and was not fooled;
but she was still his bride, and all-important to him.
He frowned, wondering why he did not wonder.
There must be a reason, and he ought to have remembered it, but somehow it eluded him.

"My every thought has been for you," his all-
important bride was pouting. "True, when you arrived today I pretended to be angry—surely you

could not have been deceived by that? I wanted Tarlenot to fight you, so you would put him in his place. You must have understood that! Could *he* ever have beaten you, even on the sickest day you've ever had?''

''Why, yes, he could, and handily.''

She avoided his reaching hand and jumped to her feet. ''How can you dare to think that I have ever meant you harm? If you will be rude enough to ask for proof of my intentions, I can only point out that here you are, restored to life and health and power. And who is responsible for your restoration, if not I?''

''Very well, you saved me. But for your own reasons. You wanted this.'' Again he pulled the charm out of his pocket. Looking down at the soft, shiny thing resting so lightly in his open hand, he could remember vaguely that he had felt misgivings about picking it up for the first time, but he could not remember why. He asked: ''What do you want it for?''

''Put it away, please.'' When he had done that, Charmian sat down again and took his hand between hers. ''I want to use it. To make you Viceroy in the Black Mountains, in Som's place.''

He grunted in surprise, beyond mere disbelief.

''Be at ease, my lord,'' she reassured him. ''The wizard Hann, who is with us in this enterprise, has made this apartment proof against Som's spies.''

''*I* came in quite unnoticed.''

''Not by me. I wanted you to enter, my good lord.'' Her small hands pressed his fingers tenderly. ''Ah, but it is good to have you sitting with me once again. You will be Lord of High Lords here, with Zapranoth and Draffut as your vassals and only the distant Emperor himself above; and I will be your consort, proud beside you.''

He made another boorish noise.

Unruffled, she pressed his arm. ''Chup, do you

doubt that I would like to be the lady of a viceroy?"

"I don't doubt that."

Her nails spurred his forearm. "And do you think that I would want some lesser man than you beside me, one who could not hold such a prize when we had won it, or try for something higher still. By all the demons, you underrate me if you do!"

Viceroy, Lord of High Lords . . . armies numbering tens of thousands under his command . . . beside him, Charmian, looking as she did now. He could no longer *wholly* doubt what she was saying. 'Has Viceroy Som no need of you, to hold his place and help him try for something higher still?"

Her eyes flashed anger, mixed with determination. "I want a living man, not dead . . . but you are right, my lord, Som is the key. We must dispose of him." She said it easily. "He gave me shelter when my father fell, thinking I would be useful to him one day; I convinced him you would be useful too. He does not know that you have brought the means of his downfall."

Chup's manner was still scornful. "And what are we to do with Som the Dead? How shall we topple him?"

Her eyes, that had gone to feast upon some distant vision, came back to his unwaveringly. "The circlet woven of my hair must go into his private treasure hoard, unknown to him. Only thus can he be made vulnerable to—certain magic that we shall use against him."

"He must have protection against such charms."

"Of course. But Hann says that the one you carry is of unequalled power."

Chup said: "You speak much of this wizard Hann, and what he says. What does he gain, by helping you?"

Charmian pouted. "I see I must soothe down your pointless jealousy again. Hann wants only vengeance, for some punishment that Som inflicted on him long ago. I know that Hann gives no impression of great skill at magic, yet he is stronger in his way than Elslood was, or Zarf—"

"Then why can he not make a stronger charm than Elslood wrought?" He thought he could feel it in his pocket, like a circle of heavy fire.

She shook her head impatiently. "I do not understand it perfectly, but it seems that Elslood, wanting me to care for him, stole some of my hair and wove the charm. But he tapped some power greater than he understood, the charm only made him dote all the more on me. Never mind. We need not struggle with these technicalities of magic. All that you need worry about, my lord, is getting the charmed circlet woven of my hair into Som's private treasure hoard."

"How?"

"I have already gone far in learning ways and making plans for that. But the execution of the plan requires someone like yourself, my lord; and who is there but you?"

"How?" His voice was still heavy with his skepticism.

She seemed about to tell him, but first she recounted once more the joys of being viceroy. Her soft voice wore him down, so that he passed the midpoint between doubting and belief; all things were possible, when his bride whispered that they were.

Now she was telling him what he must do: "Now hear me, my lord. Three things must fall together ere we strike. First, the human guards who watch the outer entrance to the treasure vault must be those we have suborned. Second—are you listening?—the new breed of centipedes in the second room must not yet have hatched. Thirdly, the word for quieting the demons in the inner vault must be the one we know . . ."

Demons again. He ceased to listen. He was wearying quickly of all these endless words, even if they came from her, when she herself was here. Shaking his head to break the spell of words, he reached for her.

"My lord, wait. Hear me. This is vital—"

But he would not wait, nor hear her any longer, and with a small sigh of vexation she let him have his way.

On the next day, when he had truly rested, there came to him officers of Som's Guard, who wished to question Chup about the military situation in the West. Chup related the rumors common in the Broken Lands, for what they might be worth. He told the officers what he had observed of troop movements, from his beggar's post, and of other matters bearing on the military, the conditions of roads and livestock in the Broken Lands, the feelings and prosperity of the populace, the state of the harvest. He could give the Guardsmen little comfort, except as regarding the relative smallness of Thomas's force. Thomas would need great reinforcement before he could attempt an attack upon this citadel.

Chup was soon sitting at ease with the officers, military men like himself. He was now dressed like them in a uniform of black, except that he had as yet no rank, and of course no Guardsman's collar. In the course of exchanging soldiers' talk he asked about the collars. He could not imagine how it would feel to enter a fight with the knowledge that you could be glued together again if you were hacked apart; would it be a spur or a hindrance to the most effective action? Would a man who wearied let himself be killed to gain a rest?

One of the officers shook his head, and raised one finger. It ended in a tiny abnormal loop of flesh, instead of a fingernail. "The healing's not that safe or certain. Things sometimes go wrong, up in Lord Draffut's house. A man who's badly mangled going in may well come out too crooked to walk straight.

And those who've been too long lifeless when the valkyries pick 'em up may never again be smarter than little animals.''

The other officer nodded his scarred head. ''Still,'' he said, ''I think none of us are likely to turn in our collars.''

''See much fighting here?'' Chup asked.

''Not since we came here, and Draffut handed out his collars; he was here first, you know, before the East or West . . . We do grow somewhat stale, those of us who stay inside these mountains. Nothing but a peasant uprising from time to time. But we practice. We'll handle this Thomas if he comes.''

Chup was invited to visit the officers' club on a lower level of the citadel, where wine and gambling and fresh peasant girls were available. He got up and strolled with the two men to sample the wine; as for the dice and the women, he had no money at the moment, and could not imagine himself wanting any woman but one.

Walking the main, buried corridors of the citadel, Chup took note of the fighting men he saw. He supposed the garrison might number a thousand if all were mobilized; but the five hundred elite Guardsmen should be easily able to hold the natural defenses of the place against Thomas's four thousand or so. A few of the Guardsmen were grotesquely misshapen with old scars, of wounds no man could ordinarily survive, though they were active still; this confirmed what the officer had said about the uncertainty of being healed.

Chup had other things to watch for on his walk to the officers' club and back again, through rooms and passages carved from the mountain's rock. In one large chamber, decorated with some ancient artisan's frieze of unknown men and creatures, he spotted without paying it any obvious attention the entrance to the passage that Charmian had told him to watch for. It was an unmarked tunnel leading downward and yet farther into the mountain. It was this way that, by many turns and branches she had described, would lead him to Som's own treasure hoard.

Again and again during the next two days she repeated her instructions to him; by then he had ceased to doubt her word on anything at all. And then she awoke him in the night, to tell him that the time had come, the three requirements had fallen together. Tomorrow he must try to reach the treasure vault of Som.

He strode into the high, frieze-corniced room with the air of a man upon some important errand, as indeed he was. The room was an intersection of two corridors, and held people passing continually to and fro. No one paid attention as Chup turned aside into the downward way that led toward the treasure; it led to other things as well, and was not guarded here.

Chup walked unarmed with any blade or club; he must not kill today, must leave no traces of his passage. For weapons, he carried Charmian's knowledge of Som's secrets, gathered he knew not how, but trust her to manage that, in a world of men; and his own boldness, and speed of mind and body; and three words of magic; and a pocketful of dried fruit, innocent to the eye and taste. Hann had demonstrated that a human might eat of it without effect.

A few people passed Chup, coming toward him through the tunnel he descended. Then the way branched, once and again, and now there were no other walkers. The branch that Chup had been taught to follow was a narrow way, and it went on without another intersection for some distance. Now and then it broke out of its walls into a large cave, where it formed a suspended walkway across chasms whose depths were lost in darkness. Sunlight filtered down into the big caves through hidden openings somewhere high above. Along the buried parts of the way, a few cheap lampstands cast some illumination. There were no signs, nor any evidence that any goal of much importance lay in this direction.

So far, all was as Charmian had foretold. And now, here, just as she had said, the path bridged a wider crevasse than usual, and then branched once more. The right way, she had told him, led up into the viceroy's private quarters. The left side, narrower, was the one that Chup must take.

Now at last there were posted warning signs. Chup had no doubt of what they meant, though he did not stop to try to puzzle out the letters. He also ignored another, blunter, warning: a bundle of mummied hands that were no doubt supposed to be those of would-be trespassers hung like a cluster of dried vegetables above the way. He moved his head slightly as he walked beneath, not wanting the dead fingers to brush his hair. His pulse went quicker. If he were stopped and questioned now, it would be hard to say convincingly that he had seen no warning.

A final abrupt turn, and Chup's path came to an end against a massive, unmarked door. This too he found as Charmian had described it: so strongly built that a ram would be needed to break it down. Having no sword hilt to rap out a signal with, Chup put his knuckles to the job. The door resounded no more than would a massive tree stump, but someone must have been listening for the little noise, for it was answered quickly. A dim face peeked out at Chup through a small grill. A sliding of bars and rattle of chains, and the great door moved inward just enough for him to enter.

He stepped into a barren, rock-walled chamber about ten meters square. The two men in Guardsmen's collars standing watch had been given no chairs or other furniture to lure them into relaxation. Directly across from the door where Chup had entered, a ladder five or six meters long stood leaning against the wall; beside the ladder was the room's only visible aperture besides the door, a narrow hole that led down into darkness. Thick candles in wall sconces lit the guardroom adequately.

One of the men who greeted Chup was hardly more than half a man in size, his legs being grotesquely short. The other guard was of ordinary stature, and sound of limb, but his face was the strangest Chup had ever seen on living man, a wall of scars from which one live eye gleamed like something trapped. According to Charmian, these men had been enlisted in her cause by promises of better healing when she came to power. The two of them closed up and chained and barred the great door tight as soon as Chup was through it; and then they looked at Chup expectantly, but saying nothing.

He had wasted no time either, but had crossed the chamber to look down into the hole. He could see nothing in the darkness there. "Where's the beast?" he asked. "I mean, in which part of its room?"

The scarred man made a nervous sound. "Hard to say. You've got some means of putting it to sleep?"

"Of course. But I'd like to know just where to toss the bait."

They came and stood beside him at the hole, peering down and listening, muttering to each other, trying to locate the beast. They were nervous for his welfare. If his attempt miscarried down below, their complicity in it would be discovered when Chup—alive or dead—was found. It seemed a long time before the dwarfed man raised a hand for Chup's attention, and pointed to a quarter of the room below. Bending over the pit, straining his ears, Chup thought he could barely hear a dry patter that must be made by the beast's multitude of feet.

"There, there, yes," the scarred man whispered. "It'll be behind you as you go down the ladder."

They got ready for him the long ladder—Chup saw now that it was really an extremely slim and elegant stair, complete with handrail, fit for Som to use when he went down to count his gold—and now they slid the ladder down.

Chup went down facing the ladder, about one third of its length, before he tossed his first piece of dried fruit. He heard the hundred feet shiver before he saw the rail-thin, cat-quick body; he could not tell for sure whether the bait had been taken. Hann had said that two pieces swallowed should afford Chup time enough to complete his mission. He let his eyes become somewhat more accustomed to the gloom before he tossed a second bait, and he saw this one snapped up by the first pair of delicate legs, flicked up into the tiny, harmless mouth. A moment only passed before the beast shivered, twitched extravagantly, and began to curl its body. Its hundred legs in disarray, it slid down springily to the floor, showing Chup as it bent the hundred branching slivers of its whiplike tail.

Chup cautiously went down the rest of the ladder. The centipede remained completely quiet. He left the ladder and paced toward the door that led to the next lower level; and now the dryness of fear was growing in his throat. Behind him he heard the ladder being drawn up; so it had been planned, in case some officer should come while he was down below.

There was a bloated bulk of darkness that he only just avoided stepping on, when it made a feeble movement in his path. He had been told of this also. It had been a man, and was still alive, nourishing the larvae of the centipede inside itself. Perhaps its hands would someday join the thieves' bundle over the tunneled walk; perhaps it had in fact once been a would-be thief.

In the faint light from below he could make out the way to the next lower level: an ordinary doorway led to a simple solid stair of stone, narrow and curving but quite open. What was below had no desire nor occasion to come up, and the centipede would be too frightened to go down.

Chup went down, armed with the three words of

magic Hann had taught him. They weighed now like swallowed arrows in his throat, syllables not fit for ordinary men to bear. Chup went down the curving stair, and before him the increasing light carried a hint of the color of gold.

As he had been instructed, Chup counted the turnings of the stair, and stopped on what should be the last, before the source of light ahead could come into his view. There he drew in his breath, and said, clearly and loudly, pausing after each word, the three words of the incantation.

With the first word, there fell a silence in the air, where before he had only thought the air was silent; there had been a certain quiet murmuring that he was not aware of until it ceased.

With the second word, the light in the room below was dimmed, and the air became fresh and ordinary, where before he had only thought that it was so; and time began to make itself felt, so that Chup perceived the age in all the slimy stones that built the vault surrounding him.

The third word of the incantation seemed to hang forever on his tongue, but when he had said it, time flowed on once more as it should. The golden light before him grew as bright as ever; a certain rippling watery reflection in it had been stopped so it was steady, where before he had only thought that it was so.

With that Chup went on down, walking into Som's treasure room through its sole entrance. The vaulted chamber was round and high, perhaps twenty meters across. The golden light came from the center of it, seemingly from the treasure itself. It lay in careless-looking heaps, for the most part brilliant yellow metal, coins and jewelry, bars and foldings of gold leaf; here and there the piles were studded with the sharper glint of silver or the brighter flash of gems.

The treasure was still sealed from Chup by a last encircling fence, of what seemed fragile metal wands. He had no need to cross that barrier or worry about it. Instead he looked up at once to the upper vaulting of the high chamber. By the light of the ensorceled treasure, he saw that up there the seven guardian demons hung, where Hann's three words had sent them, like malformed bats in fine gray gossamer robes. They were head down, with arms or forelegs—it was hard to specify—that hung below their heads. Several of the dangling limbs hung nearly to the level of Chup's head, so elongated were the demons' shapes. One had a gray blur of a talon run like a fishhook through the hide of small furry beast, a living toy that struggled and squeaked incessantly to be free, and very slowly dripped red blood. As Chup watched the demons, they began to drone, like humans newly fallen asleep who start to snore.

With a shudder he pulled his gaze down and stepped forward. He stood staring for just a moment in awe at the accumulated wealth before him. He thought he had seen riches before, and owned some too. But he had known only handfuls compared to this.

The moment of distraction passed; what drove him had far more power over him than greed. Taking now from his pocket the golden circlet of Charmian's hair—infinitely brighter in his eyes than any hoard of metal—he held it up before him in both hands. He was reluctant ever to let it go. But after all it was the woman he wanted, not her token. It was for the sake of their future life together that he must give away the charm; for no other reason could he have parted with it now.

He tossed it from him, over the innocent-looking fence of fragile rods, toward the piled-up wealth. As it passed from his fingers it seemed to draw from him a greater spark than ever man might get by rubbing cloth and amber; and with this spark, invisible for all its power, Charmian's image in his mind was smashed and shattered as in a broken mirror.

Under the blow, Chup lurched forward two steps, hands outstretched and groping. Like one aroused from sleep-walking he blinked and cried out incoherently. His case was all the worse for his remembering all the nightmare that had brought him here; nightmare magic, that had made him trust his bride . . .

Tightly he squeezed shut his eyes, forgetting for the moment even the dreaming, droning, blinded demons over his head as he tried to call back Charmian's face. He visualized her now as beautiful as ever. But now, freed of the potent charm, he recognized her beauty as nothing but a mask worn by an enemy.

He stood gazing dazedly through the fragile-seeming fence of wands. The gold circlet had vanished, lost in the dazzle of the yellow metal stacked and strewn there . . . and now that he was freed of it, he did not want it back. Nor her. She would be with Tarlenot now, or Hann, or someone else. And Chup realized that he no longer minded that.

The thought broke in upon him that she must have known he would be freed by tossing away the charm. Or did she think he was still bound to her and blinded by the simple magic of her attraction, like the other men she used? No, he never had been enthralled by her before he picked up the charm. She must have known that he would, at this point, be set free.

To do what? Where did his best interests lie? Was he now committed irrevocably to helping her against Som?

Remembering now her face and voice over the last few days, he concluded that she still hated him for not being manageable without magic, especially for once slapping her to put an end to a mindless hysteria of noise. Was she done with using him now, and was her revenge already set?

At best his time of safety here was passing quickly. Cautiously he turned to leave the treasure chamber.

Above his head the little furry animal still writhed and squeaked, impaled upon the demon's dangling talon. Chup put up a hand in passing to rob the demon of its toy; he tossed the small beast ahead of him up the curving stair. There it might find a crevice in which to die in peace. The curses of three thousand wizards on all demons! He could not slay them, but he would take the chance to rob one of a toy. When he had climbed round the first turn of the ascending stair he paused, and uttered in reverse order Hann's three words. The light changed subtly, down below, and no longer was there perfect silence.

When he had climbed to the darkened level of the centipede, he was glad that he had wasted no more time below, for already the beast was stirring. It was not moving yet, but trying to rise, its feet a-scratching on the pavement in the darkness. He waited briefly, to give his eyes a better chance to see.

Now that he had thought a little, it seemed to him that he would have no more usefulness to Charmian. No longer bewitched, he could do nothing for her that someone more manageable—Tarlenot— could not do almost as well. She hated Chup, he felt quite sure of that, and she was not the girl to leave her hate unsatisfied.

He could see the dim shape of the centipede now, lying on its side, curling and uncurling like a slow snake swimming in the dark. Its feet scraped but were not yet ready to support it. Chup moved in the utmost silence, stepping toward the place where they must let down the ladder for him . . . here? Would this be where Charmian meant for him to die?

The more he thought, the likelier it appeared. This whole scheme could have been accomplished in a different way. Hann could have given the two deformed guards dried fruit, and magic words. They could have taken the circlet in and thrown it on the pile as easily as Chup. Except in that case Chup would have been left above ground, live and active, and with his own will back again.

Holding his breath, he listened for any sound above. They must be standing silent and listening too. Suppose he called up for the ladder and they lowered it. When he, unarmed, climbed to the top, the two Guardsmen would be there, one on each side, with weapons drawn . . . or suppose they did not lower the ladder, but laughed at him. They could have some means to grapple his body and hoist it up, after the centipede had struck him. Either way, once he was dead, put him down a crevice somewhere. He would vanish, or seem to be the victim of an accident or some chance quarrel or casual assassination — only there would be nothing to connect him with the treasure vault.

Behind Chup now, the sounds of the centipede grew louder. Looking back, it saw it was now managing to drag itself along the floor. It moved in his direction.

And close above him now he heard the faint sound of a sandal-scrape, and the intake of a nervous breath. "Where is he?" came a Guard's low whisper. "If the demons took him after all, they're certain to report him. Then we're through!"

Chup's eyes had now adapted well enough for him to see the beast in some detail. Thin as an arm its body was, though longer than a man, about as long as the many-weaponed tail that flicked and twitched behind it. A man with good arms might easily break the beast's thin neck, it seemed. Except that as soon as he tried to get a grip that tail would come snapping like a whip in the gloom, impossible to block or dodge . . . the clustered poison-spines grew longer than fingers on that tail. How could a man fight such a thing barehanded?

Why, thus, and so. And he would have a fighting chance, if it was dazed and slow. The cold calculation of tactics led Chup on into the outline of a larger plan. He trusted what his instinct told him, in a fight; the reasons came clear later, if he took the time to think them out.

The animal was trying now to stand, was on the verge of success. Chup drew a deep breath and moved into action. He scraped his sandals on the paving, making hurried footsteps, and in a low clear voice he called out: "Let down the ladder."

From up above, the laughter came.

The centipede was still sliding toward Chup, with a whispery scraping of its feet and body on the stones. Moving more quietly than the dazed beast, Chup circled to its rear and closed in. He grabbed in the near darkness with his unprotected hand for the tail, and caught it, just under the cluster of poison-spines at the tip. He set his foot against what might be called the creature's rump and shoved it down and pinned it when it would have tried to rise. Hold-ing the tail straight was easy enough, but the mul-titude of slender legs had strength in numbers, re-silient power surprising for their size. He was in for a struggle as soon as the drug had worn off com-pletely, the more so as he must not kill this beast. The fighter's intuition on which he relied had grasped that point at once, though he had not thought it through with conscious logic: he must keep for himself the option of making Charmian's plan succeed or fail. To leave this animal dead would mean alerting Som and the plot's eventual discovery.

Up above, the Guardsmen's low voices were cheering on the beast.

"Put down the ladder, quick, by all the demons!" Chup cried out. Out of sight of those above, he was now sitting on the body of the beast to hold it down. His right hand was still vising the tail, his left hand feeling for the neck.

"Fight it out, oh great Lord Chup!" called down a voice. "What's wrong, did you forget your sword?"

He answered with a wordless cry of rage, as he shifted his grip upon the creature just slightly and stood up, lifting it across his shoulders. The weight was quite surprising for the size, it must be half as heavy as a man.

"That sounded like it did for him."

"It must have. Wait a moment, though."

The hundred legs remained in agitation, pounding softly, coldly, at Chup's head. He moved with his hideous burden, carefully keeping out of direct sight of the men above, stepping soundlessly.

One of the hidden voices said: "Toss down a bait. We've waited long enough. It got him, or he'd still be running."

Said the other, doubtfully: "He might have gone back down to the vault."

"Dimwit! The words won't work twice in one night, remember? Hann told us that. No man'll run to a wakeful demon, not even if a hundred-legger's chasing him. Throw a bait, we don't know when an inspector's going to come."

"All right, all right. Where's the beast? I'll toss one before his nose."

Chup twisted his burden off his shoulder and lowered it carefully in straining arms, just enough to let the little feet make scratching sounds upon the floor.

"There, there, hear it?" Chup heard the tiny spat of Hann's dried fruit, landing a meter or so before him. He waited, counting slowly to ten, his captive's body prisoned now under his left arm, its deadly tail still clamped safely by his tireless sword hand. Then he pressed the hundred legs down on the pavement once again, and this time let the writhing sides make contact too, to make the sounds of staggering and collapse.

"It took the bait. Go down."

"*You* go down, if you're in such a hurry. Wait till it falls, I say."

Chup lifted the animal again, and moved silently to a new position.

"It's quiet now. Go down and haul out the mighty

Lord Chup."

"We had it settled, you were going down!"

"You're the stronger, as you always brag. So now be quick about it."

A snarl of fear and anger.

"Quick! What if an inspector comes?"

It was the dwarf who eventually prevailed; the tall scarred man came down the ladder, slowly and hesitantly, frowning into the shadows where he thought Chup and the beast must both be lying. He had his sword drawn, and he spun round quickly when he heard Chup's soft step behind him. Then he screamed and jumped away and fell when he saw what weapon Chup was brandishing.

Without hesitation Chup turned and charged up the ladder, the writhing beast held above him and in front of him. He saw the dwarf's face, peering down incredulously, then tumbling backward out of sight in terror.

The dwarf was far too late in trying to draw his stubby sword. Chup by that time had reached the ladder's top, pitched the animal back down the hole, and was reaching for the little man. The dwarf's thick sword arm, caught, was twisted till the weapon clattered to the floor, then he himself was flung away across the room.

"Hold back!" Chup barked out, with his back against the door. "I mean no killing here, no valkyries buzzing down the tunnel to haul you out and bring investigators. Now hold back!"

The disarmed dwarf was sitting, scowling, where he had been tossed, and gave no impression of any eagerness to attack. Nor did the tall, scarred man, who, having beaten the maltreated centipede to the ladder on one lap or another of what must have been a lively race, now halted at the ladder's top. The tall one was armed, but so now was Chup, who had scooped up the dwarf's sword; and what Chup had just accomplished without a blade must have augmented his reputation considerably in the present company.

The men held back. Chup nodded, and reached behind him with one hand to slide back the massive bolts that sealed the door. "The scheme you were enlisted for goes forward, and if you play your parts I will see to it that you are rewarded." *As you deserve*, he thought. He went on speaking, with his field commander's voice: "The plan goes on, but now *I* am in charge, and not those who first bribed you and instructed you. Remember that. Raise that ladder."

The tall man hesitated briefly, then jumped to obey, sheathing first his sword. The dwarf was snuffling now like some schoolboy caught in an escapade.

Chup demanded: "What were you to do next? What signal were you to give her, that I am dead?"

The tall one said: "Your . . . your body, lord. To be left where it would be found; as if some feral centipede had . . . there are some in these caverns. To make your death look accidental."

"I see." Chup could now take time to think. "Maintain your guard here as if nothing had happened. If an inspector comes, say nothing. I left no traces down below. I will be back, or will send word, to tell you what to do." Now he could see the logic and the details of his plan, and he was grinning as he went out and shut the door.

VI

Be as I am

———◆—◆—◆———

The corpse's face had been shattered into unrecognizability, as if by a long fall onto rock, and the appearance of the rest of the body suggested that it had been nibbled by some kind of scavenger; reptiles, perhaps. The soldiers who had brought the body to Charmian — led by two officers who were not of her small group of plotters — stood by watching stolidly, as she attempted to make the requested identification.

She looked long at what had been the face, and at the heavy limbs that had once been powerful. They did not seem to have anything to do with Chup, but in their present state they might be his as well as not. Charmian was not squeamish about death — in others — and put out a hand and turned the ruined head. The build and hair color of the dead man were Chup's, and the tattered black uniform might be. She could see no marks of weapons on the body.

Half a day after Chup had set out upon his mission for her, she had sent word to Som's chamberlain inquiring whether her husband had been detained on any business. Word came back that nothing was known of his whereabouts. Half a day after that, the search was begun in earnest. Now another day later, this. Events were proceeding as she had planned.

"Where was this man found?" she asked.

"Wedged in a deep crevice, lady, in one of the deep caves. He might have fallen from a bridge." The officer's voice was neutral. "Can you make an identification?"

"Not with certainty." She lifted her eyes calmly; no one high in the councils of the East would be expected to show much grief for the loss of any other. "But yes, I think this is the body of my husband. Tell the Viceroy Som that I am grateful for his help in searching. And if it was no accident that killed the Lord Chup, then those who did it are as much Som's enemies as mine."

The officers bowed.

And half a day after they and their men had gone, wheeling their gruesome charge upon a cart, other messengers came from Som, more cheerfully garbed and with far merrier words to speak—it was a summons for her, to appear before the viceroy, but it came couched in the welcome form of gracious invitation.

Soon after those emissaries also had departed, leaving her time for preparation, the wizard Hann sat watching Charmian. They were in a central room of her elaborate suite. Hann sat a-straddle of a delicate chair turned back to front, his sharp chin resting broodingly upon his wiry, somehow unwizardly forearms, crossed upon the chair's high back.

The clothes that Charmian was to wear, close-fitting garments of raven black, hung thin and shimmering beside a screen. She herself, swathed in a white robe and soft towels and newly emerged from her bath, sat primping before an array of mirrors. She would make an imperious motion of her finger or her head, or merely with her eyes, and Karen or Kath would jump to adjust the angle of a mirror or lamp, or Lisa or Portia would fetch a different comb or brush, jar or phial, most of which their lady considered and rejected. Samantha was upon some errand for Charmian, and Lucia had earlier been judged guilty of some gross error and was not here; there was blood drying on the small silvery whip that lay at one end of the long dressing table. Charmian's face, utterly intent on appraising itself in all its multiple reflections, was for the time devoid of youth and softness, was ageless as ice and equally as hard.

Hann, observing her thus disarmed and charmless, was able to appraise her with something of the feeling he had when watching another magician pull off a perilous feat; professional respect.

He need never have worried about her nerves, he told himself. This girl-woman had matured considerably in the half year since she had come here as a frightened refugee. From the start she had been enormously ambitious; now she could be cold and capable, self-controlled. She probably could command an army, given a tactical adviser and mouthpiece to pass on orders—a man like Tarlenot. And she would have the nerve and ruthlessness to manage the other powers that were the viceroy's, even the power called Zapranoth—given the aid of a wizard of great skill, Hann.

The rulers of the Empire of the East would not care if Som were overthrown by one of his subordinates; that would mean only that a more capable servant had replaced a less. And now it did seem that Som's hand was faltering. (Only in the back of Hann's mind the question waited: why had the body been so mutilated, impossible to certainly identify? Well, why not? The Dwarf and Scarface swore that they had put the Lord Chup down a crevice as planned. And there were little scavenger beasts, that strayed out from the dungeons where they bred . . .)

Charmian was dismissing her attendants. As soon as the last of them had left the room she turned to Hann a questioning look. Hann, understanding, quickly made use of the best developed of his powers to quickly scan the suite and its environs. In this branch of magic he thought that he was unexcelled. The voices of invisible powers, inhuman and abject and faithful, muttered their reports to him, speaking close and softly so none but he could hear.

"Speak safely," he said to Charmian. "No one is listening but me."

Fingering a tiny perfume bottle, she asked: "How did our viceroy and master acquire his name?"

Hann was perplexed. "Som?"

"Who else, my learned fool? Why is he called 'The Dead'?"

He sprang up from his chair, aghast. "You don't know *that?*"

A light danced in Charmian's eyes. Looking at Hann in her mirrors, she was quite relaxed, save for her fingers on the little phial. "You know that I have met Som only twice, both times briefly. I realize of course that the purpose of his name must be to frighten those who hear it. But in what sense is it *true?*"

"In a very real sense!" Alarmed at her ignorance, Hann tilted his head from side to side in agitation.

"In a real sense, then. But tell mé more." Charmian's voice was soothing and deliberate, her eyes tranquil.

Hann absorbed some of her calm, turned his chair around, and sat down properly. "Well. Som does not age at all. He is immune alike to poison and disease, if what I hear is true." The wizard frowned. "He has reached some balance, struck some bargain with death. I admit I do not know how."

Charmian appeared to disbelieve. "You speak as if death were some man, or demon."

Hann, who had been to the center of the Empire of the East, said nothing for a moment. He had tied his fortune to this girl, and now her inexperience and rashness were beginning to frighten him. There was not time to teach her much. "I know what I know," he said at last.

She inquired, calmly enough: "And what else do you know of Som?"

"Well. I have never seen him enter battle. But it is said on good authority that any man who raises a weapon against Som finds himself smitten in that very moment with the same wound that he is trying to inflict."

On hearing this, Charmian's many mirror face
marred their foreheads with thoughtful frowns
"Then when I have put my ring of magic through
Som's nose, and led him from his throne, how are w
to do away with him? If no weapon can kill him . . .'

"There may be one."

"Ah."

"Though what the weapon is, I do not know. No
does Som himself know, I believe." Through th
powers that served him Hann had recently heard o
recent threats to Som, by some mysterious power o
the West, threats implying that the one effectiv
weapon was known and would be used when th
time came. "I do not know, but I could quickly learn
if I was given all the tools and wealth I needed for m
work."

"When I am consort of a new viceroy, you shal
have all you need and more. Now what else must
know of Som before I go to him?"

Hann went on worriedly: "There is sometimes th
smell of death upon him; though when he is in
clined to deal mildly with those around him, h
covers up his stink with perfumes.

"And —I warn you. When you see him at close
range and from the corner of your eye, you are liable
to see not a man's face but a noseless skull. Can you
smile and coo at that and not show your disgust?'

Once more she appeared to be concentrating
completely on her reflection, adding a final some
thing to her lips. "I? You do not know me, Hann.'

"No! I admit that I do not." He jumped to his feet
again and began to pace. "Oh, I know that you are
able. But also that you are very young, and from the
hinterlands. Inexperienced and untraveled in the
world."

Her mirrors all laughed at him in light and easy
confidence.

Annoyed, and worried all the more, he pressed
on: "I know, back in your father's little satrapy, men
were ruining themselves to win your favor. Some

here, also . . . but remember that not everyone here will be so easily manipulated."

She gave no sign that she had heard.

He raised his voice. "Do you suppose you have enthralled and bedazzled *me*? I am your full partner in this enterprise, my lady. It is magic that is drawing Som to you; see that you do not forget it."

"You do not know me," Charmian repeated softly. And with that she pushed away her clutter of towels and jars and phials and turned to him from her mirrors. The room seemed brighter, suddenly. Even clothed as she was, in the loose concealing robe . . .

"Never have I seen . . ." said Hann, in a new, distracted voice; and after the four words fell silent, marveling.

She laughed, and stood up, with a single swaying of her hips.

Hann said in a blurred voice: "Wait, do not go just yet."

Her lips swelled in a pretended pout. "Ah, do not tempt me so, sly wizard. For you know how weak I am, how subject to your every trifling spell and whim. Only the knowledge that I must go, for the sake of your own welfare, enables me to tear myself away." And with that she laughed again, and vanished behind the screens where her attendants were, and Hann was left with no more than the memory of a vision.

By the time she had finished dressing and set out, the time of her appointment was near at hand, but she did not hurry; the audience chamber was not far off. On her walk deep into the citadel she was bowed on and escorted by a series of the viceroy's attendants, some of whom were human. Others were more beastlike or more magical than men, and had shapes not commonly encountered away from the Black Mountains. Charmian no longer marveled at them, like a backwoods girl; twice before she had walked this way.

At her first audience with Som, nearly half a year

ago, the viceroy had told her simply and briefly that
it suited his purposes to grant her asylum. At her
second audience she had stood silent and apparently unnoticed amid a number of other courtiers
as Som announced to them the opening of a new
campaign to recover the lost seaboard satrapies
and particularly to crush the arch-rebel Thomas o
the Broken Lands; little or nothing had been heard
of the campaign since then. On neither occasion
had Som shown her any more interest than he might
have bestowed upon an article of furniture. She had
soon learned from the gossip of the other courtiers
that he was dead indeed regarding the pleasures o
the body.

Or so they all thought; what would they say today?

Looking into Som's great audience hall from just
outside the door, she was vaguely disappointed to
see that it was almost empty. Then as she was bidden enter by the chamberlain she saw that the viceroy had just finished talking with a pair of military
men, who were now walking backward from his
presence, bowing, noisily rolling up their scrolls
of maps. Som was frowning after them. Charmian
could not discern any change since her last audience in the man who sat upon the ebony throne.
Som was a man to all appearances of middle size
and middle age, rather plainly dressed except for a
richly jeweled golden chain around his neck. He
was rather sparely built, and his aspect at first
glance was not unpleasant, save perhaps for his
rather sunken eyes.

The soldiers backed past Charmian and she heard
them stumbling and colliding with each other at the
doorway as they left; but the viceroy's aspect softened as his eyes refocused on her.

The chamberlain effaced himself, and Charmian
was alone with her High Lord in the great room
where a thousand might have gathered — alone save
for a few Guardsmen, heavily armed and standing

motionless as statues, and for a pair of squat inhuman guardians—she could not tell at once if they were beasts or demons—that flanked his throne at a little distance on each side.

Som beckoned to her, with a gesture whose slightness she found enviable: that of one who knows he has complete attention. With humility in every move, her eyes downcast, steps quick but modest, she walked toward him. When still at a humble distance, she stopped, and made obeisance deeply, with all the grace at her command.

All was silent in the vast hall. When she thought it time to raise her eyes to the ebony throne, Som was gazing down at her, solemnly, with the stillness of a statue or a snake. Then like a snake he moved, with a sudden flowing gesture. In his dry, strong voice he said: "Charmian, my daughter—I have come to think of you as in some sense a relative of mine—you have lately begun to assume importance in my plans."

She dipped her eyes briefly and raised them again; so might a girl perform the gesture who had but lately begun to practice it before her mirror. A perfect imitation of innocence would never be convincing, here. "I hope these thoughts of me are in some measure pleasing to my High Lord Viceroy."

"Come closer. Yes, stand there." And when he had gazed upon her from closer range for a little while, Som asked: "Is it then your wish to please me as a woman? It is long since any have done that."

"I would please my High Lord Som in any way he might desire." There was perfume in the hall, of high quality certainly but stronger than the delicate scent she had put on herself.

"Come closer still."

She did so, and sank on one knee before him so close that he might have reached out a hand and touched her face. But he did not. For just a moment her nostrils caught a whiff of something else beneath the perfume; as if perhaps a small animal had crawled beneath the viceroy's throne and died.

"My daughter?"

"If you will have me so, my High Lord Som."

"Or should I say 'sister' to you, Charmian?"

"As you will have it, lord." Waiting for the next move of the game with her eyes cast down submissively, she saw (not looking directly at him) that Som had no nose, and that his sunken eyes were black and empty holes.

"My woman, then; we'll settle it at that. Give me your hand, golden one. In all my treasure hoard I have not such gold as you have in your hair. Do you know that?"

The statement gave her a bad moment of suspicion. But when she looked straight at her lord again, she saw an ordinary man's face, smiling thinly and nodding. However, she could not hear him breathe. And his hand, when she touched it, felt like meat that had been kept somewhat too long in the kitchen of a palace. Her hand did not for a moment tense, or her face change. She would take the fastest, surest way to power, though it meant embracing dead meat, and waking in the morning beside a noseless skull on a fine pillow.

In his dry voice, lowered now, he asked her: "What do you mark about me?"

Truthfully and without hesitation she replied: "That you do not wear the collar of the Guard, High Lord." It was a sign that Hann had mentioned, meaning that Som enjoyed some protection better than the valkyries.

The viceroy smiled. "And do you know why I wear it not?"

Impulsively she answered: "Because you are mightier than death."

He gave a silent, shaking grimace that was his laughter. He said: "You are thinking that it is because I am already dead. But yet I rule, and crush my enemies, and have my joys. Dead? *I have become death*, rather. No weapon, no disease, not even time, has terrors for me now.''

She only vaguely understood him, and she could not think what to reply. Instead of speaking, she bowed her head and once more pressed to her lips the sticky tissue of his hand.

The viceroy said: "And all that is mine, my golden one, I have decided to share with you.''

With unconcealed joy Charmian rose in response to the viceroy's tug on her hand. Som's dead hands pulled her to him, and she kissed him on the lips, or where lips should have been and seemed to be. "As your willing slave forever, gracious lord!''

Holding her at arms' length now, and smiling in great pleasure, he said: "Therefore you will become death too.''

These last words of his seemed to stay circling like birds in Charmian's awareness, uncertain whether or not they meant to land. When at last they came fully home to her, her new triumph shattered like glass. Not yet did her distress show in her face or voice; her surface was her strength, where terror would reach only when it had already conquered all within.

She only asked, like a girl expressing sweet wonderment at a reward too great: "I shall become as you are, lord?''

"Even so,'' he assured her happily, patting her hand between his, with faint sticking sounds. "Ah, I could almost regret that such goldenness must perish at its peak, like the beauty of a blossom plucked; but so it must be, for the woman who shares my endless life and power.''

With a shock of terror as sharp as the pain of blade or fire, she caught herself barely in time from trying to pull her hands away from his. In the back of her mind she was aware that other presences, human she thought, were coming into the audience chamber. But she could pay them no attention now.

She must express her joyful acceptance of Som's offer, without the least appearance of hesitation. But moment by moment her understanding of his meaning grew more certain and her fear grew more intense. Never for an instant had she expected this. She would rather die a thousand times, a million times, than become as he was. She could smile without a tremor at his dead face, she could embrace it warmly if she must. But to see the like of it in her mirror was unimaginable, was fear more pure than she had ever known.

No longer knowing whether she could conceal her horror, faint with the dizziness of it, she whispered: "When?"

"Why, now. Is anything the matter?"

"My High Lord—" Charmian could scarcely see. Would not some crevice open in the earth to swallow her? "It is only that I would preserve my beauty for you. That you may continue to enjoy it."

He made a gesture of impatience. "As I said, it is annoying that your appearance must be so much changed. But never mind. It is only mortal men who find those superficialities of great importance. What draws me to you is primarily your inner essence, so like my own—now, there is something wrong. What is it? Is the process causing you discomfort?"

"The process, my High . . . now? It happens to me now?" She was only half-aware of losing control, of pulling free from him and moving back a step.

He peered at her in evident astonishment. "Why, yes. I am impatient. Once having decided that you should rule beside me, I had the magicians begin the process of your transformation as soon as you entered the chamber. Already the change is far advanced—"

There was a rushing passage of the world, and screaming. Vaguely Charmian realized it was herself who screamed, and that the sound of pounding steps on wood and stone came from her own running feet. She had no longer any plan, no thought except to flee the death that moved and spoke and would engulf her with its own decay. A tall shape loomed before her, very near; she had run into it and rebounded before she saw it was a man, and knew his face.

The living face of Chup.

Still mad with panic, she tried to run around Chup, but he caught her by the arm. She had never seen his face so hard, not even on that day so long ago when he had slapped her. Now his voice came as if ground out between two stones: "Does it surprise you, Queen of Death, to see that I am still alive?"

Then Charmian understood what Chup's presence here must mean, that all her plotting had been discovered, her hopes destroyed. Her fear was so extreme she could not move or speak; she sank down in a faint before attendants came to carry her from the chamber.

Som, relaxed now upon his throne, spent a little time in the enjoyment of his almost silent, grimacing laughter. Chup waited, standing motionlessly at attention, until the viceroy had composed himself and beckoned him to come nearer.

"My good Chup, all your warnings to me have been borne out by investigation. The wizard Hann has been arrested. The circlet of the lady's hair has been found where you left it, in my treasure vault, with no trace visible of how you put it there. Needless to say, my security measures will be extensively revised. Fortunately, I am less susceptible to love-charms than these unhappy plotters thought; so it was shrewd of you to cast your lot with me."

Chup bowed slightly.

Som went on. "Unhappily, the man Tarlenot has departed on a courier's mission, on Empire business; it may be difficult to get him in our grasp again. But he left behind him his Guardsman' collar, which shall be yours, along with some substantial military rank."

For the first time since entering, Chup allowed himself to smile. "That's how I'd choose to serve, my High Lord Som. I am a fighter, with little taste for these intrigues."

"And you shall have your command." The viceroy paused. "Of course there is one matter first—your pledging to the East."

Ah, said Chup to himself, without surprise. I might have known.

Som continued: "When you were a satrap in our service, unlike others of your rank, you never came here to make a formal pledge. That has always seemed to us rather odd."

There was no satisfying the powers of the East. Always the certainty of great success was one more step away. Chup said, rather wearily: "I have been six months a crippled beggar."

"You were a satrap, free to come, for a much longer time than that." Som's voice was no longer so relaxed. "Before you lost your satrapy."

There was no good answer Chup could give. As a satrap, he had certainly been busy fighting, and he had told himself that he served his masters better in that way than by partaking in mysterious rituals. But they had never seen it exactly that way.

Now Som was looking at him from his sunken eyes, and Chup thought that he could smell the death. The viceroy said: "This pledging is more important than you seem to realize. There are many who ask to bind themselves completely to the East, to share in its inner powers, and are not allowed to do so."

As a soldier long accustomed to orders and the ways of giving them, Chup understood that there was now but one thing for him to say. "I ask to be allowed to make my pledge, High Lord. As soon as possible."

"Excellent!" Som took from around his own neck a richly jeweled chain, which he tossed carelessly to

Chup. "As a mark of my good favor, and the beginning of your fortune."

"Thanks, many thanks, High Lord."

"Your face says there is something else you want."

"If I may retain for the time being the lodgings of that treacherous woman. And her servants, those who had no part in her plotting."

Som assented with a nod. The chamberlain was evidently signalling him that other business pressed, for he dismissed Chup with a few quick words. After backing deferentially from the chamber, Chup hung the chain of Som's favor around his neck, and made his way to what had been Charmian's apartment. With the chain around his neck, he was now saluted by soldiers of the common ranks. People of more standing, some of whom had not deigned to notice him before, now nodded or eyed him with respect and calculation.

When he reached the apartment he found it swarming with men and women in black, each of whom bore a skull insignia upon his sleeve. In the past Chup had noticed only a few of these uniforms and had not thought of their significance. They were searching Charmian's rooms, thoroughly, leaving casual wreckage in the process. Chup did not attempt to interfere until he found their leader, whose sleeve bore a much larger skull. This woman, though she maintained an air of arrogance, was like everyone else impressed with the chain that hung about Chup's neck. In answer to Chup's question, she led him to a service passage in the rear of the apartment. There waited Karen, Lisa, Lucia, Portia, Samantha, and Kath, chained together and huddled against the wall.

Chup said: "You may release them, on my word. I am to occupy these rooms, and I will require a good staff, familiar with the place, to restore order from this mess that you have made."

"They have not been questioned yet," the leader of the skulls said, finality in her voice.

"I am somewhat aware of how the plotting went, and who was involved, as our Lord Som can tell you. These were innocent. But they will be here when you want them for your questions."

It took a little more argument, but Chup did not lack stubbornness and pride, and there was Som's favor hanging down upon his chest. When the searchers in black at length departed, the six girls, unchained, were left behind. When they were alone with him the six of them came slowly to surround Chup. They said nothing, did nothing but gaze at him.

He bore this silent, disturbing scrutiny only briefly before issuing curt orders for them to get to work. The shortest, Lisa, turned away at once and started in; he had to bark commands, and kick a couple of the others, to get them moving properly. Then he walked out into the garden, turning ideas over in his mind.

On the next day Som's chamberlain came to Chup, and led him down into the mountain. Through devious and guarded tunnels they passed, until the tunnel they were in broke out into the side of a huge and roughly vertical shaft. This chimney had the look of a natural formation; it was about ten meters wide here, at a level well below the citadel. It seemed to widen gradually as it curved upward through the rock. Sunlight came reflecting down through it, from what must be an opening at the unseen top, beyond a curve. A precarious ledge winding round the inside of the shaft, made a narrow pathway going up and down. At the level where Chup and the chamberlain now stood, this ledge widened, and from it several cells had been dug back into the rock, and fitted with heavy doors.

Only one of these doors was not closed. Gesturing at it, the chamberlain, as if imparting necessary information, said: "In there lies she who was the Lady Charmian."

When Chup had nodded his understanding of this fact, if not of its importance, the chamberlain said quite solemnly: "Come." And started down the rough helix of a path that wound both up and down the chimney.

Chup followed. The two of them were quite alone on all the path, as far as Chup could see, peering down a long drop. From below, round a lower curve in the gradually narrowing chimney, in regions where the daylight scarcely reached, there came up a roseate glow. "Where are we going?" Chup asked the silent figure ahead of him.

The chamberlain glanced back, with evident surprise. "Below us dwells the High Lord Zapranoth, master of all demons in the domain of Som the Dead!"

Chup's feet, that had been slowing down, now stopped completely. "What business have we visiting the Demon-Lord?"

"Why, I thought you understood, good Chup. It is the business of pledging. Today I will explain how your initiation is to be accomplished. I must take you nearly to the bottom, to make sure you are familiar with the ground."

Chup drew a deep breath. He might have known they'd put demons into this, the one peril that could make him sweat from only thinking of it. "Tell me now, what is the test to be?"

He listened, frowning, while the chamberlain told him. On the surface of it, it sounded easier than Chup had expected. He'd have to face Zapranoth, but not for long and not in any kind of contest.

But there was something—wrong—about it.

Still scowling, Chup asked: "Is there not some mistake in this? I am to serve Som as a fighting man."

"I assure you there is no mistake. You will not suffer at the hands of the High Lord Zapranoth if you do properly what you are sent to do."

"I don't mean that."

The chamberlain looked at him blankly. "What, then?"

Chup struggled to find words. But he could not make it clear in his own mind what was bothering him. "The whole business is not to my liking. I think there must be some mistake."

"Indeed? Not to your liking?" The chamberlain's haughty glare could have withered many a man.

"No, it is not. Indeed. Something is wrong with this scheme. *Why* am I to do this?"

"Because it is required of you, if you wish to participate fully in the powers of the East."

"If you cannot give me any more definite reason, let us go back to Som, and I will question him."

It cost Chup some further argument, and the nearly incredulous displeasure of the chamberlain, but at last he was led upward again, and admitted to see Som once more.

This time he found the viceroy apparently quite alone, in a small chamber below the audience hall. In spite of half a dozen torches on the walls, the place seemed dim and cold. It was a clammy room, nearly empty of furniture except for the plain chair Som was sitting in, and the small plain table before him. On that table there stood upright mirrors, and at the focus of the mirrors a candle guttered, topped with a wavering tongue of darkness instead of flame, casting all around it an aura of night instead of luminance. Som's face turned toward the candle was all but invisible, and what little Chup could see of it looked less human than before.

In answer to the silent interrogation of that face turned toward him, Chup came to attention. In a clear voice he said: "High Lord Som, I have taken and given orders enough to understand that orders must be followed. But when I think an order is mistaken, then it is my duty to question it, if there is time. I question the usefulness of this initiation, in the form I am told it is to follow."

Som the Dead was silent for a little time, as if such an objection were outside his experience, and he had no idea how to deal with it. But when he answered, his dry voice was hard to read. "What is it you dislike about the pledging?"

"Excuse me, High Lord Som. That I dislike it is beside the point. I can carry out orders that I find unpleasant. But this . . . I see no benefit in this, for you, for me, for anyone." That sounded weak. "Excuse me if I speak clumsily, I am no courtier . . . That's just it, High Lord. I am a fighter. What can a thing like this prove of my ability?"

Som's voice did not change; his face remained unreadable. "Exactly what did my chamberlain tell you was required of you?"

"I am to take the woman Charmian from her cell. Tell her that I'm helping her escape. Then I am to lead her down into the pit, where dwells our High Lord Zapranoth. There I am to give her to the demon, to be devoured—possessed—whatever Zapranoth may do with human folk."

The answer was quick and cold. "The chamberlain spoke our will correctly, then. That is what we require of you, Lord Chup."

A good soldier, if he had ever got himself in this deep, would know that this was the moment to salute, turn and leave. Chup knew it; yet he lingered. The hollows of darkness that were Som's eyes remained aimed at him steadily. Then Som said: "The strong magic of a love-charm once bound you to that woman, but my magicians tell me you are free of that. What are your feelings for her now?"

In a flash of relief Chup understood, or thought he did. "Demons! I'm sorry, lord. Do you mean, have I affection for her? Hah! That's what you're testing." He almost laughed. "If you want me to feed her to the demons, well and good. I'll drag her to the pit and toss her in, and sing about my work!''

"In that case, what is your objection?'' Som's voice was still cold and hard, but reasonable.

"I . . . High Lord, what good will it do to test my skill in lying and intrigue? To see if she believes me when I promise to help her? You'll have other men in your service far more cunning in such matters than I am. But you'll have few or none who'll fight like me.''

"The test seems useless to you, then.''

"Yes, sir.''

"Does a good soldier argue all orders that seem to him useless? Or, as you said before, only those that seem mistaken?''

Silence stretched out following the question. Chup's stubborn dissatisfaction remained, but his will was wavering. The more he tried to pin down what was bothering him and put it into words, the more foolish his objections seemed. What harm could he suffer, in obediently carrying out this test, that could compare with all he stood to gain from it? Yet, encouraged by Som's seeming patience, he made an effort and tried once more to speak his inner feelings.

"This thing that you would have me do is small, and mean . . . '' Then try as he might he could not form his shapeless revulsion any further. He made a weak and futile gesture and fell silent. Despite the clamminess of the chamber, sweat was trickling down his ribs. Now his coming here to argue seemed a hideous blunder. It wasn't that he cared what happened to her . . . the face of Som was growing hard to look at. And there were no perfumes here . . . but Chup was long used to the air of battlefields.

The viceroy shifted in his seat, and lo, was very manlike once again. The dark flame had burned down to only a spark of night. "My loyal Chup. As you say, your talents are not those of a courtier; but they are considerable. Therefore will I not punish you for this insolent questioning; therefore will I condescend this once to explanation.

"The test you do not like is given you *because* you do not like it, because you have shown reluctance to do things that you think of as 'small and mean'. To pledge yourself formally to the East is no meaningless ritual. In your case it will mean changing yourself, importantly, and I realize full well it can be very difficult. It is to do violence to your old self, in the name of that which you are going to become."

Time was stretching on in the odd little room. Like a man dreaming or entranced, Chup asked: "What am I going to become?"

"A great lord with the full powers of the East to call upon. The master of all that you have ever craved."

"But. How shall I change myself? To what?"

"To become as I am. No, no, not dead and leathery; I was playing with the woman when I told her she would be so. That is given only to me, here in the Black Mountains. I mean you shall become as I am in your mind and inward self. Now will you take the test?"

"My lord, I will."

"You are obedient." Som leaned closer, looking intently from his sunken eyes. "But in your case I wish for more than that. Loyal Chup, if you still had some affection for the woman, then merely to throw her to the demons might well suffice for your initiation. But as things are, it is not the woman, it is something else, within yourself, you must destroy ere you are ours completely."

Som rose from his chair. He was not tall, but he seemed to tower above Chup as he leaned yet closer, with his smell of old death. "You must be for once not brave, but cowardly. Small and mean, as you describe it. It will be difficult only once. You must learn to cause pain, for the sake of nothing but causing pain. Only thus will you be bound to us entirely.

Only thus will there be opened for you the inner secrets of power and the inner doors of wealth. And how can I give command of my Guard to one who is not bound to me and to the East?''

"The Guard . . ."

"Yes. The present Guard commander's aged and scarred well past his peak of usefulness. And you know Thomas of the Broken Lands, who is planning to assail us here, you know him and how he thinks and fights.''

Not only an officer, but once again the commander of an army in the field . . . "My High Lord, I will do it! I hesitate no more!''

When Chup had gone, the viceroy returned to brooding on his other problems. What power was it, almost equal to his own, that dwelt in the circlet of gold hair and almost awoke in him the old desires of life?

His wizards would find out, in time.

In all their divinations lately, a threatening sign, the name of Ardneh, loomed up from the West. A name, with nothing real as yet attached to it. But it was in that sign, they said, that the Broken Lands and other satrapies along the seacoast had been lost . . .

VII

We Are Facing Zapranoth

━━━━◆▶◀◆━━━━

Thomas had been right about the reptiles, Rolf was thinking now, as he trudged up a small hillock to where his commander stood looking upward at the black, night-shrouded cliffs. Rolf's breath steamed in the air before his face. The onset of winter's chill, more noticeable at this altitude than it had been near the seashore, had kept the reptiles close to their roosts, had prevented their scouting out the army of the West during the days as it lay hiding in a hundred fragments. Night by night they had crept closer to Som's citadel.

Rolf reached the spot where Thomas stood, alone for once, his head tipped back. There seemed little to be seen, gazing upward, except the stars above the cliffs, whose tops seemed but little below the twinkling sparks.

"I think it's going to work," Rolf reported. He had recently been given his first command, a work party to set in order and inspect the balloon-craft that the djinn produced. All through this night the technology-djinn had labored at Gray's direction, making airships. Loford and the other wizards had concentrated on preventing the army's discovery by demon or diviner dwelling on the cliffs above.

Gray had now learned to manage the djinn successfully, Rolf reported. At the foot of the cliffs were twenty balloons tugging gently at their mooring ropes, each of the twenty capable of carrying five armed humans. The balloons were to ascend connected in pairs by stout lines, and longer cords would fasten each pair to the ones behind it and ahead, so the hundred riders would find themselves together at the top.

"Once we begin it, it had better work," said Thomas, nodding, when Rolf had finished detailing his report. Thomas himself was one of the hundred ascending by balloon to seize a foothold on the cliffs. Rolf was going up, to order the maneuvering and landing of balloons, and Gray, as wizard and technologist both. The other ninety-seven had been hand-picked from the fiercest warriors. At first Thomas had contemplated lifting his whole army in an aerial assault. But testing and maneuvering, by night and day, on various smaller cliffs between here and the Broken Lands, had dissuaded him. The number of things that could go wrong had proven almost limitless, and the time available for practicing was not. In maneuvers, the stunt had been worked successfully with as many as fifteen balloons. He had decided to risk twenty to seize the upper ending of the pass.

Thomas now had nothing more to say. Rolf, who had known him from his earliest days of leadership—not so long ago—wanted to offer more encouragement, but hesitated to interrupt what might be a necessary pause for thought. The pause was not long before Thomas turned suddenly and strode off down the hill. Rolf hurried after.

Most of Thomas's other officers were waiting for him, in a body, and he strode in among them briskly. "All here who are supposed to be? Once more: our flares will burn with a green fire, to signal you to start to climb the pass. We'll sound horns at the same time, as we've rehearsed. Once you get the word, by sound or light or both, that we've seized the top of the pass, come up as if a hundred demons were behind you."

"Instead of waiting for us at the top, aye!" There were sounds of nervous laughter.

Gray's tall figure loomed up. In one hand he

raised what appeared to be an ordinary satchel. "The demons at Som's command number far fewer than a hundred. And I have the lives of two of the strongest of them in here."

"Zapranoth? Zapranoth's life?" The murmured question came from several at once.

Gray, perhaps irritated, raised his voice slightly. "These are the lives of Yiggul, and of Kion. I have had them in my possession for some time, though for the sake of secrecy I have said nothing about them until now. And I have let them live, so I can destroy them when Som has called them up, thrown them into battle, and is depending on them. I am sure many of you know their names: they are both formidable powers."

There was silence.

Gray lowered his satchel. "You will see me blow them away like clouds of mist, before they have had time to do us the least harm."

"Not Zapranoth's life," one low-voiced listener said.

"No!" Gray snapped. "His life eludes us still. But these two are the strongest of the other demons. With these two gone, my brother and I can beat off the smaller fry like insects. We will not need the lesser demons' lives to drive them off."

There was no comment.

Gray went on, a little louder still: "Then, with all the others gone, we will be free to deal with him. Myself, Loford, the other stout wizards here. Zapranoth is mighty, well, so are we. We will hold off him or any other power, until your swords have won the day."

"And that we will do," Thomas put in with great firmness. "Any questions? Remember what you've been told about the valkyries. Let's move, the light is coming." He gripped hands all round with his officers, and led the way toward the moored balloons.

Rolf trotted to take his place in the basket of the leading balloon. He felt weak in the knees, as usual before a fight, but he knew that it would pass. It crossed his mind as he and Gray were boarding their separate balloons that he had never seen the wizard sleep. If Gray felt any fatigue from his night-long supervision of the djinn, he did not show it. Gray was compelling the djinn to accompany his balloon, and had even forced it somehow to dim the intensity of its fiery image; Rolf could see it like a floating patch of campfire embers in the shadow of the great hulking gasbag of Gray's balloon, some thirty meters distant. Tests had shown that the lifting gas provided by the djinn would not burn, but the problem of arrow-proofing the bags had not been entirely solved. They were protected to some extent by draped sheets of chain-mail whose rings were lighter than metal, made, as were the bags themselves, of something that the djinn called *plastic*.

Rolf had argued at some length for using to the full the tremendous powers of the djinn, delaying the campaign as long as necessary to exercise its abilities and try out the results; it seemed to him that in a few months enough Old World arms, armor, and techniques might be acquired and understood to give the army an overwhelming advantage against the East.

But Gray had vetoed such a plan. "For two reasons. First, not all Old World devices will work now as neatly and reliably as they did in the Old World. This is true in particular of certain advanced weapons. I do not fully understand why this should be; but I have my means of knowledge, and it is so."

"We could experiment—"

"With devices far more perilous than balloons? No, I do not think that we are ready. The second reason, and perhaps the stronger"—here Gray paused for a moment, looking round as if to make sure that he was not overheard—"is the chance that our djinn will perish in this battle. We are facing Zapranoth, and such a blow is far from impossible.

It would leave us without help in operating and maintaining our Old World weapons. No. Better that we fight with means we understand, depending on no one but ourselves."

Waiting now in the basket for the signal to ascend, Rolf grinned nervously at the impassive Mewick at his side. "Mewick, will you one day teach me to use weapons?" he asked in a low voice. It was something of an old joke between them, for Rolf at least. Mewick shook his head at Rolf in faint reproach and let his expression deepen into gloom.

The first balloons were loaded; the crews who were to do the launching were moving about briskly and capably in the gloom. Rolf did not see when Thomas gave the final signal for the attack, but those who were required to see did so. Two men standing by the mooring ropes each tugged and released a knot, and Rolf beheld the dim cliffside, ten meters from his face, begin abruptly to slide down in silence. Gray's balloon kept pace, its basket rocking gently, the dim fire of the image of the djinn suspended near it. The line connecting Rolf's balloon to Gray's drew gently taut, then slackened again. The longer lines, that the next craft were to follow up, were paid out from their reels outside the baskets.

The edge of sky that Rolf could see past the bottom of his balloon was now brightening with a hint of dawn. Higher the two baskets swung, moving in the perfect silence of a dream, emerging now from the deeper shadows at the base of the cliffs, so that the rocky walls before them rapidly grew more distinct. Turning for a moment to the west, Rolf could see the plains and desert, night-bound still, stretching far into vague, retreating darkness. His homeland, and the ocean, would be visible from here by day. But there was no time now to think of that.

Up and up . . .

Rolf's drawn sword snapped up in his hand to guard position, as the utter quiet was shattered by the strident cawing of a reptile. The creature had been dozing on the cliff face, a pebble's toss from the balloons, and it had wakened to see the strange shapes soaring past. Sluggish with chill, wings laboring, it came out in a dark, slow explosion from the rocks, and fled them upward strainingly. Mewick and others who had their arrows nocked were quick to draw and loose at it, and it was hit but not brought down. Clamoring all the louder, it flew on up above the great gasbags and out of sight.

From somewhere farther up there came a slow-voiced, cawing answer, and then another, higher yet. Then there was silence once more, until it almost seemed that the citadel might have returned to sleep.

Up and up. The men hanging in the baskets, straining to see and hear, had little to say to one another. Rolf found himself gripping the wicker rim, inside the quilted armor-padding, trying to lift the craft into a faster climb. He could see Gray murmuring to the djinn.

Rolf was expecting that at any moment they would top the cliff, but they had not done so before there came sure proof that the enemy had awakened. It was a small squadron of reptiles on reconnaissance. Their cawing and snarling was heard above, and then the soft thumps of their bodies striking atop the gasbags. The craft continued to rise steadily. The mail of plastic links had proven too tough for reptilian teeth and claws, and their bodies were not weighty enough to hold down the balloons.

When the reptiles flew down below the bags to find the baskets, arrows and slung stones bit at them accurately. They screamed and raged and fled; some fell, transfixed by shafts, turned into weights with fluttering fringes dropping through the brightening sky.

Now came the first sign that Som's fighting men were reacting to the attack. Rolf saw black-trimmed uniforms running on ledges on the cliffs. A slung stone thunked on the padding-armor right in front of him, and he crouched lower. A fur-clad Northman in Rolf's basket loosed an arrow in reply, and on the cliff face a man dropped, toppled and slid on the steep slope, trying to cling to it with the shaft in him, plowing up a little avalanche.

Rolf knew they could not have much farther to ascend, but still the top came as a surprise. The cliff face fell back abruptly into a tableland, rough and split by many crevices, but essentially flat. At the rear of this horizontal reach, Som's low-walled citadel sprawled, backed by the next leap upward of the mountain. Across the little distance that separated his balloon from Gray's, Rolf heard the wizard barking orders to the djinn. The two balloons, each trailing a long spider-filament of line, slowed and stopped their ascent just above the rim of the cliff. Just here, almost beneath Rolf now, the narrow pass delivered the road it had caught up on the plain below.

Modest earthworks on one side of the debouching road defended the pass against a climbing army, and in fact formed the only real defense short of the citadel's own walls. These works manned by half a hundred men might easily hold the road, it seemed, against Thomas's four thousand, so great was their advantage of position. Ten or twelve men were in the trenches now, pulling on black helmets and gaping confusedly at the balloons. Their fortification offered no protection against attackers dropping from the sky.

Gray was smoothly ordering the operations of the djinn. Gas hissed from the bag above Rolf's head; the basket he was riding skimmed rock, just in from the cliff's edge. He pitched out a metal grapple on a line, and leaped right after it. The balloon bobbed up with the removal of his weight; for a moment he stood there alone, the sole invader of Som's stronghold. But in the moment it took him to catch the grapple and fix it in one of the many crevices in the rock, Mewick was standing beside him, short sword and battle-hatchet at the ready. Then with thudding sandals others were landing, at their right and left. Gray swung from his bobbing basket, agile as a youth. Across ten meters of empty ground the ten invaders faced the unfortified rear of the strong point that looked so indomitably down the pass; ten black-helmed Guardsmen, more or less, stared back as if uncertain they were real.

Excepting Rolf and Gray, the aerial troops had been hand-picked for guts and viciousness, and those proved first in fighting skill had been selected for the first balloons. The struggle for the earthwork began without an order, in the space of one short breath, and it was over in the time one might draw a long breath and release a sigh; only one fighter of the West had been cut down. Rolf sprang forward with the rest, but all the enemy were slaughtered before he had a chance to strike a blow. Still gripping his unmarred sword he turned to Gray; the towering wizard with a motion of his arm was already sending out the signal of green fire, bright as a small sun in the morning sky, leaping and shining in the air above the pass.

Rolf turned and cried out: "Sound the horn!" A Northman, blood from a scalp wound running in his eyes, had the twisting beast-horn already at his lips he gave a nod, and winded it with all his might.

Sheathing his weapon, Rolf ran back to his balloons, made them secure with double grapples, and deciding where the second pair should land. He was none too soon, for they were close below and rising rapidly. When they arrived, he helped to land them pulling on the thin ropes that the first balloons had trailed, while their fierce passengers leaped out and set themselves to hold the pass and landing place Rolf stayed at the landing place, seeing that the new balloons were tied down, and looking for the next When he glanced toward the citadel, he heard

alarms and signals there, and saw folk running on
the walls, and reptiles in a sluggish swarm above
them. The main gates had been open, and still were;
at any moment a force must sally out to push the
Westerners from the cliff. Rolf looked the other way,
down the road that became a twisty ribbon marking
the bottom of the pass, but the army of the West was
still invisible. It would be hours before their legs
could bring them to this height.

In the earthworks, men had already methodically
separated the slaughtered Guardsmen's heads from
their bodies, gathered the freed collars and thrown
them down the cliff; the valkyries, coming down
from the high mountain, hovered and sniffed but
could find no one to save. Rolf and the others,
taught by Gray to expect the flying things, still
stared at them, Rolf with particular fascination.

"Demons!" someone called out. It was not an ex-
pletive, but a warning.

Faces turned to Gray. He had already seen the
disturbances in the air a little way from the citadel,
hanging low, more like the roiling of heat above fires
than like rainclouds. Opening his satchel, he pulled
out of it a flowery little vine, wrapped as if for sustenance around a piece of damp and maggoty wood.
In Gray's other hand was a silvery-gleaming knife.

As the two presences drifted nearer in the lower
air, sweeping reptiles in a timid swarm before them.
Gray brought the blade near the tender, innocent
green tendrils of the vine. He muttered a few words
in a low voice—and cut.

Silver flashed in the sky above the citadel, like a
reflection or mirage of an enormous axe. The blow
that struck one of the demons came in utter silence,
but was irresistable nonetheless; its image in the air
split in two spinning halves. Gray scarcely looked
up; his hands, those of a gardener, kept at their
work, severing and plucking leaf from stem, slicing,
splitting, and demolishing the vine. Gray breathed
upon the rotten wood, and green flame sprouted

from it. In unburned hands he held it up, watching
the clean flame devour the clinging fragments of the
petals, leaves and stems. "Yiggul," he said with feeling, "trouble our fair world no more." And he
chanted verses in a language Rolf did not know.

Fire burned now in the sky as well consuming the
scattered pieces of the demon. Its companion
paused in his advance, but then came drifting on
again.

"Now, Kion, let us say farewell to you." Gray
reached into his satchel once more.

The roiling disturbance in the air, the size of a
small house, shook for a moment as if with fear or
rage, then came toward Gray like a hurled missile.
Some of the men around the wizard threw up their
arms or ducked their heads; others, just as uselessly, raised shield and blade. Gray shot forth his arm,
and the object he had pulled from his satchel—it
looked like some trinket of cheap metal—was held
above the chunk of burning wood. The hurtling
demon was transformed into a ball of glowing heat.
Rolf heard, more in his mind than in his ears, a
scream of pain beyond anything he had yet heard
upon a field of war. Kion's course was bent from
what he had intended. He struck the earth far from
the Western men, spattering flames and rock about
his point of impact, where he left a molten scar; he
bounded up again, twisting and spinning like an
unguided firework, and all the while the scream
went on unbreathingly, and Gray's unburning hand
continued to hold the bauble in the fire. The metal
of it, tin or lead mayhap, melted in beautiful silvery
drops that fell into the flame and there unnaturally
disappeared. And as the bauble melted, so diminished the fireball that had been the mighty
demon Kion, flashing madly from one part of
the sky to another until it vanished in a final streak
of brilliancy.

Gray pressed his hand down on the fiercely burning wood, and it went out like a candle. "What are these others here?" Gray asked in a low voice. "Do they propose to try our strength, after what we have just done?" Rolf saw that there were indeed a scattering of other disturbances in the air, man-sized waverings visible to him only now when the larger two were gone. He heard, or felt, the thrummings of their power. Alone, he might have fallen down or fled before the least of them. Standing here with Gray and Loford, now, he found he minded these minor demons no more than so many sweat-bees or mosquitoes. And now as if they had heard Gray's challenge, and chose not to accept it, the swarm of them began to disappear. Rolf could not have said just how; one moment the air above the citadel was thick with them, then they were fewer, and soon they were no more.

"So, then, masters of the Black Mountains," mused Gray, still in the same low tone of conversation, that you would not think was audible ten meters off. He stood straight, dusting his hands absently against one another. "So. Do you mean then to let our differences be settled by the sword? In the name of my bold companions here I challenge you: march out and try with blades to pry us from this rock!"

Rolf heard no answer from the citadel, only a shouting from behind him, where more balloons were ready to discharge their fighting men. He ran back to take charge of the docking. Thomas, in a gleaming barbut-helm, was arriving in the ninth pair of airships, a position he had hoped would allow him to oversee both ends of the operation.

When Rolf turned back toward the citadel he could see through the open gates that men were marshalling inside as if to sally out in strength. Confusion had been replaced by the appearance of purpose.

"Som is on the battlement," said someone. "See,

there. I think he wears a crown of gold.''

Rolf shivered. The day was chill. Winter was near at hand, and this place was high.

''If he takes the field,'' warned Loford, ''do not strike at him, but only ward his blows. The wound you would inflict on Som the Dead is likely to become your own to bear.''

Gray, too was shivering, calling for a cloak.

Why should the sun seem dimmer, when there were no clouds? And Rolf had a feeling in his guts like that of being lost, alone, at night amid a host of enemies . . . and now, why should he think there mighy be something wrong with the mountain, that it might crumble and collapse beneath his feet? Loford, Thomas, all of them, were beginning to look at one another with dread.

Gray said softly: ''Zapranoth is coming.''

VIII

Chup's Pledging

Chup nodded once to the expectant-looking
jailor—who stood near the door of Charmian's cell.
The man responded with a facial contortion that
might represent a smile, and took two steps backward to a spot well shaded from the feeble glimmerings of dawn now probing down the demons' chimney. There he let himself down carefully and lay
still. Only his feet remained clearly visible, like
those of a man laid low by stealthy violence.

At the cell door, Chup paused a moment to try to
seating of his new sword in its sheath, and give a
loosening shake to the nerve-tight muscles of his
shoulders. He thought in wonder that if he were
plotting a real escape for Charmian, instead of this
safe pledging trickery, he would not be quite as
tense as this.

The heavy bar grated as he raised it from the cell
door, and he reminded himself to strive more realis-
tically for silence. Cautiously he turned in the lock
the key he had been given. The massive door swung
outward at his pull. Chup's shadow fell before him
into the uncleanness of the cell. There Charmian
huddled on the floor, wearing the same black clothing of her audience with Som, shimmering garments, slit revealingly, foolish now as rags would
have been at the Emperor's court.

When she recognized Chup, the sharp terror in
Charmian's face turned dull; she had evidently expected visitors even more menacing than he.

He stepped back from the doorway and said in a

low voice: "Come out, and quickly." When she did not move at once he added: "I'm going to try to free you."

The words sounded so utterly false in his own ears that it seemed impossible that clever Charmian could believe them for a moment. But she stood up and came toward him, though hesitantly at first. Her blond hair hung disheveled, half-concealing her face. Without a word she came out of the cell, and stood against the wall, her face averted, while Chup played the game of dragging the shamming guard into the cell and barring up the door again. Then at a motion of Chup's head she followed close behind him as he set foot upon the downward path.

They had gone down perhaps two hundred paces, when Charmian in a small voice broke the silence: "Where are we going?"

He answered, without turning. "We must go down, in order to get out."

Her footsteps behind him stopped. "But down there is where the demons nest. There is no way out, down there."

Startled, he too stopped, and turned. "How do you know? Have you come this way before?"

She seemed surprised by the question. "No. No, how could I have?" Still she was not looking directly at him.

"Then follow me," he growled, and started down again. After a moment her soft footfalls followed. She must believe his masquerade, or she would be screaming at him or pleading. But the evidence of success brought him no satisfaction.

Pretending to be cautious and alert, looking this way and that, pausing now and then as if to listen, he led her down toward the pit. He felt weary and awkward as if he had been fighting to the point of physical exhaustion. It will mean changing yourself, Som had said, you must do violence to your old self. Yet what Chup was supposed to do was basically quite simple, and on the surface there was nothing in it difficult for a bold man. He was to bring her down (by fair words and promises, not by force—that had been emphasized) to the Demon-Lord's chamber at the bottom of this hole. There where she expected a door to freedom he was to give her to the demon. And then he was to run away. If he did not run away, and briskly, the chamberlain had warned him, Zapranoth in his demonic humor might nip him too.

His pledging was a task for one who giggled and ran away, and Chup now liked it less than ever. He did not see how he could succeed, how Charmian could fail from one moment to the next to guess the truth. Well, let her. But no, she still followed him obediently. He realized suddenly how desperate she must have been, how ready to grasp at any hope.

His pretended alertness suddenly became real. From below, where all had been ominous silence, there arose now a murmuring strange sound which he did not at once identify but which he did not like.

The first whisper of it froze Charmian in her tracks behind him. "Demons!" she whimpered, in a voice of certainty and resignation.

Chup had been assured there would be no interference, no distractions, while they were going down. He took a step back, fighting his own fear of demons, trying to think. Thinking was not easy; the sound grew rapidly louder, and at the same time more plainly wrong. It put Chup in mind of the gasping of some unimaginable animal; it made him think of a terrible wind sent blowing through the solid earth.

Now there was light below, a pinkish glow, as well as sound. Chup could make no plan. As if seeking each other's humanity, by instinct he and Charmian put their arms around each other and crouched down on the narrow path. The sound was almost deafening now, a climbing clamor flying upward from the pit. With it came the aura of sickness that accompanied demonic power, an aura stronger

than Chup had ever felt before. The brightening
roseate light seemed to drive back the feebly growing glimmerings of the sun. He clenched his eyes
shut, held his breath—and the rush, as of a multitude of beings, passed by them and was gone.

"Demons," Charmian whimpered once more.
"Yes . . . oh, it seems that I remember them, rushing
by me in this place. But how?"

"What do you remember? Have you been down
this pit?" he rasped at her. He wondered if she was
planning some deception. But she only shook her
head, and continued to avert her face.

He pulled her to her feet and led her down the
curving path once more. What else could he do?
Daylight enough came trickling from above to show
the way. They came to a doorway, but when Chup
peered in there was nothing but an alcove, no way
out. No way out . . . but he must go on to pass his
pledging, to reach the power of the inner circles of
the East.

What else could he do? Down and down they
went, though very slowly now.

Soon it began again, the noise far down below
them, climbing fast.

"It is Zapranoth," said Charmian.

This time a bass quaver, that told of madness
rampant in the foundation of the world; this time
the whole world shuddered and sickened with the
coming up, and the light it cast before was blue and
horrible.

Charmian began to scream: "Lord Z—"

Chup grabbed her, stifling her mouth beneath his
palm, and cast himself and her once more down
upon the narrow curving ledge, this time at full
length, with both their faces turned toward the wall
of rock. With a twisting and a stretching of the uni-
verse, with impacts of great footfalls smiting air and
rock, the blaring, glaring Lord of Demons trampled
past them. If they were seen, they were ignored, as
two ants might have been.

Chup did not see the demon. His eyes had shut themselves, and at the moment of the demon's closest presence all his bones seemed turned to jelly. This must be Zapranoth. Against this, no use to think of showing bravery; compared to this, the demons rising earlier had been small. And the demon who, days ago, had entered his beggar's hovel to heal and threaten him—that one had been a nasty child making faces, nothing more.

When the world was still and sane and tolerable once more, he raised his head, gripped Charmian by the hair, and turned her face toward him. "How did you know that it was him? From far away, when first he started up?"

She looked convincingly bewildered. "I don't know . . . my Lord Chup, I do not know. By his sound? But how could I ever have heard him, met him, and forgotten it? You are right, I knew at once that it was he. But I don't know how I knew."

Chup got slowly to his feet. There was one small comfort: the game he was to play could not proceed until the Demon-Lord came back from whatever unforseen errand had called him out. Chup would have to find some means of stalling until then. But at the moment he could think of no plausible excuse for staying where they were. Slowly he led Charmian downward once again.

They had gone but two more turns around the gradually narrowing chimney when there came a different and more human sound, from far above. It was faint, but to Chup's ears unmistakable—the cry and clash of men at war. Chup listened, knowing now what had called the demons forth. No one in the citadel had thought it possible for Thomas to make a direct assault; well, it was not the first time he had been underestimated.

So the wait for Zapranoth might take some time, though it seemed likely that he ultimately would return triumphant. It was hard to imagine that Thomas could raise a power equal to the Demon-

Lord, even if he could get his army up the pass. Chup grinned the way he did when he felt pain. He led Charmian on down until they came to another doorway opening into another blind alcove. There he took her by the arm and pulled her in.

"What is it?" she whispered, terrified anew.

"Nothing. Just that we must wait a bit."

He expected her to ask him why, and wondered how he could answer. But she only stood there with her eyes downcast, face half-hidden by her hair. Surely this behavior was a pose, part of some plan she was evolving. He had seen her terrified before, but never meek and silent.

Considering what to do next, he sat down with his back against the wall, watching the entrance to their alcove. Almost timidly, she slid down beside him. In her new, small voice she said: "Lord Chup, when I was in the cell, I hoped it would be you who came for me."

He grunted. "Why?"

"Oh, not that you would come to help me, I didn't dare hope that. Even now . . . but I knew that if you came to take revenge, you would be quick and clean about it. Not like Som, not like any of the others."

He grunted again. Suddenly anxious to know what it would feel like now, freed of all enchantments, he pulled her near, so that their mouths and bodies were crushed together. She gasped and tensed, as if surprised—and then responded, with all her skill and much more willingness than ever before.

And he discovered that to him, the touch of her meant nothing. It was no more than hugging some huge breathing doll. He let her go.

To his surprise, she clung to him, weeping. He had never seen this act before; puzzled, he waited to learn its point.

Between her sobs she choked out: "You—you find me then—not too much changed?"

"Changed?" Then he remembered certain things,

that made her puzzling behavior understandable. "No. No, you are not changed at all. Our mighty viceroy was lying about the destruction of your beauty. You look as good as ever, except for a little dirt." For the first time in days Chup could hear his own voice as an easy, natural thing.

Charmian stared at him for a moment and dared to believe him. Her sobs changed abruptly into cries of joy and relief. "Oh, Chup, you are my lord—high and only Lord." She choked on fragments of strange laughter.

Feelings Chup had not known were his came fastening on him now like mad familiars. He could not sort them out or put them down. He groaned aloud, jumped up, and pulled Charmian to her feet. He seized her shoulders, gripping them until it seemed that bones might crunch, while she gasped uncomprehendingly. Then, still holding her with his left hand, he drew back his right and swung it, open-palmed but with all his rage. "That, for betraying me, for using me, for trying to have me killed!"

The blow stretched her out flat, and silenced all her cries. A little time passed before she stirred and groaned and sat up, for once ungracefully. Her hair no longer hid her face. Blood dripped from her mouth and there was a lump already swelling on her cheek. She finally could ask him, in the most dazed and tiniest of voices: "Why now? Why hit me now?"

"Why, better later than never. I take my revenge my own way, as you said. Not like Som, nor any of the others here." Gripping his sword hilt, he looked out of the alcove, up and down the spiral path. Let them come against him now, he was Chup, his own man, and so he meant to die.

When he saw no understanding in her dazed face, he went on: "Shake your head and get it clear. I was not to lead you out of this foul place. I was to play the court jester for Som and Zapranoth; thus should I prove my fitness to join the elite of the East. They will not have a free man's service. They must have

pledgings, and grovelings, and for all I know, kiss-
ings of their hinder parts as well. *Then* will they
open to their tested slave the secrets of power and
the doors of wealth. So they say. Liars. Gigglers at
cripples, and pullers of wings from flies. I know not
if Som stinks of death—or only loadbeast-drop-
pings!"

He felt better for that lengthy speech, and better
still for the action that had just preceded it. Now
there ensued a silence, while his breathing slowed
and Charmian's grew steadier, and she ceased to
moan.

And now once more he heard, from far above, the
clash and cry of many men at arms.

Charmian, her voice now nearly normal, asked:
"Is that Thomas's assault we hear? The one our
generals thought could not be made?"

Chup grunted.

"They of the West bear me great hatred," Charmian said. "But if I've any choice I'll go to them
instead of Som."

"You'd be wise, if you could do so. They in the
West are living men, and many would fall down
swooning at a flutter of your eyelids. What is it
now?"

Some thought or memory had brought a look of
new surprise into her face. "Chup. I have never been
down into this cave before—and yet I think I have.
Things as they happen seem familiar. The winding
path, these alcoves. The sounds the demons make
in passing, and the feelings that they bring—the
wretched feelings most of all." She shivered. "But
how can I have known them, and not remember
plainly?"

His thought was practical. "If you have been in
this cavern, or seen it in some vision, then remember a way out of it, that we can use."

She gave him a long, probing look, with something
in it of her old haughtiness. Her bruised face did

somewhat spoil the effect. "Have you finished now with taking your revenge on me?"

"I have more important things to think of. Getting out of here, now that I've spoiled my pledging. Yes, I'll help you out if you'll help me. But turn treacherous again, and I'll kick you down the pit at once."

She nodded soberly. "Then I'll help you all I can, for I know what to expect from Som. What must we do?"

"You ask me? I thought you might recall an exit from this hole. And quickly. While the battle's fierce, we're probably forgotten."

Doubtfully and anxiously she stared at him. "I think—whether it is memory or a vision that I have—I think that there is no way out for us below." Her voice grew dreamy. "At the bottom of this chimney there are only huge blind chambers in the blackened rock. And strange lights, and the demons roaring past. I would have run back, screaming, but my father gripped my—" She broke off with a little cry, her blue eyes widening.

"Your father led you down here? Ekuman?" Chup did not bother trying to understand that; if it was part of some new and elaborate deception, he could not see its point. He prompted: "How did you get out? If there's no way below, we must go up again. Where does the top of this shaft break out of the mountain?"

She had to make an effort to recall herself, to answer him. "I don't know. I don't think that I was ever at the top of this chimney. It seems to me we entered and left it at the level of the cells . . . Chup, why would my father bring me here?"

Not answering, Chup led her out of the alcove, and started on the long ascent, at a good pace. Little was said between them until they drew near the level of the cells again. Here Chup proceeded cautiously, but there was still no one else in sight. The

cell that had been Charmian's was once more unbarred and open. Every available man must have
been mobilized to fight; but how long that situation
might last was impossible to guess.

He gripped Charmian's arm. "You say you entered
and left the shaft here. Remember a way out of the
citadel that we can use."

"I . . ." She rubbed her head wearily. "I can remember no such way. We should go on to the top.
There must be some exit there, to sunlight if not
freedom."

Chup went up quickly. The sounds of combat
were noticeably louder here.

Still they met no one. The chimney straightened
to show them the gray-blue sky, over a mouth ringed
by ragged outcroppings of rock. The path seemed to
go right up to the mouth and out to unbarred freedom.

Chup and Charmian had only one more circuit of
the chimney to climb, to its outlet barely ten meters
above them, when there appeared there against the
sky the head of a man in Guardsman's helm and
collar, looking down. Before Chup could react, the
man had seen them. He called out something, as if to
others behind him, and withdrew from sight.

"Perhaps I should go first," suggested Charmian,
in a whisper.

"I think so." He would rather not try to fight his
way up this narrow path, against unknown odds.
"I'll walk a step behind you, as your aide." The men
above could not be certain of Chup's and Charmian's current power and status, not even if they
knew she was a prisoner last night. So things went in
the intrigue-ridden courts of the East.

Charmian ran combing fingers through her hair,
put on a smile, and took the lead. With Chup following impassively they marched another half-turn up
the chimney, which brought them into plain view of
the pathway's narrow exit at the top, and of the men
who guarded it. These were looking down with, to
say the least, considerable suspicion. There were

eight or ten of the Guard in view, and Chup noted with inward discouragement that they included pikemen and archers.

Anger in her voice, Charmian called up: "You there, officer! Why do you stare in insolence? Bring cool water to me! We have slipped and fallen and nearly killed ourselves upon your miserable path!" There must be an explanation of her soiled garments, and of Chup's anger marked upon her cheek and lip.

The faces of the soldiers turned from hard suspicion to noncommittal blankness. On Chup's breast the chain that Som had given him still swung, massive and golden, and he made sure it could be seen, at the same time he favored the officer with his best haughty and impatient stare.

The Guards officer—a lieutenant—softened considerably from his first hard pose. He could not keep his new perplexity from showing. "My lady Charmian. I had heard that you—" He shifted his stance. "That is, you or no one else is to be allowed to pass this way, according to the orders I have been given."

"The lady wanted a good look at the fighting," Chup said, guiding her forward with a touch. From the way some of the soldiers kept glancing over their shoulders he guessed that the action was in plain sight from where they stood.

The lieutenant protested. "Lord, why did you not watch from the battlement instead?" But he made no attempt to block their way. Instead he turned to one of his men, ordering: "Here, find some water for the lady."

Charmian and Chup had now come right up to the top of the path, and stood among the soldiers. They had emerged in the midst of the broken plain, roughly halfway between the citadel and the sudden drop-off of the cliffs. Looking out over a breastwork of piled rocks, they had a good view of the fighting, perhaps three hundred meters distant. The fight was not at the moment being carried on with blades, but it was none the less a deadly struggle. Holding the roadhead at the pass were some fourscore men of the West, Chup saw, along with the balloons that must have surprised the defenders. The Guard, or most of it, was drawn up on the plain in battle ranks, but only waiting now.

Above the ground between the battle lines, drifting, like some foul cloud of smoke, was Zapranoth. The power of the Demon-Lord was being turned away from Chup, but still he thought he felt its backlash here, and looked away toward the citadel. Small figures were on the parapet; he thought he could see Som. Above the fort, a single valkgrie droned toward its lofty home.

Charmian finished her thirsty drinking from a canteen handed to her by an awkward soldier. "Oh, captain," she now smiled, dabbing prettily at her sore lips, "I had heard you were a man of gallantry, and I believed it true, and I have climbed that horrible path to reach you. I wish to see the ending of the battle close at hand, not stand with all the timid females behind a wall. Surely if I go out a little way, a little closer, I will still be safe, with you and all these stalwart men of yours at hand?"

"I . . ." The lieutenant floundered, trying to be firm. It was so easy for her. Chup marveled in silence, shaking his head slightly while he took his turn at the canteen. Distant Guardsmen chanted a war cry, and somewhere a reptile cawed.

Charmian was going on. "We do not mean that you should leave your post. The Lord Chup will go with me, but a little way out upon the plain here . . . I will tell you the truth, there is a wager involved, and I feel I must reward you if you can help me win it."

The lieutenant had no more chance than if Chup had come upon him here unarmed and alone. In the space of half a dozen more breaths Charmian was being helped over the barricade of stones, her escorting lord beside her. As they walked out upon the empty, crevice-riven field that stretched away toward the fighting, he heard the reptile again, cawing somewhere behind them; and this time he thought he could make out a word or two within its noise. Chup took his bride by the arm, as if to steady her on the hazardous ground, and she heeded the silent increase of his fingers' pressure. They walked faster. With a stride and a stride and another stride, the barricade, the soldiers, and the power of the East fell meter by meter behind them. Not that the way in front was clear.

" . . . escaaaaped!" came the raw reptile cry, much louder now. "Rewaaaards for their bodies, double reward for them alive! Trraaitor, Chup of the Northern Provinces! Prisoner escaped, Charrrmian of the Broken Lands!"

Chup ran, dodging with every second or third stride to spoil the archers' aim. Charmian, close behind him, screamed as if they had caught her already. Now ahead of him there loomed across his way a chasm, one of the splits that ran in deeply from the mountain's edge. It was too wide at this point for even a desperate man to try a jump. The farther Chup ran the more treacherously uneven grew the footing, and he dropped to all fours to scramble over it, even as an arrow sang past his ear. From the officer's bawled orders not far behind, he knew that close pursuit was right at hand. The reptile now shrieked in triumph right above him. Charmian cried out her panic with each breath, but her cries stayed right at Chup's heels.

He reached the edge of the deep crevice. To follow along it on this footing of broken, tilting rocks would be a slow and tortuous process, and the pursuit could not fail to catch up to easy arrow range at once. To jump across the chasm was impossible. To attempt to scramble down its nearly vertical side would have seemed at any other time like madness, but now Chup unhesitatingly began to slide and grab. Better a quick fall than the demon-pits below the citadel. But all was not lost yet: on a slope this steep there must be overhangs, to offer some protection against missiles from above; and Chup could see now that at a distant bottom the crevice ran out in a dry watercourse and got away from Som.

Chup swung from handholds, danced and bounded, leaping down the slope. Another arrow twirred past him, going almost straight down, and after it the hurtling blur of a slung rock. He started falling, slid and grabbed in desperation, and got his feet upon a ledge that was not much wider than his soles. A moment later he was clutched by Charmian sliding down beside him and almost pulled into the abyss. To his left the ledge all but vanished, then widened into what looked like opportunity, a sizable flat spot under a large overhang. With Charmian still clutching at his garments, he lunged that way. Somehow the two of them scrambled to that spot of comparative safety, on footholds that would have been suicidal if attempted with cold calculation.

They were sheltered from missiles on a flat space big enough to sprawl on carelessly, while they gasped for breath. Somewhere, ten or twenty meters above them but out of sight, the lieutenant was bawling out a confusion of new orders.

The reptile found them almost instantly. It hovered over the chasm on deft and leathery wings, screaming its loathing and alarm, carefully staying out farther than a sword might sweep. Charmian with a wide swing of her arm threw out a fist-sized rock; through luck or skill it caught a wing. The beast screamed and fell away, struggling in pain to stay in the air.

But it had already screamed out their location to the men above.

Chup stood up and drew his sword and waited for the men to come. From the renewed sounds of battle farther off, he soon picked out a closer sound, the scraping and sliding of sandalled feet on rock, too desperately concerned with footholds to be furtive.

"Both sides!" Charmian cried out. A man was sliding down toward them on each side of their almost cavelike shelter. But each attacker had to think first of his own footing. Chup put the first one over easily before the man could do more than wave his arms for balance, then turned quickly enough to catch the other still at a disadvantage. This one, going over, dropped his sword and managed to catch himself by his hands. Only his fingers showed, clinging stubbornly to the ledge, until Charmian, screaming, pounded and shattered them with a rock.

Chup sat down once more resting while he could. As Charmian knelt beside him, he said: "They'll have a hard time getting at us here. So they may just wait us out." He leaned out for a quick glance at the slope below them, it was worse than that above. "I don't suppose you got out by this route the last time you were here."

"I—don't know." Somewhat to Chup's surprise, she lost herself again for a time in silent thought. "I was only a child then. Twelve years old, perhaps. My father led us—" Her face turned up, wide-eyed with another shock of memory. "My sister and I. My sister. Carlotta. I have not thought of her from that day till this. Carlotta. I had forgotten that she ever lived!"

"So. But how did you get out? Not down this cliff somehow?"

"Wait. Let me think. How very strange, so many memories wiped out . . . she was six years younger than I. Now it comes back. My father took us both down the long spiral path. Into the demon chambers at the bottom. There . . . he pushed us both forward, so we fell, and he turned and ran away. I saw his flying robes, while Carlotta lay beside me, crying. Ah, yes. That would have been my father's initiation, his pledging to the East. Ah, yes, I understand it now."

"What happened?"

Almost calmly now, Charmian stared into the depth of time. "We lay there, frightened. And before we could get up, he came for us."

"He?"

"Lord Zapranoth. For his initiation, our father, had to give us to the Demon-Lord." Charmian's eyes now turned on Chup, but still her mind was in the past. "Lord Zapranoth reached for us, and I jumped to my feet and took Carlotta and pushed her in front of me, and I cried out: 'Take her! I am yours already. Already I serve the East'!" Charmian giggled, a pearly ripple of pure music, yet it made Chup draw back slightly. "I cried: 'Now take Carlotta as *my* pledging!' And Zapranoth stayed his hand, that had been reaching for us." Charmian's merriment faded suddenly. "And then he . . . laughed. That was a thing most horrible to hear. Then he put out his hand again, and stroked my h—"

Breaking off with a little shriek, Charmian clutched at the golden hair, that hung disheveled before her eyes, as if it were some alien creature settled on her head. Then she recovered herself somewhat, brushed back her hair and let it go. "Yes, Zapranoth stroked my hair. And later, when Elslood tried to make a love-charm from it—" She stopped.

"All Elslood's magic was confounded and reversed," Chup finished. "And he and every man who carried the charm was drawn to you by it. But never mind that now." He put out his hand slowly, not quite far enough to touch the gold that he had handled with rough carelessness not long ago. He said: "Do you suppose, that on that day—the Demon-Lord—might have left his *life* in this?"

The thought was no surprise to Charmian. "No, Chup. No. Hann examined my hair closely, when we were planning how best to use the charm, trying to find the source of its unusual power. Hann would have found a demon's life if it were there. We could have made the Demon-Lord our servant." She smiled. "No, Zapranoth would not have been fool enough to give his life into *my* keeping. He understood me far too well. When he had touched my hair, he said to me: 'Go freely from this cave, and serve the East. It has great need of such as you.' Yes. Now all the memories come back. My father was much amazed when I caught up with him. Much amazed to see me, and not entirely pleased. Oh, he looked back hopefully enough to see if my sister had also been released. She was the one he favored, truly cared for. But her the demon kept.

"And I think my father also was made to forget what happened here; at least he never spoke of it, or of Carlotta—Chup, what is it?"

He had got to his feet as if to face the enemy again, but he did not raise his weapon, only stared down fixedly at Charmian. Without taking his eyes from her he sheathed his sword and gripped her hands and pulled her to her feet. She twisted as if expecting another blow. But he only held her fast, demanding: "Tell me this. What was his aspect, when you saw him then?"

"Whose?"

"Zapranoth's." Chup's voice was not much louder than a whisper. "What did he look like then, what form did he take?" His eyes still bored relentlessly at her.

"Why, the form of a tall man, a giant, in dark armor. It matters little what form a demon takes. I knew him today, even at a distance, because the feeling he brought with him, the sickness, was the same—"

"Yes, yes!" He let her go. Caught by a powerful thought, he turned away, then turned right back. "You said that your sister was six years old, when the demon took her?"

"I don't know. About that, yes."

"And was she fair of face?"

"Some thought so. Yes."

"That could be changed—a small thing for the Demon-Lord," he murmured, staring past her into space. "What was the season of the year?"

"Chup, I—what does it matter now?"

"I tell you it does matter now!" He glared at Charmian again.

She closed her eyes and lined her perfect forehead with a frown. "It must have been six years ago. I think—no, it was in spring. Six and a half years ago, to this very season. I do not think I can calculate it any more closely—"

"Enough!" Chup slapped his hands together, rough triumph in his face and voice. "It must be so. It must be. The young fool said she came to them in springtime."

"What are you babbling of?" Charmain's temper edged her voice. "How can this help us now?"

"I don't know yet. What happened to your sister?"

Before Chup could finish the question there came a faint sound behind him and he had turned, sword drawn and ready. But the shape that dropped now to the narrow ledge was only a small brown furry creature, half the length of a sword from head to tail.

"Chupchupchupchup." Stretched as if in supplication on the ground, just outside of thrusting range, it opened a harmless-looking, flat-toothed mouth to make a noise between repeated gasps and hiccups. It took Chup a moment to understand this was a repetition of his name.

"Chupchupchup, the High Lord Draffut bids you come." The creature's speech was almost one long word, like something memorized and all but meaningless to the speaker. A beast as small as this one could not have much intelligence.

"I should come to the Lord Draffut?" Chup demanded. "Where? How?"

"Chup come, Chup come. Tell man Chup, now he is hunted, the High Lord Draffut bids him come to sanc-tu-ar-y. Haste and tell man Chupchupchup."

"How am I to come to him? Where? Show me the way."

As if to show Chup how, the little four-footed

animal spun around and bounded off, going up the side of the cliff again with ease, darting between rocks where a man could not easily have thrust an arm. Chup took one step, and then could only stare after it, hoping it might realize he could not follow.

He turned to Charmian. "How do you reckon that? If it's a trap, the bait's being kept safely out of reach, so distant I can't grab for it."

She shook her head, and seemed both envious and mystified. "It seems that you are genuinely offered sanctuary. I've heard that the small animals run the Beast-Lord's errands now and then. Does Draffut know you as an enemy of demons? That might account for it."

Before he could reply there came again the whispery slide of men trying to get at them from both sides. Perhaps they had seen the little messenger run past, and feared their prey was plotting an escape. As before, Chup smote the foe upon his right before the man could get his weapons up. This time the man on the left side was impeded by Charmian's falling at his feet. She had ducked for safety and lost her footing, and now she was clutching at her enemy's ankles while he was forced to concentrate on Chup. Much good his concentration did him with his feet immobilized; Chup's swordpoint tore him open and he toppled. Charmian let go his ankles quickly as his weight cleared the edge.

Chup spun back purposefully to the man he had struck down upon his right. It was the lieutenant of the Guards whom they had duped into letting them pass; he now had dropped his weapons and clung with blood-slippery, failing fingers to the rock. Chup cautiously pulled him in from the brink and cut his throat. Charmian watched, at first without understanding, as Chup continued cutting through the neck, gorily separating head from body.

When the collar of seamless-looking Old World metal was free, he wiped it clean on the lieutenant's uniform and held it up. With two motions of his foot he sent the headless body into the abyss.

By now she understood, or thought she did. Anger was in her voice, perhaps from envy or from fear of being left alone. "You are a fool. The valkyrie will take no unhurt man to the Lord Draffut. And none who does not wear the collar properly around his neck."

"You are not entirely right in that, my lady. I have talked with the soldiers. The valkyries *will* take a man whose collar is off. Provided he is so wounded that his head is severed from his trunk."

Now her face showed that she fully understood his plan. Her anger grew. "Not every dead man is brought to Lord Draffut's domain in time to be restored, nor heals properly."

"Nor has a personal invitation from the High Lord Draffut. Listen, lady, I think you will not be worse off if I go. If more soldiers scramble down here, you may do as well with your eyelashes and sweet voice as I would with a sword. As things stand now, you can't get out of here."

That was true; now she was listening.

He pressed on. "Your situation may be greatly helped if I can go. What I was saying when the animal came is more important now than ever. What happened to your sister?"

"The Lord of Demons took her, as I said. Devoured her, I suppose."

"You *saw* the tall black man do that?"

"I . . . no. He laid his hand upon her, and her screams were quieted. I did not linger to see more."

With a quick movement Chup reversed his sword, and held the pommel of it out to Charmian. "Take this."

She stood in hesitation.

Chup said: "If the Beast-Lord hates demons, as you say, I had better go to him, and quickly."

"Why?"

"To tell him where to find the life of Zapranoth. Now take this and cut off my head."

Holding out the sword and waiting, Chup felt content. True, she might murder him good, or his plan might fail for other reasons. But since he had turned his back on Som and on the East, he felt like his own man again, and that feeling was enough; perhaps it was all that a man like him should try to get from life.

He fought on now to win, to live, because that was his nature. But he was tired, and saw no future beyond this battle. Death in itself had never been a terror for him. If it came now—well, he was tired. Half a year of paralytic near-death he had endured, out of sheer pride, unwillingness to give in. Then, when as if by miracle, his strength and freedom had been returned to him, he had come near throwing them away again, to serve the East—and why? What power or treasure could they offer that was worth the price they asked?

"Strike off my head," he said to Charmian. "A valkyrie must be coming for this collar by now; there'd be one already here if they weren't having a busy day."

She was still hesitating, fearing, hoping, thinking, desperately deciding what course was best for her own welfare. She reached out and took the sword, then asked him: "Where is the demon's life concealed?"

"Lady, I would not trust you with my beheading, save that you must see how it is in your own interest for me to reach Draffut with what I know. If we can kill or threaten Zapranoth, and tip the battle to the West, then you may sit here safely until Som is no longer dangerous. Unless, of course, *you* would rather bear the message; in which case I must cut off your—no. I thought not."

He turned and knelt down slowly, face toward the cliff. Charmian was at his right, holding the long blade point down on the ground. He said: "Now, about this little surgery I need . . . I suppose a single stroke would be too much to ask for. But more than two or three should not be needed, the blade is heavy and quite sharp." Without turning to see her face, he added: "You are most beautiful, and most desirable by far, of all the women I have ever known."

From the corner of his eye he saw Charmian losing her hesitation, gathering resolve, straightening her thin wrists in a tight two-handed grip to lift the weapon's weight. Chup studied the details of the rock wall straight before him.

He had knelt down facing this way so that his head would not roll over—

Enough of that. He was Chup. He would not even close his eyes.

On its way, the sword sang thinly. His muscles cried for the signal to roll away, his nerves screamed that there was still time to dodge. His ruling mind held his neck stretched and motionless.

Before the Citadel

Out near the middle of the tableland that divided the forces of the East and West, in a part of the rough plateau that was shattered and split into a dozen peninsulas divided by abyssal crevices, the High Lord Zapranoth came bursting up into the morning air like some foul pall of smoke, from a huge chimney-opening in the ground. Rolf, turning from his work of grappling down great gasbags, looked up at Zapranoth and saw that which made him squint his eyes half shut and turn away—though he could not have said what it was about the smoke that was so terrible. Looking around him, he could see that only Gray, and Loford who now stood beside his brother, were able to face the demon with their heads raised and eyes wide open. They were standing in the rear of the invaders' little line, near Rolf and the balloons. The smoky image of the technology-djinn was fluttering and darting to and fro above the gasbags, like some frantic bird confined in an invisible cage.

Now Gray raised both his arms. Before the face of Zapranoth there appeared a haze or reflection of light gray, a screen as insubstantial as a rainbow, but as persistent. It stood steadily before the demon as he drifted gently nearer. Now it was possible for the soldiers of the West to look toward him—and toward the citadel, through whose open gate the Guard and its auxiliaries were pouring out, quick-march. Arrows began to fly both ways across the field. When the defenders of the citadel had finished a quick and practiced deployment in four ranks, Rolf estimated there might be nearly a thousand of them. He was too busy to give much time to pondering the odds, for the last balloons were landing now and he and his assistants had all they could do with work and dodging arrows. Each wore on his left arm a light shield woven of green limber branches; such shields were thought capable of squeezing and stopping piercing shafts that could bite through a coat of mail.

"Sound the trumpet once more!" Thomas now ordered with a shout. The Northman with the horn, his head now bandaged, turned back to face the pass—its thread of road still empty—and once more blasted out the signal.

This time there came an answering horn, though it sounded dishearteningly far away.

"There is our army coming, friends!" Thomas shouted in a great voice. "Let's see if we can do the job before they get here!"

As if the distant horn had been a signal for them too, the Guard swayed now in formation to the shouting of its officers, and as one man stepped forward to attack. At a range of a hundred and fifty meters there came from their rear ranks a volley of arrows.

Rolf and those around him, finished at last with tying down balloons, took up their weapons and moved into their places for the fight. Some, holding shields, raised them to protect Gray and Loford. The two wizards still were standing motionless, and gazing steadfastly upon the ominous but also nearly motionless bulk of Zapranoth, high in the air above the middle of the field. Loford was swaying slightly on his feet; there was no other overt sign as yet of the struggle of invisible powers that had been joined.

The horn from down below, within the pass, now sounded once more, noticeably closer; and again as if its signal had been meant for them, the Guard of Som the Dead began to run and came on in a yelling charge.

The broken ground delayed them unequally, so that their lines were bent. Rolf, with bow in hand and arrows laid out before him on the ground, knelt in the middle of a line of archers. He took little time to aim, but loosed into the oncoming swarm of men in black, nocked and drew and loosed again. The air was thick with dust and missiles, and his targets moved confusingly, so it was difficult to tell what damage his own shots were doing. Certainly the ranks of black were thinning as they came. A steady droning sprang up in the air above, as the valkyries whirred industriously, in madly methodical calm they dipped into the fury of the fight below to lift the fallen warriors of Som and take them to the high place of Lord Draffut. Some machines flew through the image of the Demon-Lord, with no awareness shown on either side. It was as if each were unreal to the other, and only humans must know and deal with both.

There was no thought of saving arrows; if this attack was not stopped there would be no need to worry about the next. The man next to Rolf went down, killed by a flung stone. Others were falling in the Western ranks, but those thin lines did not pull back. Behind them was the cliff edge, or defeat and death retreating down the pass. They braced themselves instead, and readied pike and battle-axe and sword.

By now some of the enemy were come so close to Rolf that he could hear them gasping as they ran, and see the hair on hands that lifted swords to strike. Rolf threw his bow behind him and rose up in a crouch, shield on arm and sword in hand.

An Eastern officer, marked by the plume upon his helmet, came running past in front of Rolf, with great arm-wavings urging his men on. Rolf leaped forward to get in striking range, but was checked by another Guardsman charging at him. This foe was running blindly, already berserk with battle, his eyes seemed to look unseeing through Rolf even as he swung a mace. Rolf dodged back, then stepped in—not as neatly as the nimblest warriors could, but well enough to avoid this weapon, only half-controllable. Rolf cut his sword into the Guardsman's running legs, felt shin bones splinter, saw the man go plowing forward on his face.

One of the Northmen on Rolf's left started his own countercharge, striding into the foe, making a desert round him with a great two-handed blade. Those of the enemy who did not fall back before this giant tried to spread around him and get at him from the sides. Rolf hung back a step until he had outflanked the liveliest of these flankers, then lunged in for the kill. The man was more than half armored, but Rolf's sword point found a soft place in between the hipbone and the ribs. As that man fell, another came, but this one straight at Rolf. This new opponent was the better swordsman, but Rolf would not yield an inch. He warded one stroke after another, somehow, until the Northman's long sword on its backswing wounded his enemy from behind. The odds were more than evened, and the foe went staggering back until the ranks of black had hidden him.

Then all at once there were no more of the enemy menacing, but only the retreating horde of their black backs.

"What? What is it?" Rolf demanded. Mewick had come from somewhere and had taken him by the arm.

"—bind it up," Mewick was saying.

"What?" All the world, for Rolf, was still quivering with the shock of battle. He could not feel nor hear nor think of anything else.

"You are hurt. See, here. Not bad, but we must bind it up."

"Ah." Looking down, Rolf saw a small gash on the upper part of his left arm. He could not feel the slightest pain. His shield woven of green limber withes, that had been on his left arm, was all but gone now, hacked to bits. He could not recall now which of his enemies had dealt these blows, nor how he had avoided being killed by them.

The soldiers on both sides were reforming lines, just out of easy arrow range, and binding wounds. And while the valkyries went droning on, without rest or hesitation, some men of the West hurried, at Thomas' orders, to behead the enemy who had fallen among them, gather their metal collars and throw them over the cliff. This was the only way they had discovered to prevent their foemen's restoration. No blow from any weapon that a man could wield could stay a valkyrie from gathering up a fallen man; the Westerners learned this quickly, and then saved their breath and effort and the edges of their blades. They only grumbled and dodged the vicious, blurring rotors that smashed the pikemen's weapons down and broke their fingers when they tried to interfere.

One of Mewick's countrymen was calling: "Look —our boys in sight now, at the bottom of the pass. Look!"

Men turned and gathered, looking down the pass. Rolf joined them, his arm now bandaged and his mind a little clearer. He felt no great emotion at the sight of reinforcements coming.

"They're running now that they're in sight," said someone. "But it seems they've been all day about it."

"Only a few in sight yet, with light weapons. The mass of 'em are still far down."

There was short time to celebrate, even had there been greater inclination. The Guard was fast reforming. Their ranks were still impressively superior in size to those of the invaders, whose small force seemed to Rolf's eye to have been drastically diminished. He started to count how many were still on their feet, and then decided he would rather not.

Now once again the Demon-Lord was drifting slowly closer, his image rolling like a troubled cloud. The screen of protective magic that Gray had thrown up before Zapranoth yielded to the demon's pressure but stayed squarely in his path.

Neither Loford nor Gray had ducked or dodged or moved a hand to save themselves as yet. Around them tall protective shields had been held up, by the minor wizards who had abandoned any thought of dueling Zapranoth themselves. More than one had fallen, by stone or arrow, of these men protecting Gray and Loford. Neither one of the two strong wizards had been struck by any material weapon, but anyone looking at their faces now might think that both were wounded.

A darkness like the dying of the sun fell round the two tall magicians now. It was the shadow cast by Zapranoth as he loomed nearer. And now, for the first time on this field, his voice came booming forth: "Are these the wizards of the West who seek to murder me? Ho, Gray, where is my life? Will you pull it out now from your little satchel?" Still the thin gray screen before him held, but now it flared and flickered raggedly, and still he slowly pressed it back.

"Come now," boomed Zapranoth, "favor me with an answer, mighty magician. Admit me to your august company. Let me speak to you. Let me touch you, if only timidly."

At that Loford gave a weak cry and toppled, senseless, and would have struck the ground headlong if some standing near him had not caught him first.

Now Gray stood alone against the pressure of the dark shape above. He cried out too, and swayed, but did not fall. Instead he straightened himself with some reserve of inner strength, and with his arms flung wide set his fingers moving in a pattern as intricate as that a musician makes upon a keyboard. There sprang up gusts of wind as sudden and violent as the firing of catapults, so men who stood near Gray were thrown to the ground, and dust and pebbles were blasted into the air, in savage streams that crisscrossed through the heart of Zapranoth before they lost velocity and fell in a rain of dirt into the citadel three hundred meters distant.

The image of the demon did not waver in the least. But these howling shafts of wind were only the forerunners, the scouts and skirmishers, of the tremendous power that Gray in his extremity had set in motion; Rolf saw this, glancing behind him over the cliff edge to the west. There where the sky some moments earlier had been azure and calm, there now advanced a line of clouds, roiling and galloping at a pace far faster than a bird could fly. These clouds, confined to a thin flat plane a little above the level of the citadel, converged like charging cavalry upon the waiting, looming bulk of Zapranoth.

An air-elemental, thought Rolf, with awe and fear and hope commingled; he would have shouted it aloud, but no one could have heard him through the screaming wind.

The violence of that wind was concentrated at the level of the Demon-Lord, well above the field where humans walked and fought. Men found that they could stand and swing their weapons though they staggered with the heavier gusts. And now the Guard came charging on again. Rolf put on his arm a shield taken from a fallen Easterner, gripped his sword hard, and waited in the line. While over their heads a torrent of air and cloud-forms thundered from the west to beat like surf upon the image of the demon, men lowered their eyes and worked to injure one another with their blades, like ants at war on some tumultuous wave-pounded beach.

The earlier fight had seemed to Rolf quite short. This one was endless, and several times he despaired of coming through alive. Mewick, howling like the wind, fought this time on Rolf's right hand, and saved him more than once. Somehow he was not even wounded in this attack, which failed as the first one had.

While the warriors fought, the violence of the wind gradually abated; and even as the black-clad host fell back once more in dissarray, the weightless bulk of Zapranoth again came pressing forward.

"Gray!" Thomas, stumbling on a wounded leg, came forcing his way through to the wizard's side. "Hang on, our men are coming!" Even now the first gasping and exhausted troops of the climbing Western army were nearing the top of the pass; the bulk of that army, on its thousands of laboring legs, was now in sight though far below.

Gray slowly, with the movement of an old, old man, turned his head to Thomas. In Gray's face, that seemed to be aging by the moment, there was at first no hint of understanding.

Thomas raised his voice. "You, and you, support him on his feet. Gray, do not fail us now. What can we do?"

The answer came feebly, as from the lips of a dying man: "You had better win with the sword, and quickly. I will hold the demon off till my last breath . . . that is not far away."

Thomas looked round to see that the vanguard of his main army was just arriving at the top of the pass, brave men too exhausted for the moment by their running climb to do anything but sit and gasp for air, and squint up doubtfully at the looming shape of Zapranoth. The winds had driven the demon some distance from the field; whether they had inflicted pain or injury upon him no one could tell save Gray, perhaps. Of the screen of white magic Gray had earlier thrown up, there were only traces left, flickering and flaring like the last flames of a dying fire.

Rolf found it was no longer bearable to look straight at the Demon-Lord.

"One man run down," Thomas was ordering, pointing down the pass to the approaching reinforcements. "Tell any with the least skill in magic to push on before the other, and hurry!" He turned his helmet's T-shaped opening toward Rolf. "Ready the balloons for the attack upon the citadel itself! We must not sit here waiting for the demon to set the course of battle."

Rolf sheathed his sword and turned and ran shouting to rally his crew to the balloons. At his direction men put down weapons, eased off armor, took up tools and ropes. The technology-djinn, still constrained by the spells that Gray had put upon it, obeyed Rolf's orders when he called them out.

When he could look up from his work again, Rolf saw that the Guard of Som had been reformed once more on the plain. The ranks of black were not greatly smaller than they had been at the start of the day's carnage; Guard replacements were trotting out from the citadel wearing torn and bloodstained garments in which they had already been slain once today. But the Guard had missed its chance to push the stubborn West from its small foothold on the height; the trickle of reinforcement up the pass had thickened steadily. Soon it would become a flow of hundreds and of thousands.

There were wizards of diverse but minor skills ascending with the army; each of these as he arrived was hurried to the side of Gray, who still was conscious, though standing only with the help of strong men on each side. But one by one these lesser magicians fell away, nearly as fast as they arrived and sought to relieve Gray of some part of the invisible power of Zapranoth. Some crumpled soundlessly. Some leaped and fell, groaning as if struck by arrows. One man tore with his nails at his flesh, screamed wildly, and before he could be stopped, leaped from the precipice.

Rolf took it all in with a glance. "We are ready!" he shouted to Thomas.

"Then fill your baskets with good men, and fly! We will be with you there."

Most of the survivors of the original assault force, being the type of men they were, had already boarded for the next attack. The wind seemed right. But Zapranoth was coming, rushing now toward them like a toppling wall. Rolf, in the act of boarding his balloon, looked up and cried out at the sight. With the majesty and darkness of a thundercloud great Zapranoth now passed above them; it was as if the skirts of his robe spilled madness and dragged lightning. Two of the balloons burst thunderously, even as the djinn in its invisible cage became a blur of terror. Above the djinn there lowered a drifting fringe of cloud, that in the winking of an eye became a closing pair of massive jaws. With the devouring of the djinn, Gray cried out in despair and pain, and his head rolled loosely on his neck.

Men were running, falling, waving weapons in the air. In the confusion Rolf lost sight of Thomas, who had not yet given the last order to cast off. But there was no doubt what must be done; the balloons were ready, a little wind still held. Even without the djinn they could rise up and drop again upon the citadel.

"Cast off!" Rolf shouted left and right; ropes were let go, and his flotilla rose and flew. The demon that had just passed by now turned, but did not strike at the balloons; perhaps Gray was not yet wholly overcome. As the craft passed over the formation of the Guard, stones and arrows made a thick buzzing swarm around them. Shafts pierced every gasbag, though the padded baskets shielded the men inside. But their flight was not intended to be far.

Lowering again, they reached the citadel's low wall, and for the most part cleared it. Along the top of the wall, behind its parapet, one lean man in black came running toward the invaders as if to fight them all, while others ran away—by his behavior Rolf knew Som the Dead. But in another moment Som was left behind.

Inside the walls, the silent flyers skimmed above a different world, one that was still ordered, peaceful, pleasant to the eye. Trees, hedges, and the rooftops of low sprawling buildings skimmed the basket bottoms. There fled before them women in rich silks and furs, and a few servants in drab dress.

Only one person besides Som remained to watch them boldly. One young servant girl who had mounted a low roof gazed at the balloons, and past them at the battle. Rolf passed near enough to get a good look at her face.

It was his sister Lisa.

X

Lake of Life

———◆——◆———

There was a steady swell of sound, a moaning endless tone so long prolonged in his strange loneliness that Chup could not imagine or remember when he had begun to hear it; and this odd swelling was a light as well, of which he could not remember his first sight, so bright he did not need his eyes to see it, but not too bright for eyes in spite of that.

And it was a touch, a pressure, of an intensity to make it unendurable if it had been felt in one place or even many, but it bore in all directions on every fiber, inward and outward, so all the infinity of opposing pressures balanced and there was no pain. Chup lived encompassed in this swelling thing like a fish within the sea, immersed and saturated and supported by inexhaustible sound, pressure, light, odor, taste, heat of fire and cold of ice, all balanced to a point of nothingness and adding up to everything.

So he lived, without remembering how he had come to be so living, remembering only the soft and singing promise of the sword. He did not waken, for he had not slept. Then: I am Chup, he thought. This is what the beheaded see.

What had jogged him into thinking was the feel of someone prosaically pulling on his hair. He did not open his eyes now, for they were already open. He could see light and soft pleasant colors, flowing downward. Up he rose, pulled by his hair, until he broke with a slow splash of glory back into the world of air, in which his senses once more functioned separately.

He was in a cave. He could not at once be certain of its size, but he thought it was enormous. The overhead curve of its roof was too smoothly rounded to be natural. The upper part of the cave was filled with light, though its rounded sides and top were dark; the lower part, up to what was perhaps the middle, was filled with the glowing fluid from which Chup had just been lifted, an enclosed lake of restless energy. Chup knew now that he had reached his goal, what he had heard the soldiers call the Lake of Life.

Like some gigantic bear reared on two legs, immersed to his middle in the lake, there stood the shaggy figure of a beast. His fur was radiant, of many colors or of none, as if of the same substance as the lake. Chup could not see the creature's face as yet, because he could not turn or lift his head. Chup's head swung like a pendulum, neckless and bodiless, from what must be this great beast's grip on his long hair.

He could, however, move his eyes. Where his body should have been below his chin there was nothing to be seen except receding strings of droplets, not gore, but drops of multicolored glory from the lake. Falling dripping from his neck stump, out of sight beneath his chin, the droplets splashed and merged into the glowing lake whence they had come. Chup understood now that he, his head, had been immersed and saturated in the lake, and that had been enough to restore life, with no least sense of shock or pain.

The grip upon his hair now turned his pendulum-head around, and now he saw the High Lord Draffut's face. It was a countenance of enormous ugliness and power, more beast than human certainly, but gentle in repose. And now Chup saw that in his other hand the Beast-Lord held like a doll the nude and headless body of a man. Like a child washing a doll he held the body down, continually dipping and washing it in the Lake of Life. With the splashing and the motion the brilliance of the liquid intensified into soft explosions of color, modulating in waves of light the steady gentle lumination of the air inside the cave.

And now, in his enormous shaggy hand, very like a human hand in shape but far more powerful and beautiful, the High Lord Draffut raised the headless thing and like a craftsman turned it for his own inspection. Like that of one newborn, or newly slain, the muscular body writhed and floundered uncontrolled. On its skin Chup could count his old scars, like a history of his life. He marked the jaggedness of the neck stump, where Charmian had hacked and sliced unskillfully. From its severed veins the elixir of the lake came pumping out like blood, and tinged with blood.

The hand that held Chup's head up by its hair now shifted its grip slightly. Turning his eyes down once again, he beheld his own headless, living body being brought up close beneath his head. Its hands grasped clumsily, like a baby's, at Draffut's fur when they could feel it. Closer the raw neck stump came, till Chup could hear the fountaining of its blood vessels. And closer yet, until there came a pressure underneath his chin—

His head had not been breathing, nor felt any need to breathe; now there came a choking feeling, but it entailed no pain. It ended as the first rush of lung-drawn air caught coldly in his mouth and throat. Then with a sharp tingle came the feelings of his body, awareness of his fingers clutched in fur, of his feet kicking in the air, of the gentle pressure of the great hand closed around his ribs.

That hand now bore him down, to immerse him completely in the lake once more. Once he was below the surface, his breathing stopped again, not by any choking or impediment but simply because it was not needed there. A man plunged into clearest, purest water would not call for a cup of muddy scum to drink; so it was that his lungs made no demand for air. Then in two hands Chup was lifted out, to be held high before an ugly, gentle face that watched him steadily.

"I came—" Chup began to speak with a shout, before he realized there was no need for loudness. The lake gave the impression of filling all the cave with waterfall-voices, as sweet as demons' noise was foul, but yet in fact a whisper might be heard.

"I came as quickly as I could, Lord Draffut," he said more normally. "I thank you for my life."

"You are welcome to what help I have to give. It is long since any thanked me for it." The voice of Draffut, deep and deliberate, was fit for a giant. His hands turned Chup like a naked babe undergoing a midwife's last inspection. Then Draffut set him, still dripping with the lake, upon a ledge that—Chup now saw—ran all the way around the cavern. This ledge, and the huge cave's walls and curving roof, were of some substance dark and solid as the goblet in which the demon had brought him his healing draught long days ago. The ledge was at a level but little higher than the surface of the lake. Seeing at a distance was difficult in the cavern's glowing air, but at its farthest point from Chup the ledge seemed wider, like a beach, and there were other figures moving on it, perhaps of other beasts who tended other men.

The Beast-Lord said: "I cannot command the valkyries, or I would have sent them for you. If I could choose what men I help, I would help first those who fight against the demons."

Chup opened his mouth to answer. But now that he was no longer bathed in the fluid of life, a great weakness came over him, and he could only lean back against the wall and feebly nod.

"Rest," said Draffut. "You will grow stronger quickly, here. Then we will talk. I would give all men sanctuary, and heal them, but I cannot . . . I sent for you because you are the first man in the Black Mountains in many years who has cared for a fellow creature's suffering. A small beast brought me the news that you had saved it from a demon."

For a moment Chup could not remember, but then it came to him: in the cavern of Som's treasure hoard. Still he was too feeble to do more than nod.

He tried again to study the figures moving in the cavern's farthest reaches, but could not see them clearly, so vibrant was the air with light and life. The ledge Chup rested on was of a dull and utter black, but covered tightly with a film as thin and bright as sunlight, a glowing, transparent skin formed of the fluid of the lake. The film was never still. At one spot there would begin a thickening in the film, a thickening that swelled and pulsed, rose up and broke away, becoming a living separation that went winging like a butterfly. And from some other place there would spring a similar fragment, perhaps bigger than the first, big enough to be a bird, flying up and sagging as its wings melted, but not dying or collapsing, only putting out new wings of some different and more complex shape and flying on to collide in the singing, luminous air with the butterfly, the two of them clinging together and trembling, seeming on the verge of growing into something still bigger and more wonderful; but then diving deliberately together and melting back into the gracefully swirling body of the lake, with their plunge splashing up droplets that fell again into the patterned film that glided shining and without ceasing over the black substance of the ledge.

Feeling some returning strength, Chup raised one hand to touch his neck. Running his fingers all the way around, he followed the scar, thin, jagged, and painless, of his death wound. Once more he tried to talk.

"Lord Draffut, is the battle over?"

Draffut turned his head toward the far end of the

Lake. "My machines are still working without pause. The battle goes on. From what I have heard from beasts and men, the foul demon is likely to prevail, though if the issue were left to swords alone, the West would win."

"Then there is little time for us to act." Chup tried to rise, but felt no stronger than the splashing butterflies of light.

"Your healing is not finished. Wait, you soon will be strong enough to stand. What do you mean, we must act?"

"We must act against the one you call 'foul demon'—if you are as much the demons' enemy as you claim, and I have heard."

Draffut lifted his great forearms high, then let them down, like falling trees, with a huge splash. "Demons! They are the only living things that I would kill, if I could. They devour men's lives, and waste their bodies. For no need of their own, but out of sheer malignity, they steal the healing fluid from my lake, and taunt me when I rage and cannot come to grips with them."

Chup was now able to sit straighter on the ledge, and his voice had grown stronger. "You would kill Zapranoth?"

"Him soonest of them all! Of all the demons that I know, he has done human beings the greatest harm."

"I know where he has hidden his life."

All was silent, except for the sweet seashell roaring of the lake. Draffut, standing absolutely still, looked down steadily at Chup for so long that Chup began to wonder if a trance had come upon him.

Then Draffut spoke at last. "Here in the citadel? Where we can reach it?"

"Here in the citadel he hid it, where he could keep his eye upon it every day. Where we can reach it if we are strong and fierce enough."

The Beast-Lord's hands, knotted into barrel-sized fists, rose dripping from the lake. "Fierce? I can be fierce enough for anything, against obstacles that do not live, or against demons, or even against beasts if there is need. I cannot injure men. Not even—when it must be done."

"I can, and will again." With a great effort Chup rose up, swaying, to his feet. "Som and his demon-loving crew . . . as soon as I can hold a sword again. Lord Draffut, the human Lords of the East are more like demons than like men." Lifting a weak arm, Chup pointed to the distant beachlike place, where people were being cared for by tall inhuman figures. "Who are those?"

"Those? My machines. At least they were machines, when I was young. We all have changed since then, working in this cave, in constant contact with the Lake of Life. Now they are alive."

Chup had no time for marveling at that. "I mean those being healed. If you would fight the demons, fight the men who help them. Turn against the East. Order your machines, beasts, whatever they are, to stop healing Som's troops now."

At that, Lord Draffut's eyes blazed down upon him. "I have never seen Som, let alone acknowledged him as lord, and I care nothing for him. Men come and go around my lake, and use it. I remain. Long before there was an East or West, I lived. From the days of the Old World I have healed human wounds. Weapons were different then, but wounds were much the same, and men change not at all—though to me they then were gods."

Were what? Chup wondered, fleetingly; he had not heard that word before.

Draffut spoke on, as if relieving himself of thoughts and words too long pent up. "I was not in the Old World as you see me now. Then I could not think. I was much smaller, and ran behind human beings on four legs. But I could love them, and I did, and I must love them still. Turn against the East, you say? I am no part of that abomination! I was here before Som came—long before—and I mean to be

here when he has gone. I walked here when the
healing lake was made, by men who thought their
war would be the last. When they went mad and ran
away, I was locked in, with the machines. I—grew.
And when new tribes of humanity came, I was ready
to lend them the collars, and the valkyries' help,
that they might be healed when they fought. And—
after them—came others—"

The High Lord Draffut slowed his angry speech.
"Enough of that. Where is the life of Zapranoth?"

Chup told him, things that he had heard and seen,
and how the pieces seemed to fall together. The
telling was quickly finished, but Chup was standing
straight before he'd finished; he felt his strength
increasing by the moment. "The girl's name is the
same, you see. Lisa. Though I would wager that her
face and memory have been changed. And she has
been here just half a year."

Draffut pondered but a moment more. "Then
come, Lord Chup, and I will give you arms. If there
are men I cannot frighten from our path, then you
will fight them. If what you say is true, no other
obstacle can keep me from the life of Zapranoth.
Come! Swim!" And Draffut turned and swam away,
cleaving the lake with stretching overhand strokes.
Chup dove in and followed, faster than he had ever
splashed through water.

XI

Knife of Fire

Rolf's balloon skimmed lower, dragged against tall shrubbery, and scraped free, but then continued sinking. In the quiet he could hear the gas escaping from a dozen arrow punctures in the bag. Mewick pointed silently at the next hedge ahead of them; this one they would not clear.

Rolf swung up to the basket's rim, and leaped in the instant before they struck the hedge. He hit the ground with sword already drawn—but there were no opponents yet in sight.

In all directions, other balloons were coming down, seeding armed desperate fighters throughout the inner courts and buildings of Som's citadel. But some balloons had missed the walls, or were still going up. Lacking the djinn's help, or guiding ropes to follow, there was no pattern in the landing. Mewick was to assume leadership of the five man squad in Rolf's balloon, once they had landed. But Mewick, like the rest, now stood perplexed for a moment beside the hedge; it was hard to see which was the best way to move to join up most effectively with other elements of the assaulting force. And from this garden they could see no vulnerable target where Som might be hurt with a quick attack.

Only Rolf had glimpsed a goal, and he turned toward it when it seemed as likely a direction to take as any other. He ran toward the place where he had seen his sister, Mewick and the others pounding after him, across empty lawns and over deserted terraces.

The girl was still on the roof. Her face was turned away, toward the battlefield, where like the smoke of burning villages the Demon-Lord hung in the air.

"Lisa!"

She looked round when he shouted, and he knew he had not been mistaken. But there was no recognition in her eyes when they met his, only confusion and alarm.

Rolf started toward her, but then stopped as a squad of men in black appeared, coming in single file round the corner of the building where she was.

He called out once more: "Lisa, try to come this way!" But there was no way for her to manage that right now. The Eastern squad was coming on to block the way. They were only auxiliaries, without the collars of the Guard, and armed with a varied selection of old weapons, but they were eight to face Rolf and his four companions. The eight soon proved to lack the willingness for battle of the five; one of their number they left behind, bleeding his life out in a flowerbed, and others, fleeing, clutched at wounds and yelled and left red trails.

Rolf tried to get another look at Lisa on her roof. But there was no time. Beyond a tall hedge and a wall of masonry, some thirty meters distant, a huge collapsing gasbag showed where another Western squad had landed. These now seemed heavily beset, to judge by the shouts and noises there. Another force in black, ten or twelve men maybe, could be glimpsed through hedges as they hurried in that direction.

Drops of gore flew from Mewick's hatchet as he motioned for a charge. "That way!" And they were off.

The shortest route to this new fight, lay over a decorative stone wall, head high. Rolf sheathed his sword to hurl himself up at full speed and with two hands free to grab. He drew again even as he lunged onward from his crouch atop the wall, and as he leaped struck downward with full force, to kill a

Guardsman from behind. They were in a walled-in garden, with more than a score of men contending in a wild melee. Rolf landed awkwardly, off balance, but bounced up into a crouch at once, just in time to parry a hard blow that nearly knocked his sword away.

Above the garden the huge gasbag, draped with its plastic mail, was steadily collapsing, threatening to make a temporary peace by smothering the fight. But yet there was room to wield weapons. The five beleaguered crewmen of this balloon welcomed with shouts the arrival of Mewick and his squad, and doubled their own strokes. But this time the enemy were Guardsmen, and more numerous than the squad of auxiliaries had been.

The fight was savage and protracted. The West could gain no advantage until the crew of a third balloon had managed to reach the scene, and fell upon the Guardsmen's flank. When at last the Guard retreated, there were but nine men of the West still on their feet, and several of these were weak with wounds. Rolf, bearing only the one light wound suffered earlier, helped others with their bandages. He then began to hack off fallen Guardsmen's heads, but Mewick stopped him.

"We must move on, and find some heart or brain within this citadel where we can strike; let dead men be."

One of the Northmen had got up into a tree to look around. "More of our fellows over there! Let's link with them!"

Over the wall again they went, to where another dozen or fifteen Westerners had joined together, and were setting fires. Mewick was quick to argue with the leader of these men that what they were doing had little purpose, that some vital target must be found. To make his point he gestured toward the battlefield outside the citadel. There the High Lord Zapranoth remained immobile above the Western force; and what the demon might be doing to the men who swarmed like ants beneath his feet was not something that Rolf cared to think about.

But the leader of the vandalizing crew, gestured to the clouds of smoke his men were causing to go up; these, he shouted, were bound to have an effect when they were seen.

And he was right. A hundred black-clad soldiers or more, diverted from the fight outside, came pouring back into the citadel. Som dared not let his fortress and its contents fall.

This Eastern counterattack came with a volley of arrows, then a charge. Rolf once more caught sight of Som himself, entering the fight in person in defense of what might be his own sprawling manor. The Lord of the Black Mountains, gaunt and hollow-eyed, wearing no shield or armor, shouting orders, came striding at the head of his own troops, swinging a two-handed sword. A Western crossbowman atop a wall let fly a bolt at Som. Rolf saw the missile blur halfway to its black-clad target, spin neatly in midair, then fly back with the same speed it had been fired. It tore a hole clear through the bowman's throat.

After that, there were few weapons raised at Som, though he ran straight at the Western line. Hack and thrust as he might, hoping to provoke a counter, those of the West who came within his reach restricted themselves to parrying and dodging his blows. Fortunately he was no great swordsman, and could do little damage to such a line as faced him now, shields at the ready. Once his sword was knocked out of his hands. He grabbed it up again, his face a mask of rage, and leaped once more to the attack. This time the Western line divided just in front of him; Mewick had quickly hatched a scheme to cut off Som and capture him, by a ring of shields pressed round him till he could be immobilized and disarmed. But the opening appeared too neatly before Som, or perhaps some magic warned him; he fell back into the shelter of his own ranks, and thenceforward was content to let them do his fighting. They came on sturdily enough.

Once more, for a time, the fighting was without letup. Then there came another small body of Western troops, fighting their way into the mass, bettering the odds just when it seemed they were about to worsen too severely. The forces separated briefly, the West dragging back their wounded where they had the chance. Rolf, looking again for Lisa, saw that she had remained at her vantage point on the roof. Perhaps she felt safer up there. Looking beyond her, he saw the sign of defeat still in the sky—the brooding shape of Zapranoth.

One of the party who had just joined them had thrown himself down, exhausted, and was answering questions about the progress of the battle outside. Rolf realized that this man and his group had just come from there, had somehow managed to fight their way over the citadel's wall or through its gate.

"—but it does not go well. The old man withstands the demon still, how I do not know. Surely he cannot live much longer. Then Zapranoth will have us all. Already half our army has gone mad. They throw away their weapons, chew on rocks . . . still we have numbers on our side, and we might win, if it were not for Zapranoth. None can withstand the demon. None . . ."

His voice fell silent. The men around were looking at him no longer, but up toward the mountain.

Rolf craned his neck. There, on the high, barren, unclimbable slope, amid the doors where valkyries shuttled in and out, a new door had been opened. It looked as if an outer layer of rock had been cracked away as the door, of heavy dull black stuff, had been swung out. Framed in the opening, there stood what seemed to be the figure of a man, but having a

beast's head, and garbed in fur as radiant as fire.
From inside the mountain, behind this figure, there
streamed out a coruscating light that made Rolf
think of molten metal.

And now he saw that the figure could not be human, for there was a real man beside him; smaller
than an infant by comparison, but armed with a
bright needle of a sword, and clothed in black like
some lord of the East.

"Lord Draffut!" cried out someone in the Eastern
force.

"Who will heal us if he should fall?" another
called.

Other shouts of astonishment came from the
Guard. They, like their enemies facing them, were
lowering their weapons momentarily and looking
up to marvel.

Lord Draffut bent, picked up the man beside him
in one hand, and held him cradled in one arm. Then
striding down the slope Lord Draffut came, walking
boldly on two legs where it seemed no man could
have climbed. It was as if he walked in snow or
gravel, instead of solid stone; for at his touch, rock
melted, not with heat but as if quickening briefly
into crawling life, to quiet again when he had
passed.

Though the Lord Draffut carried no weapon but
one armed man, his attitude and pace were those of
one who came on eagerly to enter battle. Yet from
the ranks of the East there came no cheers. All men
still watched in blank surprise, half of them with
weapons dragging in the dirt. Som himself was peering up as if he could not credit what was happening
before his eyes.

Draffut's great strides quickly brought him close
to the citadel. Then he had entered it, sliding down
the last near-vertical face of rock that served as its
rear wall. Behind him stretched a line of tracks left
in the dead solidity of the mountain.

The men of the West who were inside the citadel contracted their defensive line now, and gripped their weapons tightly; there was no place for them to run. Then gradually they understood that Draffut and his rider were not coming straight toward them—not quite. The tiny-looking man in black raised his bare sword and pointed, and the striding lord he rode accomodatingly made a slight correction in his course. The rider's black garments, it could now be seen, were trimmed with such a motley of other colors as should belong to no proper Eastern uniform.

Rolf was perhaps the first to recognize this man in black-and-motley garb, and no doubt the first to understand that Chup was pointing straight at Lisa on her rooftop. The girl had turned to face Chup; and in the lower sky beyond her, the weightless bulk of Zapranoth was turning too, like a tower of smoke caught in a shifting wind.

The Guardsmen, as Draffut approached their ranks, began shifting to and fro uncertainly, not knowing what the Beast-Lord meant to do, still unable to imagine what had called him forth. Draffut majestically ignored them; they scampered from his path, and like a moving siege-tower he passed through where their ranks had been.

Lisa on her rooftop sprang to her feet, but made no move toward Draffut or away. Her building was not occupied at the moment by either East or West, but the Eastern forces were the closer to it. Draffut after he had passed them paused briefly to set down Chup, who stood with his sword in hand and glaring at the Guard. Draffut himself strode on toward the girl. Taller than the roof he reached toward, he stretched out one mighty arm toward her—

And recoiled. Beneath Rolf's feet the ground leaped like a drumhead, beaten by the shock that had made the Lord of Beasts go staggering back.

Between the girl upon her building, and the High

Lord Draffut, there now stood one who was the tallest of the three. Seemingly sprung from nowhere,
this figure was covered in dark armor, even to seg-
mented gauntlets and closed visor. In the reflections of this metal armor, silent lightnings seemed
to come and go. The world around this Dark Lord
seemed askew to Rolf, and Rolf had the impression
that under the Dark Lord's feet the rocks had
stretched, like taut canvas bearing weights.

And in the instant of his appearance, the cloud-
image of Zapranoth, that had for so long loomed
above the battlefield in domination, had vanished
from the sky.

Now, scattered all across the plateau, inside the
citadel and out of it, bodies of fighting men let
weapons rest, and held their breaths, waiting for
they knew not what. Only the valkyries above still
droned on imperturbably, taking up the slain and
mangled and returning to find more.

Had there been listeners a kilometer away, the
High Lord Draffut's voice would no doubt have
reached them plainly when he spoke. "Lord of Demons, drinker of men's lives! I hear no taunting from
you now. You must maintain a solid form if you will
try to stop what I intend to do today—a solid form
that I can grasp."

The voice of Zapranoth, even louder than Draffut's voice, began before the other had ceased. "Foul
upstart beast-cub, calling yourself lord! Lord of
vermin! Lord of cripples! Though it may be that I
cannot end your life, you will soon wish that it had
ended yesterday."

The two blurred toward each other.

Rolf did not truly see them come together, for
there flashed out from their contact a moment of
blind blackness to engulf him. The men around Rolf
were all blinded too, if he could judge by the multitudinous outcry that sprang up. Even as the men
were blinded, came the shock; Rolf once more felt it

in the mountain underneath his feet, and this time
in the air around him, too, more like a blow than like
a noise.

He fell and blindly clutched the earth. When vision came back, it was to show men of East and West
all crawling, seeking refuge, intermingled for the
moment without fighting, as predator and prey seek
safety from a flood upon a floating log, and keep a
truce.

Rolf tried to rise, to get away, but before he could
regain his feet there sounded in the voice of Zapranoth an awesome bellow of rage. With this cry the
mountain lurched beneath Rolf, and its surface split
like a torn garment. A fine crevice, nowhere wider
than a man's body, ran faster than the eye might
follow it across the walls and gardens and terraces
of the citadel; in one direction it shattered the outer, battlemented wall, revealing the field before
the citadel, where the army of the West had been
stopped and where most of its soldiers still lay
stunned; in the other direction the flying split raced
up through the upper mountain, defining hidden
faults by making them its path. The splitting ceased
before it reached the domain of the Lord Draffut. Up
there the coruscating light still flooded from an
open giant's doorway, and through their smaller
passages the valkyries still flew in and out.

Now when he looked back at them Rolf saw the
two mighty fighters plain. The Lord of Beasts was
biting down upon the armored shoulder of the Lord
in Black. Draffut's drawn-back lips revealed enormous fangs, and these were sunken in. Rolf saw that
wherever Draffut touched the black armor, it moved
and flowed and yielded to the resistless life that
poured from him. Around the demon's waist his
huge beast-forearms, bright with glowing fur, were
locked like mortised logs to hold and crush.

And yet the being in black seemed mightier. For
all the Dark Lord showed of pain, he might have felt

nothing from the bite that seemed to pierce his armor. With his own great arms Zapranoth strove to loosen the hold about his waist. He tested out one counter-grip and then another, working without haste or hesitation. At last he got both his dark-metaled hands clamped to his satisfaction upon one arm of glowing fur. If the metal of his gauntlets ran and dripped with life, he did not heed. Now Zapranoth's enormous shoulders tilted, and he strained. Slowly—very slowly—he began to win.

Rolf cried out, and bit his lip, and tried to move. Some power would not let him take a step toward the fight. He threw his sword at Zapranoth; the spinning blade vanished in midair.

Slowly—ever so slowly—Zapranoth was breaking the grip about his waist. When that was done, maintaining his own grip on Draffut's arm, he bent it farther. Draffut's jaws did not relax their bite, but through them came the muffled outcry of a titan's pain.

Rolf yelled again, and hurled a rock, and picked up another, larger one. Somehow his frenzied rage enabled him to run forward. Caring nothing now for his own fate, he tried to strike the demon with a rock. Turning in their struggle, the giants brushed him aside unnoticed. He felt an impact, and his body soaring. The ground flying up to meet him was the last part of the battle that he knew.

Chup, like all other mortal men, had been knocked down by the repeated rolling of the earth. He had continued to keep in sight the ugly young girl who clung to the swaying rooftop, her bright eyes fixed now on the giants' struggle. Then the opening crevice had split the mountain between Chup and the object of his attention. Even while the earth was still heaving like a ship's deck, Chup gathered his resolve and crossed the narrow chasm with a lunge, nearly falling into it though it was scarcely wider than his body.

Behind him he heard Draffut's muffled cry of agony, as his arm was mangled in the demon's grip. Chup did not look round. He ran on toward the building where Lisa was. Now it was so close that the roof and the girl on it were out of his field of vision.

"Will you still nurse at my shoulder, beast?" It was the roaring voice of Zapranoth. "I have no milk to yield! Bah! If I tore your arms off, no doubt you would nuzzle at me still." A brief pause. "But I can see a way to cause you greater pain than that, vile animal. All you care for is your Lake of Life. Now look! See what I do!"

Chup did not look, but jumped to grab the roof. His fingers slid on marble and he fell; when he hit the ground again, he did look back. Despite the untroubled speeches of the demon, his right arm in its armor was now hanging almost motionless, below the unrelenting pressure of Draffut's fangs. But Zapranoth's left arm was free, and with a barrel-sized armored fist he now smote down into the split that climbed the mountain. Twice he struck, a third time and a fourth. With each blow the mountain shook and rumbled; with each rumbling the crack widened by a little and lengthened generously. Draffut, his limbs broken-looking, his fur now dulled and matting, seemed helpless to do anything but cling to the demon with his jaws.

With the last blow of the demon's fist, the lengthening crevice broke into the doorway from which Draffut had come down; and with that the rumbling of the tortured mountain ended, in a sound as of a great clear bell. For a moment all was still. Then through the broken, distant doorway the Lake of Life came spurting, a flood of fiery radiance, leaping, pouring down, dazzling even in full sun.

At the draining of the lake, there came from Draffut's tight-clamped jaws a howl more terrible than anything that Chup had ever heard. Beneath the loose fur of the Beast-Lord's neck, his muscles bulged, as if he tried to tear the demon's shoulder off. Now Zapranoth, too, let out a wordless cry. Struggling as savagely as ever, the two of them rolled away, while both armies fled in panic from their path. Meanwhile the lake came down the mountain in a thin but violent stream, sliding into crevices and up from them again, leaving in its pathway rock that knew the taste of life and moved, before it sank as if reluctantly into being not-alive again.

At this latest shuddering of the earth, the building before Chup, like many others in the citadel, collapsed. The walls bulged out and crumbled almost gently, the roof caved inward with a noise that was not loud amid the greater thunders of the mountain. Chup stayed on all fours, crawling forward into the fresh ruin. He quickly found the girl, covered with dust from the masonry that had collapsed beneath her, but showing no sign of any great hurt. Sprawled on her belly on a mound of stones, she drew in gasps of air as if readying a scream. A place on her forehead bled a trickle, and she stared dazedly at Chup and past him.

A burning brazier inside the structure had been crushed, and Chup poked together its spilled coals, lighted no doubt when this day had been a peacefully chilly autumn morning. He fed in splinters from a broken beam until he had a hardy little fire. When the girl looked at him with some understanding, and began to sob, he asked: "Remember me, young Lisa?"

She only sobbed on. She moved a little, but she was still dazed.

"Don't be afraid. This will not hurt you much." He tried to hide the dagger from her with his arm as he moved it toward her head. There seemed to be no doubt where the exact place of hiding was. The dark brown mass of Lisa's hair was bound up carefully, like the hair of ten thousand other peasant girls across the countryside.

This was the girl who had appeared, seemingly from nowhere, at the house of Rolf's parents, at the same time that Charmian's sister had been left with the Lord of Demons. Rolf's people were obscure farmers, then seemingly remote and safe from wars and magic. No one searching for a hidden thing of power would have had reason to search them.

But six years passed, and war came there. By accident Tarlenot carried off the girl as he had taken others. Whatever rough disposal he might have made of her, her hair would not have been so tidily cared for. In a dream or vision the Dark Lord came, and worked hypnotically; and Tarlenot forgot his own designs, and took the girl right to the citadel. There were no more safe farms; Zapranoth would hide his life where he could see it, and be quick in its defense. So Lisa had been taken to serve a sister who did not know her because both of their minds had been altered by the demon, and because the appearance of the younger girl had probably been changed as well . . .

She closed her eyes and moaned when Chup set his dagger's edge to the tough cord by which her hair was bound. When the cord parted, a feeling like the shock of combat ran up the dagger to his hand. It was the first hard evidence that he was right. Lord Draffut, he implored in silence, clamp down your bite and hold the demon occupied. Hold him but a little longer.

The dagger Draffut had given Chup was virginally sharp; he held it like a razor, and severed the first long strands. The girl came out of her daze, then, to scream and try to fight, and he reversed his grip on the dagger and clubbed her quiet with the hilt.

He dragged her limp form closer to his little fire, and laid the first of the cut hair carefully beside the flame. With proper shaving gear, or at least water, the business would have gone more smoothly. But

Chup had little inclination and no time to be squeamish; beads of blood came upwelling from the scalp as he shaved rapidly and thoroughly. The girl moaned, but did not move.

Chup noticed first a strange, deep silence all around him. But he did not look round. Then, somewhere nearby, there spoke the voice of Zapranoth, in all its power and majesty: "Little man. What do you think that you are doing there?"

Chup's hands began to shake, but without looking up or pausing he forced them to shave another swath. He could sense the power of Zapranoth above him, descending onto him—the full power of Zapranoth, whose mere passing in the cave had turned his bones to jelly. Chup sensed also that as long as he kept his full attention on his task, he could balance on a perilous point above annihilation.

"What you are doing is a nuisance to me. Cease it at once, and I will see to it that your death is quick and clean."

Once pause, at this stage of his work, and he would never work again, nor fight nor play nor love. Chup knew it by some inner warning: do not stop, look, turn. Hands that had mangled the Lord of Beasts would close upon his merely human flesh. Though Chup's own hands threatened to disobey him, he made them shave more hair and set it by the fire.

"Put down your knife and walk away." Zapranoth's voice now was not loud so much as it was overwhelming. It seemed impossible that anyone could say—or even think or hope—a word in contradiction. Chup felt his concentration slipping. In a moment he would answer, he would turn, he would face Zapranoth and die.

"Powers of the West!" he cried aloud. "Come to my help!" His hands meanwhile kept at their work.

"I am the only power who can reach you now, and

what you are doing arouses my displeasure. Put down your knife and walk away. I repeat, you shall have a clean death if you do—clean, and far in the future, after a long and pleasant life"

Lisa-Carlotta' face was changing, as the last of her hair was taken off. The ugly proportions of her nose and jaw and forehead flowed and melted into shapes of beauty, as some pressure that had steadily deformed them was removed. She whimpered, in a new and lighter voice. In spite of her dirt and her raw, oozing scalp, Chup thought he could see Charmian's sister in the unconscious face.

"Put down your knife," said Zapranoth, "or I devour you. You will join your whining Beast-Lord in my gut, where both of you can cry forever."

Chup turned, but just enough to feed a little more wood into the fire, still not looking up toward the demon. Then between thumb and finger Chup lifted a lock of Zapranoth's life from the dark brown pile beside the flame. He tried to think how Western wizards worded their spells, but he could not remember ever hearing one of them. True, it might not be necessary to say anything at all, with Zapranoth's life right in his hands. But he suspected that against such an adversary, all the help that he could get would not be too much.

In his insistent, overwhelming voice the demon said: "Far from here is a mountain that I know of, having hidden in it gold in amounts undreamed of even by Som the Dead. I see now, Chup of the North, that I have greatly underestimated you. I am prepared to bargain, to avoid the trouble you can cause me."

And Chup fed the first of Zapranoth's life into the fire, saying: *"You will fall by the flame. The knife of fire is in your head."*

The words were rather good, Chup thought, pleased at his own unexpected power of invention. From outside there came what might have been an indrawn breath, but was a sound too deep for human ears to fully register. Then Zapranoth said: "I am convinced, Lord Chup. From now on we must deal as equals."

Very good, thought Chup. What to say next?

"Your ears are cut off."

"I submit to you, Lord Chup! You are my master, and I will serve no other, so long as you permit me to survive! As good beginning to my service, let me take you to the golden mountain that I spoke of. Deeper inside it even than the vault of gold, lies buried an emerald so great —"

Chup opened his mouth and found words coming to him. *"Opening him with this knife of fire. Separating flesh —"*

The scream began in the mighty voice of Zapranoth, but ended in the shrilling of a woman. She cried out then: "Ah, mercy, master! Burn me no more. To you I must show myself in my true form." And Chup without stopping to think looked out of his ruined building, and saw a young woman stretched out on the ground, clothed scantily in her own long hair of fiery red, and in her one body she was all the women he had ever yearned to have, yes, Charmian among them. To Chup she stretched out her imploring arms. "Ah, spare me, lord!"

He craved no more the gold and emeralds of the East, but this temptation could have moved him. Still, he knew better than to heed another lie. He burned more hair.

"Separating flesh, piercing hide. I give him to the flames."

The woman screamed again, and in mid-scream her voice belonged to something else, surely nothing human, and surely not the powerful Lord of Demons; but yet it was Zapranoth's. With shaking hands Chup fed more hair into the crackling flame. He was somehow making up the words he needed, or they were being sent to him.

"In the name of Ardneh —"

Where had that name come from? Where had he heard it, before now?

"In the name of He-Who-Wields-The-Lightning, Breaker of Citadels,
I fetter Zapranoth.
I fetter him with metal.
I make his members
So that he cannot struggle.
I force him to vomit what is in his stomach."

Chup looked outside. The image of the woman was gone, and in its place lay something huge, that made Chup think of greasy ashes, and of a mound of corpses on a field of war. The thing was fettered in mighty hoops of shining metal, and the labored breathing of it sounded like the wind. The greasy ashes stirred and struggled, made heads and tails and many-jointed limbs, but could not get from out the binding bands. And now a mouth larger than any of the others appeared, yawning as if forced open from inside, and from it there tumbled forth all manner of wretched people and beasts. The people wore the clothes of many lands, or none at all, and rolled about and lay stunned and crying like newborn babes, though most of them were grown. Among them were some soldiers of the West, their weapons still in hand. And there was one huge figure, that Chup recognized . . .

Tumbling back to life from what had seemed the bitterest of nightmares, the High Lord Draffut gave no immediate thought to his own condition, or to the outcome of the battle, or to anything except the ruin of his lake. Disregarding the ruin and confusion that surrounded him, he raised his eyes at once to what had been his high domain. The radiant cascade of the lake had slowed to a mere trickle. It was draining with the new finality of death.

He rushed at once to climb the slope behind the

citadel. Power remained in him to melt the rock to life, and make it form holds for his hands and feet; the power absorbed through ages of his dwelling in and near the lake, that would not let him die, that healed his bones almost as fast as they were broken. Only this life-power let him bear the shock when he had mounted to his lake and found it a drained shell, cracked at the bottom like a broken egg. The dull, black fabric of its inner lining, the only material the Old World had devised that could resist the quickening force of pure life-principle—this shell remained, now for the first time in his memory marked by no shifting patterns or gay butterflies. The healing machines, their lives already fading, hopped and struggled feebly, like dying frogs in a drained pond.

Draffut did not stand long within the broken doorway, gazing at the utter ruin of his life and purpose. The cries from down the slope came to his ears. Human cries, from the battlefield, of men in deadly need and fear. He moved to answer them, without stopping to consider what he might be able to do.

Down the slope again he went, walking at first, then quickening his strides into a run. Before him like a trodden anthill lay the demolished citadel and its swarming men. Here and there they were still fighting one another. But there were no more valkyries in the air.

Close before Draffut one of them lay motionless, smashed by a fall, rotors bent and body broken with the violence of its crash. A look through the sprung-open belly doors showed Draffut that the man inside was cold and dead. Draffut, raging, picked up the machine, shook it and shouted at it. Where his hands touched the metal it stirred with faint life; but that was all. Only now did the magnitude of what had happened come home to the Lord Draffut with full force. Even if he could somehow repair or vivify this machine, there was nowhere for it to go, no healing possible for the dead man inside. Nor for any of the others who now lay upon the field, or who might fall tomorrow.

Far down the mountainside, near where the great crack in the mountain had shattered the citadel's outer wall, a bright gleam caught Lord Draffut's eye. It was the many-colored radiance of the lake, trapped in a small pool in the rocks. At once he tore the battered flyer apart, pulled out the corpse inside. Cradling the body tenderly in one arm, he hurried on.

Reaching the small pool, not much bigger than a bathub, he found that some of the wounded of both armies had sought it out already, were sprawled beside it drinking, or splashing the fluid on their wounds. Picking his way carefully among these injured men, Lord Draffut reached a spot beside the radiant pool. He dropped into it the dead man he carried, then set himself to disperse healing to as many as he could.

With every passing moment, more wounded, mostly Easterners, were crawling and staggering to the place. A groaning, demanding throng grew rapidly around the Lord of Beasts. The level of the fluid in the pool sank rapidly as well—rock could not hold it in for long—and Draffut crouched low beside it, scooping up healing handfuls which he poured into mouths or onto wounds. The dead man he had carried here was sitting up and groaning now.

Draffut splashed a remnant of the lake onto a mangled arm-stump, whose owner shouted with the ending of his pain; perhaps a new and proper arm would grow. Another man, his belly opened, came sliding in blood to reach the pool, and Draffut poured for him an end of agony.

Amid the general cries of pain, and with his dazed concentration on his task, Lord Draffut did not notice when a different, heartier voice, raging and commanding, was raised in the rear of the rapidly growing throng about him.

"—back to your ranks, malingerers! The enemy still holds the field. You who can walk, rejoin your units, cowards, or I'll give you wounds . . . Guardsmen! Take up your arms and fight for me!"

Nor did Lord Draffut, in his dazed state, fully notice what was happening when this shouter came raving, scattering wounded Guardsmen from the pool with blows of the flat of his sword. Draffut was aware only of one more victim reeling toward him, with sunken eyes and the stink of terrible gangrene. Draffut scooped up for this one a generous handful, and threw it accurately. From his hand the fluid of the lake leaped out, a clear and innocent serpent in the air. Only in that instant did the sunken eyes of the raving, raging man meet those of Draffut, in a look that the Beast-Lord would long remember; and only in that instant did Draffut know who this man was.

The splash of liquid struck. A maddened shout ceased in mid-syllable, a sword dropped clanging to the ground. Then nothing more was heard or seen of Som the Dead. He and his portion of the Lake of Life had vanished from the world of men.

" —with the knife of fire I cut off feet and hands,
Shut his mouth and his lips —"
The bellowing of Zapranoth grew louder and more desperate, and at the same time became more muffled.

"Blunted his teeth,
Cut his tongue from his throat.
Thus I took away his speech,
Blinded his eyes,
Stopped his ears,
Cut his heart from its place."
The fire swam before Chup's eyes, and the

exhaustion of the magician, a feeling new to him, seemed to weaken his every bone. Once more he begged the powers of the West to send him words, for it was growing very hard to think. Then summoning his strength, he shouted:

"I made him as if he had never been!"

Silence had fallen all across the riven plateau of the battlefield; in silence the army of the East had begun to turn to desperate flight or to surrender. Looking where Zapranoth had been, Chup could see no more metal hoops, no more heap of greasy ashes, nothing.

But in his mind still spoke the Demon-Lord: Master. Yet a very little of my life remains. Save that, and from it all the rest can be remade. My powers can be restored, to raise for you an army to lead, to build for you your kingdom—

Chup with great care gathered the last hairs, while beside him Lisa-Carlotta moved her mistreated head and once more opened her dazed eyes.

"His name is not any more.
His children are not.
He existeth no more.
Nor his kindred.
He existeth not, nor his record;
He existeth not, nor his heir.
His egg cannot grow.
Nor is his seed raised.
It is dead.
And his spirit, and his shadow, and his magic."

Thus was the Lord of Demons, Zapranoth, destroyed, and thus did Chup of the North earn a place in the army of the West. His bride was searched for, especially where some said they had seen her pass, descending along a new path created by the splitting of the mountain. But she was not found.

When the last drops of his lake were gone, the great Beast-Lord Draffut fled to somewhere where there were no cries of wounded men.

"Lisa?" Rolf of the Broken Lands had come to

speak to the unrecognizable girl who, they said, had been his sister once.

"Rolf." She knew him, but her voice was dull. She was inconsolable—not for her own pain, not for the East's defeat, nor for any of the fallen—save one.

"My Dark Lord," she said. "My strong protector. He was all I had."

Book Three

Ardneh's World

I

Ominor

———◆◆———

They were preparing a man for death by slow impalement, for the amusement of the Emperor, who sat in meditative silence amid the blooming drowsy richness of his garden. On the sloping lawn a little below his simple chair, the sharpened stake had been erected in a space framed by formal plantings of tall flowers, among which bees buzzed richly. A few meters beyond that the garden ended at a low sea-wall of stone, and beyond the wall the vast calm lake began. So close was the wall to where the Emperor John Ominor was waiting that with a little effort he might have made a jewel—there was no other kind of stone in easy reach—go splash.

In his view the lake stretched east to meet the sky, and in that sky there frowned a lone high thunderhead, its cloudy base below the watery horizon. Something in the appearance of the cloud suggested a giant air-elemental, but of course that could not really be. The demons charged with the defense of the palace would long since have taken the field against any such intruder, and the sky above the lake would no longer be innocent and summery.

The man who was to die—there was supposedly some evidence to link him with a plot against the Emperor—let out his first unbelieving cry, as the sharpened wood began to have its way with him. Ominor had not been paying close attention, he had larger matters on his mind today, but now he uttered a small sound of satisfaction and leaned back a little in his chair.

The Emperor of all the East appeared to be neither old nor young (though in fact he was very old indeed) and was not noticeably thin or fat. His coloring approximated the human average. His clothes were simply cut, and were for the most part white, with here and there fine trimmings of deep black. Around his neck on a transparent chain there hung a sphere of black, the size of a man's fist, shining as if with oil. It was nowhere pierced by any fastener, but held to the chain by being enclosed in a light basketwork of silver filaments.

While listening to his entertainment, John Ominor gazed out across the near-monotony of the watery plain. Much closer than the thunderhead, but infinitely smaller, a pair of wings were beating, with gradual enlargement. A courier reptile, who perhaps embodied the final relay of a message that had started halfway round the world. This pleasant confirmation of his power crossed the Emperor's mind vaguely; time enough later to discover if the messenger brought good news or bad. His gaze dropped to a fishing boat, that sculled past no more than half a kilometer from shore. His eyes followed a fisherman now, but yet his mind was elsewhere.

Today Ardneh was coming to the palace.

By electronics and witchcraft the Emperor had sought round the whole earth for his most tenacious enemy. At first the objective of the hunt had been simple: to find and kill. Then, when it had become apparent that finding Ardneh's life might be endlessly difficult if not impossible, the searchers' efforts had been bent toward arranging contact, negotiations.

Of enemies John Ominor had plenty, both within and without the power structure he controlled; but Ardneh was unique.

The noises of the impaled man were wholly animal now, and the Emperor turned to watch for a few moments. But he could not relax and enjoy himself, as he had planned to do for a few moments before confronting his visitor. The meeting was now less than an hour away. And Ardneh was beginning to loom too large.

True enough, most of the West looked to Prince Duncan of Islandia as their foremost leader. And Duncan was certainly formidable; he was now maintaining an army on this very continent, where Ardneh's seaboard territory, the Broken Lands and a few other contiguous provinces, gave Duncan a strategic base in which to rest his forces between campaigns. Ominor of course continually planned reoccupation of the seaboard, but somehow could never quite amass enough troops and demons and materiel for the job, not while he was distracted and his strength was drained by a hundred other guerilla conflicts and rebellions around the world. And Duncan would never remain for long in his coastal stronghold, but pour his army out again like some uncontainable liquid into the heart of the continent, where among the vast forests and plains Ominor's generals would fail once again to bring him to decisive battle.

Not far from the sea-wall, and from where the Emperor sat, there stood a summerhouse roofed with dark glass and sided with viny trellises. Glancing toward this shelter, the Emperor saw that his councilors were beginning to assemble within it.

Eight high subordinates had been summoned to attend the confrontation with Ardneh. All wore fine black garments edged and piped with white, negative images of the Emperor's own distinctive garb. When he had counted the six men and two women into the summerhouse, John Ominor rose from his chair and without haste walked down to join them. The two torturers left off their careful work for a moment to fall with foreheads to the ground as he passed near. Ominor glanced with passing amusement at the victim on his stake, boldly upright as if in insolence, and unlikely to be punished for it.

Inside the summerhouse, the eight remained with foreheads against the sandy floor until he had taken the chair at the head of the long table. Then they seated themselves in order of precedence. He was certainly the most ordinary-looking of the nine assembled.

There were no formalities; Ominor simply looked enquiringly at the man who sat at his right hand. This was his chief wizard, the High Sorcerer of all the East, who had many names but was at present known simply and conveniently as Wood.

Wood understood at once what question he was required to answer. He said flatly: "Ardneh is not a human being." Today Wood himself was wearing his most human aspect; he appeared old and gnarled, like some ancient tailor with bowed legs and stringy-muscled arms. He had a big, bent nose, and oddly bulging eyes that very few folk cared to meet.

"Some elemental power, then," the Emperor commented. When confirmation of his statement was not immediately forthcoming, the Emperor added quickly: "Surely Ardneh is not a beast?" Ominor's speech as usual was loud and quick, and as usual it was difficult for his hearers to gauge the exact degree of his impatience.

Wood answered quickly, daring to look his Emperor in the eye. "My Supreme Lord, Ardneh is neither man nor woman, and surely he is no beast. He is therefore a power, but I hesitate to call him elemental. And I think he is not a djinn. He fits no known category. I must confess that there are things about him I do not yet understand."

"An understatement, surely. Keeping in mind this persistent lack of understanding, what do you propose we do today?"

"That we proceed as planned, my Supreme Lord." The answer came without noticeable hesitation. Wood could scarcely have maintained his rank just below the Emperor without considerable courage, as well as the proper amount of prudence. Around the table the seven other councilors were waiting, still as carven images. Abner, High Constable of the East, commander of Ominor's armies, sat straight backed at Ominor's left hand, a thick muscle bulging in his neck as he looked with unreadable eyes past the Emperor at Wood. The Emperor was silent, watching Wood as he might have watched a prisoner on trial. But it was the way he looked at everyone.

Wood went on: "If Ardneh is so powerful that we cannot defend ourselves from him here, at the center of our world . . ." With a little shrug he let the sentence trail off.

For a few moments no one in the summerhouse spoke. From the middle distance came the gurgles of the wretch who labored hard at dying on his stake. Then Ominor lifted his weighty gaze from Wood, and flicked it toward the foot of the table. "You who labor in the uncommon arts, what can you tell me today that I have not already heard?"

The junior of the two technologists present only bowed his head in answer, while the senior stood up as spokesman, stammering: "V-very little, Supreme Lord. The electronic direction-finding stations continue in operation, and sites for two new stations have been established since our last meeting. But where the life of Ardneh may be hidden, that we still cannot say." Candor, even about failures, was the least dangerous course to take with Ominor. All who survived as his top aides had learned this well.

Most of the others around the table were indicating by their expressions how scornful they were of such esoteric methods as the two technologists were striving to employ. Technology was well enough in its place, making wheels for wagon or chariot, forging swords with hammer, bellows, and anvil. But no one understood electronics, no, not even the technologists who played with Old World gear.

Ominor was not so scornful. The Western enemy had more than once used unorthodox technology with good success.

"Let me hear what the rest of you have to say," the Emperor ordered now, sweeping his eye around the circle. "Can any one of you give me a reason why we should amend or delay our plan for meeting Ardneh?" None could; they murmured one by one, bowed, and shook their heads. The Supreme Lord touched that which hung around his neck, the sphere of blackness on its crystal chain. "And this is what I had best offer Ardneh as a bribe?"

Again the councilors murmured, in a consensus of approval. No one knew exactly what the sphere was, though it was certainly some Old World artifact. Its interior structure, visible only to wizards and quasimaterial, inhuman powers—and presumably to its makers as well—was complex and incredibly beautiful. Demons, djinn, and elementals exposed to the sphere seemed to find it the equivalent of a giant ruby or emerald in human values.

Facing back toward his chief wizard, Ominor returned to an earlier theme: "And what danger will he be to us here, Wood, if he does come?"

"No danger at all, Supreme Lord. My demons and subordinate magicians at every level are alert. Some of the supposedly neutral powers who acted as go-betweens in arranging this meeting are—as you know, Supreme Lord, but some of your councilors may not—secretly in our service. Ardneh has been too distrustful of them to let them find out much about him, but they report no indication that he is planning any attack on us today. Would that he did attempt to strike at us! To do that he would have to gather his full presence here, not only, so to speak, send us his eyes and ears and voice and little more. The more powerful his manifestation, the more he will render himself vulnerable. My demons are ready, their jaws will close upon him." Behind the wizard Wood, above the innocent lake, the air shimmered for a moment, and there were visible in it three pools of shadow, distinct for a moment despite the sun. Then the air steadied, and all was azure summer once again. Wood went on: "I earnestly desire that he will try to attack us here today, but I fear he is too clever."

But Ominor did not seem satisfied. His manner was that of a probing judge. "Our potential visitor, whom you say your powers are set to spring upon, slew the great demon Zapranoth, in the Black Mountains, as easily as a man might crush a toad. So you have reported to me."

Wood blinked, and then it almost seemed he smiled. "Zapranoth of the Black Mountains, Lord? Yes. But do not attach too much importance to that. To the least of these three powers in the air behind me now—to the least of them, Zapranoth was vassal. Of demons greater than these three above the lake there is only—one." Wood's voice dropped on the last word, but still it seemed to have a special emphasis.

The plan for a direct confrontation with Ardneh had been Ominor's own idea. A month ago he had broached it to his council arguing thusly: The power called Ardneh was certainly a sore annoyance to the East, though (as yet, at least) he could not be considered a mortal threat. Ardneh seemed to seldom or never appear in his own form, if he had one. Instead he worked in one human avatar after another, subtly possessing or influencing men to his own ends, which seemed to be in general agreement with those of the West, though

Western wizards were thought not to have any certain control over Ardneh. Usually Ardneh worked so smoothly and carefully that his chosen host or partner seemed to feel that he was acting on his own. Only the greatest wizards on both sides of the war, and the high leaders they advised, were fully aware of how much the recent successes of the West were due to Ardneh.

Growing impatient of managing any direct attack upon this subtle foe, Ominor had settled on subversion, laced with treachery, as a logical alternative.

Now in the garden the cries of the impaled man were weakening rapidly. The torturers had prudently withdrawn a little distance, to be well out of earshot of the conference in the summerhouse, and as a consequence the victim seemed likely to enjoy a relatively rapid death.

Ominor, as the executioners had judged, was paying no further attention to the diversion. Having completed his brooding, almost accusatory survey of his aides, he got to his feet and said: "Then let us bring him. On with it."

The conference broke up. The lieutenants of the powerful councilors hastened to them to receive orders. Soon all the garden back to the ivied palace wall was cleared of common soldiers, slaves, and everyone else not concerned directly with the coming confrontation. The torturers before they left were told by Wood that they might let their victim stay, told by Wood who nodded to himself as he spoke and thought that he saw opportunity here.

Explaining his thought to his Lord of Lords, the wizard said: "Ardneh has in the past once or twice possessed such a victim and acted through him. We shall have him, if he dares to try that trick today."

Ominor thought briefly, then nodded his agreement. Followed now by a deferential train, he left the summerhouse and moved a short distance to where Wood's assistants were beginning to set the stage for the encounter. This was on a flat paved place some ten meters square, bordered on one side by the low balustrade that guarded the sea wall's outer edge, the lake rippling and chuckling some four or five meters below. The Emperor beheld several of Wood's most able aides, master wizards themselves in any company but his, on their knees on the pavement, with chalk and charcoal making most careful diagrams.

Now the word was sent at once through intermediary powers to Ardneh that he was expected, under truce, as soon as he could manifest himself.

Some time passed. "What is going on in the mind of our guest?" the Emperor asked, breaking a little silence that had fallen on the group. "Is he having second thoughts about the wisdom of paying us a call?"

Wood lifted his gnarly hands, let them dangle in front of him as if seeking to dry them in the breeze. His two little fingers moved slightly, twitching like insects' antennae. "Supreme Lord, he is near." Wood's bulging eyes, looking blind now, seeing more than any other eyes present, gazed out across the lake, "My Emperor, he is approaching. When you can see something near at hand above the water, speak and he will hear."

Ominor at first saw only the distant fishing craft, and the towering cloud unchanged. Then, following a subtle gesture from Wood, he brought his attention closer to the shore, and noticed a patch of ripples somehow different from all the rest. At any other time he would probably have taken them for some effect of wind. But steadily they came closer, not blending like other waves into the general motions of the water. The Emperor was magician enough to feel it now. A hint of arrogant immensity. The presence of hostile power, aloof, quiet, waiting. The ripples, slowing their progress gradually, drifted to within a dozen meters of the low balustrade. Ominor's accustomed eyes could tell now that above the ripples there was — something.

In his loud voice filled with certitude he said:
"Hear me, dullard of the West! It must be plain by
now, even to you, that the hour of your complete
destruction cannot be far away. Yet I admit that it
lies in your power to cause me some inconvenience
still. And rather than see such abilities as you possess turned into nothingness, I would bring them
into my domain. I am willing that you should receive some substantial rank in the hierarchy of the
East, one that is probably higher than you dare to
expect."

He had spoken slowly enough for his hearer to
have readily interrupted him with an answer at any
of the several places. But there was no answer. The
Emperor glanced at Wood and at his other waiting
councilors, but got no help. Whether Ardneh's silence was born of an attempt to impress them, or of
fear, or of some other cause, there was no clue.

Under these conditions Ominor had no intention
of going on with a long-winded speech. At the moment he had only one more thing to say: "In token of
my sincerity. . ." And pulling from around his neck
the crystal chain with its impressive burden, he
whirled it once around his head and sent it flying
out over the water, spinning in the sun. He watched
for the bribe to vanish, into seeming air or in the
grasp of some materialization. But the Emperor was
disappointed; the treasure only splashed and sank,
prosaically as a lump of rock, going quickly out of
sight in the deep water.

Where no more strange ripples moved. The air
was empty once again.

Close by his side, Wood said: "Supreme Lord, the
creature is gone. All contact has been broken."

The Emperor felt his tension slide away. Through
him in a flash there passed understanding, con-
tempt for his enemy, and elation. "He did not take
the prize."

"No. It lies somewhere in the water there."

The Emperor jutted out his chin, his teeth bared

in a smile. That Ardneh might take the bribe and then refuse to honor it had been considered; it would have meant no serious loss. Of course it had been expected that he might refuse with some contemptuous speech or gesture. But to cut and run, in panic . . . it could scarcely be anything else. The quasimaterial powers were if anything more concerned than humans were with saving face. Overawed by the Emperor and his wizards, frightened by the palace guard of monstrous demons . . .

Suddenly suspicious, Ominor asked Wood: "Do you suppose he smelled the poisoned bait?" The ebon sphere had been laden with the most subtle and powerful curses Wood could devise.

"Nay, great Lord." Wood too was smiling in this moment of success, having proven his ability to control the greatest of enemies at close quarters.

Turning away from the balustrade, the Emperor walked deliberately back in the direction of his palace, massed behind its palisade of trees.

Without turning or pausing, the Emperor ordered Wood: "Make some suitable plan to rid us of this creature Ardneh. We know now he can be no mortal threat. Still . . ."

"Yes, Lord of Lords." Turning momentarily to a subordinate, Wood said in an aside: "Use great care in recovering the poison bauble from the water. Better set a guard, and let it lie awhile. Who so comes into possession of it in the next hour will need all my skill to keep him healthy."

The Emperor's train moved on at an easy pace toward the interior of the palace grounds. There was a feeling of general relief in the air. Ordinary servants were beginning to reappear, soft gongs were striking a time-signal for mid-afternoon. Between beds of unusually luxuriant flowers Ominor paused, and the lawn chair he had been sitting in earlier was instantly unfolded and placed ready for him.

There were several business matters to be at-

tended to. All were comparatively minor things
however, and within half an hour the Emperor was
signing the last required paper, with relief because
he felt inexplicably tired. Raising his eyes, he saw
coming from the central parts of the palace an oddly
mixed group of about half a dozen men. A pair of
them were high-ranking wizards, two at least were
household stewards, some were members of his
personal bodyguard. All were moving with a sort of
reluctant haste toward John Ominor, as if none of
them wanted either to be first with whatever news
they bore, or to give any appearance of delay.

He stood up and his legs nearly failed him. In his
guts there twisted something like the leaden claw of
death. Another poisoning plot uncovered, then
Perhaps too late, this time. Wood came from some
where, maybe out of the air, to stand before him
gesturing, and the pangs in his midsection began to
ease, reluctantly.

And now Ominor saw what those coming from the
center of the palace were holding up on its crystal
chain. He heard their disjointed, fearful explana
tions of how it had just been cut from the belly of a
huge, fresh-caught fish, one marked for the Em
peror's dinner.

Wood's chief assistants were coming running to
join him, to help to combat the deadly spells they
had so recently set in motion. As soon as he felt a
little better, Ominor called to him the High Consta
ble, Abner.

The soldier towered above his chair. "My Em
peror?"

"The wizards have failed me. There is a mission I
want you to undertake. We must learn, begin to
learn, what Ardneh is."

II

Summonings

In Rolf's dream the demon uttered a deafening warcry and slew the world, cutting the life from it with one sweep of a great two-handed blade. The blade drew with it the blackness of oblivion, drew a curving black wall that completed itself to make a sphere and put an end to all light everywhere. Rolf cried out in fear, and leaped backwards to save himself, knowing that to save himself was what he had to do to save the world.

Before he was fully awake he was on his feet, starting up with sword in hand from where he had been lying cloak-wrapped in the long grass, stretched out sleeping on soft earth. Dazedly he realized that his outcry had not been confined to the world of dreams; his nine comrades in the patrol had been awakened, were gathering with hasty caution round him in the dark; and others elsewhere might have heard the yell also.

"I dreamed, I dreamed, I dreamed," he kept on whispering, till he was sure the other soldiers understood. They muttered and grumbled and listened in the night, for the approach of some alerted enemy.

At last, amid some sour, whispered jokes, Mewick, the patrol commander, ordered as a precaution that all should mount; they were to move camp by a kilometer or so. This was quickly accomplished, for here on this vast, grassy plain one spot was much like another, and there were no tents and little baggage. Then with the camp re-established, riding-beasts once more picketed and a pair of sentries posted, Mewick came to where Rolf was sitting and squatted down beside him.

Neither spoke for a while. It was a warm and moonless night, with a thick powdering of stars showing irregularly between smooth-flowing, barely visible clouds. The insects of early summer racketed in the tall grass.

After a few moments Rolf whispered: "It was a warning, I believe."

"Of what?" Mewick's voice was soft, as usual. "Shall I call Loford here?"

"I can talk to him now, or in the morning. But there is little I can tell him." Already the dream was disintegrating in the grip of clumsy waking memory. "There was danger, and a sense that I must act at once, to save myself. Not just fear, but a sense that my life was—valuable."

Mewick nodded, considering. "Talk to Loford in the morning, then. But are you going to jump up yelling again the next time you go to sleep?"

"Sleep seems far from me now," Rolf said. "I'll take a turn at sentry-go."

"No. You stood your watch. Sleep now. The dawn is not far away."

Rolf shrugged, and stretched out on the ground, pulling his cloak round him, making sure that his weapons were in easy reach. He closed his eyes, though he felt sure that he was not going to get any more sleep . . .

. . . and this time the demon-monster's sword was coming right at *him*, with body-splitting force. His leap and yell were no more under voluntary control than the gush of blood from a new wound. His waking convulsion left Rolf on his feet with sword in hand once more, knowing that once more he had put his comrades all in danger . . .

An Eastern soldier, real and solid as the grass and earth, was crouching just three meters off, sword half raised for the easy stroke that would have

drained Rolf's sleeping life into the soil. A dim, tense
outline in the deceptive, grayish predawn light, the
man got his blade up in the way of the hard overhand cut Rolf aimed at him. But the parry was not
made with sufficient force, and the man's face and
shoulder erupted blood. He grunted, and could do
nothing else before the next blow came to kill him.

The others of what happened to be an exception-
ally competent Western patrol were springing up at
hair-trigger tension from what could have been no
more than light, uncertain sleep. Tall Chup hewed
right and left and the Eastern men he struck fell
back like children knocked aside. And Mewick
seemed to be fighting on both sides of Rolf at once,
opponents toppling before his battle-hatchet and
short sword as if it were a dance they had rehearsed.
And years of hard experience had made Rolf a better
fighter than most. As soon as he had finished his
first opponent, he turned with methodical swift-
ness to find another.

A white flash came inside his skull, a painless,
noiseless, stunning blast. With a moment of intense
clarity of thought he knew that he was wounded,
and waited with a certain detachment to find out if
he was slain. He felt no agony, no sickening shock,
but still his legs betrayed him and he fell.

Ardneh. The half-familiar, subtle and inhuman
presence was with him suddenly and reassuringly,
more powerfully and personally than ever before,
unmistakably the same as that which had brushed
him when he rode the Elephant.

Ardneh, he thought, do not make me fall, help me
to rise. But down he went, to lie on his face in the
deep grass while struggling feet ripped through it
all around him. Rolf could not move, but his mind
was clear, and knowledge was sent him from a voice-
less and unseen source. It was Ardneh himself who
had wakened him with warning dreams, to keep him
from being slaughtered in his sleep, and Ardneh
also who had just struck Rolf down. He was being

kept out of the fighting, for some purpose he could not yet plainly see.

Something that was of awesome, overriding importance . . . but right now his field of vision was cut to a one-eyed view of grasstalks, and his own left hand. He could feel that his right hand still held his sword, but it was not by any conscious management of his.

The fighting and chasing around him seemed to go on endlessly. Time was slow at the bottom of the tall grass. He was given reassurance, in Ardneh's subtle, wordless way, that the West was winning the skirmish. Ardneh had many other demands upon his energy. Rolf was going to be left to himself now to recover, which should not take him long.

An age or two had passed before he heard the voices of some of his friends, dourly cautious, commenting as they found the body of one of their sentries, slain by stealth. The other sentry had come through all right, it seemed, as had the animals. Now feet trampled close to Rolf again, surrounded him, and stopped.

Mewick's soft voice announced it simply: "Rolf is dead."

Hands turned him over; when his living face appeared under the now-brightening sky, voices exclaimed in surprise.

Rapidly, now that he had been moved, the life flowed back into his limbs. He sat up, breaking out in a cold sweat. To a flurry of questions, he answered with such explanation as he could give. He did not understand it very well himself.

Loford, who was the only wizard present, listened with grave headshakings and then conferred with Mewick. Then Loford drew from his bag of magical apparatus a thin slab of wood in two parts, hinged like a folding game board. Loford cleared a little flat space on the ground and put down his board, and on it he cast straws once, twice, thrice, to see in which direction the patrol should move next. No divination was infallable, of course, but Mewick wanted all the help he could get in reaching a decision.

With each cast the indicated direction was the same. Northwest. Mewick, watching closely, wore a deeper frown than usual. There was, or should be, little that way but unpopulated wasteland for a thousand kilometers or more.

In response to an inquiring look from his commander, Loford said succinctly: "Ardneh." Then he murmured the words of the appropriate spell and tried again.

Northwest.

"North." The word came firmly, in the voice of the young seeress, Anita, whose advice was so often hesitant. Prince Duncan of the Offshore Islands, who had been leaning forward in expectation of a struggle to catch some mumbled obscurity, eased back now in his camp chair. Here, many kilometers west of Mewick's patrol, the dawn was yet no more than a faint promise, and a lamp was lit inside his tent.

The girl Anita, mumbler though she usually was, had been proven the most reliable oracle that Duncan had yet been able to conscript. With Duncan's chief wizard Gray now standing at her shoulder, she sat in a chair opposite Duncan's, her breathing deep and slow and her eyes fixed somewhere over the Western commander's shoulder.

"Anita." Duncan's voice was insistently reasonable. "Why should we march into the north?" The map of the continent, spread out in his mind's eye, could give no reason, except possibly to confuse the enemy. Nothing lay to his north but a thousand kilometers of wasteland. To Duncan it seemed likely that some enemy power was working through the seeress now despite Gray's precautions, trying to lead them into a trap.

Anita answered: "To win the war. More I must not

tell you at this time." The voice was the girl's own, which was unusual for one possessed by a power; and this sudden cool assumption of authority was startling, whoever the power might be.

Duncan's head lifted. "Are you Ardneh?" he asked sharply.

"I am," said the girl, looking at him with an empress' manner. When herself, she was too shy to meet his eyes for long.

Behind the girl's chair, tall Gray turned startled eyes to meet Duncan's, then slowly nodded: in his opinion it was Ardneh. For the moment Duncan could say nothing. Ardneh had never made contact with him before, but Duncan had pondered long, trying to decide what course he should take when the meeting did take place, as seemed inevitable. He had come to no decision, but now he must; what attitude should he—and, in effect, the entire human West—take with regard to the being who called himself Ardneh?

It was very quiet inside the tent. The army lay, to protect it against discovery by spying reptiles during the day, within a forest of high-crowned trees. Duncan could now hear the small creatures that dwelt in the branches above his tent, beginning their stirrings of the day.

Ardneh was unique. No wizard of West or East could understand him. He was subtle, but the power . . . In the struggle with Zapranoth, the very mountains had been cracked. That much Duncan had seen for himself, afterward. It was as if the obscure Old World quotation were true indeed, that some put into Ardneh's mouth: *I am Ardneh, who rides the Elephant, who wields the lightning, who rends fortifications as the rushing passage of time consumes cheap cloth . . .*

But could the West take this unidentified power as unquestioned leader, king and Lord?

Duncan arose and moved to the doorway of his tent, a moderately tall young man with sunbleached long hair and a face that worry and weather had made look older than it was. Moving outside, he ignored, because he was not conscious of it, the salute of the runner waiting before his tent, who sprang up ready for duty. The camp, almost soundless and invisible in the pre-dawn dark, stretched unseen before Duncan.

Now, on Ardneh's unexplained—wish, order, whatever you wanted to call it—he was supposed to swing his whole army north, a move for which there seemed to be no military justification. No, there could be no thought of making such a move on trust.

Duncan spun and re-entered the tent. Facing the girl who was still in trance, he snapped: "What will happen if I do not move the army as you say?"

Without hesitation Anita replied: "You will lose the war."

"How am I to know that you are to be trusted?"

"By its fruit the tree is known."

Duncan grunted. He thought a moment more, then barked orders to his wizards, directing them to prepare alternate means of divination. He watched while they roused the girl from trance, and remembered to say a kind word to her as she was taken out, flustered, shy, and unremembering. Then he called for and quickly ate a hearty breakfast, meanwhile hearing reports brought in by birds just in from their night's scouting.

The daylight was not yet full when Duncan left his tent again to stride out through the sprawling camp. He passed among rows of quiet tents, and of men and women sleeping cloak-wrapped on the earth. Some were up and about, readying food for the morning meal, repairing gear, cleaning, washing, inventorying, sharing out supplies. Up in the trees, if you looked for them, the returned birds were visible, brownish gray and shapeless, hiding heads and eyes against the glare of day.

Now the rows of tents were left behind. Passing a sentry who informally nodded to him in recognition, Duncan entered denser forest. Soon he had reached gloomy thickets through which the eye could scarcely find a pathway. But now as Duncan continued to step forward one bush or another bent itself aside for him. he kept unhesitatingly to the path thus indicated. He had come some fifty paces past the last human sentry before he got a direct look at his pathmaker: a forest elemental, almost tree-like in appearance, raised great gnarled limbs at some distance to Duncan's left. It was guiding him in turns and doublings, supposedly preventing the approach of any unfriendly power.

At length the parting of a final screen of bushes disclosed before him a wide, still glade. In the middle of the glade there stood three men, or at any rate three tall forms, seemingly garbed more in darkness and in light than in any human-woven cloth. They were his three chief wizards, Duncan knew, but which of them was which he could not have guessed. The three turned simultaneously to face the Prince as he stepped out of the bush.

He could not see their faces clearly and did not try. As had been prearranged, in a loud voice he demanded: "Ardneh, Ardneh, Ardneh! Who is he? What is he? Will it be to my advantage to trust his word, to heed his will, to follow where he leads?"

One magician threw back his head, cowled and faceless, and replied: "If we do not trust and heed and follow him, I see the end of the war."

"That has a hopeful sound."

"The end of war, the backs of Western men bent hopelessly under the Eastern lash, their babies slain, their women and their lands despoiled. That is the future I see if we reject the power called Ardneh now." The faceless speaker bowed his head.

A second spoke: "Lord Duncan, if we do trust the power called Ardneh now, I see no swift end to the war. I cannot see an end at all."

"Bah! All things in this world have an end. Still,

better an augury of uncertainty than one of doom. What else?''

The second wizard continued: "I see that fearful things must fall upon our people, if we heed the call that Ardneh sends today.''

He who had spoken first to Duncan raised his head again at that, and said: ''You do not tell what all of us must see, that fearful things must fall upon us, soon, whatever the good Prince chooses.''

Duncan put in, impatiently: ''It is war, and we all know what that short word means. Can you add to it aught of fear that we have yet to learn?''

And the second seer: ''This much; I see Ardneh—not clearly, but I know that it is he—caught in the grip of some power of evil stronger than he is, caught and dying whilst our army flees from trying to help. This the result if we listen to him now, accept his leadership. If we do not, I cannot see his death, or even the appearance of this enemy of incredible strength.''

The two magicians who had so far spoken fell silent now, looking at Duncan, then turning to follow the direction of his eyes with their own.

The third wizard, who seemed now to stand the tallest, broke his silence. ''Lord Duncan, it is all true, what both of them have told you. If we accept the leadership of Ardneh, I see Ardneh ringed about with enemies and dying, and I see you despairing in retreat. And then . . . that vision ends in some great violence. If we do not accept and follow Ardneh, the vision is even clearer, and, at least to me, even more terrible. For in it the West and all it stands for is no more . . . ''

''Hold!'' Duncan commanded. ''All of you! If by your arts you can see these things, must not Ardneh be able to see them too?''

The three conferred together, whispering. Then the first replied: ''It would seem to be not beyond his powers.''

"Well, then, if he is truly on our side . . ." Duncan lost the thread of what he had meant to say. Perhaps he was distracted by the way the three faceless wizards were now all turned toward him with a certain new tension in their postures, as if they had suddenly seen something new and peculiar about him.

It occurred to him also that he should take more time to think about the patrols he had routinely scattered in all directions to see what . . . no, especially he must consider those working far to the north and . . . actually, one patrol in particular required some thought. One of the men in it was a black-haired youth, short but strong-looking, named Rolf or something like that. Yes, perhaps he had heard of this Rolf before—some matter connected with technology. Ardneh might well now want this Rolf to do something technological again, since whatever it was before had worked out so well.

As Duncan thought further he seemed to see deeper into the matter. It came to him, as a remembered secret that should be shared with few or none, that this new technological mission for which Rolf (and the patrol that included Rolf) should be diverted would probably involve a certain object black as shiny ebony, a somehow gem-like thing about the same size as a man's clenched fist. Ardneh had probably handled a similar thing recently, seen and handled such a thing for the first time, and in the course of that handling had obtained a clue as to the existence and whereabouts of this larger and vastly more valuable one, the true worth of which was not yet appreciated by any human being. It was now in the possession of some adherent of the East, somewhere in a northern desert where the patrol of which Rolf was a member, if they were fast enough and lucky enough, might be in time to intercept . . .

So smoothly and with such seeming rightness did this train of thought flow through Prince Duncan's mind, that only after it had progressed thus far did he awake to the fact that it was bringing him new knowledge, that it must have its origin in some mind other than his own.

Ardneh? he demanded, silently, but with a concentrated urgency of thought that was the equivalent of a shout. There was no answer, save that the flow of ideas about the gem-like thing, whose existence he had never before suspected, broke off.

Ardneh, you cannot manage me that way. I will not be controlled. But even as his challenging thought went forth he knew that no effort had been made to control him. He had only been taken partly into Ardneh's confidence.

The air within the glade had cleared. The wizards once again had faces, and were pressing round him anxiously." . . . Lord Duncan, Prince," tall Gray was repeatedly demanding. When he saw that Duncan was aware of him, he added: "He came to you directly. Prince, did you not feel his weight?"

"Yes, yes. Now I have felt him. Listened to him. Whether I believe him is still another question."

They pressed him for more information but there was little more that he could tell; Ardneh was still a mystery. He led the others back to the camp, where he plunged alone into his tent for a time to argue with himself amid maps, reports, intelligence estimates. There were strong arguments on both sides, but already in his heart he was more than half convinced that soon he would be moving the army north.

III

Banditry

———◆◆◆———

Full summer had come, and Abner, High Constable of the East, with the dust of hard journeying upon his clothes, sweltered standing in the small room high under the sun-beaten roof of the caravanserai. Around him a few quick and silent servants hurried, nimbly adjusting their movements in the cramped quarters to the Constable's bulky, careless presence. Dust raised by hasty efforts at cleaning still hung visible before the small, high windows in the prison-like walls. The servants were unpacking things and moving the Constable in with practiced efficiency, while he looked around him with distaste. The place had looked more inviting from the outside. It would have been better, the Constable was thinking now, to have camped in the open again; his escort was strong enough to have nothing to fear from bandits, and there could be no sizable Western force in the area. But his companion had wanted to spend a night or two indoors, and to humor her he had agreed.

Of course he could change his orders and move out again, but he had had a weary day in the saddle and was not minded to wait longer for his bath and such pleasures as the evening might afford. So let it be. In the next room of his little suite, which was of course the least dilapidated of the establishment, he could hear the buckets of bath-water already being carried in. Standing by a window and tall enough to peer down from it, he could see in the courtyard below how the weary loadbeasts of his retinue were being unloaded, watered, and bedded for the night.

The south wall of the courtyard below was pierced by a single central gate, the only way in or out. On the other three sides were buildings, all the same three-story height. The building the Constable stood in, and the one opposite, were divided into small apartments and barrack-like chambers, the ground floors usable interchangeably by animals or by humans of the lower classes. The building that formed the third side of the enclosure, opposite the gate, contained a tavern, a brothel, a store, and the small quarters of the Master of the Station and his few permanent guards. All the buildings had windows only on their inner sides, facing the central square, and in their outer walls mere arrow-slits.

Probably a couple of hundred people were now inside the walls, two-thirds of them in the Constable's retinue. Nor had they seen another living human during the last two days. This remote region of the continent seemed to have been forsaken even by the war. Here and there moved roving bands of outcasts, deserters from East and West. But as for Duncan, his maneuverings, like Ominor's, were many kilometers to the south.

The Emperor of the East had assumed command of his own armies in the field, freeing his Constable for another mission, that of learning about Ardneh. The magicians had failed miserably. Abner had the Emperor's trust, as much as anyone could be said to have it. He was journeying widely in this desolate part of the country to interview people, mostly Eastern officers, who in the past in one way or another had had something to do with Ardneh. More such Eastern people were to be found here than anywhere else, because those who had survived a struggle with Ardneh-inspired forces tended to be under a cloud of failure, and those whose failures were deemed mild tended to be assigned to

remote places where nothing important depended
on them. Those whose failures were thought grave
by Ominor were seldom in any condition to be in-
terviewed.

Of course Abner might have summoned to the
capital the people he wanted to talk to, eyewitness-
es who had been engaged in the various battles in
which Ardneh was known to have taken a hand. But
then they would keep re-working their stories to put
themselves in a more favorable light. He had to convince them that information was what he wanted,
not more scapegoats. Just talking directly to the
High Constable was intimidating enough for most of
them.

A few had other reactions. One of these had engaged the Constable's interest for reasons that had
nothing to do with Ardneh; she had been traveling
with him now for half a month. Two days after he
met her he had sent home his other concubines.

The stone walls of the caravanserai were thick,
but the fit of the massive wooden doors was far from
tight, and now from the apartment next to Abner's
there came plainly the slide and thump of baggage
being moved, and the voice of the Lady Charmian in
the shrill tones she used with servants. Abner listened. In the very ugliness of that voice, which at
other times could hold all the female sweetness in
the world, there was a fascination. Even by its in-
congruity the voice evoked the unbelievable beauty
of her face and body. Truly a most remarkable woman, even in the eyes of a man who had his pick of
what the East and the subjugated lands could offer.
And it was a nice touch that he could blend his
business with his pleasure. Charmian had been at
the debacle of the Black Mountains. Not that she
had been able to tell him much of Ardneh.

Abner squinted against the lowering summer sun
in the northwestern sky. Along the shaded porch of
the brothel-tavern, some of its girls were quarreling

and had reached the stage of pulling hair. At the
other side of the courtyard, three travellers, evidently some kind of traders, were being let in
through the massive, narrow gate.

. . . yes, the woman was already assuming a
ridiculous importance in his life. Not for the first
time, he suspected magic. When he heard the door
close behind his servants and knew he was alone he
reached for amulets of great power that hung
around his neck inside his outer garments. With
these devices given him by Wood himself, Abner
probed for any indication of a love-charm being
worked. But to his passes and mutterings now no
answer came. The woman's magic was no more than
feminine beauty and cleverness. No more? Those
were quite enough.

When Abner had met Charmian she was living
with the commander of a small cavalry post, in a
place even more desolate and isolated than this
caravanserai—a great come-down for her. Obviously she saw Abner as a miraculous chance to not
only regain lost ground but leap far ahead of the
places she had fallen from. The lady wanted power
and position, and would spare no pains to get them.
The cavalry commander had been unable to hide his
chagrin at his loss, when Abner had invited the lady
to accompany him, even as she herself had been
openly overjoyed. Well, someday Ominor might
claim her for himself; but neither he nor Abner
would ever be so openly dismayed at the loss of this
or any other woman . . .

Rolf, Chup, and Loford, having passed the brief
scrutiny of the Master of the Station and been admitted through the gate—no very strict precautions
against bandits were being taken, it seemed, because of the unusually large party of armed men
who lay within the walls tonight—were sent on to
find such lodgings as they might. They had put on

clothing suitable for merchants and had counter-
feited the general appearance of such as well as they
were able. Their apparent caste thus achieved
might at another time have gained them lodgings in
the second or possibly the uppermost floor of one of
the dormitory buildings, but today a small room on
the lower level of servants and stables was the best
that they could do. The Constable's retinue and a
party of well-to-do slave dealers had taken over everything else from the top down.

Even with some guidance from Ardneh it had
taken Mewick and his patrol several weeks to find
Abner's trail. They had been following him closely
for four days now, being too few to attempt an open
assault on such a large party. Rolf still felt the certainty, send wordlessly by Ardneh, that the strange
object they were to seize was in the baggage of
Abner or someone traveling with him. Ardneh's influence had become so convincing that Mewick had
turned his patrol in the desired direction even before orders to do so came by bird-messenger from
Duncan. The orders when they came were explicit,
brought by birds who told how Duncan was starting
to turn his whole army north: the seizure of the
jewel was to be attempted at all costs to the patrol.

Abner's decision to stop at the caravanserai offered at least some prospect of a chance. Thus, the
plan to send three men behind the same walls as the
Constable. The very added security of the walls
might induce the enemy to let down his guard, and
make some action possible.

Once in their ground-floor room, which they had
claimed by evicting a miscellany of beasts of burden
into the open courtyard, the three putative merchants had no difficulty, looking out through their
uncloseable window, in picking out the high narrow
windows of the Constable's chambers in the building opposite. It was certain that he would have
taken the poor best that the place could offer; and
Chup and Loford had had enough experience with

caravanserais of similar design to know where the most desirable rooms must be.

After seeing to their animals, and stowing their meager baggage in the most easily watched corner of their room, the three of them held converse in voices inaudible more than an arm's length away.

Chup mused: "It will not be easy, I think, to get near enough to strike."

Loford could look the mild tradesman part quite easily, and had been the spokesman at the gate. He answered now: "It is too early yet to tell. Give them a night of carousing, and see if by tomorrow they have not begun to be a little slow to notice things, a little lazy."

Rolf said: "Also, remember this. Just getting near and striking will not avail us anything."

Chup shook his head a centimeter or two in disagreement. "To kill Abner would be something, a deep wound for the East. Worth taking a chance for, whether or not we can do the job for which we came."

Rolf, putting flat authority into his quiet voice, said: "No, to kill Abner is nothing if we cannot get the stone we want and get away with it. So Ardneh says." Beyond that he could give his friends no explanation, for Ardneh had given none to him. Should Rolf be captured and questioned, still he would be able to say no more. But he spoke with conviction, having faith in Ardneh.

The other two exchanged a look of age and experience above his head. "Well," said Chup, "what you say about getting away is suitable to me. I have no objection to my own survival.'

Loford put in: "Suitable, and interesting. Sometimes it pays to plan from start and finish toward the middle. Suppose we have what we came for, and are getting away—will we absolutely need the animals that we rode in here on?"

"No," said Rolf. "Mewick and I discussed that. There are at least three good spare animals with the patrol. If we can rendezvous with them outside the walls all should be well."

"And I," said Chup, "came thinking we might go out over the roof." He patted his midsection under his loose merchant's garb. "I have some rope coiled here. That gate seems to be well watched, and not easy to open in a hurry."

"Let us suppose," said Rolf, "we are going over the wall with a rope. What is next to be considered?"

Chup: "Since the plump wizard here is going with us, I suppose we must consider how to strengthen the strands, with a little magic perhaps." Chup was better suited for this kind of work than any normal man could be; the prospect of desperate action actually cheered him up. Were it not that some in the West still mistrusted the sincerity of his conversion, he would have held a high command. "As he must have done for the backbone of his riding-beast."

Loford did not seem disconcerted. "Would I could strengthen your wits as easily, dull swordsman. About getting away . . . Rolf, is it any clearer now, where the thing must ultimately be taken?"

"Let me think." Trying to find what Ardneh wanted was like trying to find a half-forgotten memory of one's own. Glimmerings came, as if grudgingly. "Farther than we'll be able to ride from here in a single night. More I cannot see."

Loford: "What I am getting at is this. Could not a bird take it? As described, the stone is easily light enough for one to lift."

This time Rolf had to think longer. At last he shook his head. "No. Rather, it will be much better if we do not have to do it that way. Better for it to go by bird than not at all, but . . . it is important also that *I* go, there is some job for me to do, at the same place where the stone is needed." He shook his head again.

Loford scratched his head. "Then we must try to guard you too, and send you on unscratched if possible . . . what is it makes your jaw drop, swordsman? Have you managed a clear thought?"

Chup stopped his fixed staring at the high windows opposite, gave his head a shake, and blinked. "It may be that today I rode too long staring into the sun. I thought I saw —a woman."

"Well? And why not?" Loford asked reasonably.

Chup only shook his head again, and went back to observing the apartment where the High Constable lodged.

Rolf turned to Loford. "A while ago you said that by tomorrow they may be growing a little careless. But will they not also be on their way?"

"I think not." Loford slouched massively on the low windowsill, and with a slight nod indicated the far side of the courtyard. "A groom has begun paring at the hooves of several of the loadbeasts we followed today." That meant no long journey could be contemplated for those animals tomorrow. "We should have tonight and tomorrow to get ready, and tomorrow night to strike and run."

They could not decide on a scheme for getting a closer look at the Constable's quarters. After a while Rolf said: "One of us at least should go to the tavern, hear what the soldiers in the Constable's escort have to say." After a moment he added. "I wish that one of you two would go."

Chup gave him a quizzical glance. "Do the painted women make you nervous, young one?"

"No—yes. Because always in the background there's one who owns them. And that people should be owned does bother me, though it seems sometimes not to bother the slaves. I am made nervous in such a way that I want to kill that man."

Chup emitted a little snort. "Well, I am not likely to tremble with nervousness in yonder house of joy, nor draw curious glances my way by killing someone. I'll volunteer to go, and brave whatever hardships duty may put in my way."

When Chup had taken off his sword, and strolled

away, Loford asked: "There is something else we are
to do?"

"I think so. Yes. It will be here in the courtyard —
something or someone that I should watch or wait
for." Not long ago, he would have thought the hunch
was purely his; but he was beginning to grow accustomed to Ardneh's subtlety.

Taking an empty waterbag, Rolf strolled out into
the courtyard, leaving Loford to defend their quarters against sneak thieves or possible late arrivals at
the caravanserai. The scene was generally quiet
now. A servant trotted past on some errand. Animals
made plaintive sounds. A few men, apparently
herdsmen or lower-class traders of some kind,
peered ruminatively from the windows of the lower
rooms. From what Chup had called the house of joy
came a burst of women's laughter, and then the
thumping of a tambourine. Somewhere the
slavemaster would be sitting, his eyes like stone
though his mouth laughed or sipped at wine.

Rolf went to the well, hauled up cold water from
its depths, and drank. He took his time filling the
waterbag. Watching the building in which the Constable was lodged, he saw a pair of white bare feet
descending the uppermost visible portion of the
mostly enclosed stair, bearing above them a
shadowy figure that upon emergence into the
brighter courtyard revealed itself to be that of a
servant girl. She was a tall girl, quite young and
despite her slenderness apparently quite strong;
over her shoulders rode a yoke holding two large
buckets that would be quite weighty when they
were filled. Her hair and dress were both of undis-
tinguished brown, the former bound up out of the
way under a servant's cap. Her face was hard to
judge, its dominant feature at the moment being a
purplish swelling on her cheek that came near to
closing her right eye. At best, Rolf thought, she
would be plain, her nose and mouth being some-

what large though there was prettiness still in the undamaged eye.

Rolf remained standing near the well while he replaced the stopper in his waterbag. The girl approached, set down her yoke, and began working at once to get the buckets filled. The well was equipped with a rope and windlass by which the wayfarer could lower his own container to the water far below. When the girl began to haul up the first heavy pail from the depths of the well, Rolf caught a hint of her exhaustion in the way she leaned against the crank, pausing momentarily after making a beginning against the weight.

Then he put his own burden down, and stepped around the well, saying: "I will lift it."

She stood straight for a moment, looking directly at him—she was a centimeter or two taller than he—without any readable expression in her face. Then she pulled once more on the crank herself.

He put her aside from the windlass, moving himself so firmly into position to turn the crank that she had little choice but to stand aside. Only when he had the filled bucket in his hands did he turn to her again, looking at her carefully for a moment before he set it down and took up the empty one. "You have been ill-used, girl," he said then.

"My mistress insists on being well served," she said steadily, without any obvious feeling of any kind in her voice. Nothing about her speech suggested that she was a servant. There were half-familiar accents in it that Rolf could not quite place at first, until he realized that they reminded him of Duncan's speech, which he had often heard in camp, the tones of the nobility of the Off-Shore Islands in the west.

"I would use you better than she does," he said at once, somewhat surprising himself. He spoke out of policy, of course, offering a drop of sympathy to the maltreated servant in hope of getting some information from her in return; but he meant what he said. And with a faint double shock, two things came to him in rapid sequence; first, that Ardneh had wanted him to go out into the courtyard in order to meet this girl; second, that he had a good idea who her mistress might be, what Lady of the East it was whose servants were more likely than not at any given time to bear the marks of her displeasure, who employed plain-faced maids to make her own great beauty glow the more by contrast.

In the same voice the girl replied: "I doubt that the Lady Charmian would sell me." This only confirmed Rolf's premonition, but still he came near dropping the second water-bucket. Demons of all the East! He must warn Chup before Chup was recognized. But it would hardly do to run away from the girl just yet, when it seemed she might be starting to communicate.

He set the bucket down. "I doubt that I would pay the Lady Charmian in any coin she would willingly accept."

The girl seemed to look more closely and humanly at him then, but only for a moment. Saying nothing, she bent to fasten her buckets to the yoke. When she would have lifted it, however, Rolf stepped in her way again, and with a grunt took up the double load.

"You have been kind," she said, still distantly, "but it will be better for you if you are not seen aiding me. And better for me if I am not seen receiving kindness from a man."

Rolf nodded slowly. "What *will* help you, girl? And what's your name?"

"Catherine, sir. And thank you, but there is no help for me." The calm in her voice was no longer as true as it had been. She came to him and her tall body brushed his as she took the yoke on her own shoulder.

He let it go, but walked beside her as she moved

back toward the stair. "You have not been long in the Lady's service, have you?"

"Not long?" She checked herself. "No—days only, not months or years. What is it to you?" When they reached the bottom of the stairwell they were for the moment alone out of sight of others, and she paused and looked at him somewhat more carefully than before.

Rolf was thinking rapidly. Whether Ardneh was putting his present thoughts into his mind he did not know; certainly he had no feeling of being controlled. "You will not live long in her service. No one does. She will kill you, or cripple you too badly to be of any—no, wait, I am not speaking to torment you. I said that I would use you better. And I will."

She turned her face away, then back to him again. Her whisper was long in coming, but when it came it had a desperate intensity. "There is no way that I can get away from her!"

He kept his own voice low and quick and calm. "And if there were?"

Again Catherine paused. Then: "If she has sent you to entrap me and torment me, I do not care. I must take the chance. I say I will go anywhere, do anything, to get away!"

Now he must think more swiftly still, but now it seemed no help from Ardneh was forthcoming. He could not settle on a detailed plan alone. Feet were moving somewhere above them on the stairs. "Come down again, later. If you can . . . ?"

"There will be more water to be fetched. Slops to be carried out."

"Good. I will meet you, or a friend of mine. He'll call you Catherine, so you know him. Go up now. Have hope."

She gave one abrupt nod and turned her face away, and went on up the stair, despite her burden moving more quickly than she had when coming down.

In the room where he had left Loford waiting, Rolf
saw to his surprise that Chup had returned already,
and was standing against the wall where he could
not be seen from door or window. Rolf had hardly
begun to speak when Chup interrupted him with a
gesture. "Yes, I know my beauteous bride is here,"
he said leaning cautiously toward the window to
glare at the building opposite. "I thought I saw her,
earlier, up there. And then hardly had I gotten into
the funhouse yonder when I saw an Eastern soldier
that I used to know—his mind was on other things,
to our good luck, and I can almost pledge he saw me
not. He was talking to some friend about the Lady
Charmian, enough to make it plain that she is here.
Around my neck like some evil charm she seems to
hang."

"What did you do? Turn in the doorway and come
back?"

"Not quite, for I was fairly in, and to just spin and
run out again might look a little odd. Stood with my
face in a corner, practically, for a while. You might
say that I cut my revelry quite short."

Rolf went to the window for a good look round,
then turned back in. "It seems you were not recognized, or they'd be after us already. Now I've some
better news to tell."

He quickly related to the others his conversation
with Catherine. They resumed their planning, with
at least one of them always watching to see if
Catherine came down again.

The help of Charmian's personal servant should
be a great advantage if only they could hit upon the
most effective way of using her. But whether or not
the jewel was in Charmian's possession or with
some other member of the Constable's party was
still uncertain; the raiders had to make sure of its
location before they could hatch any detailed plan.

When darkness fell it became difficult to see the
stairway from the window of their room, and Rolf
went out into the courtyard and strolled about,

keeping watch. When Catherine came down again, she was carrying pots to be emptied. Rolf walked to intercept her at the refuse pits, which lay at an angle of windowless wall between tavern and stable. It was a dark and noisome place, and for the moment they had it to themselves.

Her face looked fearful, but her gaze did not fall away from his. She said: "If you were joking earlier, tell me now."

"Catherine, I was not. I will take you with me from this place. But there is something else that I must take, and I need your help for that."

"Anything."

"It is probably in your mistress' jewel box, or in the Constable's."

Catherine did not seem in the least surprised. She had had a little time to think things over and form her own idea at what Rolf must want. "The Constable has no strong-box with him, to my knowledge, and I have seen him wear no jewels. I know where the woman's jewel-case lies, but I have never seen it opened . . ."

The lid, massive and strong but elegantly lined within, was standing open at that moment, Charmian having performed the necessary ritual, reciting the three secret words and using the physical key required. She was choosing her jewelry for the evening, while one of her two servant girls, quivering a little as usual, stood by to help with other details.

Considering the hard times that had recently overtaken her, there was a fair amount of wealth and beauty arrayed in the form of bright gems amid the soft compartments of the little chest. In the bottom, looking at odds with everything else, lay a spherical lump of dark stuff the size of a man's two fists. It was mounted in a filigree of silver and gold, no part of which pierced the ebon sphere that it enclosed. As usual, when she looked at it, Charmian frowned; the commander of the cavalry outpost had given it to her, as the best he had to give. No doubt most people would think most of the smaller diamonds more valuable, but Charmian was not so sure; it was quite beautiful in its own different way. But its size! A giantess three meters tall might have worn it as a fine ornament, but what was a woman of ordinary stature to do with such a massive jewel?

She had considered other possibilities, of course. Sensitive to most of the auras of magic, she could feel nothing of power or danger from the thing, no life-potential much above that of any other lump of stone of equal size.

There was a faint sound at her door, the creak of a board under a quiet but heavy tread. The breathing of the maid became suspended, but Charmian did not turn. Let him surprise her thus. Let Abner see how many spaces remained to be filled with wealth inside this one modest treasure-box of hers. While she kept on looking into the box, readying herself to be surprised, she wondered still what the black thing was. When someday she had joined the court of Ominor, when first class wizards were at her service, she would have to have it properly assayed . . .

Abner's great hand came delicately stroking her bare shoulder and she gave a little cry and start, seemingly as spontaneous as the last time he had "surprised" her. She was looking round, her eyes innocently and prettily wide, when his face altered, and his hand on her flesh turned to stone. Her surprise turned real.

He was staring into the open jewel box, and his voice was no longer the voice of an infatuated man, but that of an Eastern Lord. "Where did you get *that*?"

Having seen Catherine back to the foot of the stair, Rolf returned to the room where Chup and Loford waited. There he passed on to them the information that the girl had given. Now in the dust of the floor they could sketch the layout of the rooms in both

Charmian's and the Constable's apartments, and the usual position of the jewel-box in the former. There were other matters to be thought about as well, what soldiers and servants were likely to be where, and how doors were fastened and windows barred. There were a few more questions to be asked of Catherine next time Rolf met with her.

"And one more thing," Chup added. "Do you really mean to bring the girl away with us?"

"We will bring her back to the patrol," said Rolf after a moment. "After that it will be up to Mewick."

Chup nodded slowly. "But if we do not get her clean away, we cannot leave her able to answer questions."

Loford was standing by gloomily, with nothing to say for the moment. Rolf hesitated, but only briefly. "Agreed," he murmured with a nod.

After a moment Chup went on: "Speaking of ladies likely to be thought superfluous, there is the matter of my bride." He fell silent for a little while, staring moodily out the window. Somehow it did not seem to him prohibitively strange to still call Charmian his bride. "I find I do not care if we leave her alive or dead."

The others made no response to that. He felt he could not leave it at that. "Well, I know this is war and not a personal matter . . . I just mean that I will kill her if it seems the best move to make, though I feel no urge to do so."

Still the others remained silent. He himself wondered why he was going on like this about her. Was he making the point that she meant nothing to him one way or the other, or only raising doubts about it?

He had no doubt that she hated him now, that horrible things would happen to him if he ever fell into her power. Well, she was like that. For a time he had hated her, too. Now she was no more important than some poisonous insect, to be avoided or, if the opportunity came, squashed flat.

Rolf and Loford were looking off into space in separate directions, doubtless waiting to make sure that Chup had finished what was for him a lengthy speech.

Loford said at last: "I am glad that your feelings are not involved here." And Rolf: "We will not go out of our way to kill her, then, if she is not at hand when we take the jewel. Of course, if she should get a look at us, it will be better if we do not leave her able to answer questions."

"Of course," said Chup at once. But still he frowned. It was odd. He could picture himself killing Charmian, or almost anyone else. But he could not picture in his mind how she would look when she was dead. Yes, it was odd.

They went back to refining. From all that Catherine had told them, three expertly violent men with the advantage of surprise should be able to get into Charmian's apartment, dispose of the immediate resistance, and get the gem into their hands. When it came to getting away, though, difficulties multiplied.

Chup wished aloud: "If only this girl Catherine could steal the gem for us, bring it out to us."

Loford shook his head. "From what Rolf tells us, there's not a chance of her getting into the treasure box. Charmian's not one to be at all careless with her valuables."

They talked it over, assuming themselves inside the apartment, the jewel in their possession. Now there were poundings on the single door, demands to know what was going on inside.

Chup: "Maybe no one will notice a few screams and a little commotion. That kind of thing's no novelty in my Lady's rooms."

"But suppose they do?"

"Then . . . I wonder if the Constable truly dotes on her? I wonder if she could serve us as a hostage?"

That idea and others were debated. The discussion went on far into the night, when it was set aside for rest. The three men took turns at watching throughout the remainder of the night.

Shortly before dawn, Loford strolled outside as if to stretch some stiffness from his limbs. There, as pre-arranged with Mewick, he spelled out the essentials of the plan they had decided on, using gestures natural to a man who had waked up with some aching joints. They meant to be coming out from the rooftop tomorrow night, with the gem in their possession. He hoped that his gestures were being watched by one of the great birds, circling on hushed wings well above the walls. If they were lucky, a bird or two had been able to join Mewick's patrol tonight.

The remainder of the night passed uneventfully, and so did the greater portion of the following day. Late in the afternoon Catherine made what would be, if things went well, her final trip down to the well. This time Rolf did not meet her, but watched from the concealment of his room as she gave the unobtrusive signal meaning that nothing had arisen to require a change in plans or a final consultation. As expected, the Constable's party showed no signs of leaving. They had been on the road for many days, and men and beasts alike were doubtless ready for a day of rest.

Night fell, and in their little ground-floor room three merchants became Western warriors once more, removing extra weapons and equipment from their packs to be distributed about their persons, then covered with long travelers' cloaks. Then there was nothing to do but hold final vigil at the window.

Time dragged. Chup was just beginning to ask: "Are you sure that she will come—" when there she came, Catherine emerging from the dark mouth of the stair opposite, making her way across the ill-lit courtyard. She too had put on a long cloak, but her feet were still bare. Rolf hoped she was carrying at least a pair of sandals for the trip; there was no way to be sure when they would meet Mewick and the others and be able to ride.

The plan called for her to come to them openly, as if she had been sent to the three merchants with a message.

"Gentlemen, you are asked to come," she said in a low voice when she had reached their open door.

"Asked?" Rolf echoed. He was not sure for the moment whether Catherine was only playing her role, or whether Abner or Charmian actually wanted to see the "merchants" about something.

"It is I who ask you," she said with feeling, looking from one of them to the other. The hood of her cloak was thrown back, and her brown hair was looser than it had been. Her eye looked a little puffier, if anything, than yesterday.

"We are ready for some bargaining," said Rolf, and stepped forward to the doorway and took her gently by the elbow, both to reassure her and to keep her from turning thoughtlessly and starting back at once—the three merchants must take a little time to ask a question or two, gather their sample wares, see to their own appearance, before calling on such an eminent lady. Catherine's arm had a lifeless submissiveness in Rolf's grip; it was a feeling that he had met before, on touching slaves, slaves who had had reason to take him for an Eastern master. It came to Rolf that in a sense this girl had now become his slave, his property, and there was a twinge of forbidden pleasure in the thought.

The proper moments for delay soon passed, and the four of them set out across the courtyard, the three men unhurriedly walking ahead.

"I could learn nothing more that will be helpful," the girl whispered to Rolf, from her position close behind him.

"All right." He tried to sound calm and reassuring. "Do what I say, without hesitating. We will bring you out."

A moment more and they were ascending the stairs of the building in which Charmian and the Constable were lodged. As they passed the open doorway of a second-floor apartment, through which several junior officers of the East could be seen gaming around a table, Loford said, as though continuing a conversation: " . . . we can procure what your Lady wants, if we have it not in the goods we carry with us. We stand ready at any hour of the day or night to serve so illustrious . . . " He let his voice fade to a meaningless mumble as they passed the door and started up the next-to-final flight of stairs. The uppermost flight, and the doors and landing at its top, were still invisible. As they turned the corner and started up the final flight the expected sentry at the top came into view, looking down coldly at them.

"Right up to the top, your honors, please," said Catherine clearly from just behind Rolf, and could not keep the strain out of her voice. Behind the sentry were the two doors she had described to Rolf; the right one would lead to the Constable's quarters, the left to the Lady Charmian's. From behind the right door male voices could be heard, in low and serious talk, too muffled for words to be distinguishable.

The sentry was Rolf's to cope with, for Chup's greater effectiveness with the sword might be needed to meet the unexpected at one door or the other, and Loford might be needed just as suddenly for magical action and was too clumsy in any case to be trusted with a knifing.

On the topmost landing the men stood awkwardly, for it was not large, and the cold-eyed guard refused to give much ground. He was not truly suspicious yet. Catherine slid among the men to Charmian's door, to tap and call softly. It seemed Charmian did not like even her maids to take her by surprise. Rolf stood rigidly waiting until he heard the bar lifted inside the door, then saw the door open a crack to frame the eye of another servant girl inside; he turned then, with unhurried smoothness that was practised but still not easy, not for him, brought a long dagger from under his cloak without any unnecessary flourishes, and pushed it up firmly beneath the sentry's breastbone.

The sound life made in going out was not loud, and was covered by the whimpering little cry of the surprised servant-girl as Chup pushed in the door she had unlocked, and pushed his way inside, Loford right on his heels. Rolf with his unarmed hand caught his falling victim around the waist, and half-carried, half-dragged the dying man along into the apartment. Catherine, still waiting at the door, pulled it shut and barred it once everyone was inside.

Chup and Loford were not pausing, but strode on ahead of Rolf across the little dingy room, toward the one door on its farther side, their heavy soft treads shaking the floor slightly, setting muted jinglings sounding amid the feminine trappings hanging in an open portable wardrobe. The maidservant who had opened the door was still cowering on the floor where Chup had shoved her, paralyzed with shock and fright. Rolf let his murdered sentry down, showed the girl the bloody knife, whispered in her ear: "One squeak and we will cut your throat," and pushed her into the big wardrobe amid the hanging garments, where she fell to the floor in what was almost silence. He flashed a look of reassurance to Catherine, still leaning on the barred door, and turned after Chup and Loford who were entering the other room.

Some sound, or instinct, must have warned the Lady Charmian. When her husband and the men behind him came through the one door of her little bedchamber, she was standing as if waiting for them. She wore a long, soft lounging garment of some pink satiny stuff; her feet were bare on a soft, thick black rug that must have come to this place with her. The incredible golden cascade of her hair hung well below her waist. Rolf saw her eyes of melting blue, familiar as if he had last seen them only an hour before, go wide as she recognized Chup.

"Silence gives life," Chup told her briefly, and went past her to the strongbox, which was just where Catherine had said that it would be, standing on a low, crude chest just below the high window with its heavy bars. Chup flicked the side of the box with his swordpoint, once, hesitantly, felt the muted shock of guardian powers, and drew quickly back. Loford shouldered past him to bend over the box, mumbling. Chup moved to where he could watch Charmian and at the same time look back into the outer room of the apartment, where Catherine still waited with her back against the door. Rolf, standing in the doorway between the rooms, could see and feel the mutual hatred pass between her and Charmian.

And now Charmian's eyes, with a different look, reached for Rolf's eyes, brushed them once, then fell away, very quickly and shyly. No, her eyes said, it was useless to try to beguile him. She had been too cruel to him long ago; and that was sad beyond bearing, because now, looking back, Charmian could see that he was the one man with whom she might have been happy.

She said it all with that one glance, no matter that it was all impossible nonsense. The falsity of it was irrelevant while she was saying it.

Loford had turned and was extending a massive hand toward the Lady Charmian. "The key," he said, in almost courtly tones. The strongbox now looked a little larger, the shape of it was somewhat altered, since the wizard had bent over it.

"You are but bandits, then," Charmian said, while her hand made slow searching motions among the pockets of her robe, as if to find a key. "I warned my Lord the Constable to give more thought to such.

Now perforce he will admit that I was right." Rolf understood that she was bargaining for her life, telling them as well as she could in the hearing of the servant in the wardrobe, that they would not be named by her as Western soldiers if they would spare her life.

She might be able to make almost anything believable. "I would that you were more than bandits," she went on, speaking now to Chup, with eyes again as well as words. "I dreamt once that a man had come to carry me away, so that from that day on I would never have to serve another man but him. And in that dream—"

"The key," Chup grated in an ugly voice. "Or I will spoil your lying face." Charmian knew him. She seemed to collapse before the threat, shrinking back against the wall.

"The key is in the bedside table," she said simply.

Chup kept his eyes on her until Loford had gone to the chest with the key and come back holding up the dark round thing in its silver filigree. Rolf had never seen anything just like it before, but felt Ardneh's certainty that it was the right thing. Rolf nodded, then added: "Don't forget the rest."

They had discussed this point beforehand, too. If they were to be taken for bandits they must not leave a single jewel that they could carry away. Loford went to scoop up other wealth from the box, and stuff his pockets with it. The black jewel, meanwhile, he had tossed to Rolf, who put it into a small empty pouch that waited ready at his belt.

There came a startling, though quiet, trying of the outer door, followed after a moment by a rattling and wrenching that made it thud against its hinges. An indistinct male voice called out, in what might have been anger or alarm. The absence of the sentry from the stair would certainly awaken Eastern vigilance.

Chup's eyes were still riveted on Charmian's. In a low voice he demanded: "Is that the Constable?"

She gave a little shiver, an involuntary movement that Rolf thought he had seen her make once before, when men were about to kill each other for her amusement. It seemed a joyous movement. She said: "It is his way; it sounds like him."

Rolf stepped quietly back to Catherine and took her by the arm. "Let me get in place behind the door," he whispered. "Then open it and let him—" He broke off there, for outside at least one more heavy voice had joined the Constable's, and the tramp of yet other feet was somewhere on the stair.

Pulling Catherine by the arm, he hurried to the inner room again. There was only the one door, and the windows were narrow and heavily barred. It was well they had made alternate plans. Loford had his sword out and was digging an escape hole in the flimsy ceiling; in a moment Rolf was working at his side. Dried mud fell in his face, and lengths of reed and sapling began to dangle brokenly.

The noise at the door turned into a determined assault. Chup said something that Rolf could not hear to Charmian. Charmian turned to the door and cried out loudly: "Stop! These men will kill me if you force your way in. Stop, they wish to bargain with you!"

The banging and chopping ceased. "Bargain?" roared a man's deep voice. "With what? Who are they, what do they want?"

"They are bandits," Charmian cried weakly. Glancing toward her, Rolf saw that she had retreated from Chup's sword until her head was pressed against the wall, but the sword had advanced until it now poised rock-steady a centimeter from her face. Loss of beauty would be worse than loss of life to her.

There was a pause outside, as if of disbelief. "Well, wondrous stupid ones, so it would seem." More feet now on the stair, a platoon gathering hurriedly; and overhead now, soft footsteps on the roof; it had not taken the Constable long to order his forces. Now he bellowed, with vast authority: "Ho, in there! The trap is shut on you; unbar this door!" Chup forced his erstwhile bride into the big wardrobe where one of her servant-girls was still cowering in silence. What he said to Charmian at parting Rolf could not hear, but she went in with quiet alacrity.

Loford had ceased prying at the ceiling, and sheathed his sword, but stood still looking upward at the damage while he made the gestures of his magic art. Now he signed to Rolf to cease work also; Rolf did so. But by Loford's art, the noises they had made when working went right on without a pause, the subdued splintering of light wood, the trickling falls of powdery fragments to the floor were heard, though the hole they had begun in the roof now got no bigger. Now Rolf attacked the floor with his dagger. He labored to pry up a board; Catherine dropped to her knees beside him and wrenched with strong sure hands as soon as he had raised one end enough for her to get a purchase on it. By the art of Loford, who worked on silently above them, the shriek of yielding nails was made to come from overhead.

The Constable's voice renewed its demands for entry.

"Not so fast!" Chup roared back. "What'll you give us for your woman's life?" And he thumped with the flat of his sword on the wardrobe, from which the voice of Charmian hastily called out, serving to demonstrate that she was still alive.

Rolf and Catherine by this time had one floorboard completely up. A quick look down through the gap assured him that the room below was deserted. The soldiers lodged in it would have been called to duty when the alarm broke out.

The Constable's overbearing voice called out some threat, and the battering at the door resumed, more violently than before. The renewed noise from the door, with that induced by magic overhead, effectively covered the ripping up of another board.

The whole was big enough now for Rolf, and he was through it in a moment, with Catherine right behind him. Loford had to tear up yet another plank before the gap was wide enough to accommodate his bulk; luckily the ceilings were low and he had not far to fall. Chup was right behind.

Catherine picked up a bow, and looped over her shoulder a quiver of arrows that had been left in a corner of the room. With her cloak she might manage to conceal the weapons, and she pulled up its hood now to hide her face. Rolf was at the door, peering out through a crack until one set of hurried footsteps had passed their landing going up, and another down; and then he led the way out onto the stair, flattening himself against a wall. The Constable's men were gathered on the stair and landing above, still assaulting the heavy door of the top-floor apartment.

Rolf, Catherine, Loford, Chup. In single file on the stair, the four of them glided swiftly down. At the bottom of the stair, weapons under cloaks, they passed out swiftly through the doorway into the courtyard where torches flared, disturbed animals stamped and moved and grunted, and travelers, slaves, grooms, tavern girls, all milled around, gaping upward with mixed alarm and interest.

The four moved in a regular walking pace across the courtyard to the stair on the other side; over there was the only way out. They were about half-way across, moving deliberately amid people and restless animals, when behind them Charmian's screams for help were suddenly added to the noise. She must have at last dared to peer out of the wardrobe, to find herself practically alone amid unnerving sounds. When the screams came Rolf took Catherine's arm in a hard grip, but he need not have bothered, for her step remained steady. Without interference from anyone in the ragged little crowd of gapers, the four reached the desired doorway and began to mount the stair. This building was less solidly built than the one they had just come from, though of the same general plan.

Doors stood open to their right and left as they ascended, one floor, two, but for the moment no one was in sight. The rooms had evidently been emptied of soldiers and onlookers alike by the alarms.

Now Chup took the lead, and pulled back the hood of his cloak. As they rounded the last landing going up, the expected sentry appeared at the top of the stair, the door to the room behind him standing open.

Chup in his best Eastern-officer voice demanded: "Here, fellow, are any men loitering in those rooms?" and kept on climbing as he spoke.

"No, sir! No malingerers here."

"Then who is that?" Chup barked. He pointed behind the sentry into a dark corner of an empty room as he came up to the man, bringing a sure blade from beneath his cloak as the man's head turned.

Now, the four could go unhurriedly up a ladder from the topmost stair-landing to a trapdoor that opened on the roof. Rolf, once more in the lead, flattened himself down as he crawled out into the open night. On the roof across the court the Eastern men waiting in fruitless ambush were being less cautious, and he could see them easily in silhouette. All was quiet in that direction now, a state of affairs that could not last much longer; the Constable would be finding his trap empty, and would be howling on their trail when he saw the great hole they had made in the floor.

Chup had the soft thin coil of rope unwound from his midsection, and now lay on his back with his feet against the low parapet, making himself a human anchor to hold the rope while the others slid down. Rolf went first. The rope was long enough to reach the ground with a little to spare. As soon as sand was under his feet, he tugged once on the rope and waited with drawn sword. Catherine came next, dropping her bow when halfway down but picking it up before she scrambled to Rolf's side; and then Loford, grunting and mumbling as the rope burned his sliding fingers. Then came the rope itself, a whispering coil; then Chup, dropping unaided from rooftop to sand.

IV

Distance

━━━━━━◆◆━━━━━━

In single file the four of them marched in silence, save for the soft crunch underfoot of sand, and the faint whisper of the wind. Now Loford followed Rolf, and then the girl, with Chup alert to hear pursuers in the rear. They left the caravanserai kilometers behind, while the stars spun slowly around the one that marked the Pole. Rolf strode on into the unknown with confidence, though he had only a hazy idea of what kind of country lay in that direction, and no idea at all of the goal that Ardneh wanted him finally to reach. No one spoke, except that once or twice a faint whisper-mutter with the rhythm of magic in it came forward to Rolf's ears, and soon thereafter arose what might have been perfectly natural pushes of wind against their faces, wind howling back down along their trail with strength enough to pull sand over their footprints.

Rolf now and again looked up, trying to catch sight of wide bird-wings against the stars. But there were none.

"We had best get clear of this open sand before morning," Chup growled once, low-voiced, from the rear. Rolf only grunted in reply. The need was obvious. Rolf stepped up his pace a little more. Now he could hear Catherine's breathing. But the girl kept up without faltering.

The hours of the night turned on. There was no pause for rest. No hint of dawn had yet appeared in the clear sky when Rolf noticed that the character of the country was changing. The gentle dunes grew

steeper, and among them there jutted up hillocks
and humps of worn, eroded clay. Grass and bushes,
appeared in a thin scattering, then became noticeably thicker. As the eastern sky began to brighten
subtly, the clay hills came to dominate the land.
These turned into a plateau across which the
travelers walked, scrambling frequently through
small ravines that lay across their path, or following
those that ran for a time along it. Some of these
narrow ravines were steep enough to have small
overhangs along their sides, and these, when the
morning sky began to brighten up in earnest, afforded some possibility of hiding for the day.

Rolf chose a place, which was then improved by
digging back a little into the clay bank, the exca-
vated material being carefully scattered where it
would not show. Now, lying on the narrow ledge
that they had made, it was possible to see back for
nearly a kilometer in the way that they had come,
and for some forty or fifty meters along the ravine in
the other direction. And from this direction, now, at
last, came Mewick and the other members of the
patrol; or most of them, rather. There were five riders, not six, approaching.

The four who had just lain down in weariness
sprang up again. Mewick reined in below their
ledge, saying: "The birds have just now gone to shelter for the day. We would have caught up with you
sooner, but—" He made a gesture of weariness,
dismissing causes pointless to enumerate now. He
and his mount, and the men and animals behind
him, looked tired, and some had new bandages to
show. "There is cavalry on your trail, not two
kilometers back. They dared to follow you out by
night, and we were not enough for a real ambush.
We only delayed them a little and I lost Latham."

It registered now with Rolf whose face was missing, whose animal was being led in the rear with
the other spares. The shock of a friend's loss came
and was set aside in the pile of losses that must

someday be dealt with somehow. Now Rolf only asked: "How many of them?" As he spoke he was packing his meager gear into a roll, getting ready to bundle it onto the back of the best spare riding-beast.

"Fifty. Thereabouts," said Mewick wearily. "Through divination or otherwise they must have some inkling of the importance of what you took; else I think they would not have come onto your trail at night, no. The Constable is leading them in person. Has Ardneh any offering of guidance now?"

"Only that I must go on, with what I carry." Rolf finished tying his bundle onto the beast and swung himself up into its saddle. His eye fell on Catherine, and saw in her a desperation made calm only by her great weariness. The mention of Ardneh had probably meant nothing to her, he realized. Most probably she feared only one thing more than being with this bandit gang—there was still no reason for her to think them anything but bandits—and that one thing was being left behind by them, to be retaken by the East. "Mount up, girl," he ordered, pointing to another ready animal. "Come with me." Only after he had spoken did he realize that there was a deeper purpose than compassion, or any selfish want, behind his words.

Mewick raised his eyebrows, then nodded, handing Rolf provisions and a water bag. "So it must be. We here will do what must be done. Which way does Ardneh bid you go? We will try to turn the ones who follow aside."

"I am still heading just a little west of north. I *think* it will be many days yet before I reach the goal—whatever it may be."

Mewick and others raised their hands, murmuring good wishes. Arrangements for future contact would be left to nighttime and the birds—or to Ardneh, if he should take a hand overtly. Rolf dug heels into his mount and set off along the ravine to the north; a glance back showed Catherine riding

competently and close behind him. If, as her accent
suggested, she were really of some noble family in
the Offshore Islands, it was natural that she should
know how to ride.

The cleft of the ravine grew shallow, and bent off
in the wrong direction. Rolf heeled his riding-beast
to a faster pace as he urged it out onto the flat
surface of a plateau. Steadily they put distance between themselves and the place behind them where
Mewick was trying to arrange an ambush of an
enemy force that outnumbered his by something
more than five to one. Rolf knew that Mewick and his
six men would not stand and be wiped out, not if
they could help it. They would strike and retreat
and strike again, if they were able. If they could get
through the day, the night would offer better hope.
But it was early morning now . . .

Rolf and his companion had come about a kilometer across the open plateau, and were almost in
reach of another favorably oriented ravine, offering
some chance of shelter from the sky, when there
came drifting from a height the raucous cry that
meant they had been spotted by a reptile.

No use to gallop now; Rolf held to a steady pace.
The reptile was overtaking them on effortless wings,
staying high out of bowshot; directly over their
heads, it marked their position for the pursuers on
the ground.

When Rolf and Catherine topped a slight rise,
they could look back and see the mounted Eastern
force, coming now onto the broken plateau, nearing
the place where Mewick and the others must be in
wait. It seemed the ambush could be no surprise, for
there were more reptiles, concentrating over something Rolf could not see—over seven Western soldiers, no doubt. He felt an urge, not courageous but
simply irrational, to turn back and be with them. But
that was not to be.

Catherine drew abreast of him as they rode on.
She asked: "Your whole band is scattering in dif-

ferent directions?'' When he did not answer, she asked him: ''What did he call you back there? Ardneh?''

''My name is Rolf.''

''Rolf, then. There is something I would ask of you.''

''Wait.'' He urged his mount over a difficult stretch of terrain, then stopped for a brief halt, to rest the animals for the space of a few breaths and to see by what route the pursuing cavalry was following. ''Now. What was it?''

Catherine said: ''If we are going to be taken by them, kill me first.''

It was only surprising for a moment. ''If that time ever comes, I will have other matters to think about. But cheer up, it has not come yet.''

The enemy riders had turned suddenly away from what seemed their logical course, and were slowing down. No reason was visible at this distance; but the concentration of reptiles, somewhat nearer, seemed greatly agitated. The one who had been flying directly over Rolf and Catherine, evidently assuming that they could be found again without any trouble on this bright morning, suddenly darted back to join the others.

''Now!'' Seizing the chance for whatever it might prove to be worth, Rolf turned his beast off running at a tangent to the course they had been following. He had begun to alter his true course, a little west of north, as soon as he thought the leatherwings had spotted them, and now he took it up again. And now, far ahead, he could already see how the country shaded out of barren badlands and into a higher and grassier plateau.

The moments of freedom from reptile observation fled by, and Rolf could make no profit from them. There was no reasonable place of concealment in sight, nowhere they could vanish, to be gone when the reptile came back to find them, as it must. As he rode, Rolf anxiously tried to reach Ardneh's thought, to find guidance. Nothing helpful came, nothing except the impression of a titanic weariness: a vague image of a faceless, beleaguered giant, hard pressed by a thousand enemies. What Rolf was doing was important, and worthy of Ardneh's help, but no more so than ten or a score of other struggles in which Ardneh was simultaneously involved. At this moment there could be no help for Rolf, except the continuing sense of the direction he was to travel.

The summer day stretched long ahead of them, before the night would bring a reasonable chance of shelter and of rest. Again there sounded the shouts of men at war, louder than might have been expected when fifty were facing only seven. Looking back, Rolf saw a gray maelstrom of wind and dust settling upon, or very near, the area where the fighting must have been. Loford must have managed to raise a desert-elemental. The Eastern troops would be powerless to advance as long as it blasted and blinded them with sand, but the Constable would be sure to have able magical assistance with him and the elemental might be soon dispersed. Meanwhile, the reptiles were being driven from the fighting by the terrific winds; now instead they came on after Rolf and the girl.

Given a great-enough advantage in numbers, the leatherwings were willing to attack armed humans and there were a score or more of them now in sight. Rolf asked: "Can you use that stick of wood you carry?"

Catherine unslung the bow from her back and groped for an arrow, meanwhile guiding her mount with her knees. "Once I could shoot with some skill. It has been a long time since I had the chance."

Rolf grunted. He was an indifferent archer, but almost certainly he would do better than she with sword.

The reptiles circled them at low altitude, a ragged-looking swirl of gray-green wings and yellow teeth; then, from all points of the compass at once, they closed. Catherine's first arrow missed, but she had time for a second, and one of the creatures tumbled heavily into the sand, a clean kill. Then the cawing cloud engulfed the riders. Rolf swung his blade with brutal energy. The riding-beasts plunged and screamed when they felt teeth and talons. Again and again Rolf's sword met resistance, parting leathery hide, stringy flesh, and light bones. Then suddenly the flock was gone, those who could still fly whirling at a safe distance to screech their rage, leaving half a dozen dead and wounded to litter the thirsty sand. Catherine had sheltered under her great cloak when the enemy came within clawing range, and she was unscratched though the cloak had been rent in several places. Nor was Rolf injured, but the animals, shivering and muttering, were each bleeding from several wounds.

Still, the riding-beasts trudged stolidly on, and this was not the time and place to stop and tend them if it could be avoided. Rolf was momentarily expecting the enemy cavalry to come into sight, the elemental had perhaps been dispersed, though a pall of dust still hanging over the area made it difficult to see what was going on back there. But no riders appeared. Once again, fainter than before, Rolf heard the sounds of fighting. Time was being bought for his escape, at what cost he did not care to think.

The reptiles continued in their circle. Catherine rode silently at his side, watching them with her chin up, an arrow nocked and ready in her bow.

The morning progressed, the reptiles gradually withdrawing farther and at last breaking their circle and landing, one of their number remaining airborne to observe Rolf and Catherine from a distance. Rolf called a rest stop, and devoted it mainly to caring for the animals, whose wounds were bloodier than he had thought. Insects were buzzing around them already. With Catherine helping efficiently, he did what he could to clean the wounds, and bandaged those in places where a bandage could be made secure. Then the two humans walked on for a while, leading the animals, before remounting.

Considering the damage the reptiles had suffered in their first attack, Rolf was not surprised that they forebore to launch another. When about midday they returned in a menacing cloud, Catherine loosed another arrow at them. They clamored insults but flew no closer.

Slowly but steadily the kilometers flowed by beneath the plodding beasts. Twice during the afternoon Rolf halted to rest and tend the animals as well as possible, and for long stretches he and Catherine walked. Far behind, there was still dust on the horizon. He groped for Ardneh's presence once more, and this time received a feeling of reassurance; help was to be granted, or was being granted now. What kind of help was not explained, but Rolf felt somewhat easier. He was further cheered when at last the reptiles screamed their final insults and began their forced retreat, to the safe roosts they must seek out before the coming of the night.

Rolf shortly called a halt. The mounts were swaying and stumbling with fatigue, and the place they had come to offered grazing as promising as any they were likely to find. It was a nearly dried-out watercourse, marked along its edges by abundant grass, a few bushes, and even scattered trees.

The animals' wounds included several ugly punctures that seemed likely to become infected. When they had done what they could for the beasts, and eaten a little themselves, it had grown dark. 'Rest,'' Rolf grunted. Catherine, looking too tired to answer, collapsed into a silent heap.

He was too tired himself to try to stay awake when the likelihood of an enemy coming seemed vanish-

ingly small. He arranged his weapons handily and
began to doze off in the warm night, his back against
the curved bank of the dry channel. Vaguely he
wondered about Catherine, how she had come to be
a slave, what she would want . . . he was too sleepy
to think long.

Waking abruptly to the racketing of insects, he
quickly surveyed the night-world about him before
he moved. The starry powder of the Milky Way made
a vast diagonal blaze across the sky. It took a second
or two before he saw what had somehow awakened
him. Perched high on the opposite bank of the
ravine, a great bird rested motionless, its feathered
bulk cutting a dark pattern from the light of stars.
When Rolf turned his head toward the bird he saw
the huge wings open and reach out, balancing, far
wider than a man's spread arms.

Its voice was musical, and so soft he had to listen
carefully to make sure of all the words. "Rooolf o
the Brooken Lands, rest no moore this night. Those
who pursue you are not far away, and they will come
on with the first of the morning light."

Rolf glanced up at the stars to gauge the time. He
had only slept for three or four hours, but felt considerably refreshed. The riding-beasts, used to
birds, were dozing on their feet where he had picketed them a little distance off. He got to his feet and
began to gather his few belongings. He asked the
bird: "What of my friends who fought to buy me
time?"

"The one whoo spoke to me was a tall, fat wizard,"
the bird replied. "He said to tell yooou that Metzgar
had fallen, but that the others fared well enough."

"Ah." Tall Metzgar, of the long beard, and long
stories . . .

"Also I must tell youuu that more friends, and
enemies, are beginning to move into this country
from the south. But all of them are kilometers and
kilometers away as yet. Also, Duncan wants to know
what you are doooing now."

"Tell Duncan I am going on," said Rolf. He shot a quick look at Catherine, but she gave no sign of having moved since she lay down. He introspected for a moment, and found something new. "And tell Duncan, and the fat wizard, that now I must angle more toward the West. I am going to travel an hour or so and try to hide again before dawn. If the pursuers can be led straight on north, or east, it will be a considerable help."

The bird hooted once, assentingly, then rose with a silent effort and disappeared among the stars, just as Catherine stirred. A moment later she sat up, looking groggy and bewildered.

"Get up," he ordered. "We have more distance to cover before the dawn." She sighed and got to her feet slowly but without complaint. Only now did he notice that she had evidently not managed to find a pair of sandals. Well, if the animals held out, it would make little difference.

There was not much water left in the bag, but the country was no longer desert-dry and Rolf was not much concerned on that account. The animals seemed strong enough, but restless, as if their wounds were paining them. Catherine dozed in the saddle from time to time; Rolf would see her head start to sink forward, then jerk erect as she caught herself into wakefullness. It was not a good time for talking; the ears had to be kept free for more important matters.

Before the sky had begun to pale in the east, they came to another mud-bottomed creek bed. This was wider than the last one and filled with tall, reedy flowers. These were full-leaved enough in places to form fairly secure screens against aerial observation. Rolf made a screen for the animals against the high bank of the dry creek, under which they were willing enough to lie when he had given them some water. He and Catherine found dry spots close together at a little distance from the animals, and after bending a few flower-stalks overhead for better concealment lay down and promptly slept.

When Rolf awoke again the sun was full and bright, hurling splinters of its light between leaves into his face. Insects murmured undisturbed in the full drowse of summer day. The girl, curled up in her brown servant's dress, face hidden resting on her rolled-up cloak, still slept. Her back was to Rolf, her breathing regular, her legs pulled up inside her dress. He noticed that the bottoms of her bare feet were calloused hard.

He arose silently and went on a brief scouting expedition, fifty meters or so up and down the mud-bottomed gully, not getting far from the tall flowers. He studied the sky with great care but saw no reptiles. He found a place where it seemed a little digging might reach water. And he stood looking long to the northwest. There were some trees in that direction, and a great deal of long grass, but the cover seemed inadequate for an attempt at traveling by day. They had finally managed to lose the enemy and there was no sense in being spotted again at once. He tried to weigh in his mind the odds that the Constable would bring his men this way, find the creek-bed, follow it, and flush them out, before darkness fell again.

He could hope that Ardneh would warn him again in time, but he could not be sure. It seemed to him that he had scores of kilometers yet to travel.

He went quietly back to Catherine, who had stirred in her sleep, stretched out her legs, and turned her face up. Now she looked very young. Her face was not pretty, he thought, even apart from the still-swollen and discolored cheekbone and a few odd scratches and smears acquired in the last day and night. Her nose was just off-shape enough to deny her prettiness in any case. And her stretched-out body now looked a little awkward.

But she was most certainly a girl. He had not had the leisure until now to consciously consider her as such.

An insect whirred close above her face. Waking suddenly, she sat up with a start, regarded him with bewilderment for a moment, and then sank back, remembering.

"I have got away from her," she said then, softly, looking all around as if awakening from some evil dream, and making sure of reality. Then she looked at Rolf and added: "Your friends have not caught up with us. Are we to meet them somewhere?"

"Nor my enemies, either." He regarded her silently for a few moments. "Your black eye looks better than it did."

Her gaze dropped as if in sudden shyness. "What will we do now?"

"Eat some food. Dig a hole in this mud, we'll probably be able to get some drinkable water. It may take a while, but we'll be here all day with little else to do. Don't want to travel with the reptiles watching, not once we've lost them."

She got up stiffly, brushing back from her eyes long hair that had come unbound. "Shall I start digging right away?"

"See about getting a little food ready. I'll dig. The animals are going to need more water soon."

Rolf took a long knife and dug for a while in the likeliest-looking place he could find, a sandy area against a bank. At first only soupy muck appeared, but after some diligence in scooping out the hole and patience in letting it refill, a supply of usable water was available. After he led the animals to drink, he and Catherine sat eating dried food and finishing the contents of the waterbag.

She was not very talkative, he thought. In fact it seemed to him that the silence was definitely growing awkward, before she suddenly announced: "I am sure that my family will pay some ransom for me if you were to find a way of returning me to the Offshore Islands. We are not poor, and our city was never overrun by the East."

Rolf munched for a while in thoughtful silence.

The less he told her now, the better, he decided. She might become separated from him in some way, and fall again into Eastern hands. He said: "It doesn't seem likely that I'll be able to take you home. Not very soon."

Eagerly she edged a little closer to him, again putting back her long brown hair. "You wouldn't have to take me all the way. If you could show me how I can reach one of the armies of the West, I would—I would pledge that my family would reward you." When he was silent her eagerness faded. "I know, it would mean having to wait for your money. And why should you believe me at all?"

"I have heard your accent before. I believe you, about your family. But I have other business that must be taken care of, that cannot wait."

She said no more for a while. But after they had led the animals back to deeper shelter, she said: "I do not know if you are waiting here for your friends, or what. I suppose you don't want to tell me."

Rolf threw himself down in the spot where he had slept, and after a moment Catherine sat nearby, next to her rolled-up cloak. She went on: "Maybe you have to divide your loot with them. I don't know how such things are managed among bandits. But if you are not planning to meet them, or if you have given them up for lost, then you might come with me, and join the West. I am sure that they need sturdy men."

"Hm. Or even if I wanted to run out on my friends, not split the loot with them at all, I could do that." He paused, wickedly enjoying her confusion. "But there are good reasons why I cannot do that. Not right now."

She was downcast, but persistent. "I understand, you have that great jewel to profit from. Why should you get mixed up in battles? Maybe you even were once a Western soldier, and deserted. I know some men become bandits that way. I do not know or care, I only know that you have helped me more than you can know, and I want to thank you for it. Since you have done it, for whatever reason, you might as well have the reward. My father is a burgomaster of Birgun, which as you may know is one of the chief cities of the Offshore Islands, a city never touched by the East and still powerful. Prince Duncan's home is not far from there, and I am sure that you have heard of him.''

"A friend of yours, no doubt.''

"I have seen him. Not much more than that.''

"If your city was untouched, how did you come to be a slave?''

She looked off into the distance. "A long story, like many others you must know. I was traveling away from home, and caught up in an Eastern raid . . . I am sure my kinsmen must be searching for me, and their gratitude will be great toward anyone who brings me back.'' Her eyes came back to Rolf. "And no one in the Islands would think you a thief for having taken some Eastern jewels at the same time.''

Both were silent for a little while. Then Catherine went on, as if more to herself than to Rolf: "There is also the man to whom I was pledged in marriage, but it has been so long . . . more than a year since I was lost. He may well be married to another by now, or dead, for he was a soldier.'' She seemed calm enough about it, as if all that former life were decades behind her instead of only months; and Rolf understood her; his life too had been broken off in the same way.

Evidently encouraged because he was at least tolerating her talk, she asked: "Do you know anything of how the war is going?''

He thought a little, and made an answer that any alert bandit should be able to give. "Duncan keeps an army in the field, keeps the fight going. Ominor can't seem to drive him off the mainland, or plant him in it either.''

A sparkle shown in Catherine's good eye. "I tell

you, the West is going to win. If they have not been beaten by this time, it never can be done."

"The same thing might be said about the East," Rolf said drowsily, and closed his eyes. "I'll think on what you've said. No more of it for now. Try and get some more sleep. Later in the day the Constable may be coming near, and we'll need to be alert."

They spent the remaining daylight hours in their hideaway, resting, watching, trying to help the animals. The beasts were in pain from their infected wounds, and one of them was limping noticeably. Rolf glimpsed a reptile in the distant sky, but he could not tell what business it was about. In the last hour before sunset he grew restless and impatient, listening intently at every far-off sound. As soon as it was dark, having eaten again, they set off into the northwest, leading the animals until the day's stiffness should be worked out of their muscles.

At the first rest stop the girl said to him: "Let me ask you bluntly. Do you mean to keep me with you? What will you do with me?"

"Have I not used you better than your previous master did? Of course. What are you worried about? The less you know of my business, the better off you are, I think."

"I see that." She spoke softly and reasonably. "It is only that I have hopes of traveling west, of getting home. I did think of running away from you, but I do not fear you anymore. And I know nothing of the land here, or where the armies are."

"Let me think about it, I say again. Don't worry. You are not getting any farther from your goal."

For the remainder of the night Catherine said no more about her hopes and fears, and had very little to say on any subject. Rolf set a steady pace that covered a good many kilometers, though now both animals were limping and the humans walked more than they rode. Toward dawn they came upon a running stream with tree-lined banks. After drinking their fill, they were searching for some good cover against the coming hours of daylight, when out of nowhere a great gray bird came down, first a soundless shadow and then a somehow unreal though solid presence, big as a man, squatting in the grass before them. Catherine half-raised one hand, as if to point, then froze.

"Greetings, Roolf." The bird's voice was as soft and musical as that of the previous night's messenger, but Rolf thought this was a different bird; most of them looked much alike to him. The bird went on: "Strijeef of the Feathered Folk sends his greetings."

"Take mine to him, good messenger, if you will. What other news?"

"Only that, to the south of you, humans and powers are gathering still, of the East and of the West. It seems that both armies may follow yooou intooo the north."

"Are there any orders for me?"

"Prince Duncan sends you this word: I am to take what you are carrying, and fly on with it ahead, if you can tell me where to go with it; if Ardneh does not object."

Rolf thoughtfully fingered the pouch wherein the great jewel lay. "No. Tell the Prince the answer must still be no. If it seems I am about to be taken, then come to me if you can, and I will give you this. Not otherwise."

The bird was silent for a bit, then fixed enormous yellow eyes on Catherine. "I must take a report back on this one whooo travels with you."

"She does so by Ardneh's will. She is an enemy of the East, that much I am sure about. And a former neighbor of Duncan's, it would seem. Come, bird, the light is growing. Rest with us through the day; we can find some good place among these trees. We will talk. Then tomorrow night you can bear my answers back to Duncan."

A little later, when they were securely hidden in a

thicket, Rolf looked closely at the stunned face of
Catherine, who had not said a word since the bird
came down. With a rare full smile on his own face,
he said: "Welcome. You see that you have reached
the armies of the West."

V

Little Moment of Revenge

After speeding Rolf on his way with a final wave, Chup crouched down between Mewick and Loford on the little sheltered ledge they had scooped out of the side of the ravine. Looking to the southeast, he could see the Constable's force just coming into sight a kilometer away. Despite the distance, Chup thought that he could distinguish Charmian's long golden hair. An illusion, she would have it bound up for the ride. He told himself he should have killed her when he had the chance . . . Mewick was plucking at his sleeve, and motioning that it was time to move. Down in the bottom of the ravine, Chup mounted and followed the other six men remaining in the party, riding in a single file angling up the side of the ravine. Mewick was leading them to the northeast, at right angles to the course that Rolf had chosen.

About a dozen reptiles were in the sky, Chup noted as they reached the top of the slope and trotted toward the next ravine. The leatherwings were beginning to concentrate above the little Western force. Chup caught another glimpse of Abner's force, advancing steadily, beginning now to come into the broken country.

The chances of perpetrating an ambush seemed vanishingly small at the moment. To Loford, just ahead of him, Chup called: "What's in your bag of tricks, stout one?"

Mewick at the head of the file heard him, turned and called: "Let us see what we can find in our

arrow-bags first.'' And then he led them down one
ravine in a sudden dash toward the enemy column
that sent the reptiles speeding ahead to croak their
warnings, and then back up another, smaller, narrower ravine, on a winding, reversing course that
took them out of sight of the reptiles. Mewick there-
upon abruptly called a halt, and with virtuosic gestures bade his men draw and nock arrows and aim
into the air. When the first reptiles came coasting
back over the hilltop close above, to discover what
had happened to the vanished subjects of their sur-
veillance, the ready volley brought down one and
winged another. While the flock was still recoiling
in noisy outrage from this ambush, Mewick led his
men on up the winding ravine at a headlong gallop,
once more unobserved by the foe. Following some
instinct of his own that seemed as accurate as aerial observation, he halted again suddenly, dismounted, and scrambled up a slope to peer through
grass at the top. Letting out a hissing noise of satisfaction, he once more pantomimed his wish for
archery, this time even correcting his men's angle of
aim, and then, with an unmistakable slashing gesture, bidding them loose their arrows blindly. Before the shafts could have tallen from the sky upon
any targets, Mewick was in the saddle again and
leading the retreat. There was a pained outcry from
somewhere below.

The little volley of arrows had fallen scattered
among and around the front of the enemy column,
and one of them had drawn blood. More important,
it stopped the enemy's forward progress for the
moment, and assured its somewhat slower and
more cautious movement in the future.

Mewick now led his men toward the north, for the
time being making no effort to do anything but keep
between the enemy and the course he wanted them
to think that Rolf was following.

The morning wore along uneventfully. The two
groups of mounted men made their way steadily

northward on parallel courses. Around the line of
march the desert badlands reared up strange barren shapes of rock, among which smaller rocks lay
jumbled and dry ravines lost their way.

Mewick somehow found a reasonably straight
way through. Then suddenly he stopped, staring
intently at the reptiles in the sky. "Demons of all the
East!" he muttered fiercely. "But they are getting
away from us. West! We must get west, and catch up
with them!"

Riding hard, they topped a rise and caught sight
of the enemy column moving away to the northwest,
seemingly right on the trail of Rolf who had evidently not managed to shake the reptiles after all.
Abner had maneuvered himself between the fugitives he was trying to overtake, and the annoying,
elusive handful of men who were trying to delay
him.

Mewick kept his men moving forward briskly.
"Wizard?" he asked.

Loford, riding now in the middle of the file, was
letting his mount find its own way, while his large
blue eyes looked into distances that were not of
earth or sky, and his fingers fumbled in a bag he had
withdrawn from his pack. His gross body jiggled
unheeded with the rapid ride. He took from the
cloth bag a smaller bag of leather, curiously decorated in many colors, and from that in turn a length
of sandy-colored twine, twisted into many strange
knots. He rode on for some distance, fingering this
absently, then suddenly seemed to come to himself,
and with a throat-clearing got the attention of all
the others.

"Hum. As the signs and powers now stand, the
only thing of any consequence that I can manage
successfully is to evoke a desert-elemental. But even
at best to call one up will mean some difficulty and
danger for us all. At worse—well things could get
quite out of hand."

Mewick shook his head. "You had best try. Our

swords and arrows are too few, unless we can get between them and Rolf once more."

"I am wondering," Chup put in, "how strong a wizard they have with *them*. Not that our pudgy fellow here is easily overmatched, but the Constable of the East will surely be well attended in that regard."

"As to that," said Loford, unperturbed, "we will soon enough find out. Now let me do my work. No, keep moving. Just a little silence; I can raise an elemental as well as almost any other man, while I ride on beast-back if need be."

With fingers suddenly turned extremely skillful, he tilted the little leather bag so that there ran from it a thin stream of ordinary-looking sand, falling to be lost along the trail. Holding the bag in one hand while it slowly continued to spill, he used his other hand and his teeth to tug at certain places in the curiously knotted twine. One by one knots fell away and straightened out. Counting knots as they disappeared, Chup caught his breath. "We'll all be sandblasted to the bone," he muttered. But he made no real protest; heroic measures were called for.

Loford's art took quick effect. Looking to the northwest, beyond the enemy force, Chup watched the sandy land seem to shake out its dunes like wrinkles from a blanket, rising with the appearance of a single deep ocean swell as far as eye could see to right and left. Chup, who had seen similar things before, knew it was not in fact the whole earth lifting up, only surface sand raised by a great wave of wind, yet involuntarily he tried to brace his feet more firmly in the stirrups.

Reptiles chattered and shrieked alarm. From near the head of the distant Eastern mounted column, one tiny mounted figure detached itself, spurring with seeming confidence toward the oncoming wall of sand that here and there took on vague shapes of hands and jaws. It would be the Constable's wizard. The tiny man-figure raised its arms, and Chup heard Loford grunt as if he had received a blow. The stout magician turned his animal aside, slid awkwardly from the saddle, and sank down on one knee, eyes squinted shut, while his comrades reined to a halt around him.

"Ah, Ardneh," Loford groaned, "Ardneh, help! He means to turn what I have raised against us."

The galloping Eastern wizard seemed to be under no such strain as Loford suffered. Riding easily, he moved his outstretched arms forward and down toward the oncoming elemental; Chup, watching, had the impression of a tremendous quelling, quieting force. But it might almost have been the useless gesture of a child. The wavefront of wind and wind-blown earth poured on remorselessly and struck. For a moment or two there remained a tiny isle of calm, around the mounted Eastern magician, not much wider than his arms could stretch, in which air fell quiet and lifeless before his counterspell. But then he and his defended island vanished; the elemental rolled on unimpeded, reaching out monstrous half-living paws of sand and air for Abner and his fifty men.

With a cry of relief, Loford staggered to his feet. Then the elemental's peripheral winds and dust were beating on the Western men. Chup felt the sting and lash of sand, and the air was a sudden shriek around his ears. The bright sun, and his friends, were suddenly gone, concealed within the desert as it walked. When things cleared for a moment, he glimpsed the dense core of the elemental squatting some hundreds of meters to the northwest, right where Abner's force had been. Abner's force was still there, from the look of things. Out of the solid-looking clouds of raging sand came Eastern men individually, riding, staggering, crawling; and here and there fled blinded and demented animals. This elemental would not kill, at least not quickly and not often, but it would surely disable any human fighting force it settled on.

Chup cried out: "Ah, for a score of men to charge them now!" But to charge and fight in the heart of the storm would be to put oneself under the same disadvantage as the enemy, and he knew full well the impulse had to be restrained. Mewick instead used the time gained to best advantage by getting his few men once more between Rolf and the disorganized foe. The reptiles, hit harder than any land creatures by the elemental's blasts, were swept from the sky for the time being, and Mewick found a place against the steep side of a sheer jutting rock, where his men might hope to remain unobserved should the reptiles manage to come back, and from which they might sally out to sting the Constable again if and when he came on in pursuit of Rolf.

Chup huddled with the others between sheltering rocks, muffling his face with his cloak against the sand. Once more Loford groaned. "Now they too are getting help from greater powers," he muttered.

The wind died suddenly, rose again, then came and went in fitful gusts. Squinting into the sky above the enemy, Chup could see that the Eastern wizard had at last been able to call upon some effective force. The elemental was broken into a multitude of smaller whirlwinds, each of which raised a cloud of sand and dust, but which taken all together lacked the purpose and power that the single great creature had possessed. He could see, too, that Loford had not abandoned the struggle. The numerous whirlwinds danced around a common center, and seemed to be striving continually to reunite.

"The wind is no longer so bad we cannot walk or ride," Mewick shouted to his men, making himself heard above the shrieking air. "Let us see if we can strike another blow!"

Abner had lost two men to the elemental, one blinded permanently by sand, the other left crazed and unable to do more than whimper to himself. It was midday before he had his forces properly marshalled again, the hopelessly wounded disposed of and their riding-beasts and other useful property distributed among the well. The wind was now no worse than a bearable storm. He considered dividing his force, feeling reasonably confident that there was no superior enemy body anywhere near, but decided against it when his wizard assured him that the winds must continue to decline.

The Constable cast a final look at his assembled force (the woman Charmian, dressed like a soldier and muffled against sand like the others, smiled bravely and admiringly at him; well, he couldn't have left her at the caravanserai, there was no telling when he'd be able to go back) and got it moving forward again. Scarcely had they gone a kilometer, however, when there came a few more arrows down upon them, from a hilltop close ahead. One more man was hit. At the Constable's order forty cavalry charged the hill with leveled lances, but its top was now deserted, and behind it several ravines offered concealment for a small force and the possibility of further ambushes. The Constable's horn sounded a recall.

Again they moved on to the northwest. The first reptile able to return to the column, between disabling wind-blasts, reported flatter, grassier country ahead, into which the two fleeing Westerners were making steady progress, while the seven others remained between the fleeing two and Abner. The Constable consulted his weary wizard, who confirmed him in his opinion that the two more distant fugitives had the huge important gem with them. The Constable ground his teeth and profaned the names of demons in his anger. He felt by no means certain of getting back the gem. Though the long hours of a summer afternoon still lay ahead, the sun had by now definitely passed its highest point.

There now arrived a reptile-courier from the Emperor of the East himself, who was with his main armies in the field a good many kilometers to the south. The courier bore an answer to the Constable's urgent dispatch of the early morning, informing the court that an object had been stolen similar to, but even larger than, that which had been used in the unsuccessful attempt to neutralize Ardneh. The answer from Ominor now was that the object was certainly of great importance, and the Constable must take personal command of the attempt to get it back. Also that he must conduct his search to the northwest — divination at the highest level gave assurance that the thing was being taken in that direction. Also, that reinforcements were being sent as quickly as possible to the Constable's aid. The first of these, a flight of a hundred additional reptiles, began to arrive shortly after the courier.

The West, too, Abner thought sourly, would doubtless be throwing in reinforcements, and there would come a hundred more birds to harass him through the night. As the reptiles came in, he sent them to scour the country far ahead, to try to discover where the fugitives were heading.

Half an hour's steady forward progress followed, before one of the scouting reptiles came screaming that the small Western force was drawing up in a line on a hilltop directly in their line of march.

"Seven men? I wish they would make such a stand."

When he had got a little closer and could better see the hill, he realized the Western maneuver was not so foolish as it had sounded. The slope was very wide from left to right, and too steep for mounted men to charge up it at any speed in the loose sand. Once more they would take casualties from arrows and find the foe gone when they reached the top. But to go clear around the hill would let the enemy succeed in delaying them, without paying anything for the privilege . . . Abner quickly decided to spread his men out and charge the hill. He would accept two or three casualties to inflict one; he would be delayed little if at all; and there was always the chance the fools would stand and fight.

The skirmish went about as he had expected, except that the Western arrows came down a little more thickly than he had hoped, so Abner left four men upon the slope. And when the crest was reached, the foe was gone, except for one who lay in the sand with the shaft of an Eastern arrow protruding from his head.

At any rate the country from here on was definitely flatter; the harassing enemy would have to remain at a greater distance. He could see the six riders on a distant rise, as if beckoning him to follow. Above them (at a safe altitude) many reptiles were cawing loudly and circling in the sky; but his wizard motioned in a slightly different direction, and in that way Abner directed his troops.

The hours of light remaining were still long, but inexorably growing shorter. Some of the reptiles sent to scout far ahead of the two fugitives began to return, saying they could find no settlements, no buildings, nothing that looked as if it might be the fugitives' goal. Grass grew tall and thick in that land, the reptiles reported, and trees in ever-increasing numbers. There were many places where the two-legged beasts could go to earth once darkness had fallen, and finding them again in the morning might not be easy. How far ahead were the fugitives now? Several kilometers. It was hard to say exactly; the reptiles' horizontal-distance sense, like that of the birds, was poor.

Abner moved his troops at a hard pace, though both men and animals were weary. He had the feeling he was gaining. No more hills obtruded themselves to give the six skirmishers another place to make a stand. They kept half a kilometer ahead of Abner in the open country, and seemed for the time being powerless to do more.

Just when it seemed that the day was going reasonably well after all, there sprang up another wind from dead ahead, erecting another wall of dust whose sudden creation bespoke the working of more Western magic. But this wind brought little pain to sore Eastern faces; it was far weaker (or perhaps more subtle) than the desert-elemental had been. This had been born in the sea of grass that lay ahead, beyond the desert. It did not blind and abrade with particles or threaten to kill with heat.

Abner's wizard was hard at work in his saddle once more, gesturing with a talisman of some kind in each hand. Whether he was having any success was hard to judge; the wind appeared about the same, able to do no obvious harm. The Constable tried to recall the characteristics of prairie-elementals, which he assumed this was. He seemed to remember that bleakness and tangled grass and natural wind were three components, but there was something else too, something he could not quite remember. His schooling in this branch of magic had been sketchy, and was now far in the past.

They had left the desert behind them, and were struggling through the first of the grasslands, when he remembered the most pertinent characteristic of prairie-elementals: distance itself.

His eyes told him what was happening, now that he thought to look closely for it. Beneath the feet of his riding-beast, and those of the other animals in his troop, the grassy land was elongating in the direction of their travel, like an optical illusion in reverse. Three steps forward were required to cover the real distance normally contained in two.

With a shout the Constable called his magician to his side, dragged the wretch from his saddle, and beat him half a dozen vicious blows with the flat of his sword. "Blunderer! Traitor! Could you not tell me what was happening? Or are you too thick-witted to be aware of it yourself?" He yearned to strike with the working edge of the blade, but was not ready to leave himself effectively wizardless in the face of the enemy.

"Ah, mercy, Lord!" the beaten wizard cried. "There be powers against me here such as I have never faced before."

Charmian had ridden forward from her place near the rear of the little column, and seeing that the Constable glanced at her but did not at once order her back, was emboldened to take part. To the unhappy wizard she said savagely: "One fat lout from the provinces opposes you, a man I have met before and know to be nearly devoid of skill, compared to what my Lord Constable's wizard should possess. My Lord Constable is ill-served indeed."

"I tell you I am blameless," the magician cried. He had fallen on his knees before the mounted Constable, while behind them the column halted.

"Who has defeated you? What mighty power?" the Constable demanded. "If you cannot tell me even that much, why should I not take you for a traitor, or an imbecile incompetent?"

"I know not what or who!" The magician's eyes were wild. "I knew not even that I was being beaten, until your mighty Lordship struck at me, as—as indeed I must be grateful for, that I was not slain out of hand."

Charmian's expression had changed as she listened, and now she put out a hand to Abner. "Wait, my good Lord, if it please you. There may be something to what this man says. There is one among our enemies who is subtle and powerful enough to confound most wizards in this way."

"So." Abner's rage was quickly transformed into calculation. He knew by now that Charmian was intelligent, or rather that she could be when it suited her; and she had come close to Ardneh in the past. "What more can you tell me on this point?"

She looked at Abner with an apparent anxiety to please. "Little enough right now, my Lord. Let me talk with this fellow for a while, as we go on, and it may be I can learn something worth your hearing."

"So be it." With a savage gesture Abner got the

stalled column moving again—two-thirds speed was better than none—and then, grimacing, he got paper from his saddlebag and reluctantly prepared to send a message asking Wood for help.

Charmian now had perfect reason for riding next to the wizard, and holding with him a lengthy whispered conversation of which no one else could hear a word.

"So, fellow," she began, in a tone remote and commanding. "I have saved you from the punishment your clumsiness merits. If you wish me to remain your friend, there is a simple thing you can do for me in return."

He looked at her with fear and calculation. "I am eternally in your debt, fair lady. What is there I can possibly do for you?"

"It might seem unimportant to my Lord the Constable, and I have not bothered him with it. But it is a meaningful matter to me." She began to explain.

She had not said much before the wizard was shaking his head, and holding up a finger to stop her speech. "No, no. If it were possible to cast a spell and bring down some disabling woe on those two fleeing from us, I would have done so long ere this. It was one of the first things the Constable asked of me, before taking the field in pursuit of them. But it cannot be done so simply. Conditions are not right in many ways—"

"I care little or nothing about harming the man," Charmian broke in. "It is the girl, Catherine, who betrayed me." Her voice dropped lower still, hate tightening it like some rack-rope in a dungeon. "It was she who got them to manhandle me. I saw her smirking, gloating, over her little moment of revenge . . . well, I mean to have the last laugh over her. I must and I will. Find me a way to give me my revenge upon that girl, and I will reward you well." She shifted her body in the saddle and saw his eyes go wandering over her, as if they had no choice but to do so when she willed it. "But fail to do so, and I will

tell the Constable that which will bring his full
wrath back upon you; it hangs balanced over your
head already, and needs but a gentle touch to bring
it down. I will say that it was not Ardneh at all who
defeated you, but some trivial power."

"It was Ardneh, or his equal. It must have been."
Charmian did not appear to have heard.

The magician—he was using no name at all at
present, a procedure not unheard of among those of
his calling—rode on in silence for a little time, siz-
ing up with sidelong looks the woman who rode
beside him, taking her measure in more ways than
one. "No, no," he said again. "From here there is no
way that I can visit on this fleeing servant girl the
tortures that you have in mind. We have no hair of
hers, or nail clippings, or even anything she
owned—hey? I thought not. Even a comparatively
mild curse would take—no, there is no way."

But Charmian was quick to catch him up. "Would
take what?"

The nameless magician evidently regretted starting to say whatever it was that he had left unfinished. How could he have made such a clumsy
slip?

"Disagreeable fool, you are going to have to tell
me sooner or later."

Imagine a vast buried sea of power, into which a
man might hope to sink a secret well, not in safety,
but still with reasonable hope of not being caught in
a disaster, because he and a few others had managed to do it successfully a few times in the past.
The Nameless One pondered briefly and fatalisti-
cally the secret syllables of a Name forbidden to be
spoken. Wood knew that name, and Ominor of
course, and four or five others in the highest councils of the East. It was seldom even alluded to—the
Nameless One had heard Wood do so only once, on
the day of Ardneh's visit to the capital.

Charmian prodded him: "It would seem to be a
worthless power, or whatever it is, if it cannot be

used." And again: "Remember, I meant what I said, both my promise and my threat."

The Nameless One believed her. "All right, then. We will see. I will try what can be tried."

Throughout the remainder of the day, the Constable gained upon his prey, but not enough. As sunset came, the wind abated and the prairie-elemental died; but the night belonged to the West, and Abner reluctantly gave orders to make camp and set a vigilant guard.

VI

Ardneh

———◆—◈—◆———

Rolf was saying: "You told me yourself that your Offshore man is likely wedded by now to someone else. What does it matter, then, if you should come and sit by me?

It was morning again, the second since their flight had begun. The bird had gone into hiding for the day in a nearby tree, where he—or she, Rolf was not sure—was now practically invisible. Since talking with the bird, Catherine and Rolf had slept a little, and had drunk their fill of fresh running water.

She looked at him now with what was almost a smile. "Is it some military matter you wish to discuss?" Catherine had been kneeling on the stream's grassy bank trying to see her face in the water below. The swelling on her cheekbone had gone down, but the discoloration was if anything worse than before, mottling from purple into green.

"Well . . ." He spread his hands. "We could begin with military secrets. You are at least four meters away, and to shout them across such a space would put them in danger of being overheard by the enemy." He looked up and around him with a great show of wariness. Catherine almost laughed.

They were in a little grove cut through by the stream. Looking out of the shade of the trees Rolf could see in all directions, fields and gentle hills of grass dotted here and there with other copses or single trees. It might be the patchy remnants of a receding forest or the struggling outposts of a new one.

Rolf sat with his back against a fallen trunk, facing across the stream, which was here only six or eight meters wide, and very shallow. With his right hand he patted the smooth grass beside him, indicating to Catherine where she was invited to sit.

She had given up trying to study her face in the water, but as yet she came no closer. "I do not know, sir, whether I should. Still, I suppose you are now my commanding officer, and if I flout your orders I am liable to find myself in some military court."

A cloud of irritation passed over his face. "No, don't joke about that. Giving orders, I mean." She sat back with her feet tucked under her, looking at him steadily. "I mean, I have seen people I knew executed by military courts. I'm sorry, I didn't mean to squelch a joke. You must have had few chances for them, since . . . when were you taken by the East?"

"A lifetime ago." No longer close to laughing, she got up slowly, and with her hands rubbed her bare arms as if she were peeling, scraping, something off. "But let's not talk about that now. I wish this stream were deep enough to swim and soak in it." Her servant's dress was stained, as were Rolf's clothes, with travel and hard usage, and her bound-up brown hair was dull with dust. But she looked less tired by far than she had before their flight.

"We could look for a deeper place," he said. "I would enjoy a swim myself, I think." He felt a little pulse begin, inside his head.

"Leave these trees, in daylight?"

"I meant tonight. At dusk."

She came nearer then, though not quite as near as his patting hand had indicated, and sat down. Her eyes flicked at him, unreadably; at nineteen he had long since given up trying to understand women.

He said: "I should never have mentioned that man you were to wed."

"No. I am thinking only of the girl I was, and how I have been changed. How when I was young I flirted and laughed and teased."

"When you were young? What are you now, about seventeen?"

"Two years ago I was fifteen, I think. But now I am no longer young."

"So, you are really such an old woman." Now his voice was growing more soft and tender. "Then you must be a fit companion for an old man like myself."

And somehow he had traversed the little distance that had been between them, and his fingers had begun a gentle stroking of her bare arm, up to the coarse slave's-cloth at the shoulder.

Her look seemed to say to him that his behavior was far from being unendurable; that, perhaps, if it went on a little longer it might begin to give her pleasure. His arm would have needed less encouragement than that to start unhurriedly going around her. It had always seemed to Rolf something of a wonder how this hard and angular limb of his always managed to adapt itself so neatly and exactly to the soft job of girl-holding. This one was certainly a soft girl now, regardless of how lean and strong she had appeared only a little while ago. Now in response to a firm pressure of his fingers on her cheek (safely below the blackened eye) her face turned round to his more fully. He found her lips.

Her smooth face rubbed willingly under his straggly beard. Time passed, then seemed about to be forgotten. Now he would kiss tenderly the swelling on her cheekbone, before he began a line of kisses moving down her throat.

Now, what was this upon her skin?

What had happened—

What —

With an outcry Rolf sprang to his feet and backed away, stumbling and almost falling in his haste. He grabbed up his sword and half-drew it from its sheath before he was aware of doing so, and when he became aware he scarce knew whether to finish pulling out the blade or push it back.

Before him now, and lately enfolded most tenderly in his arms, was one of the most hideous human shapes it had ever been his ill fortune to behold. What had been Catherine's healthy young face had altered while he kissed it to the visage of a withered, snaggle-toothed, misshapen crone. Even where he now stood, some meters distant, he thought he could still taste the pestilent breath. Under stiff, dirt-colored hair, tied up just as the young girl's had been, were the face and neck of an unrecognizable old woman, skin wrinkled as a rag, dotted with warts and here and there a whisker. The strong smooth arms that Rolf had felt about his neck were shrunken now to quivers of loose skin in which bones slid like crooked arrows. The breathing that had moved young breasts against him now had altered to a scraping wheeze, coming from a body as shapeless as the dress that covered it.

The old woman staggered to her feet, groping before her with fingers gnarled like roots. Her features worked, but her face was so distorted by age and disease that Rolf could not for a moment guess whether it was terror, anger, or laughter that moved her now.

Moving like some crippled sleepwalker, she tottered toward him on the brink of the grassy bank. "Rolf?" she cawed out the one word, in something like a reptile's voice, and then her figure seemed to blur, and down she fell on hands and knees.

Later he could not estimate how long he had stood there, rubbing his eyes, trying to see the figure before him clearly once again. In time he discovered that the blurring was not in his eyes, but in the female shape before them. Then all at once she was as she had been before he took her in his arms; healthy and young, the purplish-green bruise upon her cheek, vital brown hair struggling to escape the tie that bound it up. It was Catherine on her hands and knees, her face convulsed in terror. "Rolf?" she cried out once again, this time in her own voice, and he threw down his sword and fell on his knees beside her.

She covered her face with her hands, until he pulled them away gently. Her whisper was still terrified: "How do you see me now?"

He put out a hand to caress her, but sudden suspicion made him draw it back. "As a girl. As you were when we first met."

"Thank all the powers of the West. Then she could not make it permanent . . . why do you still look at me so? What *do* you see?"

Shaken, he blurted clumsily: "I see a girl. But how do I know which is your true shape, this one or the other? What kind of magic is this?"

"What kind of magic? *Hers*, the evil woman's . . . she has found some way to do this foul thing to me. I know it." Now the first immensity of Catherine's terror was gone, but tears were standing in her eyes. "I heard it from her and others, that never in my life should I escape her. The Lady Demon, Charmian."

Gazing at the young form before him, Rolf suddenly could no longer believe that it might be a lie, the product of some Eastern enchantment. Catherine had none of Charmian's glamor; her youth and health was marked with human awkwardness and imperfection. She was too complete and varied to be unreal. He said, reassuringly: "There are Western wizards who can deal with any spell."

"Hold me," she whispered, and he took her in his arms again. For a while he comforted, he soothed, and all was well. Once more he kissed the bruised cheekbone, which this time did not change. And then, as his caresses ceased to be meant as comforting, he saw the first sagging wrinkle appear upon her cheek.

This time he did not retreat so rapidly or so far, but still he let her go. This time he watched the progress of the cycle with compassion, as Catherine passed through decrepit ugliness and back to youth again. Then they were silent for a little while, looking at each other like grave children.

"It is when I embrace you as a man with a woman that it happens," he said at last. And she nodded, but made no other move. A long time passed before she spoke at all.

Near sundown, as Rolf awoke from a fitful sleep and began to prepare for another night of travel, he saw a great swarm of reptiles taking shelter for the night in a grove about a kilometer to the southeast. Rolf could see no Eastern ground forces, but they must be near; the reptiles would need at least a few human defenders to survive the night if they were discovered by the Feathered Folk.

With the first true darkness, the bird awoke, and came to perch briefly on Rolf's hospitably leveled forearm, settling with a surprising spread of soft, balancing wings; it weighed no more than a small child. Pointing south with his free hand, Rolf said: "It is good we did not rest in that grove instead, for there the trees have just filled up with leather."

"Hooo! Then I must go quickly and gather my people here."

"I have some words for you to carry to Duncan, also. Some Eastern magic has been worked upon us." While Catherine stood by listening, he told the bird in brief what had happened.

"Carry word also," Catherine added, "that our riding-beasts are failing. One is too far gone to be ridden, I think, and the other not much better."

Rolf went to inspect the animals himself, but had to agree that Catherine was right. The bird took thought, and then offered: "Let them gooo free. I will send birds tonight to ride and goad them far from here, so if the East should find them tomorrow they will be misled."

The few belongings they had, weapons and cloaks and a small store of food, made no great burden. With compact bundles on their backs, Rolf and

Catherine waved goodby to the bird and stepped off once more to the northwest, at first following the stream closely. There would be no looking for bathing-spots tonight, not with the enemy only a kilometer away. He and Catherine managed to cover about fifteen kilometers before dawn. During the night they saw no more birds; probably all who could fly had been mustered for an attack on the roosting reptile horde.

There was no difficulty on the next morning—or on the next, after another uneventful night of walking—about finding places in which to hide. The country through which they traveled was gradually becoming more thickly wooded, though still the long grass was dominant. The land also grew hillier, and was threaded at frequent intervals with small streams which ended any remaining concern about finding water. Catherine got her bath at last, in privacy.

"You can take a little walk now, Rolf. I'll catch up when I'm through."

"What's the matter? Hey, why pull away?"

She looked at him steadily and pulled away even a little farther. "How can you ask that?"

"Well, but the curse may have expired by this time."

"Or it may have grown more powerful. I'll not risk it again. It was easy enough for you, you didn't have to feel your own body . . . changing. Don't try to touch me."

And he had to admit, with an unwilling sigh, that she was right.

Several more nights of travel passed without notable incident. Nightly a bird came to them, bringing news of how the rival armies had maneuvered the day before. Duncan, the birds reported, was receiving from his wizards ever-stronger omens of the importance of Ardneh to the West, and of Rolf's mission for Ardneh. The Prince had dispatched a cavalry force to overtake Rolf and act as his escort to wherever Ardneh wanted him to go. But the Western cavalry detailed for the job had been intercepted by strong Eastern patrols, who were also converging upon the area, and forced to fight. John Ominor was now thought to have taken direct command of the main Eastern army in the field, though if so he was careful to stay hidden in his tent at night, out of sight of birds.

On another night, one of drizzling rain, Rolf and Catherine came to a stream wider than any they had met so far. Squinting into the murky dark, Rolf found he could not tell if the far bank was thirty meters distant or three hundred. At the moment no bird was with them to act as guide. The river flowed roughly to the north, but as soon as Rolf began to follow its bank in that direction a sudden hard feeling of wrongness, almost a sickness, came over him. When he stopped, the malaise subsided, only to return full force when he would have gone on again. Catherine felt nothing, but he could scarcely walk. Only when he reversed himself and followed the stream south did the sensation leave him. His puzzlement ended a hundred meters upstream, where what he first took to be a very odd-shaped stone in his path revealed itself on examination to be one end of a large metal object, almost completely buried.

Since Ardneh had apparently led them to it, he and Catherine set to work with knife and hatchet to dig the thing out of the hardened earth. They had not got far before they realized they were uncovering a small boat, made of Old World metal, uncorrupted by whatever ages it had lain under the ground. In an hour or so they had the craft dug out; it proved to be practically undamaged and perfectly usable, of a handy size for two passengers. Oars or paddles there were none, but a little groping in the dark turned up a couple of branches suitable for poles if the water were not too deep. Rolf took it for granted that his proper course was still to the north, downstream. They loaded their little gear into the boat and put out into the river, finding it fairly swift and shallow. Before dawn they had made, while resting their feet, several more kilometers toward their still unknown goal.

That day they spent mostly in the boat, tied up to the shore under a sheltering overhang of bushes. For the first time in days Rolf spotted a reptile; but the enemy was cruising deep in the remote southern sky, and there was no reason to think it had seen them. Toward evening Rolf took a couple of fish with a whittled spear, and at sunset Catherine cooked them over a small fire. The food in their packs was beginning to run low.

That night, drifting north again over moonlit water, Rolf felt the conviction begin to grow in him that he was nearing the end of his journey.

The river wound its way north among the grassy hills of a land that seemed utterly empty of intelligent life. Near the end of their second night on the water they drifted past the mouth of a tributary creek, and Rolf obeying a sudden powerful impulse turned the boat into it. Poling the boat upstream was difficult, and the creek soon became so shallow that the boat scraped bottom frequently. Rolf and Catherine emptied it of their belongings and let it drift free, back to the larger stream that would carry it away from their path.

By now it was light enough for reptiles to be out, but Rolf decided to push on. Brush growing along the watercourse offered some concealment, and he had the sense that some conclusion was imminent, the feeling that it would not greatly matter if some reptile saw them now. Suspiciously he tried to analyze this feeling, and decided that it came from Ardneh and was to be trusted.

The water offered a path in which they would leave no trail. They waded on up the stream, which was only four or five meters wide here and not much more than ankle-deep.

"Why should the water be so cold?" Catherine asked him. Rolf frowned, realizing that she was right; the land was deep in summer, and such a little stream did not have depths to hold a chill. Unless it was the outflow of some deep lake . . .

A final meandering of the stream between its gentle banks brought them round a little hill, and he understood. The creek vanished unexpectedly into a hillside hole, a tunnel-mouth with a ledge at one side just above the water level.

He stood with Catherine before the tunnel-mouth for a little time, and then said: "This is where we are to go." He felt her shiver beside him; chill air emerging from some underground depth, flowed almost imperceptibly around them, and their breaths steamed despite the growing radiance of the rising sun. "Come," he said, and loosened his sword in its scabbard and moved forward. Here the water narrowed and deepened quickly and he climbed out of it to take the dry ledge that emerged from the hillside beside the stream.

Clay and dank limestone folded them about, and as they proceeded the tunnel gradually grew darker. It was far too regular to be natural, and marks showed of the hand tools that had shaped its surface.

"A mine," said Catherine. "I have never been in one before."

"Nor I. But you are right, it must be a mine." Perhaps, Rolf thought, diggers after some useful metal had by accident run into an underground vein of water, and had dug this channel for it to keep their works from being flooded. That must have been long ago, for the creek bed outside looked as old as any other on the prairie.

The passage curved, but not into the blinding darkness that Rolf had expected. Ahead, it was joined by a vertical shaft, letting in the light of day from what must be a hilltop some meters overhead. Looking up through the rough shaft when he reached it, Rolf beheld a small circle of blue sky, fringed with stirring grass.

"Look," urged Catherine, pointing downward. Half-embedded in the undisturbed clay beneath their feet were rusted lumps of metal that must once have been tools.

Rolf started to say something, then fell silent. He waited, listening, then moved silently to look back down the passage in the direction they had come. It might have been a drop of water that he had heard, falling from the wet stone and clay of the tunnel's roof. After a moment he shook his head, returned to where Catherine stood with a nocked arrow in her bow, and beckoned her to follow him. Their journey's end was near, but they had not reached it yet.

"What are we do to here?" she whispered at his back, but he did not know and did not answer. Beyond the vertical shaft, the horizontal one continued, into truly growing darkness.

Going slowly to let his eyes adjust to deepening gloom, Rolf edged forward, his feet just above the steady murmur of the stream. Here was where the stream gushed into the tunnel, from an indistinguishable crevice at one side. Not a dozen meters farther on, with the floor of the tunnel now completely dry, the miners' ancient work abruptly broke off. More crumbling tools lay, as if dropped while in use, against the tunnel's deepest face, and high in that face a hole remained, leading to a deeper darkness. The ancient diggers might have broken through, but had not entered whatever chamber lay beyond, for the hole was not big enough . . .

The aperture flamed abruptly, with cold, clear light. Catherine let out a little cry and raised her bow. Rolf started, but in the next moment felt relief. He knew Old World illumination when he saw it, hard and bright and steadier than any flame. He had seen it before, and then as now Ardneh had been his guide.

He reassured Catherine, and together they

peered into the hole. It opened into a simple room about five meters square, with gray smooth walls and flat panels in the ceiling from which the cold light flowed tirelessly. A closed door stood in the opposite wall.

Groping among the fallen miners' tools, Rolf found the head of a pickaxe that was not too corroded to be effective, and with it he worked at enlarging the hole the miners had abandoned. Maybe the Old World lights had flashed for them as well, and they had chosen to drop their tools and run, not coming back.

Catherine worked at his side, clearing away lumps of rock and clay and smooth gray paneling as he broke them loose. The hole was soon enlarged enough for them to squeeze through. The floor was of the same gray stuff as the walls. Scattered on the floor and on a few shelves along one wall were a number of metallic-looking boxes, neatly marked with words in a language neither Rolf nor Catherine could read. The room and its contents were vastly better-preserved than the less ancient miners' tools had been, but even here Time had begun to have his way. From one spot on the ceiling a waxy-looking icicle depended, and Rolf on touching it found that it was rock, with a slow drop of ground water gathering on its tip, and a small rocky stalagmite building on the floor beneath. He shivered suddenly in the chill cave air, with a sudden sense of what time might mean.

The door leading out of the room tried to stay shut when he twisted at its handle and shoved against it with a shoulder, but then it yielded with a sudden rasp. The passage beyond the door was revealed abruptly as its ceiling panels sprang to glowing life.

"Come," said Rolf, as Catherine hung back again. "I tell you it is all right. This is where we are to be."

They moved on through the new passage in the direction that seemed right to Rolf, passing through other corridors and chambers. The sound of the stream in the tunnel was lost somewhere behind them. In time they reached a room where the air was warm and their breath no longer steamed.

Time had hardly entered here as yet. There were many metal cabinets and racks, seeming perfectly preserved, filled with equipment Rolf could not begin to guess the purpose of, but which yet gave him an impression of a high degree of organization.

On the most prominent panel at one end of the room stood bold symbols that he could not read, but which he recognized as having the look of certain Old World writings that he had seen before:

AUTOMATIC RESTORATION DIRECTOR—
NATIONAL EXECUTIVE HEADQUARTERS

"Rolf."

The voice was pleasant, masculine but not heavily so. It came from somewhere in the cabinetry behind the lettering. Rolf did not even start at the sound, but only raised his eyes; he knew at once that it was Ardneh calling him. Catherine had almost literally jumped with surprise, and now stood poised as if to flee; but she waited with her eyes on Rolf.

Rolf said: "Ardneh?", half expecting a figure to materialize. But there were only the metallic-looking cabinets, from one of which the voice of Ardneh issued again.

"Do not fear me, Catherine. Do not fear, Rolf; for years you and I have known each other, dimly, but in trust."

"I do not fear you, Ardneh, no," said Rolf. He held out a hand, and Catherine came slowly to his side. "You can show yourself, Ardneh, and we will not be afraid."

"I have no flesh to show you, Rolf. Nor am I of pure energy, like an elemental or a djinn. But I am of the West, and I need your help."

"That is why we are here." Rolf paused. "Are you then like Elephant that I once knew, some war machine of the Old World? But no, you have life and thought, where Elephant was mindless as a sword."

"You are partly right," said Ardneh's voice. "I am, or was, what you call a machine, and made by men of the Old World. But I was not made to fight a war, I was made to restore a peace. And for a long time I have, as you say, had life and thought."

Rolf turned around. "Where are you, then?"

"All around you. Each shelf and cabinet contains some part of me. As you see, I depend heavily on Old World technology, and it is because of your natural talent in such matters that I chose you and brought you here. The object you have brought me is important, but your own presence, Rolf and Catherine, is equally so."

Rolf put his hand on the pouch he carried. Ardneh said: "Bring what you call the gem along the path I will now show you. There is a test that must be made before my plans go further."

The lights in the room dimmed abruptly, but brightened beyond a doorway, in one external corridor. As Rolf and Catherine entered this corridor and followed it, the brightening of the lights moved on ahead of them, from one ceiling panel to another. After many winding passages, interspersed here and there with descending stairs, they entered another room, larger than that where Ardneh had first spoken and crowded with a number of strange devices. Into one of these, a simple-looking crystalline case surrounded by a number of heavy metal rings, Ardneh told Rolf to drop the gem.

"And now leave this room," said Ardneh's voice, this time from a wall. "The test had better be made without human beings present." Leaving the chamber with Catherine, Rolf noticed doors as thick as castle walls, sliding from concealment to seal the passage behind them. Once more the overhead light danced on, leading them back to the room in which Ardneh had first spoken.

"Sit down, if you wish," Ardneh said when they were there again; and they seated themselves on the floor. "There is much I must tell you, for it is going to be necessary for you to tell others the truth about me; more than I dare now explain in the world outside these chambers, but which must be explained before many more days have passed.

"I was built by war-planners of the Old World, as part of a system of defense. But not as a destructive device. My oldest purpose is to defend mankind, and so I am of the West today, though there was no East or West when I was built. My basic nature is peaceful, so it has taken me long to develop weapons of my own to enter battle. The object you have brought me will add to the physical strength I can exert, if the test I am now conducting has a favorable result. More of that later.

"My builders meant their defense system to save the world, and in a sense it did. But they called on powers they did not fully understand and could not wholly control, and in saving the world they changed it, so drastically that their civilization could not survive. This was the great Change of which humans still speak, and it divided the Old World from the new.

"As I will show you soon, the world was changed by another machine, or rather by a part of me that has long since done its work and been dismantled. The part of me that still exists, was created to end the Change when the time was ripe. The builders did not really expect that the changes in the world wrought by their defenses would be so great that I would be needed, but they doubted and feared enough to make me and to put the powers of restoration under my control if they should be needed. They thought that fifty thousand years must pass before the proper time for restoration came. But only now has it arrived. The odds for the survival of mankind, if the restoration is accomplished in this year, in this month, are better than they have been at any time since the Change, or are likely to be in the estimable future."

Rolf asked: "And when this restoration you speak of is made, will it destroy the East?"

"I hope it will."

"Then let us restore the Old World, if you think that we of the West can live in it."

Ardneh seemed to ignore his advice, and Rolf had the uncomfortable feeling that he had been talking of things he knew nothing about.

Silently the overhead lights once more began their dance, leading them back to the room wherein they had left the mysterious gem. The heavy doors had reopened, and Rolf and Catherine entered to stare at the case in which they had left the ebon sphere. The sphere had been replaced by, or transformed into, a pearly, weightless-looking ball of light of about the same size. Looking at it, Rolf had the impression of effortless, tremendous power.

"It is what I thought it was," Ardneh's voice explained. "And my plans can now go forward."

"What?" Catherine whispered, staring in fascination.

"What a technologist of the Old World would have called the magnetohydrodynamic core of a hydrogen-fusion power lamp. From it I can draw renewed power, which is very important. Also important is what it shows. The fact that I have been able to change it from a gem back into what it was in the Old World, is a sure proof that the Change is weakening; that the restoration can be made."

Rolf sighed. "Ardneh, there is still much of this we do not understand. And you say it is necessary that we do so."

"Again, follow the lights. Watch and listen for a little while and then there will be time for food and rest."

This time they were led along yet another branching of the passageways, and to a still lower level. With every minute the buried complex housing Ardneh was revealed as larger, and there was no reason to think they had seen it all as yet.

In a room that must have been far below the level of the outside ground, but where the air was fresh and dry and comfortably warm, were couches covered in some leather-like substance that creaked and crackled with age when Rolf and Catherine lay down, but did not crumble. Above each couch and pointed at its head were clustered metal rods, suspended from somewhere in the obscurity above the lights.

The lights dimmed. "Now you will sleep," said Ardneh. And so it was.

To Rolf there soon came a dream, so clear and methodical a dream that he knew it was not natural. Although he knew he was dreaming, he did not waken. He was drifting, no more than a disembodied viewpoint, watching people who he somehow knew were of the Old World. They were strangely dressed, and spoke to one another in a tongue unknown to Rolf, as they went about tasks that he at first found completely incomprehensible. Then he saw that they were pouring lakes into buried caverns, lakes not of water but seemingly of sparkling, coruscating liquid light.

Ardneh's voice, also bodiless, said: "Rolf, those lakes were one attempt to prevent the Old World from destroying itself, by strengthening the powers of life. I was another attempt."

"I know what those lakes of life were like, Ardneh, for I saw one spilled in the Black Mountains. Is there one that Duncan can make use of, to restore his men fallen in battle?"

"I think there are no more such lakes left in the whole world, Rolf. Watch, now. This dream that you see is something made by some leaders of the Old World, to show other folk of that time how well they were to be protected against war."

And Rolf, in the strange embrace of the bed which he no longer felt, settled himself to watch the dream. With only partial comprehension, despite Ardneh's occasionally interjected words of expla-

nation, he watched as in scene after scene
strangely-uniformed men and women built, armed,
tested and concealed long finned cylinders, which
Ardneh explained were rocket-driven missiles. Missiles were carried in strange craft moving hidden
under the seas, were secreted in underground silos,
were hung soaring in patient readiness so high
above the ground that great earth itself became
nothing but a ball. Small missiles intended to destroy large missiles were made in great numbers
also, and one scene showed racks of these defensive
weapons that swung out quickly from an artificial
hillside.

Next, interspersed with views of men and women
laboring at tasks even harder to understand, Rolf
watched workers assembling the multitudinous
cabinets of Ardneh in his cave. Or at least in some
deep shelter. Rolf could not really recognize the
uninhabited shelter in which he knew his sleeping
body lay. Nor did the countryside around the site in
the Old World much resemble that of Rolf's time,
except that there were very few people in either.

"What are those things, Ardneh?"

"They are called heat-exchangers. They are sunk
deep into the earth and draw power from it.
Through the ages when all atomic devices were inoperative, I drew power from the heat-exchangers,
and I draw it still. And now, Rolf, Catherine, behold
the last days of the Old World, and its changing.
First, what those who made me foresaw might happen; next, what actually did happen, as I later
pieced it together."

Now the dream unrolling before Rolf with vivid
precision no longer showed perfectly lifelike people
and events, but instead what seemed to be a series
of drawings that moved and spoke in close imitation
of life. They were marvelous drawings, such as no
artist known to Rolf could have fashioned. But they
were lifeless nonetheless.

Rolf saw in this bloodless world of moving draw-

ings how the huge missiles were fired in sudden
salvos, taking flight from their many places of concealment. In swarms and clouds they leaped up
high, ranged around the globe of earth, and fell
again. As their blunt heads detached and multiplied
themselves, down-curving toward their targets, the
small missiles sprang up to meet them, shooting
like darts from hidden defensive nests. When an
offensive missile passed in killing range of a defen-
der, a blast seared the upper air, and both were
gone.

But the attack was too heavy; destructive devices
from halfway around the world were falling upon
the helpless-looking cities of Ardneh's builders.
Only seconds remained before disaster. At once, the
Ardneh portrayed in the moving drawings was
shown fully alerted. To him—to it, rather, there was
no sign that this Ardneh was intended to be, or
thought to be, alive—was passed control of the ultimate defense.

With the help of Ardneh and the Old World dream
machine Rolf was able to comprehend that this defense was in the nature of an experiment, involving
the use of forces that must engulf the entire planet
once they were unleashed, that were feared by some
to be irreversible. They were newly-discovered
forces that had never been tested and would not be
tested now if destruction were not certain otherwise. The ultimate defense against atomic attack
worked by robbing certain types of energy from certain atomic and subatomic configurations of matter, making the fusion or fission of nuclei enormously less likely.

A quick flicker in the drawings showed a subtle
wave of change spreading out from the Ardneh-
machine's emplacement, passing over the
threatened cities of the homeland moments before
the enemy's missiles struck within them. No murderous blasts erupted; the impacting warheads did
no more damage than so many catapulted rocks.

What had happened to the enemy country was
not apparent, but suddenly things at home were
tranquil once again. A stylized drawing-man
reached to touch one of Ardneh's control panels,
and with the neatness of a folding parasol the protective change that Ardneh had thrown out was
folded up, withdrawn, undone.

"So much for the plan," said Ardneh's voice, in
present time. "And now behold what truly happened, at the changing of the world."

The visionary narrative of attack and defense
began over again, with little change at first in the
substance of the story. Again the offensive missiles
came from around the world, launched in greater
numbers and with more deceptive aids than could
be dealt with by the conventional defense of short-
range countermissiles. The Ardneh-machine was
alerted in the first minutes of the great war, while
the enemy attack was still no more than a network of
trajectories in space, perceived and plotted by the
defenders. While destruction was still minutes
away, the counterattack was launched; whether
Ardneh succeeded or failed, it seemed that the
enemy must die.

Now disaster was only seconds away from most of
the major cities of the land. The part of Ardneh that
had been built to change the world was empowered
to act, and it functioned as it had been made to do. It
laid hold upon the matter within itself and pulled
its energies into a new shape, beginning a Change
that spread through the substance of the earth like
cracks through shattering glass. A round wave-front
of Change sprang out with the speed of light from
Ardneh's buried site. But the setting in motion of
the ultimate defense had taken a few seconds longer
than anticipated. One enemy missile fell just before
the wave-front reached it and exploded with full
force beside a populous city, ending uncountable
lives in the blinking of an eye. Other intercontinen-

tal weapons, falling like hail a few seconds later, failed to explode.

Meanwhile, on the other side of the world, surprise; the enemy was employing the same kind of an ultimate defense. But theirs was not controlled by any device as sophisticated as Ardneh, and their simpler mechanisms were never to become alive. This Rolf understood as in a dream, knowing it was so without knowing how he knew. But the enemy defenses also worked. A wave of Change springing from the other side of the world met that generated by Ardneh, and the fabric of the planet was altered more powerfully than anyone had expected.

Those few missiles that fell before the Change exploded, and the vast number that fell afterward were rendered practically harmless. One missile, however, to which Rolf's attention was now silently directed, was caught precisely in mid-explosion by the wavefront emanating from Ardneh. The fireball, the blooming nuclear blast, had just been born and it was not extinguished but neither did it follow the normal course of the explosions that had preceded it. It did not fade, but changed in shape, ran through a spectrum of colors and back again, and writhed up toward the sky as if with agonizing effort. Rolf knew that he was watching a kind of birth, and one of terrible importance.

With the passing of the wave of Change, Ardneh himself immediately began his first stirrings toward life, as did many other formerly inert components of the world.

But neither Ardneh nor any of the others accepted life as savagely, exultantly, as this.

VII

Orcus

———————◆·◆◆———————

That writhing into a furious life, begun amid a violence beyond the capability of any human being to understand, was the earliest memory of the being who would later be named Orcus, later called Lord of Lords and Emperor of all the East. His earliest memory was recorded thousands of years before John Ominor was born, thousands of years before humanity lay divided into the two camps called East and West.

For a few thousand years after his violent birth, the being who would later be known as Orcus wandered in the desert places of the earth, avoiding humans, avoiding distraction as much as possible while he groped his way toward full sentience. Child of the awesome old technology and the marvelous new magic that had begun with the Change, his substance was only partially subject to the laws of matter.

There were others more or less like him now in the world, though none so terrible of birth or power. Quickly men began to forget their technology, maimed as it was by the Change; almost from the moment of the Change they were speaking of the Old World and the New, and taking up the newly opened possibilities of magic to help them finish their aborted war. Since the Change it could scarcely be said that anything was lifeless; powers that before had been only potentialities now responded readily to the wish, the incantation, were motivated and controlled by the dream-like logic of the wizard's world.

Humans grew aware of the existence of the being who would be Orcus, and in their dogged search for magical power they tried to devise means to control him. These efforts were annoying to him, in his growing self-awareness; to avoid them, when they became persistent, he wandered away from earth. Half-immune to the laws of physics and chemistry as the Old World had known them, he drifted without sustenance and almost without effort outward to the moon, where what had been human colonies were now dead and deserted, casualties of war and the failure of technology. Above the cratered surface Orcus drifted, watching, beginning to think, as the strange bubble-houses that had sheltered the humans decayed and burst in silence. All around, soft-looking mountains two thousand thousand times as old as humankind looked down, unchanging and indifferent.

Orcus was beginning to think, and to feel sharp emotions, and to be intensely aware of the world and of himself. He began also to fear the empty moon, and the soft deep beyond, that by its immensity made him feel that he was shrinking steadily. Slowly through the solar winds of space he turned, willing himself to begin the long drift back to earth. He realized now that there, and perhaps nowhere else, he was a giant.

Now as he approached the earth again he saw humanity clearly, and began to understand and loathe them. A new generation of sorcerers had developed in his absence, men and women of greater magical skill and greater arrogance. These became aware of the demon who would be Orcus, and when they glimpsed his power they tried with fear and greed to summon him and master him. But their nets of magic burst and tore around him as he moved.

Long and slow and difficult was the groping of the demon to his full sentience and identity. Despite his hatred of the wizards' race his own development followed the same general direction as theirs, under requirements imposed by the mental potentialities of the home planet they shared. The ways of Orcus' thought were not unlike those of the men he hated, not when compared to others that he had dimly sensed in the great deeps beyond the frightening moon. (Never would he leave earth's air again.)

Orcus moved over the earth and looked at the life upon it, with a hate and pointless envy that no man or woman could match. In himself he was the East, before the East had come to be. Men were building new civilizations now; most of the Old World and its technology lay buried and forgotten (unknown to men and demons, Ardneh too was now living, thinking, waiting.) And he who would be Orcus became aware now of others who were somewhat like himself, though smaller. These were demons and protodemons born from sunlike fires as he had been, but from comparatively minor acts of violence crossed by the wave of change. None of these others could begin to match his strength, and he cowed them when he met them, never questioning his own urge to dominate. Two other demons, who might in time have grown great enough to challenge him successfully, he met separately and slew. His struggle with one of these lasted for nearly a thousand years, and nearly depopulated one of the earth's smaller continents of human and animal life, before he-who-would-be-Orcus managed to reach and snuff out the hidden life of his opponent.

Shortly after that age-long struggle he received his name. When he had made himself undisputed king of the demonic powers of the world, and therefore the chief enemy of most of the human race, magicians began to call him Orcus, after some demon-lord of ancient Old World legend. (Had there in fact been Old World demons, too? And was this

Changing from whence he came nothing new, after all, beneath the ancient moon? The questions occurred to Orcus, but he made no attempt to answer them. He really did not care, one way or the other.)

Not only evil powers had been brought into objective reality by the Change. From earth and sea and sky there welled into existence other forms of inhuman but intelligent life. The Change that had damped the energies of nuclear fire had at the same time freed the energies of life. The nameless force that lay behind both kinds of energy could not, ultimately, be repressed; that which was inherent in every atom could not be destroyed.

Gradually the elemental powers of earth and sea and air came to be looked on as allies by that portion of humanity who chose the West, against the men and women who had elected to associate themselves with demons, and who with the demons had formed that society of essential selfishness called the East. How the name of East and West had come to be used rather than, say, North and South, or Red and Green, was no longer remembered in Rolf's day. Nor would such a question ever have had any significance for Orcus.

Dominating the other quasimaterial powers of the East, and leading them in slowly intensifying war against the West, Orcus the Demon-Patriarch sought slaves and allies among the beasts of the planet as well as among the men. A race of intelligent flying reptiles had evolved in the mere thousands of years that had passed since the Change, so life-rich had the substance of the world become. These reptiles became close allies of the demonic powers, just as a species of huge, intelligent, nocturnal birds, the reptiles' natural enemies, came into being and joined the West.

Still, humanity was at the heart of the struggle. Only humans were capable of dealing with both beasts and spirits on their own terms. People had largely deserted the technology that had enabled

them to Change the world. But before their forget
fulness could become complete, the pressure of the
new war made them try to recall and rebuild what
they had lost. Thus it was that the technology of the
Old World had never entirely died.

Orcus grasped how vitally important human beings were to the struggle, but when he began to train
and organize his human slave-allies he underestimated their true potential. There was among the
first generation of his recruits a man so consistently
successful in his assigned tasks, and at the same
time so apparently common and predictable in his
motives (therefore as trustworthy as anyone in the
East could be) that Orcus promoted him time and
again. The human did well in each succeeding job
and accomplished each without giving the appearance of more ambition than a human being (in Orcus' view) should have. Eventually the man was
given command not only of other humans, but of
lesser demons as well. So John Ominor advanced,
using skillfully the centuries of extra life with which
his demon-master was pleased to reward him.

Perhaps Orcus, who had never fully understood
men, never understood himself either. He may have
come gradually to think himself omnipotent, and so
grew careless. Whatever the explanation, without a
hint of warning, he was tricked and overthrown by
the man Ominor. John Ominor, with the men and
demons he had suborned to aid him, cast down the
demon-emperor Orcus and bound him in perpetual
slumber. Orcus was not slain, could not be slain,
because his life could not be found. Nor could he be
made to reveal where it was. It was as if he did not
know. The victorious new lords of the East were
puzzled; the circumstances of Orcus' birth, that
would have explained much, were unknown to
them.

As was the existence of Ardneh.

Still the war against the West went on, as bitter as
ever, and now more slowly, for Orcus' power was

sorely missed by the East. But to awaken him
enough to use him properly would be very dangerous. He was kept bound with certain other un-
trustworthy powers, under the world, in darkness
and tormented sleep. The fitful flashes of con-
sciousness that came amid his dreams he spent
constructing scenarios of revenge.

Riding a griffin-like, demonic steed that galloped
in midair across the demon-haunted night, the
gnarled sorcerer known as Wood flew northwest
among the clouds. He had been Ominor's ac-
complice in the overthrow of Orcus, and he was
Ominor's chief wizard still. He and his mount had
risen from the vast encampment of the army of the
East, and he was flying to seek out the Constable's
small force where it was resting in its frustrated
pursuit of Rolf of the Broken Lands.

Wood's mount flew faster than any beast or man
could travel or ever had, unless it were some Old
World master of the technologies of speed. The tall
clouds of a midsummer storm glowed with muffled
lightning to right and left as Wood flashed between
them. The demon-beast, whose shaggy back he
rested on, ran silently on air. Its griffin's hooked-
beak eagle-head bobbed and swayed at the end of
the long neck, along which feather and scale commingled. Its wings spread and sailed, seemingly no
more than banners or balances as it ran on wind and
nothingness with driving, pounding legs. This steed
would carry no other human not even Ominor himself.

In the flicker of lightning, Wood's face was grim.
Out here in the northern hinterland something was
going very dangerously wrong. When the Constable
had sent his first appeal for magical help of the
highest order it had seemed likely he was trying to
cover up some blunder made by his own wizard, or
by himself. But now in Wood's own auguries the
ominous portents had grown too grave and numer-

ous to ignore. Some of the very highest powers of the West must be fighting hard to foil Abner's efforts in this obscure place.

Now already the demon-griffin's course was slanting down, angling steeply toward the gently rolling land dimly visible below. The prairie came clearer now, where the scudding cloud-shadows let the moonlight fall. Down the griffin flew toward one particular grove on the tree-sprinkled expanse, a grove where torches burned, protecting huddled reptiles against marauding birds. The arrival of Wood and his demon-steed under those trees opened all the reptiles' eyes and made of them glittering beads in the flaring torchlight. With a mixture of wariness and relief Abner's handful of human soldiers watched Wood dismount.

With a single, secret word Wood hobbled his baleful mount. Leaving it standing in the middle of the camp, he strode toward the door of the tent where the Constable's banner hung limply from a staff. Before the magician reached the tent Abner emerged from it, looking weary and on guard, to greet him with the gestures appropriate for welcoming an equal.

Entering the large tent, Wood caught just a glimpse of loveliness, of a golden, impossibly graceful body rising hastily from a couch and vanishing behind a hanging partition of rich silk, trailing unbelievable blond hair. He had to think that the timing was deliberate, that he was meant to see what he had seen.

Wood was not noticeably perturbed. Without further preamble, he demanded of Abner: "What is delaying matters here?"

Abner spread his massive hands. "Western magic. Why else should I call upon you? The so-called magician you have furnished me seems utterly unable to cope with what is being done to us."

His suspicions confirmed, Wood nodded gravely and closed his eyes. He let himself be thoroughly aware of the thin tent-floor just beneath his feet, of the grass pressed down under that, of tree-branches not very far overhead (and of the golden woman somewhere nearby, getting dressed; had she been distracting Abner from business? most men's effectiveness would have been impaired with her around), and of the soldiers and the sleepy reptiles and of his own most savage mount outside. Wood was adapting, submerging himself into the psychic climate of the place, letting its energy patterns inform his mind. At first, nothing seemed much out of the ordinary. But he persisted, and, in a little while, sighed and opened his eyes.

"Ardneh has taken the field against you," he said then to the Constable. "He is exceedingly subtle, and it is little wonder that your wizard has been unaware of what is setting all his work at naught. I could perhaps have been deceived myself had I not met Ardneh the day we summoned him to our capital. I will always know him now."

Abner nodded slowly. "Then what do you advise? Does it make any sense for me to press on with forty men against him?"

"You must press on, with whatever men you have, and gather more as fast as you can bring them here. Our whole future is turning on what is going to happen, somewhere not far from here to the north-west."

"And Ardneh? Can you clear him from my path?"

"I can," Wood said brusquely, "with the powers I shall soon invoke to help me with the job. Within a day or two, if not tonight . . . I mean to make a trial of it tonight."

He made a short gesture of farewell and strode out of the tent. When he had swung himself astride his steed, Wood cast about him by his arts until he was able to sense the location of the two fugitive humans whose capture had so far been beyond the powers of the East. They were resting now, it appeared, not many kilometers distant.

"One of them labors under some kind of minor curse," Wood commented, to the Nameless One, who had appeared from somewhere and was now standing motionless a little distance off. "Your doing, I suppose?"

"I . . . yes, great Lord." The Nameless One bowed as if in modesty.

Wood nodded, not troubling to find out the details. It was remarkable that the man had been able to accomplish even that much against the opposition that he faced here. "Well done. But now restrain yourself to a defensive posture for a time."

"As you will, Lord."

Wood dug heels into the cold flanks of his riding-demon, and into the ear that it unfolded for him, he whispered the needful word. With a roar of sound they rocketed into the air. Once above the treetops, he again turned his mount's massive, sharp-beaked head into the north. This time he was content to fly at low altitude, and he did not urge the griffin to anything like full speed. He meant to test the strength of Ardneh to the full this night, and to destroy it if he could, without undergoing a desperate risk himself. But there was no great hurry about it; he did not expect to be able to take Ardneh by surprise. To Wood, the something-out-of-the-ordinary that was Ardneh was coming clearer now, bit by bit in tantalizing glimpses like the one he had had of Abner's concubine. Subtle hints of splendid powers, and of a beauty that could not, unless it were a lie or under some evil bond, could not be any part of the Empire of the East.

After watching Wood's violent departure, Abner started to mouth an informal curse, thought better of it (Wood would never be so foolish as to try to kick Abner in the shins), and instead walked a quick tour of inspection around the perimeter of his little camp. Satisfied that his sentries were properly alert, his reptiles well guarded by burning torches, and that no other business needed his attention at the moment, he went back to his tent.

She had returned to the couch. Amid disordered draperies she stretched out in a pose half sleepy and half sensual, like some fine catlike beast. Her eyes were nearly closed, but there was a tremor of candlelight along the length of their golden lashes, and Abner knew she was looking at him, as he brought down his palm to snuff the candle out.

Now for a little while the Constable forgot the world outside his tent. Soon, however, there came some sounds of movement at its door, hesitant and tentative sounds, but threatening unwelcome interruption. He could picture the Nameless One there, or some of his officers shifting their feet, listening to ascertain if anything urgent was going on inside. They were bearing news but were uncertain of its importance. They thought the Constable should be told, but were afraid of his anger if they bothered him at the wrong time for something that turned out to be trivial. Would they go away? No, at any moment now they would work up the nerve to stop their exchange of silent gestures with the sentry and call out to be admitted.

He got up and without bothering to dress went to the door, and in displeased tones demanded: "What is it, what do you want?"

The darkness was greater in the tent than just outside, and even as Abner spoke he saw there was no sentry, only a figure taller than the Nameless One or any of his officers, tall as Abner himself. Abner was alerted before his answer came, was already moving back to where his sword hung in its scabbard on the tent's central pole.

"My wife," the tall stranger said, matter-of-factly, and drove in a sword-thrust that no man could have seen coming, much less avoided, in that poor light. But neither could the stranger see Abner well, and the blade did no more than slice tent-cloth and splinter innocent wood.

Abner had his own sword in his hand by now, and his lungs were filling for the bellow that would rouse the camp, when other screams shattered the night outside. "Rally to me!" roared out the Constable, and cut at the dim figure of his adversary, missing as his attacker had.

Now the man was inside the tent, and suddenly the darkness was no longer deep. Some neighboring tent had burst up into flames, almost explosively, and sent a tawny flaring light into the Constable's. The noise outside had mounted up as well, sounds not only of fighting but of panic, and at the moment that augured ill for the Eastern cause. Abner's place was outside, but his way was barred. His second thrust at his foe was parried with impressive speed and strength; the man blocking the doorway was certainly not going to be readily brushed aside. The enemy cut savagely back at Abner's legs, a blow that might have taken one off clean if it had landed; Abner dismissed a half-formed idea of turning and cutting his way out through the tent wall, to reach and lead his men. The first moment he turned his back upon this enemy would be the last he lived.

"Chairmian," Abner called softly, in a moment's lull after the next violent passage of arms. The next words he meant to say were *strike at him from behind*, but before he could utter them, something made him aware of the treacherous blow coming at the rear of his own skull, something hard and heavy swung by thin girlish arms. Abner started to turn and block the blow, realized that the sword would get him if he did, and tried to throw himself on the floor and roll from between his enemies, knowing even as he did so that he was too late. And he wondered, even as the sword came butchering between his ribs, how he had ever thought that the East, whose essence was treachery, could ever stand.

Speeding at treetop level to the north, Wood

dreamed briefly of glory. If he could return to the Emperor with the jewel in his possession and the crushing of Ardneh to his personal credit, certain key members of the Emperor's council might be persuaded that Wood would be a more effective Emperor than Ominor . . .

The taste of that thought was delightful, but it was a sweetness forbidden until the coming battle with Ardneh had been won.

It was an easy matter for Wood to cast his vision ahead to where the two fugitives rested. They were in some kind of cave, and the protection of Ardneh could be sensed around them. Wood could see how to reach them. It turned out, however, that reaching them was another matter. No sooner had he turned his mount directly toward the fugitives than a wind sprang up in his face. The wind quickly rose to a shrieking intensity, and Wood realized at once that its energies were more than strictly physical. It buffeted the griffin-demon and tried to turn him back. Wood dug in his heels. His mount snorted flame and continued to make headway. Then came a gust of superb violence. The demon-steed was halted in his airborne gallop, shot flying upward like a windborne leaf, sent skidding and pawing along a scudding firmament of clouds. The psychic energies that were the stuff of wizardry came forth from Ardneh's stronghold in a torrent to match that of the driving air.

Even under the spur of Wood's threats and incantations, his steed could make no headway, and soon he was forced to let it turn and ride before the blast. Most onlookers would have thought his situation precarious indeed, but Wood was not greatly perturbed. He had expected more subtlety on Ardneh's part than this. The wind was driving him back momentarily, but it should not be too difficult to cope with.

Muttering words that seemed to be torn uncompleted from his lips by the twisting wind, Wood called powers to his aid. From odd places on the earth and under it he called up a motley horde of demon auxiliaries, the strongest force he could assemble in one time and place at a few moments' notice. Ardneh must fall before this group should he dare to try to stand and fight them. If Ardneh would not fight he must retreat, and yield the two he was protecting.

The wind had slowly died as Wood had ceased to challenge it. Now, when his ill-favored troop of demons was fully assembled, grimacing and cackling like gigantic reptiles as they circled Wood on various shapes of wings amid the flying murk, he reined his mount in a wide circle and once more charged into the north.

The shell of demonic forces now surrounding Wood and his mount kept out the wind at first, when Ardneh tried to force them back again. Like some Old World missile the knot of Eastern power that Wood had formed around himself pushed its way through the blast. But the wind now rose to a new height of violence, and black clouds hurtling through it struck like fists upon the demons' shell. And now from Ardneh's striking fists there lanced out bolts of lightning. Like the wind, the lightning was deeply charged with energies beyond the physical range, and each bolt was well aimed. Some flew at the demons surrounding Wood, and some were meant for him. His utmost mental agility was needed to detect the bolts that were to be aimed at him while they were still in the process of formation, and to defuse them, drain their power before they flew, when they would be too fast for any mortal man to stop.

Some of Wood's host of conscripted warriors were fast enough to parry lightning directed at themselves. Nor could they be slain by it, for all their lives were safely hidden elsewhere. But Ardneh's hail of darts came thick and fast upon them now, painful, damaging, red-hot, impossible to stand against.

The demons' shell of force was pierced and broken, and once more Wood's powerful mount was gripped by Ardneh's wind-blast and hurled back. The griffin was flung twenty kilometers downwind before the hurricane abated enough for Wood to once more summon his demonic outriders around him. Whipped and half-stunned they came, mountainously cringing, shrinking their physical volumes as much as they could in order to make less conspicuous targets for his expected wrath. With words of terrible power Wood lashed them forward, northward, once again. This time he himself remained riding his griffin in a slow circle in this area of greater safety; trying to think, trying to probe ahead and understand.

By his arts he saw his demons driving north, beyond the clouds of driving mist that lay between. To meet them now came Ardneh's lightning, this time a single swordblade, flickering, walking along the energy spectrum through all the bands where demons had their half-material existence.

Yet again Wood's troops were thrown back, in fear and agony; and now at last they had found the enemy more terrible than Wood, and however he cursed and threatened they would not go into the north again. He sharpened his incantations yet more, wreaked suffering upon his quivering vassals, and banished them to hidden dungeons till they should be useful once again. Now, however, he was calm in all his curses and punishings. He no longer raged. He saw now that a little more effort from his demons would not have helped; they were simply not strong enough to stand against Ardneh.

How could Wood have so grievously underestimated his enemy's strength? Had Ardneh somehow managed a tremendous accession of power recently?

It was not simply that Ardneh was powerful enough to defeat them. Most shattering was the realization that the devastating defense had not even occupied Ardneh's full attention. While watching the last defeat of his demon-troop, Wood for the first time had managed — or had been permitted — to perceive the extent of Ardneh's world-wide activities. It was a frightening disclosure. Ardneh could not have possessed such strength for long, Wood realized, or the East would have lost the war some time ago instead of now thinking itself on the verge of victory.

In the form Wood's vision took, Ardneh appeared in the guise of a tall, powerful man, striding through a pack of curs that swirled snapping and growling vainly around his legs. The dog named Wood received no more attention and effort than was necessary in order to beat him off; meanwhile Ardneh's chief attention was directed somewhere else, somewhere Wood's dream-perception could not follow.

Lies, Wood told himself, and felt somewhat relieved; lies. Propaganda, put into his mind to intimidate and weaken him. But he had no evidence that it was lies. And if such a trick could be worked on him, and he could not tell it was a trick, he might well be facing an enemy who could destroy him.

—*in the nick of time he realized that Ardneh was coming at him for the kill* —

His host had been dispersed. He turned and fled, the lightning-bolts pursuing him downwind. Wood lived through it, although his demon-steed was struck so violently it lost the power of flight. All of Wood's arts that remained useful to him now barely availed to save his life, to let him tumble from his falling mount into rain-sodden bushes, amid a scene of wild storm and waving branches. Bruised and shaken and winded, but not seriously hurt, he realized that Ardneh had departed, and that he

himself was within a kilometer or two of the camp
where he had left the Constable.

Limping and cursing his way through the marshy
grass and rain, Wood knew that the ultimate powers
available to the East would have to be invoked.

VIII

They Open Doors,
They Take Down Bars

———◆◆◆———

Wood, stumbling on scratched and weary legs toward the Constable's camp, rehearsing in his mind what he might say to make his arrival there appear less inglorious, was within a hundred meters of his goal when he heard the surprise attack led by Chup burst out ahead of him.

After the first shock, Wood was not really surprised. The night belonged to the West, and it was not the first time an Eastern position thought secure had been taken unawares. He paused, trying to determine what was going on ahead. The enemy force seemed quite small. Ardneh was nowhere near. Wood had no functional demons to call on at the moment, but still, after his moment's assessment of the situation, he pressed on at a hurried walk. His personal anger was aroused, instead of the rest and food and drink he had been looking forward to, here was only another fight. But his rage was cold and eager. The smart of his defeat by Ardneh would be eased by victory here; instead of appearing humbled before the Constable, he would come in as a savior. There were fires ahead, and screams of panic. The East was not doing very well at the moment.

It was for good reason that Wood was accounted the greatest wizard of the East. When swords were out and blood was spilled, it was difficult for any magician to raise an effective spell—the Nameless

One even now lay bleeding out his life ahead, Wood's extra senses told him—but Wood's arts were still powerful, even now when his best powers had been scattered and his most potent energies exhausted. He still had one vital advantage, that of surprise, fully as important for the magician as for the soldier. . . .

On legs that no longer felt tired and injured, Wood approached the camp, where shadowy figures ran and fought before the burning tents. It took him a moment to make sure that there was no Western wizard among the attackers who might be capable of serious opposition to Wood's spells. The fat one who had earlier, with Ardneh's help, overcome the efforts of the Nameless One was there, but that meant nothing to Wood, as Ardneh himself was still absent from the scene.

Standing in the shadows of a tree near the edge of the burning camp, a vantage point from which he could see without readily being seen, Wood pronounced one lengthy word and began to make small gestures with one hand. The fat Western wizard was the first to fall, whirling round almost gracefully, elaborate talismans spilling from his hands like so much trash, before he tumbled like a chopped-through tree. One after another, as they came into Wood's view, the other men of the Western raiding party fell, backs arching, twisting in convulsions. There seemed to be less than a dozen of them in all, even fewer than Wood had thought at first. They could do nothing against Wood because he gave them no time to find him with their blades. One of their leaders came closest. A tall man, he emerged from the Constable's tent with bloodied sword held high. Seeing Wood, or somehow sensing his position, the Westerner charged like a maddened beast. But though his long strides brought him so close that Wood had to dodge back at the last moment from the killing blade, it was the Westerner who fell.

He was the last, except for one or two who might

have managed to run away; in his depleted and exhausted state Wood did not care to make the effort to be sure of that. All the others lay on the earth, their convulsions quieting as Wood led them smoothly into ensorceled slumber. Those he had felled were still alive, and he had a good reason for keeping them so.

The surviving Eastern soldiers who had survived were gathering in the center of the camp once more. Wood called to a junior officer and charged him with seeing to it that the prisoners were gathered together and kept alive until they should be needed. But no sooner had Wood finished giving these orders than he looked up to see that the golden girl he had earlier glimpsed in Abner's tent had emerged from some hiding place or other clad now in a silken robe, and was raising a dagger over one of the prone Westerners.

"Forebear, girl!" Wood called out. "We have far weightier business than your grievance against this wretch, whatever it may be. Where is the Constable?"

The golden woman threw down her dagger and turned to Wood. Now she was the picture of submission. "Alas, my lord Wood, the Constable is dead. At the last minute, when the enemy had already entered the camp, he saw the danger and met it bravely. He did what he could, but it was not enough."

Wood nodded, unsurprised, then looked around and raised his voice. "Where is the senior surviving officer, then?"

When that man had made himself known, Wood questioned him: "Have you enough able troops to defend this site until the dawn? There can hardly be a dozen live Westerners within ten kilometers of us at the moment. I will be available to help in an emergency, but not for keeping watch. There is another task upon which I must concentrate. I want to know if I can safely relax my vigilance to do so."

"Aye, aye, my Lord, I think so. We have at least twenty men still on their feet. These Westerners can move soft as demons. Our sentries had their throats cut—"

"That should keep their successors awake, at least for a few hours. Now I am going to set to work, and you must detail two men to fetch and carry for me. That you may cooperate intelligently with me, I will give you some explanation." He paused; the woman was watching him, round-eyed, and some of the soldiers were gawking dazedly. Wood took the officer by the arm and led him to one side; and he made his own image change in the eyes of the gawkers, to something that was not fit to look upon, and they hastened about their business. Then to the officer Wood said: "I have tonight met Ardneh face to face, and have found his strength grown awesome. I can only guess at how he has managed to augment his powers; now they are enough to tip the scales of the entire war against the East."

The officer was sweating, evidently wishing he was a private simply taking orders once again. Wood went on: "It will be necessary to call up some special reserves. I am referring to a group of demons who have for one reason or another been put into confinement, in a place—outside the normal world. They are dangerous and unruly creatures, and I must impress upon you the necessity of my being allowed to concentrate in peace while I am working with them."

All that Wood had said thus far was true. His great untruth had been in leaving out even the faintest hint of the existence of Orcus, the real object of the work he was about to do. Not even in his own inner thoughts had Wood allowed himself to form that name. Not for centuries now.

The officer wet his lips. "Great Lord, you will understand that I mean you no disrespect, when I venture the opinion that this project of releasing imprisoned demons, along with these discoveries regarding our enemy Ardneh, should be reported to headquarters as soon as possible. To the Emperor himself."

The officer was sharper and bolder than he looked. Understanding that the man wanted to be reassured that there was no intrigue against the Emperor in progress here — or perhaps wanted to be let in on it if there were — Wood answered patiently, "Send a message to headquarters any time you like. But I presume no reptile will fly until daylight, and I must begin the evocation here and now. Tonight. It is not a calling that can be made in an hour, or even in a day. There are many bars to be let down, sealed doors to be broken, locks to be opened for which the keys were thrown away. If we are to have help against Ardneh in time, I must begin now to call upon — the powers that are to help us. Should the Emperor for some unimaginable reason forbid me to go through with the calling, I can stop it at any point. Now if you will detail the men to help me, I must select the first required victim."

The officer was reassured, and moved away, giving his men such orders as Wood had requested.

When Wood came to the Western prisoners, he found them now laid out in a row, all still unconscious from the effects of his paralyzing spells. The woman was standing there, once more looking down at one of the still forms. The same one. It was he who had come near killing Wood. This time her expression indicated thought, rather than uncaring hate.

It was Wood's first opportunity for a long, close look at her. "What is your name, girl?"

"I am called Charmian, my noble Lord." Her blue eyes were so luminous that his spell-casting finger twitched defensively. But it was no more than woman's inborn witchery she had, as power to bedazzle men. No *more*? There were numerous demonic spells not half so powerful. Wood pondered the possible advantages and drawbacks of sending her on as a gift to Ominor; the Emperor enjoyed alluring women as much as any ordinary man.

Wood looked down. "And who is this one at your feet, who makes you frown so thoughtfully?"

"He was my husband, Lord," she said, managing to surprise him. She hesitated briefly before adding: "There is a question I would ask." His expression gave assent, and she went on: "You are choosing one of these for a ritual victim? I thought as much . . . is the victim's death to be an easy one or difficult?"

"Tonight's victim will die easily."

"Then I beg of you, dread Lord, take some other than this who was my bridegroom once. I would not have him die a quick and easy death."

Duncan's camp tonight was nearer to Ardneh, by some kilometers, than it had been the night before. Duncan each day moved his army north, following his wizards' advice and his own intuition, and keeping pace with the parallel movement of the main body of his Eastern foes.

Now in Duncan's tent, the seeress Anita, in deep trance, was muttering: " . . . they open doors to they know not what, they take down bars that were put up when they were wiser and more frightened." The girl's speech began to trail off, becoming more disjointed and unintelligible, until at last she could only cry out in unwonted fear. Duncan, weary from the dull riding and intermittent fighting of the day, tried to puzzle out what it could mean, but he could not. Neither could his wizards, who contradicted one another in sharp debate about the girl: whether to waken her or send her deeper into trance, whether what she said tonight had any useful meaning. At last she was taken out. Duncan and his councilors continued meeting through the night. There was no communication from Ardneh.

The blood of the first sacrifice was warm and fresh on Wood's hands, and in his throat the words

of power flowed like song, controlled, in harmony
with the images formed in his mind by his practiced
imagination. Energy flowed through him, from him.
Shortly after starting the evocation he had felt a
pang of worry, on realizing just how tired he was.
This was not a task to be begun when weary; mistakes might be punished terribly. But now it was all
going well enough.

It was a task that required a full mastery of magic,
but he was equal to it. More than equal. In his imagination he was now descending worn stone steps,
through a dark and narrow passage, going to visit
the dungeon under the world. Other demons were
confined there as well as Orcus, and Wood meant to
release them in passing. They were not really
dangerous—not to Wood. Now he could hear them,
feel them, smell them, moving in some imagined cell
just off his passageway. A pack of ethereal wolves,
jostling one another for the chance at taking on
reality once more. They knew their jailer was coming, and perhaps they knew he meant to let them
out.

To Wood these were not much; they were cattle he
penned up or loosed, no matter how monstrous and
powerful they might loom in the sight of lesser men.
To handle them he needed no protracted ceremonies, no human sacrifices; he could bring them
up into the world tonight, without consulting the
Emperor, and he meant to do so. It was only the
Other, whose name Wood had been avoiding even in
his thoughts, that made him worry now. It was the
process of releasing Orcus, of course keeping hold
enough on him to put him down again when the
West had been defeated, that called for supreme
wizardry and offerings of lives.

Now the first victim had been offered, and down
in the deepest dungeon cell the chained One had
begun to stir and tremble in his painful sleep. When
those stirrings became evident to Wood, their magnitude restored his memory regarding what Orcus

was truly like. Suddenly he now longer saw the gathering of the other outcast demons as a wolf-pack, even as a herd of unruly cattle, but as no more than a nest of squealing, snapping rats. Neither they or Wood had changed of course. It was only the comparison with Orcus.

Wood slowed his imagined descent of the stone steps. The bottom was near. Surprisingly, Orcus was not only stirring, not only beginning to awaken, he was already straining and struggling to be free. He radiated an incredible power and purpose. Impossible, of course, that his effort should succeed. Wood was still the jailer, armed and comfortable and with the stair behind him open for his ascent. He stood now at the ultimate cell door, looking down through bars and gratings at the wretch in chains, the giant cramped and bound. But the rousing of Orcus had begun too successfully, was proceeding a little too rapidly. To maintain the proper margin of safety, steps should be taken to slow things down.

The bloodied ritual knife still in his hand, the corpse of the first sacrifice still warm at his feet, Wood swayed a little with his weariness, swayed and frowned and changed the text that he was chanting, altered the shape of the dungeon whose symbol-structure was held so carefully in his mind . . .

Like a snake uncoiling from the uttermost depths beneath the world, the power Orcus came striking up at him. Through symbols and matter alike the shockwave traveled, launched by the half-conscious Demon-Lord, trying in blind fury to strike back at his tormentors. At the first impact of the shockwave, Wood cried out. He had a moment in which to realize that in his weariness he had mispronounced a word of his long chant, before he fell down senseless.

Even with Wood unconscious, the One who had struck him still could not escape his dungeon. The walls and bonds of magic were still too many and too strong. Orcus could not force his way back into the world of men, or even awaken fully from his sleep. But the hords of lesser demons that Wood had been about to herd back into the world were now able to force the passage for themselves. They lost no time in doing so.

Charmian crouched motionless as the vile rabble of the demons began to appear in the torchlit night before her. One after another their hulking, obscure shapes blurred into the world, and almost at once vanished again for other parts of it. Wood when he awoke, or some other magician of comparable stature, could round them up again, and no doubt would; but they were not going to stand still and wait for it.

Charmian had good reason to be afraid. That she herself was of the East might mean very little to these ill-disciplined powers. Any one of them, hungry to inflict pain, or yearning for the taste of some immaterial human essence, might destroy her on impulse — or, worse, swallow her without destroying. Imagine the emotions of a spoiled infant, combined with the force of some huge animal or elemental power, and cleverness above the human average.

To try to run away might draw attention to herself, but still she was on the brink of doing so. She was distracted by the realization that the Western prisoners still alive were now awakening. The light spells Wood had placed on them were loosened by his unconsciousness. No one had thought to bind them physically, or perhaps the thought had been that to do so might insult the chief wizard of the East.

Now Charmian saw her husband stir. An instant later Chup got to his feet. He was only a few meters away, and when his eyes fastened on her she did not dare to run.

He was a more immediate threat than any of the demons, who so far had ignored her as they came into sight and vanished again. She took a step nearer to him, and with hands clasped beseechingly cried out: "Help me, Chup! I've released you, saved your life. You must get me away from here!"

Chup continued looking at her. She read cold rage into his fixed stare, and then realized that it was only blank. Now his forehead wrinkled. With men screaming and demons flickering in the background, he gave the impression of a man with all the time in the world, trying to understand some interesting problem. Now she noted that the other surviving Westerners were wandering around wittlessly; their minds must be still half-imprisoned by Wood's spells.

Now she drew back from Chup again, but he moved with her, studying her face as if he sought some answer there. She feared to turn and run lest some predator's instinct make him chase her and attack. "Come, Chup! I beg of you. Save me! Help me get away!" The Constable was dead, Wood fallen, and demons seemed to rule the world. There was nowhere else for Charmian to turn. She pleaded, tugged at Chup's unyielding arm, and at last in her desperation slapped his face. This last made him frown at her most villainously, though he gave no sign of retaliation. The frown frightened Charmian, and she hastened to soothe him with strokings and soft words. His face smoothed and he looked content once again, while above him and Charmian the insubstantial horrors of demons came and went, casting light of purple and gold and green, and leaving waves of sickness in the air.

An Eastern soldier, probably maddened by some passing demon's touch, came bounding at them. Chairmian saw his contorted face and his uplifted sword. She turned to try to run, but slipped and fell. As the man leaped toward her, Chup caught him by one arm, seemed to wave him in midair as if he were a banner, and threw him sprawling on his face, so heavily that he did not rise.

Recovering, Charmian crawled to pick up the sword the man had dropped. Murmuring "Come, My Lord Chup, come with me. We will help each other," she held it out toward Chup, whose hand closed on the pommel as naturally as a mouth might close on food. Taking hold of his other hand, big and hard, docile and trusting, Charmian led him out away from the remains of smoldering tents and torches, away from the passing pyrotechnic demons, out into the summer night. Other humans could be heard running and crying out around them in the dark, but no one paid them any heed.

IX

Ardneh's Life

<hr>

"Wolf tracks, if I've ever seen them" Rolf announced. It was mid-morning on the day after their arrival at Ardneh's base. They had camped overnight wrapped in their cloaks in a small, ancient dormitory, where the plumbing still worked but the ancient furnishings had otherwise crumbled long ago. Ardneh, still busy integrating into his own complex being the strange artifact that had been their gift, had not yet explained to them in any detail what their chief tasks here were to be. But he had asked them to make a short reconnaissance round the old mine entrance, to see if there were any signs of their having been followed. When this request puzzled them, Ardneh explained: "It is here, inside my own physical structure, that my powers are in some ways most limited." And there came to Rolf, with seeming naturalness, the mental image of a hand trying to bandage itself.

Now he stood with Catherine at the mouth of the ancient adit. A thunderstorm had come and gone during the night, unheard by them inside, leaving fresh mud where the small stream's banks had been dry dirt. The splayed prints in the mud were those of large and heavy animals. "Only natural beasts of some kind, we can hope," Rolf added now.

"Look." Catherine was pointing at the hard rock ledge a couple of meters in from the entrance. Rolf crouched beside her. The faint smear of mud on rock was not yet quite dry. His eyes could not really make it into a large paw-print. But something, or someone, had left it there within the last few hours.

"Are there wolves that serve the East?" Catherine asked.

"I have heard stories of such, but never seen them. Ardneh will know."

"We were to scout outside; I suppose we had better not retreat at the mere sight of a track."

Rolf agreed, and they proceeded cautiously. But, once away from the mud at the adit's entrance, they could discover no evidence of enemies or large beasts. New rivulets, still gurgling with rainwater, entered the stream at several points, and a hundred meters downstream from Ardneh's cave it was now much deeper than it had been, overtopping its normal banks to comb long grass with its current.

After following the stream that far they scouted in a circle centered on the entrance to the cave. They climbed the hill, crawling cautiously round its grassy top to observe a peaceful summer world in all directions. From there the circle brought them back to the stream and its swift pools. Catherine knelt to scan the bank closely; her thighs showed white before her skirt fell back demurely into place.

The little glade felt utterly secure, isolated from friend and foe alike. A thought that Rolf had banished came leaping back, with power irresistible: *Maybe the curse has ended now —*

Two minutes later, feeling numb with fury, he was turning away from Catherine, picking up his just-dropped scabbard from the grass. The sword came out into his right hand, and with it he hacked murderously at the Lady Charmian's image, projected by his rage on a small tree. He was leaving marks to show enemy scouts that someone had been here. All right, then, he was leaving marks.

"I am changed again," came Catherine's wearily steady voice from behind him. "Changed and dressed."

Walking behind her, on their silent way back to

the cave, he thought that even her normal, youthful shape was after all far from lovely. Those bare legs moving ahead of him were not curved in the way that a man's dreams told him a girl's legs should be curved. Too thin and wiry. My Lady Charmian chooses ugly servants, always—

And Rolf felt sullen, mean, and ugly too.

Wood woke with a start, and instantly sprang to his feet. The movement came in a burst of fear-born energy that drained away as quickly as it had come, and left him tottering. He stood swaying in the cheerful sunlight, amid unfamiliar grass and trees, unable to recall how he had come to be here.

Gradually, in bits and pieces, it came back: the error made in weariness, the jolting punishment from Orcus. But that had been during the night, and it was late morning now. Or might it even be early afternoon—

With a shock Wood beheld that the grass where he had lain still remained pressed down, showing the outline of his body. Within the outline it was even yellowed, beginning to die from lack of sun.

How many days had he been lying there? Within the outline of withered grass, beetles were scurrying to find new shade. But though he must have been motionless as a corpse, apparently no living thing had come closer than that to molesting him. A magician of Wood's power was not completely unprotected even when unconscious.

Now he looked cautiously about. The only other humans remaining in the grove had made food for scavengers already. He faced no immediate threat.

Wood spewed out words of power, barking commands and questions into the air, which soon crackled with invisible presences. His first orders were for food and drink—he was ravenous and thirsty now, as well as stiff in every muscle and joint. Next he demanded information.

What he learned was, for the most part, reassuring. The horde of rogue demons had scattered around the world, which was an annoyance, but no more—obviously Orcus had not escaped. Quickly Wood set in motion the processes necessary to bring the others back under his control. Then, clumsy and aching, he set out on foot across tree-dotted grassland in the direction where, as his invisible informants now assured him, Ominor's army was presently encamped.

With no better means of travel than his old legs, the journey was slow. But the kind of steed he had once ridden was not readily replaceable, and he was saving his powers now for essentials. After an hour, however, the hiking grew oppressively difficult. He took thought, noted that the light breeze was at his back, and nodded to himself with satisfaction. With a few words he changed his shape into that of a wind-rolled, rootless weed, a feat he could manage with no great expenditure of energy.

In this guise he traveled faster than before, and by late afternoon had come within sight of his goal. Resuming his usual shape, he now made himself completely invisible, a condition hard to maintain for more than a brief time. In this way he passed sentries and minor wizards alike without being detected, until he stood inside the pavilion of the Emperor himself. Wood was surprised—though not enormously so—to discover the woman Charmian standing before Ominor. She was simply dressed now, and shy-looking, with downcast eyes. There were a few other people about.

The dialogue between the Emperor and Charmian was interesting to Wood, as it somewhat concerned him; but the first time John Ominor's eyes flicked his way they seemed for just a moment to rest directly on Wood, and after that Wood could no longer completely convince himself that his invisibility was proof against the Emperor's gaze. A fear that he could not master began to grow in Wood, and with a faint shudder he retreated, passing out

through the pavilion walls as a demon might, or
smoke; and once outside he looked for a suitable
place nearby where he might let himself be seeable
again.

To Charmian, John Ominor was saying, in his cus-
tomary loud, half-angry tone: "You still seem surprised at the sight of me, girl. What did you think I
would be like?"

"That you would be impressive, Lord. As indeed
you are."

The Emperor half smiled, and enjoyed looking at
Charmian a little longer before answering her. "As
indeed I am not, you mean. Not loathesome or
demonic-looking. Or even particularly handsome."
Though as usual the Emperor gave the impression
of impatience, yet he was in no hurry to conclude
the conversation. "I have heard of you, most memorable lady," he went on. "Attempted to attach yourself to Som the Dead, in the Black Mountains; yes,
and nearly thawed him back to life, didn't you? I can
well believe it . . . though that man always seemed
quite inhuman to me. Whereas I am an ordinary
man in all but power. The powers I was born with,
and those I have since accumulated—rather greater
than those of Som. Or anyone else. Charmian, you
will find my desires much more ordinary than those
of many other men whom you have tried to please;
that is not to say that I am easily satisfied."

"My Emperor, I wish only that I may someday be
granted the privilege of trying to satisfy your
every—"

"To take whatever I want. To punish all my overt
enemies, and to maintain fear in all who are too
frightened of me to be my enemies at the moment—what more is the East but this?"

Charmian, in silence, made deep obeisance toward the carved chair in which the Emperor sat.

Ominor said: "Before you attempt more energetic
ways of contributing to my happiness, answer me a

question or two; repeat to me how you and the man came to be out there where you were found by my patrol. What went wrong with Abner, and what has become of my chief wizard?" There came a hoarse scream from somewhere not far away, probably from another chamber of the elaborate tent. "They are still asking the same questions of the man who was with you, but it seems he is as witless as he looked. He does nothing but yelp. You may be our only witness, so try to remember things in a little more detail. Exactly where is Wood?"

"My dread Lord, I will do the best I can." Charmian had already told of Abner's fate and Wood's, leaving out of course her attack on the Constable from behind. She began to repeat the story now, adding such detail as she could remember; still she could not say exactly where it had all happened. She had wandered for two days with the dazed Chup before the Eastern patrol found them. She had no more information about Wood to give the Emperor, who was listening carefully.

Now and then another mindless outcry drifted in from Chup. In a moment of private thought it occurred to Charmian how enjoyable it would be to watch Chup's slow destruction, but then in the next moment she realized that she would miss him when he was no more. She recalled feeling a certain joy mixed with her fear on recognizing him as the man forcing his way into her rooms at the caravanserai, and again in the Constable's tent. Of course Chup might have killed her either time if she had crossed him; but this man here, on whose favor she was counting, might well kill her someday for amusement.

John Ominor asked her: "When this group of demons, as you put it, came pouring out into the world, was there any one among them notably larger or more impressive than the rest?" He seemed to think the question very important.

"I think not, dread Lord, if you can accept the opinion of one not well acquainted with demons, or able to view them without fear."

"No, of course not," Ominor mused, as if to himself, "we would have known." His eye fixed Charmian once more. "And the man with you? He is of the West, you say, and yet you seem to have known him previously?"

There was no telling how much the Emperor might already know, and Charmian now boldly gave the truth. "He was once of the East, my Lord, and he was once my husband. A deserter and a turncoat. I cannot believe his present madness is a sham; but be that as it may, I would be pleased to see his suffering as well as hear it."

Ominor grunted and flicked a glance back over his shoulder. Apparently the signal was relayed and heeded for presently the dismal outcries ceased. A moment more, and two black-garbed torturers came in bringing with them Chup, bound to an iron frame on wheels. He was stripped and bleeding here and there, where patches of skin were missing; but he was not the mangled object Charmian had imagined. His head turned to and fro, eyes glaring wildly.

Another pair of men had come in, wizards to judge by their dress. Ominor now turned to them. "Try some gentler means of restoring his memory. It could be important. If he knows aught of what was befallen Wood—"

There came a hail from outside the pavilion. A stir at the entrance, and then Wood himself appeared there. He hurried forward, scarcely glancing at Charmian, made obeisance, and quickly rose. "A word with you, at once, my Lord."

Ominor arose promptly and led the way out of the chamber, motioning Wood to come along. Charmian was left to contemplate her husband, now being treated kindly, with a mixture of anger and relief that she did not fully understand.

Ominor and Wood confronted one another within an inner chamber of black silk, a tent within a tent, guarded round by most dependable powers of secrecy, and filled with a darkness that sometimes could press upon the eye like glaring light.

Wood got to business at once. "Supreme Lord, I can rouse that man that they are working on out there; it is one of my spells that still oppresses him. Has he any information of importance?"

"Not since you are here. Where were you?"

"Mobilizing reserve forces, my lord Emperor. We shall soon have urgent need of them."

"And you were struck down in the process? So the woman told me, but I doubted . . . what, who, were you trying to call up?"

There was a pause. Wood began to answer indirectly. "My Lord, shortly before that I faced Ardneh, and I was weakened thereby. Ardneh is now mightier than we have ever suspected he might become. He may be as strong as — one other, whom we both know of, whose name I have not mentioned —"

Ominor stood up. "Are you really leading where I think you are? Was that the purpose of the ceremony you had begun?" The secret tent muted sound, but still the anger in his voice was terrible. "Of course; who else could have struck you down like that?"

"Lord Emperor, hear me out, if you would save the East! I tell you I have faced Ardneh and I know! We must arouse the One whose name should not be said, to fight for us. Or else we perish."

"*Arouse* him, you say? Not simply tap his power?"

"Yes." Wood swallowed. "Awaken him enough to send him into battle. Keep reins upon his senses and his will, and send him back below when he has served."

There was again a little silence before Ominor said: "You think it will be possible to release the one you speak of, then bottle him again like so much wine?"

"It is a risk that must be taken, supreme Lord."

"You really believe you can do that?" The Emperor's loud crude voice made it sound as if Wood's sanity rather than his ability, was in question.

"Lord, Ardneh had exhausted me before the Other struck me down. Nor could he even then escape our bondage, as you see. Before beginning again I will rest myself, and make thorough preparation. Next time I will have help—"

"Of course!" Ominor clapped his hands, as if blessed with a sudden happy thought. "To help you we must call upon those same three powers that hovered above the lake, and warded harm from our imperial person, the day that we invited Ardneh to our palace—ah, it seems so long ago. Yes, call them, let them clamp shut their jaws upon all who threaten us, as you swore they were eager to do."

Wood hung his head, taking care to indicate nothing but total submission. Ardneh had already driven those three demons from the field, in the cur-pack with the others, as Ominor must understand. Just now was not the time for Wood to say anything more at all.

Having made his point and inspired what he thought to be sufficient fear, the Emperor was ready to talk business. "Wood, despite the recent record of your failures, I find myself listening to this new plan of yours. But I am not yet convinced. I know, better than you or anyone else, the dangers of what you propose. Do not take another step along that road unless I bid you do so. However." Wood's eyes lifted. "However, if what you tell me of Ardneh is true, we may have to take the most desperate steps, and quickly. So rest now, and prepare yourself—are there any preliminary steps remaining?"

Wood was eager once again. "One more sacrifice, great Lord. I need not promise it will be far more carefully conducted than the last. That is all, and the One we speak of will be reachable for quick summoning, or for quickly being reburied as deep as ever.''

There was a silent pause. "Go and do it," said Ominor then abruptly. He stood up, ripped open with his hand the little tent of blackness, and strode out.

Returning to his private quarters, the Emperor was soon visited by one of his chiefs of technology, and by his Master of the Beasts, who came in lupine form. For once, both brought good news. In recent days the technologists' Old World devices had detected a steady increase in electromagnetic activity in a certain small area to the north. It seemed to be precisely where the Beast Master's half-intelligent scouts now reported the scent of two humans, male and female, entering a strange cave. From the same direction had come the winds that had defeated Wood and scattered his demonic horde. In that direction, also, was Duncan's army tending, as if something were there that the Prince wanted to defend.

I have found Ardneh's life. Ominor did not say the words aloud. But he dismissed his aides and stood alone for some time, looking at the map. Then he summoned his field commanders and demanded from them a faster movement to the north. Such beasts as were already near the objective were to try what could be accomplished by a prompt attack.

X

Beast-War

———◆◆◆———

"Ardneh, how long will we be here?" Rolf sat on a
chest of Old World tools. His hands were playing
nervously with a gripping, twisting device of silvery
metal. Catherine, on the other side of the room, lay
curled up on the floor as if she hoped to sleep. Not
many words had passed between the two of them
since their return from the scouting expedition. On
hearing their report of paw-prints, Ardneh had
urged that at least one of them remain awake and
alert at all times; they could not depend upon his
being able to warn them of danger, here in his own
blind interior.

Ardneh's answer to his question now took Rolf by
surprise. "The number of days is not now determin-
able. But almost certainly it will not be as long as a
month. By then the outcome of the war will have
been decided."

Across the room, Catherine's head came up, her
face turned in Rolf's direction.

Rolf opened his mouth, closed it, tried again. "It
will be over?" was all that he could find to say at last.

"The next major battle will decide the war,"
Ardneh replied matter-of-factly. "And it will be
fought here, within the month, though the war will
not end entirely for another year or two."

"Ardneh . . . fought here?"

"Around me and over me. I must bring the
strongest of the enemy to me, and break them here,
if they are to be broken at all. And Duncan must

come with his army, to be ready to strike again when I have done my utmost."

Catherine asked: "And what are Rolf and I to do?"

"There will be much. Physical repairs and rearrangements to be made, things I cannot do for myself, enough work to keep two humans busy until the issue is decided. Rolf has great natural skill in technology; also he is familiar enough with me not to be greatly awed by my presence. Therefore I decided that he should be the one to bring me the heart of the power lamp."

Catherine put out a slender hand, to touch a giant piece of hardware. "I have no great skill with things like these."

"More than you know," Ardneh's voice assured her. "You will be of help with the machinery. But your chief value to my plan, the reason I brought you here, lies elsewhere, in the future. I see it dimly, but cannot explain. You have powers that you know not of. Powers of life, that build the world."

"Magic? No, I cannot . . ."

"Not magic. Not un-magic, either. All. Reality."

Her eyes turned to Rolf, as if beseeching him for help. It was a moment of openness between them, such as they had not shared since rejoining Ardneh. But though Rolf's heart went out to that look, he had no other help to give.

Ardneh gave them no time to brood any more, but announced that the integration of the power source that they had brought was now complete. He led them now to other rooms and began to show them some of the tasks they must accomplish. There were interlocking nests of metal and glass to be opened, disassembled, moved, put together again in new configurations. There were long cables, like multi-headed snakes, to be unpacked, tested, and installed. The outward shapes of the machinery were not very complex, but still some practice time was necessary. Rolf's fingers soon got the feel of what was wanted; Catherine, less in tune with technical matters, increasingly limited her help to unpacking, fetching, and carrying, taking up tools only when necessary.

That night in the ruined dormitory, sleep would not come to Rolf. He tossed about for a while, looking again and again at the motionless, cloak-covered form on the far side of the room. Finally he sat up. "Ardneh."

It seemed a long time before an answer came. "What is it?"

"Catherine is under a spell of the Lady Charmian's." The figure on the far side of the room was still apparently asleep. "If you could counteract it, both of us would be grateful."

This time the pause was longer still. Then the voice above Rolf said: "I am aware of the spell. To counteract it would be difficult, because of the source of power that was tapped to make it. And to counteract it does not seem essential."

"Our lives here would be much easier if—"

Calm, inflexible, Ardneh's voice overrode his. "At this moment many lives in the West are more difficult than yours. And there are greater dangers to you than this discomfort that you speak of. I am too busy to even discuss the matter now. Another may help you where I cannot."

Another? Who? But there would be no use in trying to ask; Rolf could feel that Ardneh's presence had departed. Despite himself, despite his awareness of the legless, armless, dying who were far worse off, he half-willingly nursed a sullen anger.

Catherine was still asleep—or still wanted him to think she was. He tried once more to get to sleep himself, but it was hopeless. Getting up, he groped his way through dark but now partially familiar corridors, to the chill cave air of the tunnel and at last to the warmth of summer night outside. For a time he stood cautiously just inside the tunnel mouth, his ears sorting out the natural activities of the prairie night as he heard them through the murmur of the stream. Then he climbed the little hill above the entrance to the cave, and sat in the grass to contemplate the stars.

"Whooo, Roolf."

The great bird was almost within reach of his hand before his eyes could find it in the night. "Strijeef! It's good to see you again. How are you? What news?"

The bird spoke briefly of reptiles recently slain, and personal perils avoided; and then of the march of great armies, how both East and West were converging on this northern land. "Each day the great battle that is to come grows nearer. All in Duncan's army speak of it."

"So says Ardneh, also. Have you a message for me from Duncan?"

From his courier's pouch Strijeef's nimble talons brought out a small roll of paper, which he tossed to Rolf with a flirt of his murderous beak. "Yoouuu are promoted to captain, and the woman Catherine is formally enrolled as warrant officer. And there is one more bit of news, that I bring of my oown sight. Large four-legged beasts are coming here, loong before either army. A pack of beasts I doo not know, and they will be here before daylight."

It had rained during the night, and in the dismal morning the west prairie smelled more of autumn than of summer. The army of the East was striking camp, preparing for another day of northward march. From the earliest light Charmian had been outside her tent, keeping an alert eye on the tent where Wood had rested. And now at last she saw him emerge from it, wearing a soft, rich robe.

Once more a circular space, set apart from other camp activities, had been made ready for the chief wizard's intended work. In the middle of that space Chup had been left waiting through the night, still bound to his iron frame, and guarded by two soldiers.

Wood had paused, just outside his tent, in conference with other wizards. Charmian took the opportunity to approach the waiting victim. Grabbing Chup's long hair, she turned his face around to hers. He snarled, but there was no recognition in the scarcely-human sound. His eyes were those of a trapped beast.

Once she had yearned to tear those eyes out with her nails. Now she had the chance to do so. But somehow the desire had fled.

Wood was approaching now, followed by two assistants, as silent and somber as their master. At a flicker of the chief wizard's eyes toward her, Charmian darted out of the circle. Just past its edge, she paused, alone and watching as before.

As soon as a few preliminaries were out of the way, Wood came closer to the victim on his iron frame. The wizard raised and spread his empty hands. For this sacrifice he must use nothing so direct as a knife. Subtle and bloodless must be the draining of this victim's life. Its energies were needed as solvents and lubricants, to melt the seals and oil the hinges of the dungeon door through which Orcus must eventually pass if it was finally decided to free him. Wood began to work now with his most subtle arts, to extract the energies of Chup's life without the use of material weapons. Proceeding slowly and carefully, Wood ignored, or at least he did not stop to savor, the reactions of the victim whose mind must be made clear so he could understand what was happening to him. The essential oil of despair must be added to those of fear and pain. Chup, regaining his wits at last, strained at his iron bonds, and looked up with a new and understanding horror at the man who was beginning to kill him.

Wood had killed in ritual so often than now it seemed no more important to him than the cracking of an egg. While his voice chanted, and his hands gestured, his mind held steady to the useful working image. Once more in imagination he had descended to the nethermost dungeon. Now he stood there like an artisan, a workman lubricating a lock, an intricate tremendous lock that held a massive door, a door securely sealed and barred, whose key had been put so far away that it had been forgotten. Another terrible ceremony would be needed for the recovery of that key, but that was for another day.

On the other side of the door, Wood knew, the monster moved (aye, he could feel and hear it through the door), the utter beast, a slouching, slimy and wall-bulging weight, that slid against the door, and turned within its tiny cell and padded on along the tiny circle it must walk. It was fully awakened now. He felt its foul breath issuing . . . enough. When he envisioned demons breathing, more than enough. The workman's image was the one that he must keep in mind. He must oil the unopenable hinges, and the lock, and make them ready to be used. Now, twist and squeeze the oily rag (whose name was Chup) to get the solvent and the lubricant. Probe deeply now into the lock and clear the sealing force from all the parts . . .

Incredibly, the workman's hand upon the door was seized, by something from the other side. Wood's hand went dead as ice. A numbing shock flew all along his arm. He tried to step back from the door, to pull away. When that effort failed he sought to tear his mind out of the image at once, terrible though the dangers were in doing so. But still his hand was held. He could only gape in horrified disbelief as the monster, having been somehow granted some kind of fingerhold within the lock, proceeded to make good use of it, applying his full strength.

The lock went smash at once, the crossbars on the door were splintering. The weight against the other side leaned harder and the bars broke off. Slowly, leisurely almost, the door swung on its hinges open-

All Futura Books are available at your bookshop or newsagent, or can be ordered from the following address:
Futura Books, Cash Sales Department,
P.O. Box 11, Falmouth, Cornwall

Please send cheque or postal order (no currency), and allow 55p for postage and packing for the first book plus 22p for the second book and 14p for each additional book ordered up to a maximum charge of £1.75 in U.K.

Customers in Eire and B.F.P.O. please allow 55p for the first book, 22p for the second book plus 14p per copy for the next 7 books, thereafter 8p per book.

Overseas customers please allow £1.00 for postage and packing for the first book and 25p per copy for each additional book.

interzone

SCIENCE FICTION AND FANTASY

Quarterly   £1.5

- *Interzone* is the only British magazine specializing in SF and new fantasti
writing. We have published:

BRIAN ALDISS	M. JOHN HARRISON
J.G. BALLARD	GARRY KILWORTH
BARRINGTON BAYLEY	MICHAEL MOORCOCK
MICHAEL BISHOP	KEITH ROBERTS
ANGELA CARTER	GEOFF RYMAN
RICHARD COWPER	JOSEPHINE SAXTON
JOHN CROWLEY	JOHN SLADEK
PHILIP K. DICK	BRUCE STERLING
THOMAS M. DISCH	IAN WATSON
MARY GENTLE	CHERRY WILDER
WILLIAM GIBSON	GENE WOLFE

- *Interzone* has also published many excellent new writers; graphics by JIM
BURNS, ROGER DEAN, IAN MILLER and others; book reviews, news, etc

- *Interzone* is available from specialist SF shops, or by subscription. For fou
issues, send £6 (outside UK, £7) to: **124 Osborne Road, Brighton BN1 6LU**
UK. Single copies: £1.75 inc p&p.

- American subscribers may send $10 ($13 if you want delivery by air mail) to ou
British address, above. All cheques should be made payable to *Interzone*.

- "No other magazine in Britain is publishing science fiction at all, let alone fictio
of this quality." *Times Literary Supplement*

- -

To: **interzone** 124 Osborne Road, Brighton, BN1 6LU, UK.

Please send me four issues of *Interzone,* beginning with the current issue.
enclose a cheque/p.o. for £6 (outside UK, £7; US subscribers, $10 or $13 air
made payable to *Interzone*.

Name _____

Address _____

_____